"Swee

Roan dropped his hands f[...]

"Is that what you call it when a man uses a plain little old word like *honey* instead of just callin' you by name? Hasn't anyone ever called you sweet names, Katherine?" he asked softly. "Haven't there ever been any men hangin' around, tryin' to court you or just tryin' to get your attention?"

Katherine spun back to face him, and her eyes were bleak. "Take a good look at me, Roan Devereaux! Do I look like the sort of woman men come to court? I'm sure not good-looking and I'm too plainspoken for most of the men hereabouts. What have I got to offer a man in his right mind?"

She was serious! By damn, she was! And here he'd been feeling like a randy, apple-cheeked boy around her!

Dear Reader,

In her second book for Harlequin Historicals, *Loving Katherine*, Carolyn Davidson tells the heartwarming story of an isolated farm woman who meets a man who is determined to overcome her mistrust and draw her out, despite her reluctance. Don't miss this wonderful follow-up to her first novel for Harlequin, *Gerrity's Bride*.

Claire Delacroix continues to delight audiences with her stories of romance, passion and magic. This month's story *My Lady's Champion*, is another captivating medieval tale of a noblewoman forced into marriage to save her ancestral home that will transport you to another time and place.

Whether you're a longtime fan of Mary McBride or have just discovered her, we know you'll be delighted by her new book, *Darling Jack*, the touching tale of a handsome Pinkerton detective and the steady, unassuming Pinkerton file clerk who poses as his wife. And be sure to keep an eye out for multipublished author Ruth Langan's *Dulcie's Gift*, the prequel to the contemporary stories in the Harlequin cross-line continuity series, BRIDE'S BAY.

Sincerely,

Tracy Farrell
Senior Editor

Please address questions and book requests to:
Harlequin Reader Service
U.S.: 3010 Walden Ave., P.O. Box 1325, Buffalo, NY 14269
Canadian: P.O. Box 609, Fort Erie, Ont. L2A 5X3

CAROLYN DAVIDSON

Loving Katherine

Harlequin Books

TORONTO • NEW YORK • LONDON
AMSTERDAM • PARIS • SYDNEY • HAMBURG
STOCKHOLM • ATHENS • TOKYO • MILAN
MADRID • WARSAW • BUDAPEST • AUCKLAND

ISBN 0-373-28925-1

LOVING KATHERINE

Books by Carolyn Davidson

Harlequin Historicals

Gerrity's Bride #298
Loving Katherine #325

CAROLYN DAVIDSON

lives in South Carolina, on the outskirts of Charleston, with her husband, her number-one fan. Working in a new/used bookstore is an ideal job for her, allowing access to her favorite things: books and people. *Loving Katherine* is her fourth novel. Readers' comments are more than welcome in her mailbox, P.O. Box 60626, North Charleston, SC 29419-0626

With grateful appreciation, this book is dedicated to my agent, Pattie Steele-Perkins, who makes me believe in myself.

And with a heart full of love to my granddaughters, in the hope that each of them will one day find their own special hero. To Erin, Rachel, Jennifer Beth, Sarah, Cherylyn, Karen, Jennifer Lynn and Ashley; and especially to Katherine, who was but a twinkle in her daddy's eye when this story was begun. Grandma loves you all!

But most of all, to Mr. Ed, who loves me.

Chapter One

He'd been watching her for more than ten minutes, curiosity snagging him after the first glance. He'd meant to assure himself that he was indeed finally arriving at Charlie's place, hoping to see the familiar figure somewhere about the corral or perhaps coming out of the pole barn. But the sight of the lone figure, kneeling in the garden patch, had caught his eye and he'd settled down to watch for a few minutes. Katherine. It had to be Katherine, he decided.

And as for Charlie, where the hell was he? With no sign of him about, he was probably out in a far pasture, checking on his mares. Roan Devereaux nodded his head at the thought and stretched out his leg to ease the cramp in his thigh, grunting his impatience with physical infirmities.

"Seen the time I could play statue for the best part of an afternoon," he muttered, squinting against the sun, fast making its way toward the horizon. Lifting to one elbow, he disrupted the smooth line of his profile, the better to observe the woman who worked amid the hills of potatoes and the forest of tomato plants next to the cabin. She'd not glanced about or appeared to catch sight of him since he'd placed himself at the top of the hill just minutes ago.

The ride had been short, coming out from town. It was the days of travel before that had brought to mind the old injury he'd rather have ignored. His hand rubbed instinctively at his thigh and he frowned, his eyes narrowing on the woman who knelt less than two hundred yards away.

Even now, she blended into the garden, half kneeling amid the potatoes she'd been gathering, dropping them into a burlap bag.

Reaching for his hat, he swatted it against his leg before jerking it into place against the dark swath of his hair. The wide brim cut the glare of the setting sun, and his squint eased into a more leisurely perusal of the small figure below his vantage point.

"She looks like a mud hen," he decided with a rusty mutter. "Bustlin' around in that garden like a brown mud hen, if I ever saw one." Heaving a sigh, he contemplated his next move. "Guess I might as well go down and introduce myself."

His brow furrowed, his hand moved to his thigh as he eased himself to his haunches, and then he froze in place. Rising from her crouch, she lifted her head in a gesture of wary alertness that surprised him. She brushed one hand distractedly against her skirt, then raised the other to shade her eyes as she gazed at him.

Even across the distance that separated them, he felt the piercing touch of her survey and met it with his own dark scrutiny. With a lifting of her chin, she dismissed him and walked the few yards to where a basket of late vegetables lay amid the tangle of tomato vines. Then, as if she considered his presence of no account, she turned, heading with measured, firm steps toward the small house.

He grinned. "You're a spunky little thing, Katherine," he said aloud. "Dismissin' me out of hand and strollin' away like you don't give a good goldarn about whether I come or go." Turning to his horse, tied to a tree just a few feet from the crown of the hill, he hoisted himself into the saddle. His leg protested and he frowned at the reminder, settling into the worn leather of his saddle, his boots gripping the stirrups even as his knees nudged the stallion into motion.

With the ease of a man familiar with his saddle, he allowed the horse to find his own way down the slope, and within moments they rode past the neat, even rows of the garden. The scent of ripe tomatoes and the musty smell of the overturned earth in the potato patch met his nostrils and he inhaled it with a sense of nostalgia. It's been years, he thought. Years since he sneaked out to help in the kitchen garden and got swatted for his trouble when his mama caught him with dirty knees.

Saddle leather creaked and the horse snorted once, his ears flicking as he answered a nicker from the barn beyond the house. One hand easy on the reins, the other resting on his thigh, the man directed his mount, approaching the wide front porch that stretched the length of the unpainted house.

It was uncanny, she decided. The sense of unease haunting her had once more proved itself to be valid. She'd known someone was watching. But it wasn't an evil gaze. Not like the spine-chilling surveillance of Evan Gardner, invading her privacy last winter.

This time... She considered the man who rode toward her house. He was far from harmless, she thought, noting the erect posture, the easy hand on his reins, his watchful eyes. But not a danger. Yet.

It had been a frightening few moments, turning her back on him as he rose to his feet there on the ridge, a tall figure in dark clothing. She'd counted the steps it took to gain the safety of the house, her arms aching from the weight of the basket she carried and the digging and toting she'd done all afternoon.

Now she watched from behind the white lace curtain as he drew back on the reins and settled deep in his saddle, his unsmiling face shadowed beneath the brim of his hat. Her fingers gripped the stock of her father's shotgun, and she took a deep, shuddering breath as she wondered uneasily if she could fire it.

Oh, the ability was there. For hours—days—she'd hit cans and scattered rocks until she was as good a shot as the man who'd taught her. But that same man had warned her to be prepared to aim for vital parts if the time ever came for her to prove her skill.

"I will if I have to," she muttered beneath her breath as she moved to the door and lifted the latch.

"Good afternoon, ma'am." The hands were in plain sight, his own weapon sunk into the leather scabbard that fit behind his saddle.

Even that was not immensely reassuring, she decided. If she were any judge of men, he could have it pointed in her direction in jig time and the lazy ease in his greeting could turn just as quickly to a threat.

"What do you want?" she asked, putting dark, warning venom into the question.

The husky voice was a surprise. He'd expected a gentle, womanly tone. Perhaps even a waver or a breathless quiver in her words.

"Just to ask a few questions, ma'am." He lifted one hand slowly, tipping the brim of his hat in a gesture of courtly awareness.

Her eyes followed the movement and her lips tightened. "Ask away, stranger," she told him after a moment.

She was a sturdy little thing, this daughter of Charlie Cassidy, he thought, the low, throaty sound of her voice once more teasing his hearing. Or maybe Charlie'd taken a wife. The thought was unappealing, he decided, watching her closely. No, she had to be his daughter. She had something of the man about her. Perhaps that stubborn chin or the tilt of her head.

Her gun rose in silent menace as she allowed her index finger to slide into better position. "Speak up, stranger," she said abruptly, her impatience with his dithering at an end.

"Charlie around?" Even as he asked, he sensed the solitary presence of the woman here.

She shook her head in silent negation. "What do you want him for?"

He shifted in the saddle and felt the warning she offered as the weapon lifted a bit higher. Her arms must be getting weary. That old shotgun was a heavy one and she wasn't much of a size to carry it, let alone hoist it into firing position and hold it steady.

"Charlie told me once, if I wanted a good piece of horseflesh, to look him up." His hand stroked the neck of the stallion beneath him as if in apology, and a shiver of pleasure ran over the flesh of his animal. The long tail swished once, then, black and thick, it settled into immobility again.

"Charlie won't be selling you any horses."

His lifted brow disputed her statement. "He out of stock?" As if mocking his question, a horse nickered once more from the barn. His lips curled even as his eyes hardened. "Or are you doubting my word?"

"No." She looked down, gripping the stock of her weapon, her index finger easing from the trigger.

She'd turned a bit pale, he thought, and leaning a bit, he looked at her more closely. "You all right?" he asked, looking past her at the half-open door that led into the house. "Is something wrong here?"

She shook her head. "No, nothing's wrong here." She raised her eyes once more to look at his face. Brown and dingy, her dress hung straight from the shoulders, caught up only by a leather thong, keeping it from the ground, forming it loosely about her waist.

Her hair was long, a heavy braid hanging to her waist, as thick as his wrist where it left the nape of her neck. Sort of a mahogany color, he decided, amused at his own fanciful description. She'd shed the shapeless hat that had successfully hidden her face from his view earlier, revealing strong features. Her skin was tanned from exposure to the sun and her stubborn chin reminded him of Charlie's.

It jutted forward now as she faced him without a sign of fear. "The only thing wrong here is the unwelcome company, stranger. I told you Charlie isn't here. Now move on out." A movement of her gun barrel provided urging. Then it dipped just a bit and she frowned as she brought it back into line with his leg.

His bad leg. The leg that had been cut and sewn every which way already and sure as shootin' couldn't withstand another assault. He shook his head at the thought, his mouth twisting derisively as he considered her.

"Can I at least get down off my horse long enough to get a drink of water?" He leaned one hand against the horn of his saddle, shifting against the leather and easing his right foot from the stirrup.

"Canteen empty?" she asked, nodding at the leather-covered flask that hung from his saddle.

His eyes met hers with a level look that was no answer at all. Even as he swung his leg over the back of his mount, his narrowed gaze clung to her. And it wasn't until he stood before her, dark and unyielding, that she realized her query had gone unanswered.

Her mouth tightened in annoyance and she tipped her head in the direction of the well just across the yard from where he stood. From her vantage point on the porch she watched as he turned away, his eyes almost reluctantly leaving the shapeless mass of fabric that enclosed her.

With stiff movements that spoke of sore muscles, he reached to pull the bucket from the depths of the well, his back wide beneath the worn cotton of his shirt. Deliberately opening his flask, he turned it up to allow a few drops of liquid to fall, and then, with a deft hand, he tipped the bucket to fill it.

"Who are you?" she asked, her eyes intent on his every movement.

"Roan Devereaux." He lifted the dipper hanging from a length of binder twine and scooped it into the bucket, then drank thirstily while he soaked in her silence. With a twist of his wrist, he dropped the wooden pail back to the depths of the well and turned to face her.

The look of stunned surprise on her face had not had time to fade and he allowed a small smile of satisfaction to ride the corners of his mouth.

Her shotgun was pointed at the wide boards of the porch she stood on. As he watched, she straightened her shoulders a bit more, lifting her head, enabling him to see the fine color staining her cheeks.

"I owe you, Roan Devereaux," she said quietly. "My father spoke of you more than once after he came home from the war."

His nod accepted her words. "Is he ill?" His survey of the place revealed the signs of neglect that told him Charlie's hand hadn't been felt here for a while. Yet, there were horses on the place.

"He...no, he's not ill. My father was healthy till the day he died." She waved a hand at a small rise that began just to the north of the house, where a nondescript picket fence enclosed a plot of ground. "He's buried there."

"What happened?" Abrupt and harsh, his voice demanded details and the woman shrugged, turning back to the door.

"I'll offer you supper before you leave, Mr. Devereaux."

She'd turned her back on him, and without a by-your-leave stalked into the house, carrying the heavy shotgun by its barrel. His lips firmed as he tended his horse, loosening the cinch and leading the animal to the trough next to the well.

Waiting till the stallion had drunk his fill, he looked around once more. The bars of the corral delineated the enclosure where Charlie's horses ran. Several tossed their heads now, all fillies by the looks of them, eager to kick their heels. The barn was good-sized, probably triple that of the house, he estimated. Charlie'd always taken good care of his animals. His daughter looked like she needed some tending, though, Roan thought with a grim-lipped smile. Plain as a gray mourning dove, she was. No wonder she didn't have a man about. With that forbidding look she wore, it would take a needy specimen to try for her affections.

"I've dished you up some stew, Mr. Devereaux." She spoke from the open doorway, and he tipped the brim of his hat, leading the stallion toward the hitching post at the side of the porch.

"I'll be right in, ma'am," he offered, rolling up his sleeves as he headed back to the trough to wash up.

She was at the stove when he ducked to walk in the door. There was room to spare, but his height had given him the habit of allowing a bit of space over his crown. She waved her hand at the towel hanging on a peg by the wooden countertop.

"You can dry off with that," she said, turning to him with coffeepot in hand. A heavy china mug sat on the table, hugging the full bowl of steaming food she had served him. With spare movements, she filled the mug almost to the brim and then glanced at him, her manner hesitant.

He met her eyes. They were blue, darker than he'd thought, widely spaced beneath a fine forehead. Her gaze was penetrating, assessing, and he waited for her judgment.

"Want some milk, too?" she asked finally, nodding at her own brimming glass.

"Coffee's fine," he allowed, aware that she'd deemed him safe.

Nodding, she turned back to the stove, the pot clattering against the metal as she slid it to the back corner to keep it warm.

"Sit down." The words held a measure of courteous warmth, as if she had finally remembered he was a guest in her home. Her own place held a bowl of the stew, and between them reposed a plate of sliced bread, side by side with a round of butter, moisture gleaming from its smooth yellow form.

"You churned today?" he asked.

She nodded, chewing on the first bite of food. "Once a week."

"What do you do with it?" He selected a slice of bread and cut into the slab of creamy spread, smoothing it back and forth as he cradled the crusty heel in his hand.

"Sell most of it in town. Along with the vegetables and my extra eggs."

"You alone here?" His voice was lazy against her ears, the faint drawl softening his words.

She stiffened and stirred the stew with her spoon. "Looks like it, doesn't it?"

"Your brother around, Katherine?" The woman glanced up, her blue eyes widening with a faint trace of alarm.

"If you're Roan Devereaux, you should know to mind your own business where my brother's concerned."

"Your pa spoke of him."

"Did he now?" Her words were flat, disbelieving, as if such a possibility were doubtful.

Up against the wall of her distrust once more, he heaved a sigh of disgust. "You're not what I expected, you know," he said with a grunt of exasperation. "Your pa would have had me believe you were the best thing to come along in his life. 'My daughter, Katherine,' he used to say." His voice was a close imitation of her father's Irish lilt.

"Well, I am what I am," she said, grinding out the words. "My pa's dead and buried, and I owe you for dragging him off a battlefield in Virginia, Mr. Devereaux. If I can repay you in some way, I'll do what I can. But we won't be discussing my brother."

"What happened to your pa?" he asked quietly, his spoon midway to his mouth as he listened to her terse speech.

She pursed her lips and clasped her hands at the edge of the table. "He was breeding a mare and the stud went crazy for a minute. Pa didn't move quick enough. If he'd been just a few inches one way or the other, it mightn't have happened, but one hoof caught his temple and he never woke up."

"Were you here alone?" He watched as she brushed her fingers along the smooth edge of the table, intent on their progress as she touched the worn wood.

"Yes, I was alone." She rose abruptly and reached for his bowl. "Would you like more stew?"

The matter was closed. Her movement, her pinched expression and her pursed lips told him she would speak no longer of the death of Charlie Cassidy.

He handed her the heavy bowl and nodded. She might not be overly friendly, but the woman sure could cook. "What kind of meat you got in that stuff?" He tilted his chair a bit as he watched her brisk movements.

"Rabbit."

His brow rose. "You shoot it?"

Her glance withered him effectively. "No, I hit it with a rock," she said dryly.

He grinned. Perhaps with a little luck, he could get a new horse here after all. Apologies to the stallion he'd picked up for a song just outside of Lexington, but the horse wasn't what he wanted for the long road he'd soon be traveling.

And maybe with a small dose of gentlemanly courtesy, he'd even find a bed hereabouts for the night. Anything would be better than the hard ground he'd been sleeping on lately.

The canvas cot he found in the barn was too short, and he grumbled loudly as he awoke for the third time since midnight. It creaked ominously as he shifted once more, turning himself over gingerly as he sought a modicum of comfort. The other choice had been the hayloft; even given the presence of mice, it might have been the better of the two, he decided glumly, staring into the darkness.

She'd offered the shelter of the barn without much prompting. In fact, her brisk words had come as a bit of a surprise as he'd leaned back in his chair, his appetite eased by the rabbit stew.

"You're welcome to stay out back if you need a place for the night." Busy at the sink, scrubbing at the empty stew kettle, she'd spoken over her shoulder offhandedly, then swung back to her task.

Hesitating only a few seconds, he'd answered, "That's kind of you, ma'am. I'd be obliged to take you up on the offer." His elbows rested on the table, and leaning forward, he watched her. "Maybe we can talk about those horses out in the corral, come morning."

She was silent, but her movements slowed as she appeared to consider his words. Then she lifted the clean kettle from the soapy water and rinsed it with a small dipper. With deliberate motions, she wiped the inside dry with the towel she'd flung over her shoulder earlier.

"I've got nothing to sell right now." She put the pan on the stove with a resounding clang, and its moist surface sizzled on the hot metal.

"Noticed a nice-looking mare that was a good size," he observed idly, his eyes narrowing as he caught a glimpse of slender ankles beneath her swaying skirt.

"We'll talk about it in the morning," she'd said dismissively.

"Well, it's morning now," he muttered. "Pret' near, anyway." With one last turn, he kicked at the blanket that covered him and rose from the narrow cot. In the depths of the barn, he heard the rustling of straw as an animal stirred.

Probably the cow, he decided, getting anxious the way cows usually do about dawn. Time for milking soon. He wondered if Katherine was up yet, if that rope of hair was loose or already braided up and hanging down her back. Shoving long legs into his pants, he reached for the shirt that lay over his saddle, next to where he'd spent the night.

He shook the image of her from his mind as he buttoned and tucked his shirt, tightening his leather belt above his hips before he pushed open the barn door. The sky was pink, there on the eastern horizon, and an owl swooped low in a final flight before the sun sent him to his perch. From the corral, he heard the soft nicker of a horse and the answering call from within the barn. His stallion hadn't taken to being put in a stall when three fillies were just outside the upright slats of the wall next to him.

Roan Devereaux knew the feeling. He'd sensed the same yearning last night, just for a moment, when Katherine Cassidy had risen on tiptoe to light the lantern hanging over her table. The movement had drawn the fabric of her dress tautly against her form, and he'd felt a twinge of response as he watched her. Beneath the shapeless dress was a woman's body, and his own, needy as it was, had answered in a predictable manner. Something about the sun-ripened skin of her cheeks and the length of her slender neck appealed to him. Or maybe it was the intelligence that dwelt in the depths of her gaze as she glanced in his direction, silently weighing him and his purpose here. At any rate, the little brown mud hen was a complex female, he'd decided reluctantly.

"One thing's for sure, she's off limits to you, bucko," he said between gritted teeth, shoving a hand into his back pocket.

The memory of Charlie Cassidy was fresh in his mind and the respect he'd felt for the man spilled over onto the woman who was his daughter. Seeking out an old friend, more for the sake of friendship than the hope of buying a horse, he'd allotted only two days for this detour.

Louisiana was due south, and that was the general direction he'd be heading come tomorrow, if all went well. Katherine Cassidy might be a mite richer when she sold him a mare, but if she ever thought of him again, once she'd seen the last of him, he'd be remembered as a gentleman from the word go. He'd leave the lady as chaste as he'd found her, that was for sure.

Chapter Two

Katherine's eyes widened in disbelief, and a mocking smile curled the corners of her mouth. The sight of Roan Devereaux milking her cow was not what she'd expected to see this morning. But she'd been properly set back on her heels as she halted in surprise just inside the barn.

"Good morning, Katherine." His voice was low and husky.

"Eyes in the back of your head, Mr. Devereaux?" she asked dryly, leaning one arm against the doorjamb.

"No, ma'am. Just recognized your step, the way your skirt swished."

She looked down quickly at the telltale garment and frowned. "Could have been someone else," she argued idly.

He turned his head from the task he'd assumed and his eyes flashed a humorless message. "No. If it'd been someone else, I wouldn't have been sittin' with my back to the door, waitin' to be ambushed."

She nodded, accepting the mild rebuke, and stepped closer. "About done there?"

"About." His hands efficiently stripped the udder of its last drops of milk, and he lifted the bucket to one side before rising from the three-legged stool.

"Where do you want this?" he asked, inclining his head toward the results of his early morning chore.

She shook her head. "It's enough that you beat me to the chores. I'll take care of the rest of the job," she told him briskly, bending to pick up the pail of foaming milk.

His big hand halted her, his fingers grasping her wrist, circling it easily. "I always finish what I begin, Katherine. Just tell me where it goes."

The warmth of that callused hand was a revelation, she decided, her eyes riveted on the place where his flesh met hers. She almost flinched, felt her muscles flex beneath his palm as his touch transmitted a strange, pulsing heat to her skin. Then his hand slid up to grasp her elbow and her eyes rose to meet his, apprehension tightening her jaw and flashing momentarily in her gaze.

"I don't need your help," she said firmly, her chin lifting proudly.

His grin was one-sided, tilting the corner of his mouth in a suggestion of mirth that was gone before the smile could be fully formed. "Didn't say you did." His nod just escaped mockery. "Let's say I'm a little late earnin' my supper from last night."

Turning her by the hold he kept on her elbow, he effortlessly lifted the bucket, careful to keep the warm milk from sloshing over the sides. "Now, tell me where this goes, Katherine."

It was worth more to keep her dignity intact, she decided as she walked through the wide doorway. Arguing with the man would only be practical if it involved something of greater importance than a bucket of milk. She bowed her head in acquiescence and waved her free hand toward the milk house, a small wooden shed, one of several outbuildings.

"There. You'll find a fresh cloth to cover it with. I'll take care of it after breakfast."

"You're cookin' breakfast already?" His words were hopeful.

"I'll feed you before you leave," she said flatly, pulling from his grasp and heading for the house.

Behind her, he halted, the half grin in residence for a fleeting moment. "We haven't talked about a horse yet, ma'am," he reminded her.

Her gait was brisk, and only a man with a quick eye would have noticed the hesitation his words inspired. Roan Devereaux had always prided himself on the accuracy of his eyesight, and he allowed the smile to widen his mouth just a bit. Beneath the brush of his dark mustache, his teeth gleamed for a moment.

"Ma'am?"

Her stride lengthened as she left him behind. Her back was rigid, and chestnut-hued hair hung between her shoulder blades, barely moving against the dark fabric of her dress. Tied with a leather thong at her nape, it reached to her waist. It looked like the silky tail of a Thoroughbred, he noted with absurd pleasure.

Her hand grasped the railing as she stalked up the three steps to the porch. Then, turning to face him, there where he waited, watching her, she spoke, her voice low, her enunciation precise.

"I already told you, Mr. Devereaux. I don't have any horses ready for sale right now. I don't mean to be rude, but after breakfast, I'll expect you to be on your way. I'm sure you'll be able to find an animal suitable for your purposes in town. The livery stable has a good selection. Thurston Wellman will be most happy to sell you a horse."

She lifted one hand to shield her eyes from the rays of sunlight shining from above the horizon in the east. He watched her silently, with a measuring look that gave little indication of his thoughts, and she responded with a calm appraisal of her own.

Her eyes swept his form, lingering briefly here and there as she measured his considerable length. His clothing was well-worn but sturdy, she decided, his denim pants clinging to the strength of his thighs like paper on the wall. His shirt was faded to a nondescript color, but intact, neatly tucked into place, hugging the breadth of his wide shoulders, then tapering to the narrow measure of his waist. Long-legged, his stance casual and relaxed as he watched her, he bore her scrutiny well. The mouth that had twice twitched with amusement at her expense was almost hidden now, his lips pressed together beneath the brush of his mustache. His eyes were narrowed and dark. High cheekbones made her think of an Indian brave, and the straight blade that formed his nose was centered in a face too strong and rugged to be considered handsome.

"You can wash up at the well," she offered finally. "Breakfast will be ready in ten minutes." Briskly, she turned to open the door, and her skirts swayed as she disappeared into the house.

He ate four biscuits, smothered with pale gravy and flanked by several eggs. She'd risen twice to fill his mug with coffee and was surprised to see him add a generous dollop of cream to the dark brew. It was a crack in his spare demeanor, this small luxury, she thought, watching his fingers move the spoon about in the heavy white coffee mug. Katherine silenced the admiration that surged within her as she acknowledged the raw, dark beauty of the man across the table. Roan Devereaux, her father's friend, was not what she had expected.

She ate sparingly, aware of his presence in her kitchen, of each movement of those lean hands as he ate, only the small sounds of their silverware against the thick china plates marring the quiet of early morning. And then she nodded at the murmur of his appreciation as he finished the meal she'd prepared.

Pushing his chair back, he lifted his coffee to drink the last of it, savoring it slowly, watching her over the rim of his mug. "Fine food, ma'am. I'm much obliged," he said, replacing the empty vessel on the checkered tablecloth.

She rose briskly and was up and about, clearing the dishes and removing herself from his presence. He'd been the soul of good manners, she decided, eating the food she prepared and using his utensils with skill and ease. Sometime in his life, someone had taught him well, she thought, wiping up crumbs from the red-and-white oilcloth. Aware of his gaze upon her, she moved quickly, uneasy beneath the cool, measuring eyes that paced her movements.

She rinsed the dishrag and hung it to dry over the edge of the sink, then she set the dishes to soak in soapy water. Closing her eyes, just for a moment, she took a breath and, turning toward him, motioned to the door.

"I've got a heap of work to do, Mr. Devereaux. I need to be up and at it." She'd given him a bed and meals to boot. Roan Devereaux or not, Charlie's friend notwithstanding, she didn't need the strangely disturbing presence of this stranger here. Now to move him on his way, out of her house and on down the road.

"Katherine." His voice reproved her gently.

Her mouth tightened at his reluctance. The sense of unease he inspired within her had to do with that husky inflection in his voice as he spoke her name, she thought. As if he knew all there was to know about Katherine Cassidy and found her lacking. As if he sought to peel away the stark surface she wore like a coat of mail, seeking the softness of the woman beneath the brown drabness. The same warmth she'd felt at the touch of his hand on her flesh earlier reappeared as she listened to the sound of her name on his tongue. He'd rolled it within his mouth, making it appear a many-syllabled word. Not like Pa, who'd more often than not called her Kate or sometimes Katie, when his eyes regarded her with tenderness.

"Katherine," Roan repeated, rousing her from her wandering thoughts. "Can we talk about a horse now?"

She pursed her mouth and frowned at him, disturbed by her meanderings. "Like I said before, I don't have any stock ready to sell."

He shrugged and tipped the sturdy chair back to balance on the back legs. "Can I take a look?"

She shook her head at his persistence. "It wouldn't do you any good. They're all halterbroken, of course, but I've only put a saddle on two of them. They've not been ridden yet." Her pause was significant before she added her final words on the subject, as if to emphasize their import.

"And you can't have my mare."

He shrugged off the edict with a casual grin. "Where's your pa's stud?" he asked lazily, watching her hands bury themselves in the pockets of her apron.

She flushed and her eyes shifted from his gaze. "I had to sell him." The admission was painful, and her mouth tightened.

"You don't have any stock breeding now?"

"Maybe my mare."

He frowned, considering. "I didn't notice."

"If she took, she won't drop her foal till March," Katherine said shortly. "She was in season when I had to let the stud go, so I let him in with her just before . . . before I sold him."

He drew in a breath, shaking his head. She was really something, this small woman who spoke of the breeding of horses as if it were not fraught with danger. "You're not big enough to handle a stallion like your pa's," he said. "You're lucky you got it done without getting hurt."

She shrugged, dismissing his words with the lifting of her shoulders. "You do what you have to. He was strong and a good size, and he'd carried my pa to war and back. I wanted another colt from him before I let him go."

"Could be a filly," he reminded her.

Her gaze was fiercely determined and she shook her head, negating the idea. "No, I need a stud. And I'll have one, give him a couple of years."

"How many are you running in your pasture?" he asked. "Thought I saw a yearling or two."

"Three, actually," she admitted. "The results of last year's breeding. My father had great hopes for them."

"You make it sound sorta dismal, Katherine. Surely the dreams didn't die with Charlie, did they?"

She shrugged off his taunt. "I'm not made of the same stuff my father was, Mr. Devereaux. Someone had to be practical, and Charlie Cassidy was somewhat of a dreamer."

"That's not all to the bad." He dropped the front legs of his chair to the floor with a thump. To his way of thinking, Katherine Cassidy looked like she could use a little dreaming to brighten up her life. As a matter of fact, he decided with a long look at her stiff demeanor, the woman in front of him looked like she'd had all of her dreams shattered. From the top of her smoothly scraped-back hair to the scuffed toes of the shoes showing beneath her dark dress, she looked like a woman who'd buried more than her pa. She was about at the end of her rope, Roan thought. *What am I gonna do, Charlie?*

Rising from the chair purposefully, he reached for his hat, hanging on a peg just inside the door. Easing it into place, he settled it with a final tilt of the brim. His fingers slid into the pockets of his denim pants, thumbs hooked over his belt and his elbows thrust behind him.

All he needed was a gun belt and he'd look like a gunslinger for sure, Katherine thought, her eyes ranging over the man who was thoroughly upsetting her equilibrium this morning. She struggled against the tension that had gripped her upon his arrival yesterday and had remained deeply seated in the depths of her being. His touch had not eased her disquiet any, either, she reflected grimly. Whether it was a natural reaction to a stranger or some individual sense of danger attached to this particular man was the problem.

The former she could handle. The latter, which was more likely to be true, could create a situation she'd gone to great lengths to steer clear of over the years.

His eyes pinned her in place, taking a leisurely journey over the dowdy length of her, and she began to bristle instinctively. He had no right, she thought with rising indignation. No right at all to come in here and make himself at home and then question her about her livestock as if he could pick and choose.

His next words only added to her turmoil. "What are you gonna do with the three mares out in the corral?" he asked mildly, as if he sought to salve her obvious tension.

Her reply was abrupt, snapped off irritably. "Work with them."

"I'll take one off your hands," he offered easily. "Give me a few days to get in the saddle and I'll be out of your way."

"My four-year-old is too small. In fact, I don't have anything big enough for you. Just a three-year-old and she's..." Her eyes softened as she hesitated.

"Doesn't pay to make pets of animals you're bound to sell off, Katherine," he said gently.

Once more her chin tilted as she glared at him. "She's not a pet. But she sure isn't ready to have a saddle thrown on her back and a two-hundred-pound man digging his heels in her sides."

"She's a horse," he said bluntly. "She was bred to be ridden."

"Said like a man," she returned with icy disdain, anxious to be rid of this reminder of her own frailty.

"Any man in particular, Katherine?"

She glanced at him quickly, assessing the question.

He pushed for an answer. "Who made you so prickly?"

"I don't know what you're talking about."

"Maybe, maybe not. But something tells me you're a mite touchy about that sassy little filly of yours."

"That's the key word, Mr. Devereaux. She *is* mine and I intend to keep her."

He smiled agreeably. "That's your right, ma'am." His head nodded in the direction of the barn as he changed the subject with alacrity. "Thought I'd spend a couple of hours out there to pay for my keep."

"It's not necessary," she countered swiftly. She'd felt the warmth creep up into her cheeks as the play of words had swirled between them, and she felt a sudden letdown as he turned from the fray so easily. For a few minutes, she'd felt alive and vital sparring with Roan Devereaux and, in an odd way, enjoying it.

His index finger rose to tilt the brim of his hat in a courtly parody, and he headed for the door with long strides that carried him out onto the porch and down the steps before her protest could be enlarged upon.

She watched, almost unwillingly, yet drawn by the sight of him. Slim-hipped, he walked with a lithe swing that spoke of long years in the saddle and an ease with his own body. Only a slight hitch betrayed him, and Katherine's gaze narrowed as she analyzed the hesitation that marred his easy stride. Then her father's words came back to her, jolting her with the image of savage warfare they had painted.

"Roan paid for my life, girl," he'd said grimly. "That leg of his will wear scars for all of his years. He dragged me when he could hardly make it himself...till both of us were so covered with muck and mire you couldn't make out the pair of us from the mud we crawled through. Him pullin' and tuggin' on me, one hand holdin' my belt and the other clawin' for a good grip on the side of that hill."

Charlie Cassidy had spoken often—and well—of the man who'd saved his life in the midst of battle in Virginia. Her eyes softened as they focused on the barely discernible hesitation in Roan's step now as he strode across her yard.

"I owe you, Roan Devereaux," she whispered with reluctance in the silence of her kitchen. Her shoulders lifted as an indrawn breath shuddered through her. "Maybe I can figure something out." And maybe she'd better quit lollygaggin' around and get busy, she thought, shaking her head as she reluctantly turned her back and headed for the cookstove to bank the fire.

Charlie had left a fine legacy. Although where the mares were concerned, who had produced these charmers was anyone's guess. The yearlings frolicked about the pasture with long-legged freedom, heads tossing and tails flying, performing as though they sensed the admiration of their audience. Oblivious to their antics, a chestnut mare grazed, her nose lifting as she turned her head momentarily in his direction. The man who'd hooked one boot on the bottom rail, leaning casually to watch the animals gambol about in the pasture, was more than just an admiring audience. Roan had earned his respite, the sweat that drew his shirt to cling to the muscles of his back was a damp testimony to his morning's work.

He'd walked the boundaries of the pasture, checking and repairing several weak places in the old fencing, tight-lipped as he considered the amount of work that needed to be done. The condition of the posts and wire had disturbed him, and he was aware that his nailing up sagging wire and shoring up fence posts could only be considered a temporary measure.

Charlie's homestead was not what he'd expected. The horseman who'd befriended him in the last days of his service to the army had not been cut out to be a farmer, it seemed.

Charlie'd been more suited to be a roaming man, Roan thought. More geared to training horses and moving on his way than settling down here on green Illinois pastureland.

And then there was Charlie's daughter. Roan's quiet laugh broke the silence and one of the fillies tossed her head at the sound.

"Yeah, Katherine..." His voice caressed the name and his mouth twisted in a wry grin as he considered the woman. Unyielding at first glance, stiff and unbending with that old shotgun aimed in his direction, she'd glared her best at him. She was still glaring, he thought, only not quite as convincingly.

He'd glimpsed her uncertainty earlier, when he'd touched her arm. Sensed the withdrawal as she shrank from his hand. There was a lot of woman there, he decided, hidden beneath the coarse homespun dress she wore like armor against his gaze. But not just his. She made it her business to look dowdy.

"Doesn't look to me like you've earned your dinner yet."

He spun to face her, his hand brushing against his thigh in an automatic gesture. One her eyes followed with cynical awareness.

"You're lucky you haven't lost these horses before this," he said roughly, his head inclining toward the pasture. "I mended several places that were just one good shove from collapsing."

Katherine nodded. "I've been meaning to check it out. It was on my list," she said dryly.

Along with a hundred other chores, he thought, aware of the unending job she'd taken on when Charlie died.

"Well, what I did will hold for a while. But it was only a lick and a promise. Some of those posts are rotting where they stand. You're gonna have to replace them."

Her sigh was tinged with defeat. "I do what's most needed. And right now, training those horses in the corral is the most important thing."

"Who are you gonna sell them to?" He'd lay money she hated the thought of parting with any one of the sleek mares she was so fond of.

"My mare's not for sale to anyone," she told him, nodding at the chestnut animal approaching them. Katherine's hand reached out to stroke the white blaze that flashed through her mare's forelock and slashed like a narrow sword down the length of her nose. "She's a beauty, isn't she?"

Roan nodded, admiring the picture before him... the woman caught up for a moment in her pleasure with the creature she fondled. "I like the looks of the tall bay," he said, glancing back at the corral Charlie'd attached to the barn.

"The three-year-old? Well, I haven't decided about her. The four-year-old is going to the banker's daughter in town, soon as I finish gentling her real good. The black's mine," she said, her voice soft as she turned to watch the horses in the corral closer to the house.

"Charlie teach you how to train?" he asked as they began to walk back to the house.

She nodded. "Ever since I was big enough to snap on a lead rope and drag a six-week-old foal around in a circle."

They walked side by side, their attention caught by the mares who stood in the shade offered by the barn.

"My pa bought this place from the man who cleared the land and built the house. Matter of fact, we moved in just a while before he left for the war. He'd been fretting about sitting on the sidelines, and one day, he just got on his horse and told me to take care of things till he got back."

"Just like that?"

Her nod was abrupt. "Just like that."

"What did you do?"

"I've always been a dutiful daughter, Mr. Devereaux. I did as he asked. I took care of this place till he did come back. It was a good thing he'd waited so long to go to war. Things had piled up on me by the time he showed up again. I pampered that four-year-old mare and delivered the three-year-old and bought the black with the last of Pa's hidey-hole money. A neighbor lost his mare birthing that one and sold her to me real cheap. He didn't want to waste his time raising her by hand. I spent a lot of hours with a play titty on a bottle till I got her to eat by herself.''

They'd reached the pole fence that surrounded the corral on three sides, and he leaned his elbows on the top rail. The image of Katherine, here alone, struggling with the day-to-day work of caring for a farm and all the animals involved, was an overwhelming idea.

"I don't see how you handled it all," he said finally.

"I managed. We all do what we have to."

"And then?" he said, urging her. "Then he came home?"

"He came home." She took a deep breath, and her smile was tender with the memory. "He rode that big stallion up to the porch one afternoon and called me out of the house, just as if he'd only been gone for a day or so. 'Katie, my love,' he said. 'Your father's home.' Just like that," she told him with emphasis on the words. "Just as if he'd been to town for supplies."

"Was your brother here at all while Charlie was gone?"

"No. I haven't any idea where Lawson was." She glanced at Roan soberly. "I told you, I don't talk about him."

"Charlie—" he began.

"I need to go to the house." Her dismissal was abrupt. "Dinner will be ready shortly."

Katherine's retreat gave him pause, and he watched as she left his side to walk with long, hurried strides across the yard to the small house. *You were right, Charlie. She's small, and fierce, and ready to do battle at the drop of a hat. Not an inch of give to her.*

He followed her, stopping long enough at the well to pump fresh water. Within minutes, he was ready to eat, sleeves rolled above his elbows, hair damp and smoothed back from his forehead. He carried his hat with him into the house and snagged it on the peg inside the door as he passed.

She'd already set the table and was pouring a tall glass of milk as he came in.

"I like milk at noontime," she said, looking his way.

"Sounds like a good idea to me," he agreed, sliding into the chair he'd used the night before.

He ate his fill before he spoke again, his stomach welcoming the chunks of roasted venison and the abundant array of vegetables she'd prepared.

"Someone sure taught you how to cook, Katherine." Moving his chair back, he crossed one booted foot over the other knee.

She allowed her eyes to rest on him for a moment. He looked contented and well fed, sitting across the table. Deceptively idle, for even in repose, there was the look of a hunter about him, a faint menace that set her on edge. He was handy with fence-mending tools, though, she reminded herself, and for that she had to be grateful.

"I found early on if you don't cook, you don't eat," she said finally, uneasy with his compliment. "My pa was never one to lend a hand around a stove, so after my mother died, I learned in a hurry how to put a meal together."

"I wouldn't mind havin' dinner here on a regular basis for a while," he said easily. "Fact is, I've got sort of a deal in mind to offer you."

"I'm not much for making deals. The last time a man tried to make a deal with me, he came close to getting shot for his effort."

"What did he want? The three-year-old mare?"

She caught the amusement in his voice and flushed. "No, he wanted the whole kit and caboodle. The farm, the horses and me."

"I take it you weren't agreeable."

"It wasn't any bargain from my point of view."

"Well, maybe I can strike a better deal than he tried for. It'll involve some of my time and more work than I'd planned on doing right now, but it might pay you to listen up."

"Are we back to my three-year-old?" she asked suspiciously.

"She's a good-sized horse and she's ready to be saddle-broke," he said firmly. "If she's bred from Charlie's stud, I'd like to have a go at her. I can be in the saddle in a week or so, and you can have a hell of a lot of work done around here in the meantime."

"I'm not in the market for a hired hand, Mr. Devereaux."

He flicked her a doubtful glance. "Looks to me like you could use a little help, Katherine. That barn needs some work, and your tack's in bad shape."

"I'll get to it. I can't afford to hire you."

"I'll do a pile of work for a chance at that mare," he said bluntly.

She looked at him, lips pressed together, holding back the refusal it was her inclination to give. "She's worth more than a week's work," she said finally.

He shrugged. "Set a price. Tell me what you want."

"I'll have to think about it." She hesitated, wondering if she could abide letting the spirited mare go to this man. He was right, she acknowledged to herself. She'd made a favorite of the sleek filly, and now she'd pay the price.

"You'll stay in the barn," she said warningly. "I haven't room in the house for you."

"I expected as much." It had been too much to hope that she'd offer Charlie's bed. It sure had to be better than the cot he'd fought with all night long.

"She's probably worth more than you'll want to work out. I won't give her up easy. I'll want some hard cash to boot."

"I don't blame you. She's a good-lookin' horse." He leaned back in the chair once more. "Do we have a deal?"

She pursed her mouth and glared at him, impotent in her need. "I'll run you ragged for a month, and then we'll have to settle on the money end," she said finally.

"Agreed." He held out a hand across the table and she reluctantly placed her palm against his.

"Agreed?" he repeated, prompting a reply, his fingers wrapped about hers.

She flushed, aware only of the warmth of his flesh and the strength of the hand she touched. Looking at him quickly, she nodded, tugging her fingers from his grasp.

"Yes . . . agreed." She plunged her hand into the pocket of her apron, only too conscious of the triumphant gleam that lit his gaze.

Chapter Three

The man's a worker, Katherine acknowledged, a bit grudgingly but with inherent honesty. In just over two weeks, he'd been able to tighten up the barn, his hammer pounding audibly throughout several afternoons. Replacing boards, reinforcing the stalls, then coating the entire interior with whitewash, which he'd told her would reflect the light and brighten up the place.

He'd been right. And not only once. Telling her she needed to quit pampering her three-year-old pet and climb on her back had ruffled her feathers more than a trifle, she remembered.

Again, he'd been more than right. She'd babied the mare beyond reason, scratching her ears till kingdom come, confiding in her with soothing whispers, speaking the fears she could trust to no one. Except to the saucy, long-legged creature who'd stolen her heart the first time she'd seen her, all wet and gawky, swaying on spindly legs.

Wincing as she watched him saddle the bay mare, Katherine had almost turned from the sight. Then, gritting her teeth, she'd watched as his big hands gentled the skittish creature. She'd peered from beneath half-closed eyelids as he mounted the animal the first time, his words too low to be heard, whispered for the benefit of the shivering horse. He'd ridden her with tenacious skill, subduing her brief attempts to spill him from the saddle, his hands easy on the reins, lest he damage her tender mouth.

Only when the brown sides were heaving and the sleek coat was daubed with flecks of foam did he ease from her back. And then only to step quickly in front of the mare, facing the flaring nostrils and wide-eyed gaze, touching with soothing hands and speaking quiet words of praise.

Katherine turned away, her heart aching as she relinquished possession. With strength tempered by kindness and an uncanny knowledge she couldn't help but admire, he'd subdued the feisty creature, forcing her to acknowledge him as master.

"He might as well ride off on her right now," Katherine said beneath her breath, striding from the corral in the direction of the henhouse. "She's his, as surely as if he'd already paid cash up front."

Dealing with the quarrelsome hens took the edge off her unreasonable anger, and she carried the morning's gathering of eggs in her apron as she left the speckled flock to their scattered grain. From the corner of her eye, she caught sight of Roan Devereaux working his magic, rubbing with long strokes at the flank of the filly. Brown coat gleaming in the sunlight, the horse turned her head, looking over her shoulder at the man who tended her with capable hands.

"Turncoat," Katherine grumbled accusingly. "Just like a female, taken in by the first good-looking man to ride down the pike." That she accused her own gender didn't occur to her, since she'd decided long ago that she was a breed apart from the women she'd met in Tucker Center.

"Katherine." His voice claimed her attention and, turning, she frowned, aware of the triumph gleaming from his dark eyes. Even with the length of the yard between them, she still felt the masculine pull of him, the male force that spoke to some small part of her. Brushing aside the unwanted attraction, she faced him with impatience.

"What do you want? I need to take care of these eggs."

His eyes rested on the rounding of her apron, clutched closely against her belly, and he felt a flush of pleasure, for a moment imagining that she would look just so with a child growing there. Chasing the rampant thought from his mind, he gritted his teeth. She'd been thrusting herself into his thoughts with more and more frequency over these past days, and his randy condition was making him ripe for all sorts of foolishness.

She's Charlie's daughter, he told himself firmly. *You're leaving for Louisiana in a couple of weeks, owing her nothing. You'll find plenty of willing women in the next town.* Getting hard never killed a man yet, he decided. And he was sure as shootin' hard up when Katherine Cassidy set him to thinking about planting a baby in her.

He shook his head in disgust.

"I asked you what you want," she repeated impatiently. "You gonna stand there all day and gloat, or have you got something to say?"

"Gloat?" Her choice of word caught his attention, and he frowned as he considered the accusation. "What would I have to gloat over, Katherine?"

She pinched her lips tightly and slanted her eyes in his direction in that arrogant manner that reminded him sharply of her pa. "Never mind," she said. "I've got dinner cooking. You'll have time to clean stalls before we eat." Her eyes gleamed with a triumph of their own as she envisioned him pitching the straw bedding, the aroma pungent in his nostrils.

His nod was quick and he turned away, aware suddenly of her meaning. She'd watched the mare, her eyes anxious, as he rode her. She'd waited, needing to comfort the animal should he deal with her harshly. And then she'd walked away, realizing his taming had only served to bond the creature to him.

"She's mine now, Katherine," he said, his words unheard as she stalked up the steps and across the narrow porch. Her stiff posture told the tale. She was mourning the loss of her favorite, and he acknowledged her sorrow. But a flush of triumph overrode the compassion he felt as he remembered the strength of the horse between his legs. He'd craved ownership of the animal from the first. The elegance of her finely formed head and the sleek lines had drawn him. As had the fiery spirit he'd taken care to subdue without damaging the horse's mettle.

Some lucky man would have to use the same care with Katherine one day. She'd need a light hand, backed by a determined nature, if any man ever expected to keep her in line without shattering the strength of her pride and determination.

Somehow, he no longer attributed her with the stigma of dowdiness. He thought with amusement of his first evaluation. Mud hen. Mud hen, indeed. Her pa had her pegged right, he concluded. She was second cousin to a sparrowhawk, sure enough. Small and feisty, Charlie'd told him. "Plain as puddin'," he used to say. "But under them brown feathers is a heart that's bustin' with courage."

"Sparrowhawk...suits her better than I'd have thought at first," he acknowledged aloud, then grinned as he caught himself. "Talkin' to yourself is a bad sign, Devereaux. Means you been too long without a little female companionship. Makes you drifty."

The quiet of the dinner table was roughly shattered by the sound of gunfire. Roan shot from his chair as though he'd taken the impact of the bullet himself.

"Shut that door," he ordered her as Katherine flew to the open doorway.

She obeyed, her response automatic as she sensed the authority in his voice. Gone was the man of easy gestures, courtly mannerisms and gentle speech. She faced him warily, her back against the heavy planks that made up the door, and watched as he delved within the saddlebag that had taken up residence against the far wall of her kitchen.

With fluid movements, he clasped the gun belt about his hips and took on the guise she had attributed to him weeks earlier. Gunfighter. Warrior, perhaps. Whatever name he wore, his stance in her kitchen proclaimed him ready to do battle, and she acknowledged his ability with silent admiration.

"It's probably not what you think," she told him quietly.

"How do you know what I think?" he asked roughly, striding to the window to stand at one side and bend his head to peer through the curtain.

She drew in a shuddering breath. "I don't, of course. I just think it's maybe someone trying to scare me."

His look was piercing. "Who?"

"I don't know," she quibbled, and then at his frown, she shook her head. "Could be Evan Gardner, a man from town."

"Why? You got somethin' he wants?"

"Yes." A brief smile flitted across her mouth and vanished beneath the pursing of her lips. "He's the man who wants my farm. Not to mention the horses—and of course, he'd like me thrown in to boot." Her words were clipped and harsh, and he felt the anger she suppressed.

"Well, I reckon we'll just have to let him know you're not available, won't we, Katherine?" he asked in a deep drawl that offered a threat to the man who dared to encroach here.

"It might not be him," she said quickly as he strode to where she stood against the door. "It's just that no one else ever bothers me."

"Bothers you! Hell, you haven't even had a visitor since I've been here, lady. If this Evan Gardner comes callin' with his gun cocked and ready, he's askin' for trouble."

Snatching up his rifle from where it stood against the wall, he motioned her to one side and slid the latch on the wooden door.

"Come on out, Katherine." The voice was cunning, grating against his hearing. "I know you're peekin' out. I heard the latch slidin', Katherine. Did I get your attention?" Wheedling and tinged with mockery, the man's words coaxed the unseen woman to expose herself.

"Where is he?" Roan asked quietly, motioning to the window. "Can you see him?"

She slid carefully across the wall, her eyes peering through the white curtain as she sought to see the man who called from outside the house.

"He's right in front of the door, sitting on his horse," she said, catching sight of Gardner and then moving fully in front of the window. "He's put his gun away."

Roan's lips curled back in a grimace of pleasure that belied the flare of anger in his dark eyes. "More fool than I thought," he said with quiet satisfaction.

The door was flung open, and he stepped out on the porch, rifle at the ready, feet apart and braced as he faced the man who waited astride a dark mare. It was worth a bundle, Roan decided quickly, just to see the surprise and then the look of panic that painted Evan Gardner's features, even as his flesh paled abruptly.

"Who the hell are you?" Gardner croaked defensively, fighting for a semblance of dignity. His wide-brimmed hat rode low over his forehead, but yellow hair cascaded over his collar from beneath the band. Bulky and belligerent, he faced the gunman on the porch, his eyes narrowed as he attempted to focus beyond Roan, as if he hoped to espy his quarry within the house.

"I'm the one holdin' the gun," Roan reminded him with a tightening of his grip on the stock. "Maybe you'd like to tell me just who the hell you think you are, comin' here and shootin' off that weapon in a threatenin' manner."

Evan Gardner attempted a jovial gesture, his grin wide and forced. "Just a joke, mister. Me and Katherine always did tend to fool around. Just playin' a little, you understand."

Roan observed him silently, his stance unchanging, his rifle poised before him.

"Hell, I didn't mean anything by it. Katherine knows that. Why don't you ask her yourself?" His color had gone from pale to pasty as the heavily built man watched the unmoving figure on the porch.

"Katherine, come out here," Roan ordered quietly.

She approached the doorway slowly, her nostrils flaring as she sensed the danger emanating from the man who called her name.

"Yes, I'm here," she said, moving to stand beside him.

The barrel of his gun tilted upward, pointing directly at the head of Evan Gardner. "This man the one who gave you grief before?"

"I ain't been near this place since March," whined the intruder.

Roan took one step forward. "Well, if I were you, mister, I wouldn't plan on comin' back for at least another year. In fact, you might be wise to keep your distance from the lady from now on."

Evan Gardner's lip curled in a sneer, as if he realized the danger he was in had receded somewhat. "And what happens when you're not here anymore, stranger? What happens when Katherine there needs a helping hand, and I've got the only one available?"

Roan's brow lifted in derision. "Somehow I doubt she'll ever be that desperate," he said bluntly.

Evan turned his horse in a half circle and touched his spurs to the animal's sides. "Can't never tell, mister. You might not be here then." The horse responded to another urging touch and within moments had crested the hill and headed toward town.

"He from Tucker Center?" Roan wanted to know.

"Yes," Katherine answered. "He has a place just outside of town, just a small holding. He's wanted my pa's horses since the war. I guess he figures he'll take me along in the bargain. Least that's what he's bandied about town."

"Don't sell yourself short, Katherine," Roan told her with a sidelong glance. "You'd be the best part of the bargain. To my way of thinkin', anyway."

She felt a flush rise from her throat and sweep over her face with a heated rush. Turning away quickly, lest he see the telltale blush, she cleared her throat and touched one hot cheek with the palm of her hand. "I hardly think he'd make all this fuss for a spinster like me, Roan. If there was another way to take over here, he'd do it. He'd like to marry me, but just so he can have what I own. At least I'd be pretty safe. He's very much aware that if something happened to me, the whole town would know that he was the first man to suspect."

She took a deep breath, as if she could blot the whole idea from her mind, push it into oblivion. Her smile was shaky, but she persevered. "Anyway, Mr. Devereaux, he's not going to ever get his hands on me or the stock my pa left me. Not to mention the farm and the house."

"How do you plan on holdin' him off, honey?"

She stopped, her indrawn breath filling her lungs as she repeated the endearment in her mind. *Honey.* Spoken in a hushed, tender tone, so at variance with his harsh tongue-lashing of Evan just minutes ago, the word clutched at her heart. *Honey.*

"Katherine?" He reached for her, his hands heavy on her shoulders, turning her to face him. "What did I say? What's wrong?"

She ducked her head, the shining crown almost touching his chest as she sought to shelter from his inquiring gaze. "Nothing's wrong, Mr. Devereaux," she mumbled, both her hands pressed firmly against the heated flesh of her face.

One long finger inched between their bodies, brushing against the rough fabric of her dress until he found the rounded chin he sought. He tilted it upward, frowning his bewilderment at her actions. The shadows on the porch did little to hide the tinge of color still remaining, and he smiled in understanding.

"I said something to embarrass you, didn't I?" he asked gently. "What was it, Katherine? Did I doubt your ability to defend yourself? Was that it?"

She grasped at the straw he offered, and her head nodded, her eyes half-closed against his penetrating gaze. "Yes," she said quickly. "Yes, I . . . I'm a good shot. I can take care of myself. You have no reason to doubt me."

"Look, honey," he began, and watched openmouthed as she tore away from his grasp.

"Don't call me that!" she huffed. "I'm not your 'honey' or anyone else's. I'm not the kind of woman for that sort of sweetsy stuff."

"Sweetsy stuff?" He dropped his hands from her shoulders and gaped. "Is that what you call it when a man uses a plain little old word like *honey* instead of just callin' you by name?" He viewed her with suspicion as she clamped her lips together and looked away from him, her eyes intent on the barn.

"Hasn't anyone ever called you sweetsy names, Katherine?" he asked softly. "Haven't there ever been any men hangin' around, tryin' to court you or just tryin' to get your attention?"

She spun back to face him and her eyes were bleak. "Take a good look at me, Roan Devereaux! Do I look like the sort of woman men come to court? I'm sure not good-looking, and too old to be having babies much longer, and too plainspoken for most of the men hereabouts. What have I got to offer a man in his right mind?"

She was serious! By damn, she was! Standing there telling him she was too dried up to appeal to a man. And here he'd been feeling like a randy, apple-cheeked boy around here for the better part of a week already. With that slim body hiding beneath those ugly dresses she put on every morning, and that long, dark hair that made his fingers itch to twine themselves in its length. Not good-looking? With color like the pale side of a peach and skin like a newborn babe's and those dark blue eyes that reached inside and touched a man's soul... Well, it was too much to be believed.

"Ah, hell, Katherine! You don't know what you're talkin' about," he said harshly. He allowed his eyes to roam the length of her, from the darkness of her hair, fresh and clean and smelling like the soap she kept by the kitchen sink, to the leather thong that held her dress loosely about her waist.

She blinked at him, shook her head in bewilderment at his words. "I do," she said, denying him.

His hands came to rest once more on her shoulders, this time holding her firmly, lest she pull from his grasp. "Do not," he growled. And then he bent forward and claimed the mouth that had begun to form another protest.

She gasped in surprise, aware only of heated breath filling her mouth, warm flesh covering her lips, containing her in a damp, hungry embrace that sent her senses reeling. She drew in air through her nose and stared at him, her eyes unable to focus, only aware of the thick brush of his eyebrows, riding above his heavy-lidded eyes. And then he closed them, those dark, unfathomable orbs that had so easily warmed her with their regard just seconds past.

Her lips attempted to close, but he would not let her bring them together, playing along the edges with the hot sword of his tongue instead. There, just inside her upper lip, where the flesh was tender and sensitive, he brushed his weapon. Back and forth he swept with a slow movement that brought a gasp of surprise from her throat. He swallowed that, too, resuming his exploration of her mouth, his lips closing just a bit, his teeth finding a hold on her lower lip as if he would nip lightly at the delicate skin. Then, catching her unaware, he moved to whisper a series of kisses from one side of her upper lip to the other, his mustache teasing her sensitive flesh. He chuckled softly.

"Roan!" she whispered on a quick gasp of air.

"No more Mr. Devereaux?" he asked with another chuckle.

She was stunned. Speechless and inert, she hung between his hands, only the grip of his fingers holding her erect. And then those warm hands slid the length of her arms and somehow fastened themselves about her waist, finding a home at the small of her back, where he clasped his fingers to hold her captive.

"Never been kissed, Katherine?" he asked gently.

"Of course I..." She stopped. "No... you know I haven't," she admitted finally, fastening her eyes on his, afraid to allow them permission to look fully at the mouth that had plundered her own so thoroughly.

"You'll do better with a little practice," he told her cheerfully. "But for a beginner, you sure pack a wallop, lady."

"A wallop?"

"A punch," he explained, delighted by the color washing over her countenance once more. He looked at her assessingly. How had he thought her plain? The fine lines of her eyebrows cast a perfect frame above the brilliant blue of her eyes. Eyes that were viewing him with a wonderment that pleased him immensely. Her nose was almost too straight, only a small deviation at the tip marring its perfection, almost like a dimple. And then there was her mouth. He looked at it again, soft and swollen a bit, reddened from his caresses. He tugged her closer against him and she gasped, the sound a shocked whisper of his name.

"Roan!" She stiffened against him. Against her body, pressed tightly, with only the layers of clothing they wore separating her from its threat, she felt ... Her eyes closed again and her lips tightened.

"Let me go." It was quiet, but a demand echoed in those words, and he obeyed.

"I'm sorry, Katherine. I didn't mean to..."

She stepped back once, and then again, until the wooden wall of the house pressed against her back. Her face was pale now. Gone was the becoming flush, the pink cheeks stained by her guileless innocence.

"I didn't mean to frighten you," he said quietly, allowing her the width of the porch, aware he had invaded unforgivably.

"I'm sure you have things to do in the barn or the pasture ... or somewhere," she managed to say, her voice high and breathless in her ears. Here she'd been worried about Evan Gardner coming around, giving her trouble, causing her grief. Somehow she knew Evan Gardner couldn't hold a candle to Roan Devereaux when it came to causing problems for her.

In fact, if the sensations washing their way through her body were any indication, Roan Devereaux had already managed to cause more hassle than she was equipped to handle.

"And that's a fact," she mumbled beneath her breath as she watched him stride, with only an almost imperceptible limp, across the yard toward the corral.

Chapter Four

"I'll wash your clothes if you bring them to the house."

He'd wondered how she would greet him this morning. After the general all-around mess he'd made of last evening, he hadn't known what to expect. Certainly, Katherine knew what to look for from a man who was all hot and bothered. Or did she? Her total experience with males appeared to have begun and ended with horse breeding. Hell, that ought to have taught her something!

He looked at her finally, aware she'd been fidgeting about with her hands all twisted up in her apron, waiting for an answer to her offer. Her expression was calm, but a telltale tinge of pink stained her cheeks, and together with the knot she was managing to put in the front of her voluminous apron, he knew she'd dreaded this encounter.

"I reckon I'd appreciate havin' my clothes washed up, Katherine," he responded gently. "I can scrub them out myself, though, if you leave the water when you've finished your own things."

"That won't be necessary. I've done a passel of laundry in my day, keeping my menfolk clean," she answered crisply. Her eyes met his gaze for a moment and then skittered off to fasten on the low ceiling of the barn, just over his head.

"I'll bring them up to the house directly. Soon as I finish putting this stall door back together."

She nodded briefly and turned to make her way from the barn. Roan's eyes rested on the dark dress that hung so limply from her squared shoulders, and his mouth twisted in a smile of remembrance as he visualized the slim form she hid so well beneath the sturdy fabric. His hands had personal knowledge of her waist. It bore no resemblance to the length of the leather thong she had taken to using for a belt.

If any woman needed rescuing from herself, it surely was Katherine Cassidy, he thought idly, his lips twitching with humor. It'd be no small task for the man brave enough to take it on. And it was certain sure *he* wouldn't be around to tend to the job.

"Breakfast is almost ready," Katherine told him, calling the words over her shoulder as she stepped through the wide doorway into the early morning light. "Leave that door for later."

"Yes, ma'am." Obediently, he put aside his hammer, brushing his hands against the denim that covered his thighs. The grin he'd restrained for her benefit split his mouth and remained in place as he gathered up the few pieces of clothing he'd folded and stowed beneath his blankets on the cot—anything for a little padding.

That hayloft was looking better night after night. If it weren't for the fact he'd be leaving shortly, he'd even consider building a bunk against the wall and stuffing a mattress with fresh straw.

Ah, no sense in getting too comfortable. Before long, his bed would be the bare ground. Maybe a few leaves or a good stand of grass for padding. The country between southern Illinois and River Bend was pretty green for a while yet. Autumn was late in coming to the south, and with a little hustle, he could miss the cold nights that would soon be heading this way.

He sauntered to the house, his dirty clothes tucked beneath one arm. Slowing long enough to drop off his bundle next to the washtub Katherine had dragged from the porch, he hesitated. A fire burned not far from the well, a metal pail hanging over it from a tripod, the water within steaming, catching his eye. Retracing his steps, he picked up his shirt and folded it compactly. Then, with casual ease, he reached for the pail, using the shirt to shield his palm from the hot metal handle. After emptying it into her washtub, he filled the bucket from the well, replacing it over the fire to heat.

"Thank you, Mr. Devereaux," Katherine called from the doorway where she was watching. "I was about to come out and do that myself."

"Saved you a few steps," he answered, washing his hands at the horse trough. He splashed the water over his face and used his wet hands to plaster his hair down, running his fingers through it to groom the dark length into a semblance of order. Katherine tossed him a towel as he mounted the steps, and waited until he had dried his face and hands.

"Thank you, ma'am."

"Ma'am?" she asked with a lifting of one eyebrow.

"Matches the 'Mr. Devereaux' you've been spoutin' this mornin'," he reminded her with a rakish smile. "Thought maybe you were tryin' to put me on my best behavior, Katherine."

"Not much chance of that, is there?" she asked, crossing to the stove to dish up the oatmeal she'd had simmering on the back corner. A pan of biscuits and a plate of sausage from the warming oven up top completed the meal, and Roan settled down to the business of eating, blithely ignoring her final gibe.

"Tell me," he said between bites, his fork held upright as if he commanded her attention. "Tell me how you got those yearlings out there with not a mare in sight? They got birthed somehow, but I sure haven't figured out where, or what you did with their dams.''

She lifted one of her eyebrows in a gesture of triumph, and a dimple showed high on her left cheek as she suppressed a smile. ''One of my better deals—actually three of them. My father and I offered his stallion for breeding at three different farms hereabouts and asked for a foal from each of the farmers. They all had mares they wanted bred, more than a dozen between them, and Pa's stud was the best-looking horse in the area. They jumped at the chance. They ended up with free stud service for their mares, and we got the three foals for nothing, once they were weaned from their mamas.''

Roan eyed her with new respect. ''Your idea?'' he asked.

She nodded. ''One of my better ones. We needed new blood, and we didn't have much money available. Pa'd sold off everything we'd trained and saddle broke, and he was getting itchy feet again. It was hard for him to stay in one place. I think he bought this farm for my benefit, knowing how sick of roaming the countryside I was. He said it was time to put down roots and find me a husband.''

''I expect you didn't look very hard, did you? Seems to me you wouldn't have much trouble finding a man if you put your mind to it.''

She sniffed and turned her head aside. ''I've seen enough men in my time to know for a fact I don't need one to warm my bed at night. Never could see much benefit for a woman in marriage anyway.''

''Maybe you looked at the wrong men,'' he suggested mildly.

''Men are men,'' she stated, as if that were the final word on the subject.

His nod was agreeable and he set to eating, accepting her decree. Katherine watched him with furtive glances as he made his way through the abundance of food before him. The man did appreciate good meals, she thought, her eyes focused on the hands that wielded his fork and spoon with innate grace. Well formed and darkly tanned, those hands held eating utensils with ease, as easily as they used the tools from the shed.

With as much skill as they'd demonstrated touching her body last evening, she thought, remembering the heat of his palms against her waist. Even through the heavy homespun of her dress, she'd felt the warmth of him, the bold touch of his fingers tugging her against his hard body. She shivered suddenly, shifting in her chair as her errant thoughts tread the dangerous ground that lured them. Maybe she'd not have been so dead set against getting married if someone like Roan Devereaux had come along when she was more amenable to the idea.

Roan's eyes speared her quickly, snagged by the quick lift of her breasts as she gained a deep breath, fastening on the flaring of her nostrils and the dark awareness shining in her eyes. He chewed methodically, his gaze narrowing as he watched her...noting the faint flush painting her throat and creeping upward.

Wiping his mouth with the edge of his hand, he picked up his coffee, eyes never veering from the woman across the table. Damned if she didn't look flustered to beat all.

Things would be better all the way around if she didn't keep looking at him the way she was right now. He wasn't the man she needed. And heaven knew he'd got an awful itching urge to cart her off to her bed ... and then she'd be compromised, but good. And he wouldn't be as good for her as Evan Gardner. At least Evan wanted to marry her.

Hell, he couldn't sit around here any longer, he decided. She had him going in circles and she hadn't even touched him. Except with the bluest eyes he'd seen since the day he met Charlie Cassidy.

His chair scraped against the plank floor and he rose hastily. "I'll just get back to the barn, Katherine," he muttered, groping with one hand for his hat as he turned toward the door. "Mighty fine meal," he called back as he strode across the porch, his steps long and hurried.

"Here's your hat...what's your hurry?" she said beneath her breath, relieved to have him gone. "He stirs me up, and I don't like it." Her mouth pursed as she considered him, glaring at his long legs, which carried him quickly across the yard. He was limping a bit this morning. "Not that I care," she grumbled. "He can limp all the way to Timbuktu and back, for all it matters to me."

He managed to stay out of her way for the rest of the week, making his way to the house for meals and tending to his business otherwise. The pasture fence took on a new look, the posts erect once more, the poles firmly attached and anchored in place. He'd hung a new gate, after viewing the old one with a shake of his head. Sagging and swinging from handmade hinges with half the nails missing, it was a wonder she'd been able to handle it at all. The ruts were deep where she'd been dragging it across the ground to lead the yearlings in and out, and he frowned at the thought.

How much more had she put up with on her own? he wondered. He hadn't even looked around much inside the house, not enough to spot the places that needed repairing, anyway. And sure as the sun rose and set every day, she wouldn't be asking him to spend any time in her kitchen. Leastways, not any longer than it took to eat a meal and vamoose out the door.

"I've given her a good case of leavin' alone, Charlie," he said dryly, casting his eyes heavenward. Somehow it seemed likely Charlie'd headed in that direction, he thought, remembering the gray-haired soldier who'd made little fuss over his Bible reading or the quick words he spoke over his meals.

"Wish you were here, old man," Roan muttered, turning his attention to the bridle he was mending. The sun beat on his back through the dark cotton of his shirt and he relished the heat with a lifting of his shoulders. Tugging at the bit, he assured himself that the leather would hold, then, putting it aside, reached for the halter that awaited his care.

He was about done. The month was up and he'd set his hand to every chore he could find, aside from the house Katherine guarded so closely. He'd ask her politely about it before he left, in case she needed something done that wouldn't hold over the winter. Fat chance she'd give me space to work inside her sanctuary, he thought with a grin. She guarded it like a smuggler's cave.

His eye was caught by a flash of color and he looked up to see her quickstepping across the yard in his direction. The apron she wore was yellow, bright against her dark dress, and he wondered for a moment where she'd dug it from. Every other single piece of clothing he'd seen on her looked like they'd been cut from the same cloth . . . dark and somber.

"New apron, Katherine?" he asked teasingly.

She shook her head impatiently and he straightened abruptly, rising from the stool he'd dragged into the sunshine.

"What's wrong?" His eyes moved over the yard, up the hill to the small cemetery, and then darted across to the rise just east of the garden. Satisfied that no immediate danger threatened, he turned his attention to her face, puzzled by the expression she wore.

A mixture of panic and embarrassment painted her features and her hands were linked tightly against her waist. "I feel foolish," she blurted, her teeth biting against her lower lip.

Relief flooded him and he grinned at her admission. "Can't imagine that, Katherine."

"I'm not generally easy to fluster," she told him, her fingers flexing as she relaxed the grip that had fused them so tightly. Lifting one hand to her forehead, she brushed aimlessly at the tendrils of hair blowing about her face.

"Well, I'd say somethin' disturbed you in a big way," he allowed, amused at her dithering.

Her mouth pinched tightly and she glared at his teasing grin. "It's not funny, Roan Devereaux!" she spouted. "There's a whole family of mice underneath my cupboard!"

His eyes danced with delight. "Is this the same woman who threatened me with a shotgun and came within an inch of runnin' me off her place?" He shook his head in disbelief. "I didn't think there was a thing in this world that could put the fear of God in you, Katherine Cassidy. I'm glad to see I was wrong. You're pret' near as human as the next one, after all."

She stiffened and narrowed her eyes. "I'm not afraid," she denied stoutly. "I just don't know what to do with them."

He hooted with laughter. "Well, I doubt they're big enough to warrant a shotgun blast. Reckon a swat with the shovel would take care of the matter."

She shuddered visibly. "I couldn't do that."

"Well, you could always make pets out of 'em."

"Don't be ridiculous," she sniffed. "I should have known better than to expect any help from you." Her skirts tangled about her legs as she spun around and headed back to the house, her face crimson with embarrassment.

His hand on her shoulder effectively halted her progress and the warmth of his breath next to her ear caused another shiver to cascade through her.

"Aw, come on, Kate," he coaxed softly. "Don't take on so. I can handle most any kind of problem around here you can throw at me, so long as you don't get all huffy and stomp off."

Her head dipped and she caught a deep breath. "Just let go of me, Roan Devereaux, and go clean out that nest of critters before your dinner burns to a frazzle." Her voice trembled just a bit and he peeked over her shoulder, bending lower to scan her flushed countenance.

"Well, we sure can't have that, can we?" he said softly. And he then bent even lower to drop a quick kiss against her cheek. "Consider it done, ma'am." His hand squeezed gently for a moment before he dropped it from her shoulder.

"I don't want to know..." she began, calling after him as he climbed the steps to the porch.

"Why don't you go gather the eggs or somethin'," he suggested from the doorway, turning to face her. She was worrying her bottom lip again, and he fought the smile twitching at his mouth.

"Yes, I'll do that." Relief was alive in her voice as she spun away and headed quickly to the henhouse. He watched till she slipped inside the wire fence, shooing the clucking hens before her, preventing their escape from confinement.

By the time she pushed the henhouse door open minutes later, holding her apron tightly to protect the eggs she carried, he'd disappeared from sight. She hesitated, unsure whether he was still in the house, her eyes scanning the garden and beyond for a glimpse of him.

"Roan?"

"Go rescue your dinner." He was somewhere near the other side of the house, his voice carrying on the breeze.

"Yes...all right," she said quickly, intent on putting aside all thought of his solution to the problem.

She picked at her food, waiting for the sly digs to begin, certain he wouldn't be able to resist at least one reference to her being so softhearted. But she waited in vain. He ate swiftly and well, silently offering his plate for seconds, devouring the chicken and dumplings with obvious enjoyment. He sat back finally, a sigh of satisfaction the first sound to escape his lips since the meal began.

"Had enough?" She looked up, still shifting the carrots around on her plate.

His raised eyebrows saluted the movements of her fork. "Looks like you aren't much for your own cookin' today, Katherine."

She placed the utensil beside her plate and folded her hands in her lap. "I guess I wasn't in the mood for chicken. I didn't seem to work up much appetite this morning."

"Well, you can just heat up the leftovers later on," he told her. "It'll save you cookin' supper after while."

"I'd have to add a mess of vegetables to the pot and call it soup," she said with a quick smile in his direction. He wasn't going to tease her, she realized, and her smile widened.

"A pan of cornbread would go real well with that," he suggested hopefully. "You sure do make good pone, Kate."

It was the second time he had shortened her name today. She considered him. Leaning back in his chair, he looked utterly relaxed. It was an illusion, she knew for a fact. Rarely did Roan Devereaux allow himself to be off guard. As if he were aware of every movement within his range of sight and hearing, he kept watch. That he could do so and still maintain a conversation puzzled her.

Another puzzle was his calling her "Kate."

"My father used to call me that," she said quietly.

"Kate?"

She nodded. "No one else ever has, just Charlie."

"I didn't mean to be too familiar. Sometimes you just look like...like you ought to be Kate." His eyes were dark, their regard warming, and his mouth was pursed as he studied her.

"I don't mind," she said quickly. It was a familiarity that pleased her somehow. And she fought against the pleasure it brought her. *He'll be gone... before you know it, he'll be gone,* she told herself. *And you'll miss him.*

That admission was a new one. So hurting was it, she rose and gathered up the plates and forks, carrying them to the sink and depositing them with a clatter in the tin dishpan waiting there. She couldn't afford to miss him, she thought, blinking away the hot tears burning against her eyelids.

"Katherine?"

She heard his chair scrape against the floor and she blinked furiously, determined to hide any evidence of weakness. *Not on your life, Roan Devereaux,* she thought furiously. *You've already known me for a softhearted female once today. I'll be switched if you see me being foolish again.*

"It's time to be movin' on," he mused beneath his breath as he pounded the last nail into place. The stall door hung straight, the latch was in place, and for the life of him, he couldn't find another thing to do in the barn.

On top of that, Katherine was looking better to him all the time, and he surely didn't need a woman to complicate his life right now. At least, not on a long-term basis. And Katherine was definitely not a bed-'em-and-leave-'em woman.

He watched her from the barn door. Watched as she took the last of his clothing from the line she'd strung between the cabin and the milk house. His gaze was fixed on the heavy rope of hair that caught the sunlight and gleamed with hidden fire. Prettier than a spotted pony and twice as spunky, he thought with a subdued chuckle. She'd be a prize for the right man. One willing to look beyond her fierce pride and drab demeanor.

"Katherine," he called, reluctantly heading in her direction. "How about if I take a look inside the house and see what needs tending before I head out of here? Thought I'd see what I can put to rights for you."

Her head shot up and she put out one hand in an unmistakable gesture. "My house will do fine, thank you. I manage to keep it up to snuff without any trouble at all."

He lifted one eyebrow in silent question. "If you're sure about that..." he said, unwilling to push, aware of her fierce possessiveness when it came to her own surroundings.

"Are you heading out?" she asked bluntly.

He sauntered closer, his eyes intent on her fisted hands, clenched at her sides, betraying the tension she sought to conceal. Katherine was not nearly as unconcerned about being here alone as she let on, he decided.

"It's about time. I'm pret' near thirty years old and my family hasn't seen me in ten or twelve years." His laugh was rusty. "Fact is, they might not be too excited about my comin' home. But I figure it's time to let 'em know I'm still alive and kickin'."

"They'll be glad to see you, Roan," she said quietly, her eyes on his guarded expression. "I'll bet your mother watches for you every day."

"Well, you sure don't have any notion of how Letitia Devereaux carries on, I can see that," he answered dryly. "About the last thing she's thinkin' about is her long-lost son. Matter of fact, I'm probably the biggest disappointment in her life. I doubt she ever got over my fightin' for the North."

Katherine regarded him thoughtfully. "I wondered that myself," she admitted. "Just thought it wasn't my business to ask questions, though."

Roan squatted in the shade of the milk house and picked up a handful of small stones from the ground between his knees, one at a time, looking each over carefully. As if he considered his words with equal care, he spoke hesitantly.

"Slavery wasn't the issue with most Southerners, you know. But it was with me. I had a hard time with the right of one man to own another, no matter what the law said. Still do, for that matter. My father and I had a go-round more than once, after I got to be full grown. He said I had to learn my place in life and it wasn't workin' side by side with the slaves and bein' familiar with them." He looked up at her with somber eyes. "I couldn't consider the boys I'd grown up with as less than men," he said harshly. "And to my father, they were 'boys,' fit only to work in the fields." He shrugged. "We didn't see eye to eye. So I left."

"And fought on the side of the North," she said quietly.

"Yeah, that was sorta strange, I guess. When I wrote to my mother, after the war, I told her. She wrote me back while I was in the hospital in Philadelphia, where they patched my leg up for the last time."

"I'll warrant she was worried about you," Katherine told him.

His laugh was harsh. "Maybe, maybe not. What she was was ashamed of me. That I would fight against my 'own kind' was more than she could tolerate, she said."

"Why do you want to go back?" Katherine asked after a moment.

He stood, brushing his hands together as the stones fell once more to the ground. "Haven't figured that out yet," he told her with a grim smile. "Somethin' just seems to be tuggin' at me to go home. Maybe I think things will be different, now that the war's over. Maybe I need to make peace with my daddy before it's too late to put things right."

Katherine shaded her eyes from the sun as she looked up at him. "What if they don't want you back?" The thought that any parent would turn aside his child was abhorrent to her, but the possibility surely existed where Roan Devereaux was concerned.

His grin was crooked as he tilted his hat back with one finger. "They might not. Far as I know, they've still got my brother there to handle things. If there's no place for me, guess I'll just meander along and head west," he said with a shrug of his wide shoulders. "I'm not sure I'm cut out for that kind of life, anyway."

"Seems to me you did pretty well, staying here," she ventured.

He straightened abruptly and his look was deliberately forbidding. "I was tryin' to pay a debt and puttin' in time to pay for that mare in the corral, Katherine. All we need to do is come up with an amount of cash to cover the difference and I'm gonna be on my way."

She frowned at his words. "What debt are you talking about?"

He shook his head. "Never mind. The important thing right now is the money I owe you." He pulled a leather purse from his back pocket, soft and well-worn at the folds. "What's it gonna be, Katherine? How much for the horse?"

Her eyes were narrowed, her mouth tight as she pressed her lips together. "You don't owe me one damn cent, Roan Devereaux. You can get your gear together, including those clothes I just took off the line, and vamoose anytime you want. Consider the work you did sufficient price for the mare."

If the man wanted to leave this morning, let him get on his way, she thought, annoyance at his high-and-mighty attitude raising flags of color in her cheeks. She spun on her heel and headed for the house, almost tripping over the wicker clothes basket as she went. She kicked it out of her way and stalked to the porch, pulling her skirts above her ankles to climb the steps.

Roan watched, hands on hips, eyes never leaving her drab form as she entered the house. She sure was in a huff. Probably just as well. "Eliminates havin' a big song and dance about sayin' goodbye," he muttered. "I'll just leave ten dollars on the porch when I go and pick up supplies in town."

She stood to one side of the window ten minutes later and watched as he rode across the yard, brushing at the tears that would not be denied. He stepped down from the mare long enough to lay something on the porch, and then, with a last look at the doorway, mounted his horse.

His voice carried easily to where she watched, and her lips tightened as she heard his words.

"I'm much obliged, Katherine. You're a credit to your pa."

She swiped furiously at the hot tears, and her muttered words fell unheard in the silence he left behind.

"You hateful man. You're sure not worth crying over." She hiccuped loudly and sniffed, wiping at her nose with the back of her hand. "Damn you, Roan Devereaux."

Chapter Five

"How'd you ever talk Katherine Cassidy out of a mare?"

Roan eyed the livery stable owner with a tight grin. "I worked it out. She needed some repairs done and I'm kinda handy with tools."

"Huh!" Thurston Wellman expelled his breath forcefully. "Never thought I'd see the day that gal would let loose of another one of her horses, after she had to sell that stud of her pa's. She's tighter'n an old maid's pucker when it comes to her animals."

Roan waited patiently for the older man's nattering to cease. He'd known the sight of him atop the sleek mare would set tongues wagging and he'd been right. Evan Gardner had been in the general store just minutes ago, his eyebrows at half-mast when Roan came through the doorway.

"How'd you get your hands on one of Cassidy's horses?" the man had blurted out. "Does Katherine know you're ridin' her mare?"

Roan had given him a glare to end all and turned to the storekeeper. His list was long, and it took more than a few minutes to name the supplies he'd need for his trip. At least for the first leg of the journey.

In the meantime, Evan had stomped out the door, reentering minutes later. "That's surer than the dickens one of

Cassidy's horses," he'd said vengefully. "You got no right to that mare, stranger."

Roan had turned to face the man. "If you got a problem, I'll meet you out front. Are you callin' me a horse thief?" The words were spit with precision, the tone tightly leashed but edging toward anger.

Evan Gardner wisely backed off, his face ruddy, his words sputtering without coherency from his lips. "Never said, uh, didn't mean . . . sure didn't . . ."

Roan had spun to the storekeeper. "I'll be back in an hour or so. Can you have it packed and ready for me?"

With the man's assurance still in the air, Roan had left the store, brushing past Evan Gardner with a look of scorn.

Now he tended to the business at hand. The purchase of a packsaddle was next on his agenda. The stud he'd ridden through Tucker Center just over a month ago would carry his supplies, perhaps trading off with the mare if she needed spelling during the long journey.

"You got a packsaddle I can buy?" he asked Thurston Wellman. He'd loosened the girth on the mare and turned the stallion into the small corral while he'd gone to the dry goods store earlier. Now it was time to do his business and make tracks to the south.

Thurston cleared his throat, loathe to miss a sale of any sort. "I expect I can locate what you need, mister. Might take me an hour or so to come up with it, though. You got anything you need to do? Mebbe you'd like to wet your whistle over at the saloon while I check things out."

The idea of a long swallow of beer was mighty appealing to Roan. It'd been a long dry spell since he'd left Ohio, heading for Charlie Cassidy's spread. But drinking and riding a trail didn't mix well in his book. In fact, he might just bed down at the hotel for the night and make it an early start in the morning.

"Sounds good to me," he told the livery stable owner. "Maybe I'll stay overnight and head out early." He swept his hat from his head and tossed it to rest on a bale of hay. "Show me a stall for my mare and I'll unsaddle her."

"Second one on the right," Thurston said agreeably. "You can stow your tack over yonder. It'll be two bits for the night, if you leave the stud in the corral. I'll feed 'em both."

Roan nodded. He led the mare to the stall and stripped the saddle from her back. Replacing the bridle with a halter, he rubbed her down, his hands possessive as they swept the glossy length of her. Checking twice to be sure she was securely tied, he left the stall.

"I'll toss her some hay," Thurston told him. "There's some for your stud already in the hay rack outside."

Roan grunted in reply, snatching his hat on the way out the double doors into the sunlight.

Already it had started, he thought gloomily, catching sight of sidelong glances as he passed small knots of townsfolk. Noting the speculative look on the face of the local lawman as he neared the jail, he slowed his steps.

"Sheriff?" he said, greeting the robust man cordially.

"Yessir, I'm Sheriff Doober." The man straightened from his post against the wall. "You the feller asked about the whereabouts of the Cassidy place a while back? Heard from Evan Gardner you was stayin' out there. He was kinda upset, bein' an admirer of Katherine and all."

"I was there. Now I'm leavin'. My name's Roan Devereaux. I'm an old friend of Charlie's," he told him, hand outstretched in greeting.

With a degree of reluctance, the lawman met his grip. "Heard tell you got away with one of Charlie's mares," he said, his words tinged with admiration.

"Mares aren't Charlie's anymore," Roan corrected him. "They belong to Miss Katherine now, and yes, I made a deal with her for one of them."

"She's kinda low on stock, ain't she? What with sellin' one to the banker for his daughter pretty soon, she'll be scrapin' the bottom of the barrel."

Roan nodded. "Pretty close. She's got one more filly she's workin' with and the yearlings she's trainin'."

"Looks like she'd think twice before she sold off her breeding stock," Sheriff Doober said.

"Want to ride out there with me and ask her about it?" Roan offered quietly.

The other man shook his head. "No, I don't reckon I do. Just makin' conversation."

Roan nodded and walked on, feeling himself the center of attention. The town probably hadn't had this much excitement in years, he thought with a suggestion of good humor. It sounded like Katherine had a reputation for being stingy, least when it came to her horses.

He made a quick stop at the dry goods, where Orv Tucker, the owner, agreed to store his purchases in the back room till morning. "Won't be no trouble at all," he assured him.

Across the street was the hotel, the tallest building in town, with elegantly carved wooden curlicues and flourishes garnishing its framework. As though expecting his arrival, the clerk met Roan with an ingratiating smile, assigning him a room with much fuss and ado. Extolling the virtues of the establishment, the clerk ushered him up the stairs, unlocking the door with a flourish.

"Yessir, we've got the finest rooms for fifty miles," the young man boasted. "Our dining room's known all over the area. Why, we get folks come from miles away just to eat dinner here," he said, beaming with pride.

Roan waited patiently, nodding agreeably, then herded the enthusiastic clerk out the door.

"I'll send up a pitcher of hot water," came the final word from the young man as he stood in the hallway.

"You do that," Roan answered, already stripping off his shirt. He turned the glass knob once more and stuck his head through the open door. "In fact, make that a whole tub of hot water. Might be the last chance I get for a good bath for a while."

A marked contrast to the short cot and the quiet barn, he found the hotel to be a mixed blessing. The bed was comfortable but the sounds coming through the open window kept him awake half the night.

"Didn't know the saloon would be open till all hours," he grumbled to the desk clerk in the morning. "Man can't get a decent night's sleep."

"Should have closed your window, sir," the clerk ventured mildly, counting the coins Roan had given him.

"Felt like I was in a tomb, with all that velvet hangin' all over the place," Roan growled. "Can't sleep without fresh air."

Breakfast was plentiful in the hotel dining room. Ignoring the speculation he encountered on several faces, he plowed through the plate full of ham and potatoes he'd ordered. It wasn't near as good as one of Katherine's meals, he thought, wiping his mouth with the linen napkin.

He deliberately set his mind to other things, her image too vivid for comfort. "Forget the woman," he told himself beneath his breath, marching down the wooden sidewalk. "She can take care of herself just fine. You got other fish to fry, Devereaux."

Thurston Wellman, busy harnessing a mare, nodded to him as he strode into the livery stable. "Got you what you need all right. It's over there."

The packsaddle lay across a sawhorse outside his mare's stall, and Roan noted its age with concern.

"It's in good shape, Mr. Devereaux," the man assured him as he hurried over. "I checked it out first thing this morning, and it's good and sturdy. Only cost you a dollar."

Roan nodded. "Sounds fair," he allowed, digging for the coin in his pocket.

"Hear tell Evan Gardner is het up about you gettin' the mare from Miz Cassidy," Thurston confided in an undertone.

"None of his damn business," Roan said with a grunt, lifting the mare's saddle to her back.

"He's been tryin' to make her his business for a while now. He's a determined son of a gun. I'll put my bet on Katherine, though. She's a spunky little gal."

"Yeah, she can handle that shotgun like a trooper," Roan agreed. The saddle was cinched and he slid the bit into the mare's mouth, fastening the bridle in place.

"I'll bring the stallion in," Thurston offered. "We'll have you ready to go in no time at all."

"Yeah," Roan said glumly, aware that his early morning enthusiasm was rapidly evaporating.

"I did what I could, Charlie," he said beneath his breath. "I got her all fixed up and things are up to snuff out there. Hell, I got to get on my way."

The stallion didn't take well to his status as a pack animal, nudging against the mare's flanks and nipping more than once at her hindquarters. Roan cast him a look of sympathy as he jerked on the lead rope.

"You got to behave, boy. You got the better end of the deal, totin' my gear. Just leave this filly alone. She's gonna let loose with one of those heels, and you'll be wearin' a horseshoe across your nose if you're not careful."

He stopped long enough when the sun was overhead to tear a heel from the loaf of fresh bread Orv had given him. After cutting a thick slice of cheese from the chunk in his pack, he stowed the food securely and set out once more. There was no sense in stopping till near nightfall. He might even make it to the river by then.

According to the map he'd carried about for over a year, Tucker Center was just a ways east of the big river, and once he reached the Mississippi, he'd be home free. He'd just follow it south, almost all the way to River Bend. Home. His eyes narrowed as he considered what awaited him there.

"Might be nothin' left for you, Devereaux," he grumbled. "They probably won't thank you for makin' the trip. The damn horse'll probably get a warmer welcome than me. Pa was always on the lookout for a good piece of horse-flesh. He'll appreciate Katherine's mare."

Katherine. He shouldn't have spoken the name. A dull ache beneath his breastbone nudged him. A vision of dark hair glimmering in the sunlight and blue eyes sparkling with intelligence filled his mind. He shook his head, willing the memory of her to vanish, but to no avail.

"I did what I could," he growled, as if her image accused him. "No woman is gonna tie me up in knots. She's set for the winter, anyway. By spring, she'll probably..."

The angry face of Evan Gardner sprang before him. "What happens when you're not here anymore, stranger?" As though he heard the question aloud, Roan swore, biting the words off savagely. "He's a determined son of a gun," Thurston Wellman's voice echoed in his head.

"She can face him down any day of the week," Roan growled, nudging his mare into an easy lope, the stallion falling in behind. The thought was not the comfort he'd hoped for. Once fresh in his mind, the memories of Katherine would not be dislodged, and he turned over each glimpse of her as it appeared before him.

Her stubborn chin, the creamy look of her skin where her throat met the collar of her dress. The strong, well-formed hands that were equally as capable whether she held a skillet or the lead rope of a yearling foal. His mind dwelt for a moment on the surprising softness of her mouth as it had opened beneath his own, and he tilted his head back to gaze at the cloudless sky.

"Damn woman...I don't need to be thinkin' about you," he snarled impotently. His mind's eye envisioned the bulky form of Evan Gardner, imagining the man's mouth intruding where Roan's had been the first to venture.

"Never been kissed, Katherine?" He'd known when he asked, known that he'd been the first to taste the sweetness of her mouth. Damn. Evan Gardner'd better keep his hands to himself. Not to mention his slack-jawed...

He pulled the mare to a halt, his hands tight on the reins. With a grim foretaste of disaster, he sensed Katherine's vulnerability. The whole damn town was probably waitin' for Gardner to move in on her, he thought glumly. They probably all thought it was the best thing for her, havin' somebody to look after things there.

He lifted his eyes once more to the brilliant blue sky, watching as a hawk circled and swooped beyond the next rise in the trail. *Damn it all, Charlie. I can't just ride off and leave her to fend for herself. I reckon I shoulda just ridden south from Ohio and stayed out of this mess.*

And never known Charlie's Sparrowhawk? The thought pierced him with dreadful accuracy and he shook his head.

He wouldn't be able to live with himself if he left her with things so unsettled. He cast another look at the sky, shaking his head glumly. "It'll be full dark before we get there," he said to the mare, his hand stroking her neck with a gentle touch. "Guess we'd better make tracks."

"I know you're not gonna shoot me, Katherine," Evan said cajolingly, sidling toward the porch. The setting sun cast his face in shadow beneath the wide brim of his hat, but she knew exactly how he looked. She knew the greedy expression his face wore as he considered her. For too long, she'd known he was only biding his time.

"Should have realized you'd be back here as soon as Roan Devereaux left town," she taunted him, leveling the barrel of her shotgun in his direction. "Too much of a coward to hang around while a man was staying here, weren't you?"

"I don't take kindly to bein' called a coward. I'm facin' you down, ain't I? And you with a gun aimed at my belly." He reached the foot of the steps and tilted his head back to look up at her. "Let me come in and we'll just talk, Katherine," he wheedled softly, a smile turning his expression into a parody of friendly persuasion.

"Get out of here, Evan," she told him wearily. "I don't have time to argue with you." The barrel of the shotgun sagged just a bit, its weight heavy.

He halted and peered at her. "I can wait, Katherine. I'm a patient man." With little grace and much muttering, he made his way to where he'd tied his horse, mounting and riding from the yard.

It was only a whisper of sound, there outside her bedroom window. Almost asleep, she wakened with a start, her heart pounding with a breathtaking cadence. Framed against the opening, his shoulders already inside, was a shadowed figure. Katherine's mind was muddled, the edges of sleep making her movements slow as she swung her feet to the floor.

"Who is it?" she whispered into the darkness, aware even as she spoke the query that the familiar bulk belonged to Evan Gardner.

"I told you I was patient," he said with a chuckle. "I been waitin' out yonder for better than two hours, Katherine. Thought you'd be asleep by now, though."

"What do you want?" she said, her voice raspy as she struggled to her feet, dread clutching at her throat. Without a gun as an equalizer, she was no match for Evan's weight and she knew it. The thought of those thick fingers against her flesh made her shudder, and she feinted to evade his touch. To no avail. He was upon her before she could take a step, his body slamming into her with no regard for her woman's vulnerabilities.

She lost her breath as he bore her down into the feather tick, his heavy torso solid against her slender form. One hand found its way into her hair and he twisted a handful about his fist, anchoring her against the sheet while he sought to rub his mouth over her face. His lips were open, loose and wet, and she shuddered, reaching with both hands to pound against him.

It was futile. Before she regained her breath, gasping for air to fill her lungs, she knew she was in way over her head. Her gun was beside the bed, too far for her to reach, and the nearest help was down the road, almost a mile away. Tears flooded her eyes. Tears of resentment that because she was a woman, smaller and more easily bested, he could come into her home and wrestle from her what she was unwilling to give.

"Evan, no..." Her voice was muffled beneath his weight. His free hand was busy at the front of her nightgown, tugging at the buttons, his mouth vainly attempting to capture hers as she endured the pain of his fist clenched in her hair.

"You wouldn't be nice about it, would you," he snarled against her cheek. "I wanted to do this nice and easy, Katherine, but you wouldn't let me." His fingers grew impatient; he tore at the worn fabric of her gown, the material ripping with a ragged sound.

"Please, no. Don't do this, Evan," she sobbed, aghast as she felt the helpless tears flood her eyes and overflow.

"Aw, come on, Katherine. I'll make you happy," he wheezed, his hand fumbling beneath her bodice, fingers grasping for a hold against her flesh.

She felt the brush of a fingernail across the crest of her breast and gasped for air, only to release it in a scream of sheer terror. And once started, she could not be silenced.

"Listen to me, you stupid woman," he growled, both hands on her shoulders now as he sought to hold her firmly, aware only of her thrashing body beneath him. "Damn it, Katherine, I'm willing to marry you!"

"Nooo…" It was a cry of anguish, followed by a sobbing, mournful wail that reached the ears of the lone rider who approached over the rise east of the garden patch.

"I'll show you what a good husband I'll be, Katherine," Evan told her loudly, attempting to make himself heard over her muffled cries. He fought for a space between her flailing legs, his hands shifting to grasp wherever he could, ducking her fists, which aimed in his direction, more often than not landing sharp jabs.

She screamed again, the sound shrill in his ear. He straightened over her, his hand open and hurting as it met the side of her face, cracking loudly in the darkness.

"Shut up and listen to me, Katherine," he shouted angrily. "You're gonna marry me, one way or another, and I don't mind takin' my wedding night a day early."

"I wouldn't count on that." The voice from the window was quiet. The sound of a revolver's hammer being cocked was unmistakable, and the form of the man who climbed silently through the window was familiar.

Evan rolled from the bed, exposing Katherine's pale flesh to full view. Her gown was tangled about her thighs, the bodice torn and shredded, one breast exposed in the moonlight.

Roan stood to one side of the window, his eyes searching the darkness beyond her bed, narrowing as he spied movement. A form was edging across the floor, making an attempt to reach the door.

"Gardner, stand up where you are," Roan snarled. "Don't make me shoot you in the back."

"Roan?" Katherine moaned beneath her breath, her hands futile in their efforts to tug her gown into place over her breast.

"I'm here, Kate," he answered, his attention focusing on her, attuned to her distress.

It was all Evan needed, that moment of distraction Katherine had afforded him. He bolted through the open doorway and across the kitchen to the door of the house, crouching low as he leapt from the porch.

With a snarl of disgust, Roan turned back to the window and was gone, landing on the ground with one leap and moving around the house to the front.

"Gardner!" he shouted, stopping and taking aim at the fleeing figure. "Damn fool knows I won't shoot him in the back," he growled. Lowering his aim, he steadied his arm and pressed the trigger. The shot was true. Evan hit the ground, rolling to clutch at his leg and shouting his anger.

"Shoot me in the back, would you?"

Roan covered the ground between them rapidly, his eyes intent on the man who was attempting to struggle to his feet. "If I wanted to shoot you in the back, I'd have aimed higher," Roan snarled in disgust.

"You've broke my leg," Evan cried, stumbling as he put weight on the injured member.

"You're lucky I didn't kill you," Roan told him harshly. "Get on that horse of yours and get out of here before I finish the job."

Evan crawled across the ground to where his horse was tied to a tree near the barn. "You'll pay for this, Devereaux. I'll have the sheriff out here after you."

"You just do that," Roan said. "I'll be waiting."

Turning his back, he shoved his gun into its holster, aware of the unaccustomed weight of it against his leg. It had been a long time since he'd worn it there. But tonight he'd sensed the need for the familiar revolver close at hand.

His steps were light as he ran back to the house, in the door and across the kitchen to where the opening to Katherine's bedroom showed as a pale rectangle. She lay unmoving on the bed, outlined in the moonlight from the window. Her eyes were closed, arms clutched across her breasts. His heart thumped against the wall of his chest as he neared the bed.

"I'm so glad you came back," she whispered. "You didn't kill him, did you?"

"No, he's just got a hole in his leg. Man deserves to hang," he growled, kneeling by the side of the bed. His hand hovered over her, hesitant to frighten her, sensing her tightly held emotions.

"I don't want anyone to know." Her whisper was forlorn. "Roan, I'm glad you... I thought you'd gone...."

"Hush. I'm here, Katherine." His hand settled finally on tugging her gown down to cover her thighs and calves, loosening the folds where the material had been forced up by the weight of Evan Gardner's legs.

She clutched at herself more tightly, her hands against the bare flesh of her breasts. "Please pull the sheet over me."

"I'm gonna light the lamp, Katherine," he told her. "I wanna make sure you're all right." With one quick twist of his wrist, he settled the white muslin sheet over her body. Then, turning to where the oil lamp rested in the darkness on the table next to the bed, he fumbled for the matches that lay there. Muttering darkly as his fingers groped, he grasped one, and struck it against the side of the box, his eyes narrowing against the glow as it caught fire.

"Don't look at me," she begged, and the words cut him to the quick. So unlike the spunky, vibrant woman he knew, the small creature lying before him tore at his heart.

He lifted the globe and lit the wick, lowering it until the lamp's glow was subdued. His hands were warm as they touched her, one brushing the hair back from her forehead, the other clasping her shoulder. His eyes found the red welts that measured the handprint of Evan Gardner against her cheek, and his mouth tightened.

"I should have aimed higher," he growled, his fingers gently touching the bruising flesh. He scanned her shoulders, bare beneath the shredded gown, and he brushed against the small marks, which would be purple by daylight. Deliberately, he lowered the sheet a few inches, drawing back the fabric she'd attempted to pull into place, exposing the pale rise of her breasts. His eyes were hard as he saw the results of harsh fingers, the reddened places where Evan's nails had scraped her tender flesh.

"I should have killed him." He swore again beneath his breath as he pulled the sheet up and over the fullness of her bosom once more.

"I need to get up and wash," she whispered, her eyes opening as she clasped the covering in place, struggling to sit up. He lifted her against him, holding her head to his shoulder and clasping her waist as he turned her to sit on his lap. He'd managed to find his way onto the bed, and she welcomed the warmth of his big body as he shielded her with the comfort of his arms.

"I'll help you in just a minute or two," he told her, sharing the heat of his body with the chill that held her in its shuddering grasp. She shivered against him and he tightened his grip, pulling the sheet around her, wrapping her in its folds. With a rocking movement, he comforted her, his arms cradling her securely, his dark head bent low as he rested his cheek against her forehead.

Breathing deeply, he inhaled her scent, the clean aroma that followed her like a breath of spring. "Ah, Katherine, what am I gonna do with you?" he muttered against her skin.

"I'll be all right." Her voice wavered only a little. "I'll be fine in the morning."

"Yeah." His tone was unbelieving, and his mouth twisted with anger as he held her. "Yeah, you'll be fine."

Chapter Six

"I'm not leavin' you here alone." For the third time he spoke the words, and for the third time she glared her refusal of the ultimatum he offered.

Her face was swollen, the bruise fully developed. His eyes traveled over the evidence of brutality and beyond, assessing the puffiness of her mouth, where harsh treatment had damaged the tender tissue. He knew what the tightly buttoned dress hid beneath its somber layer of cotton. His eyes had seen the marks of uncaring hands, frantic to grasp at her softness. He swallowed hard, feeling the bile of disgust rise within him.

"I can't stay, Katherine, or I would. I have to go home." How to explain the need for this journey. How to make her understand the necessity of closing this chapter of his life so that he could continue the act of living. With no more questions, no more regrets.

"I understand... I know you're going to Louisiana," she said quietly, her eyes telegraphing the determination that existed within her as a living, breathing entity. "What you don't understand is my need to finish what I've begun, right here. It will be another two years before I have my yearlings ready to sell. I can't let them go before then."

"Is this some kinda vow you've made to Charlie?" he asked bluntly. "'Cause if it is, he wouldn't hold you to it, Katherine."

She bowed her head. It was far from a sign of defeat, he knew instinctively. Whether she hid the sadness that darkened her eyes when she thought about her father, or sought to keep from his sight the resolve that drove her, he would not have it.

Leaning across the table, he grasped her chin and forced her face into view. Lips pressed tightly together, eyes swimming with tears, she glared at him.

"Aw, Katherine," he sighed.

"Leave me be." Her forehead wrinkling in a scowl, she squeezed her eyes shut. The pressure forced a single tear to make its way from beneath each eyelid and begin a trail down her cheek.

The sight of those drops of sorrow against her bruised and battered flesh was his downfall.

He released his hold on her and rose, reaching her side in three quick steps. His hands were gentle as he scooped her into his arms and lifted her from the chair, ignoring the protest she cried against his chest. He turned around, seeking a place to suit his purpose, his gaze moving to the open door of her bedroom. The quilt was smooth across the plump surface of her feather mattress, the pillows fluffed and perched against the rough headboard. It was there he headed.

She wiggled and twisted in his arms when she sensed the direction he took, her mutterings muffled against his shirt as he gathered her tightly against himself.

"Hush, Katherine." He spoke it as an order, not coaxing or entreating her, but issuing the edict with no expectation of refusal.

The bed beckoned him. He turned around to sit down, his arms full of obstinate woman, his mind swimming with confusion. The only solid thought penetrating the mass of broken images in his head was to persuade this fool woman of the folly implicit in her intentions.

There was absolutely no way in hell she could stay here alone now. Not for one day would he leave her by herself with only that damn shotgun for protection.

"Why the hell didn't you ever get a dog?" he asked bluntly, sinking into the softness of the feather tick, the double weight of two bodies taking them to the wooden base.

"A dog?" She felt enveloped in the bed, drawn against his hard body, the billowing mattress surrounding them. "Why would I get a dog?"

"He mighta taken a chunk outa old Evan last night and saved you a whole lot of misery, lady." His feet rose from the floor, and turning, he shifted them both into a supine position, leaning against the headboard.

Struggling against the strength of his hold, she sought a new angle, only to find his face mere inches from her own. His grin served to multiply her frustration, and wiggling, she managed to free one arm, waving it about in silent threat.

"You gonna hit me, Katherine?" he challenged.

Her eyes flashed fire, the tears drying as if a good west wind had borne every trace of sadness with it as it passed her way. "You know I'm not," she snapped.

"You done cryin'? I carried you all the way in here to give you a little comfort, and all you do is fight me every inch of the way."

"We're on my bed, Mr. Devereaux," she told him unbelievingly. "Let me go, and leave my bedroom."

"I been here before, Kate," he reminded her, tightening his grip.

She stilled, her legs relaxing, her hand falling to rest on his shoulder, her head drooping against his chest once more. "I remember," she whispered bitterly. "But it was kind of you to remind me."

"I don't mean to hurt you," he said quietly. "In fact, I suspect you know I'm the last man on earth lookin' to give you a hard time."

She lowered her head, exposing the slender, vulnerable nape of her neck, the heavy rope of hair falling across her breast and coiling in her lap.

It was more temptation than he could resist. Lured by the pale vulnerability of that exposed skin, he inhaled deeply, allowing her scent to fill his lungs.

"Don't, Roan," she told him. "You're breathing on my neck, and I've got chill bumps—I don't want you doing that!"

He straightened, his body heating beneath her, his loins heavy with the arousal he strove to deny. Not now, he prayed desperately. Not here, not with Katherine. All he needed was to frighten her again. Here on the bed where Evan Gardner had grasped with greedy intent at her tender flesh last night. Where he'd rooted about like a boar hog in rut between her legs, bruising her and scaring her half to death.

Shifting her about, Roan loosened his hold, rubbing his face on the top of her head, freeing the wispy strands of hair she'd so carefully scraped into place earlier.

"You done cryin' now?" he asked again.

"I never cry," she told him harshly.

"Yeah, I noticed that about you. You just hold every blamed thing inside that starchy little body of yours and glare like a banty rooster, your feathers all ruffled and your neck stuck out."

"Well, thank you, Mr. Devereaux. I've never been described in more glowing terms, I'm sure," she said with mock delight. Lifting herself with deliberate care, she sat upright on his lap, no small feat, given the angle of their posture. Unfortunately, she managed to park her bottom in the exact spot he had been striving to keep from her notice.

Her eyes widened and her lips pressed together tightly as she became aware of the significance of his sudden gasp.

"If you don't mind, Katherine," he said tightly, lifting her with alacrity and rising with her. He held her with one arm about her middle, her feet dangling above the floor and their eyes on a level.

Her cheeks were flushed, at least the unbruised one, the other already so suffused with blood it made his stomach hurt to look at it. Her eyes were bright, shining with an element of surprise that tickled his fancy, and he chuckled.

"What's so funny?" she asked breathlessly, her lungs squeezed against his chest.

"Nothing," he told her cheerfully. "I'm just tryin' to decide how to tell you what's gonna happen now."

"I can solve that problem for you," she said tartly. "You're going to release me, and I'm going to gather the eggs and get ready to churn butter before I go work my yearlings."

He shook his head slowly, her eyes following the movement. With each back-and-forth motion, she bit at her lip, flaring her nostrils and frowning her finest.

"The eggs can sit out there and rot for all I care, Katherine. We're gonna have this out, here and now," he told her firmly, the facade of cheerfulness gone by the wayside.

"Let me down." Chin uptilted, she was defying him.

"Not till you listen."

"I'm listening." Her teeth gritted against one another, and she clenched her jaw tightly as she shot the words at him.

"We're gonna leave here together, Katherine. I'm not leavin' you alone again. We'll figure out some way of takin' care of your stock, and if we have to, we'll take the blamed horses with us. But I'm tellin' you for the last time, I won't leave you here alone."

"Just where do you think you're going to take me? Me and a whole herd of horses! That'll be the day, Roan Devereaux!" Her eyes snapping smartly, she twisted in his grasp and her lower lip stuck out in a determined pout. Her hands shoved against his chest as she stretched her legs to the floor, her toes barely touching the bare wood. Her mind searching for an out, she settled on the obvious.

"Well, maybe I'll just marry up with old Evan and save you the trouble of worrying about me," she spouted shrilly.

"The hell you will!" He glared from dark eyes into the stubborn blue ones that flashed fire in his direction.

"You can't tell me what to do," she said.

"I owe your daddy, and he'd turn over in that grave up on the hill if he knew I'd walked away from you yesterday."

"Well, you don't owe me!" And then her eyes softened and she leaned her head back to fill her vision with the rough outline of his face, the squared jaw and hawkish nose that denied him beauty.

"What do you owe my daddy?" she asked in a hushed tone, aware she was in the dark on this subject. All she'd heard about when it came to Roan Devereaux was the story of his valiant effort to save Charlie Cassidy's life. About his care of the man, his strength and his stubborn determination that Charlie should live to return home.

"If it hadn't been for your daddy, I'd be wearin' a pair of crutches, lady. He stood off an army surgeon with his rifle when they wanted to cut off my leg. Old Charlie pointed that gun and told that doctor to patch it up long enough for me to get to a hospital. They dumped enough carbolic acid on that wound to kill every bit of poison the bullet left behind. Charlie made 'em wrap it up and splint it tight, and then he put me in a wagon and headed out."

"Where'd he take you?" Somehow she was aware of his hands loosening their grip, allowing her to slide down the front of him till her feet were flat on the floor, enabling her to step back a bit, her eyes never leaving his face.

"All the way to Philadelphia, changin' the dressing on my leg twice a day and feedin' me soup from every farmhouse we passed. Well, pret' near, anyway," he amended. "The doctor in the hospital there just shook his head when he saw me. Guess I was a sight to behold, all skin and bones and my leg all stove up.''

''But he patched you up?'' she prodded.

''Yeah. Charlie waved goodbye, like he'd done 'bout all he could. By then the war was over, and he headed home. That doctor took me on like a personal challenge.'' Roan grinned, obviously remembering. ''I owe your daddy,'' he repeated. ''If I have to lug you all the way to Louisiana and back, I will.''

''You don't have much of a limp,'' she said, ignoring his command.

''He was some bang-up doctor,'' Roan answered agreeably.

''You still don't owe me anything, Roan,'' she repeated. ''I'll be fine here.''

''Sure you will, and I'll be a suck-egg mule if I walk away from you.''

Her nose wrinkled in distaste. ''I'm not sure what that is and I don't think I want to know. But *you'd* better know something. My daddy would do cartwheels from that grave if he thought I was trotting across the country with a man.''

''What if that man was your husband?''

''I don't...have a husband. The only offer I've had lately was from Evan Gardner, and we both know what I thought about that one.'' Remembering her threat, she cast him a quick look of chagrin.

''I'm not offerin'. I'm tellin' you what's gonna be.'' The strength that carried Charlie up that hill was on display as he placed hard fingers about her shoulders, giving her no leeway, holding her firmly in place as his words made their impact.

She shook her head. ''I can't do that.''

''What can't you do?'' he asked quietly.

''The dragging all the way to Louisiana and back, for one. And the married part,'' she blurted.

"You let me cuddle you a while ago. I even kissed you once."

"Twice," she corrected him.

His brow lowered as he searched his mind and found the brush of his mouth across her cheek when he'd agreed to rid the vermin under her cupboard. "That little peck doesn't count as a kiss. One decent kiss is all you've ever gotten from me."

"I'm not afraid of that. It's just the rest of it, the pawing and pushing and sweaty hands part I can't tolerate."

"Whose sweaty hands touched you, Katherine? Besides Evan's, I mean."

She ducked her head. "I don't want to talk about it, Roan." Her voice pleaded for understanding and he gave it, with immediate compliance.

"All right, we won't talk about it. I'll just tell you here and now, I won't be pawin' at you. All right? Not unless I know it's what you want," he added quickly, leaving an open door.

"I can't leave here just like that." Her mind spun as she attempted to digest the plan he proposed.

"Charlie wouldn't hold you to this place, if he knew," he told her bluntly. "If you want to come back, we'll head north in the spring, Katherine. We can decide then what to do with your place. In the meantime, let me take care of you, and you just worry about that string of horses out back."

Her look was doubtful. "Charlie bought this place for me. I can't just walk away from it."

"I don't expect you to. It'll take a couple days to make arrangements. I'll take you into town and we'll see the banker. You have to deliver that filly anyway. You can't get her any more trained than she is, Katherine. You've just been puttin' it off and you know it."

"You're rushing me!" she cried accusingly.

"Damn right I am."

* * *

It took three days. One longer than he'd allowed, but several shorter than she'd planned.

The banker, Ross Green, had been more than obliging. Agreeing to sell off her hens and loaning her cow to a family near town too poor to own their own, the man had sliced through her arguments neatly. Ross Green would either keep an eye on her place or rent it out, whichever was likeliest, he said.

The garden was about done anyway, Roan had reminded her, and the canned goods on her shelves would make a dandy present for the woman who'd been unbelieving when presented with the cow. Left in the pantry, they'd only freeze and burst in the first below-zero cold spell to hit. Even southern Illinois was guaranteed to be laid low at least once by a blast from the north this winter.

She'd agreed, her mind swimming with details, trudging beside Roan as he went about town on her business, shielding her bruises from inquiring eyes.

That had been the worst part. The speculation that followed her wherever she went in town. The whispers of sympathy that reached her ears as the townsfolk deduced the happenings at her farm.

Evan Gardner was laid up with the gunshot wound in his leg, the bone shattered. And he wasn't about to tell anyone how he'd gotten wounded, either, if the gossip was up to snuff.

She'd held her head high in the church, though, knowing she had nothing to be ashamed of in the sight of God Almighty. Even the vows she spoke were loud and clear, echoed by the strong voice of the man who shared them.

Three days. They'd left town with a string of yearlings and her black, three-year-old filly trailing behind, Roan's stallion having fetched a good price from Thurston Wellman.

"I can sell him twice over before sundown," he'd assured Roan. "You'll never find a better pack animal than old Sugarfoot here.'' Slapping the rump of the nondescript gelding, Thurston had sent them on their way.

''I'm sorry you felt you had to sell your stud,'' Katherine said after several silent miles had been covered.

Roan snorted impolitely. ''If you could have seen him nudgin' at this mare for a full day, you wouldn't wonder why I traded him off.''

''You didn't make much on him.''

''Didn't pay much for him.''

''Another case of earning a horse, Roan?'' she asked slyly.

He turned to glare at her. ''No, in fact, it wasn't. The man who'd owned him wasn't goin' anywhere, ever. His wife wanted to get rid of him and get a mare to pull her buggy, and I obliged her by takin' the stud off her hands. She said she didn't want any reminders of her husband around.''

''He was dead?''

''As a doornail. Lucky for me. I got the horse, and I'm assumin' the lady got her mare. He carried me to Illinois, but he wasn't the horse I wanted.''

''You wanted one of Charlie's mares.''

''Yep. Got her, too,'' he reminded her with a sidelong glance that spoke triumph.

''The bargain wasn't all that great. You got stuck with Charlie's daughter, too,'' she reminded him.

He looked at her carefully, noting the pants he'd bought for her, threatening her with dire consequences if she didn't don them in the storeroom behind the dry goods. They fit loosely about her middle, held up by a braided belt, but the fit across her fanny was snug, revealing the slender form she'd hidden for so long. She sat the horse well, her legs outlined by the denim.

He looked away, aware of the direction his thoughts were taking and determined to curtail their wanderings. The shirt he'd tossed at her was flannel, made to fit a teenage boy, and it tucked nicely into her waistband, loose enough to almost

conceal the womanly figure it covered. She'd traded her
worn work shoes for a pair of boots that came halfway up
her leg and caused her to grumble more than a little when
she pulled at them, tugging to get them on the first time.

"They'll stretch a bit," he'd assured her, admiring the
trim form that stomped about the store, fitting her heels in
place and bending to tuck the pant legs in smoothly, right in
front of him. He'd glanced away, clearing his throat noisily
and managing to catch the amused look riding the face of
Orv Tucker.

"They fit all right," she'd said grudgingly.

"Sure do," Roan agreed, glaring at Tucker's grin.

They'd been some kind of sight to see, all right, leaving
town. Her with her pants and boots, her herd of animals all
strung out and tugging at the lead ropes.

They'd settled down pretty well, he decided, glancing
back at the prancing little filly who brought up the rear. She
sure was feelin' her oats, he thought, his eyes intent on the
animal. He probably should check her out, noting the pretty
face and swishing tail as the dainty creature trotted along.
He wouldn't be surprised if she was ready to breed.

Katherine had a legacy some men would give a bundle to
own. All he'd need to do was help her keep it.

As if she read his mind, she nudged her mare forward to
ride abreast with him. "Do we have to worry about outlaws?" she asked, her forehead wrinkled with concern.

He shook his head. "Not along here, I wouldn't think.
After we cross the river at Cooneyville, we'll be headin' into
Missouri for a while. Haven't been through that part of the
country. Hard tellin' what we'll run up against."

"Where are we stopping for the night?" she was already
aware of the tenderness in her lower parts.

"It's only the middle of the afternoon, Katherine! We've
got miles to travel before we look for a place to stay."

"I sure hope there'll be a nice hotel available," she said
wistfully, thinking of the soft bed awaiting her.

"Hotel? Not likely, Mrs. Devereaux. More like a pair of blankets and a campfire under the stars." He peered at the western horizon. "I don't see any sign of rain, so I expect we'll be high and dry tonight."

"Blankets? Why not a hotel as long as we're still in civilized country?"

"We're not takin' a detour to the east just to find you a fancy room for the night, sweetheart. The country we're goin' through oughta have some farms here and there, but the best you can hope for is a pile of hay in somebody's barn."

"I'd settle for that," she said meekly, seeking the lesser of two poor choices. "It'd beat the dickens out of laying on the ground."

He grinned. "We'll see what we can do."

The farm they chose was less than prosperous. In fact, if Roan were to speculate, he'd say the young couple were struggling to keep their heads above water.

"It's almost too big a job for one man to handle," the young farmer confided as he helped Roan unsaddle the horses and turn them loose in his corral, his eyes yearning as he watched the string of yearlings.

"Can't afford a hired hand?" Roan asked sympathetically.

"No, maybe next year," Joshua Stuart answered. "If my wife hadn't come up in the family way, she'd be able to help more, but as it is, she's still at the upchuckin' stage, keepin' company with the chamber pot every morning."

Roan grinned and began the task of rubbing down his mare. Beside him, the young farmer occupied himself grooming Katherine's mare, his hands careful as he prodded gently at her belly. His eyebrows rose as he caught Roan's eye. "She gonna drop a foal?"

"Can you tell already?" Roan asked. "It won't be till next year."

"I've got a good touch with horses, mister," Joshua answered.

"I'll be sure to tell Katherine. She's been hopin' the mare took, first time out." Roan smiled as he considered Katherine's delight with the news.

It was in the quiet of the hayloft when he told her. They'd bedded down in their blankets, scant inches apart, due to Katherine's unspoken dread of mice scampering about while she slept.

"Young Joshua says your mare's gonna drop a foal, for sure," Roan told her quietly.

She sat bolt upright, searching in the dim light for his face, leaning toward him eagerly. "Is he sure? How can he tell?"

Roan sighed. "Yeah, he says he's sure. And how the hell should I know how he can tell? He just felt around and came up with the news."

She dropped back into the bed of hay and pulled the rough blanket up to her chin, her mouth forming a satisfied smile. "I knew it anyway."

"You did not," he said, denying her claim.

"Did so," she countered. "I just knew that stallion of my pa's wouldn't let me down."

"Well, I'm sure not gonna argue with logic like that." Roan turned in his blanket to face her. The moon's glow was sparse through the open window, barely allowing him to make out the pleased smile she wore. Her lips were curved, her eyes shiny, and her small hands were gathering that blanket up right under her chin.

She'd been a good sport about everything. Never complaining, only wistful when he shot down the notion of a hotel tonight. *And this is my wedding night.* he thought. Maybe he could coax her just a little.

He took a chance.

"You said you didn't mind the kissing part of marriage, Katherine," he reminded her softly.

Her head turned his way, her eyes meeting his. "Did I say that?"

"Yup, you surely did."

She shifted beside him. "Are you trying to tell me something, Roan?"

"Nope. I'm askin', nice and polite, if I can kiss my new wife good-night."

Taking in a deep breath through barely opened lips, she rolled toward him, one hand touching his cheek as she collided with his big body. Her mouth settled softly against his, her lips still parted.

As kisses went, it wasn't the choicest he'd ever shared, but the fact that it was freely given, and probably the best he was going to get on his wedding night, made it worthy of his full response.

He clasped the back of her head with his big palm and, angling her head a bit, set out to taste just a little of her sweetness. His mouth was warm, lips urgent against hers as he pressed for entrance. She sighed, providing him with the opening he'd silently requested, and he took possession with a languid sweep of his tongue, swallowing her gasp of surprise.

He'd give her credit, he thought admiringly as he wrapped his arms about her slender body, she didn't pull back or push him away but snuggled up right tight and let him have a go at it. Trusting little soul, he thought, releasing her finally, reluctantly allowing the small space between them once more.

"I think I'd like to have you layin' on my arm, Katherine," he said mildly, offering his shoulder to serve as her pillow. He'd already placed a saddlebag beneath his own head, which she'd scorned, remembering the goose-down pillow she'd abandoned in the bedroom.

She considered his request. "Why?" she asked bluntly and a little breathlessly, a trace of suspicion coating her query.

"So I know where you are, in case I hear anything out of the ordinary," he answered glibly.

"Like what?"

"Oh, an intruder. Maybe mice. Who knows?"

"All right," she said hastily, scooting over in the bedroll until she was pressed once more against his side. Lifting her head, she waited, watching him as he slid his long arm beneath her. Then, fitting her neatly into the bend of his shoulder, he curled around her, his arm scooping her tightly against him.

"There, isn't that better?"

"I guess so," she answered, inhaling the musky scent of him, only now aware that he'd stripped down to his smallclothes—at least above his waist. She'd washed that set of summer-weight underwear. She could smell her soap on the knit material. It was familiar. The musky scent was Roan's own flavor, she decided. And it blended quite nicely with lye soap. It was her last coherent thought as she closed her eyes, nestled against him, secure from marauding mice in the night.

Chapter Seven

They'd eaten a hearty breakfast. Roan, the last to leave the table, placed a silver dollar behind as they left the house to ready the animals for the trip.

"They were poor, weren't they?" Katherine's voice was filled with sadness as they rode away from the small farm. Roan shot a look at her. Her mouth was drawn down, her eyes straying once more to the man and woman who waved from their doorstep.

"Yeah, they were," he agreed. "But things'll get better for them. He said they just have to get through this year. Things will pick up once his crops come in next summer. She's in the family way, you know."

Katherine nodded. "She told me. She's been pretty sick, I guess."

"It goes with the game, you know," he told her, leaning back to check on his saddlebags once more.

She'd noticed he left nothing to chance, rechecking and redoing every knot and buckle until he was satisfied that things were as secure as he could make them. She felt safe with him. That was why she'd slept so well.

She flushed as she remembered waking to find her arm about his middle, hanging on for dear life. She'd slipped it back to her side, aware of his stirring and mumbling as he awoke.

"Don't dally, Katherine," he called back to her, urging her to narrow the gap between them. She had been slowing unconsciously, her thoughts wandering, while he'd stepped up his pace and left her to bring up the rear.

"I'm not dallying!" she told him. "Just enjoying the beautiful day. Isn't that sun wonderful?"

"It's gonna rain this afternoon. We need to get some miles under our belts."

"Killjoy," she muttered. And then raised her voice. "Well, I certainly wouldn't want to hold you up, Mr. Devereaux. I'll just hurry right along."

He glared in her direction as she urged her mare into a lope, gaining his side in seconds. "Don't be flip, Katherine. While we're on the trail, I'll set the pace and you'll mind your manners."

"Yessir!" she answered briskly, dropping back to keep company with the yearlings and the dainty filly, all of whom were acting frisky today. Strung out behind the packhorse, they'd scampered about yesterday, testing the length of their lead ropes until, tiring of the long trail, they'd settled down and cooperated nicely.

"I'm proud of you," she told them quietly, her eyes scanning each animal as she rode, looking for any untoward hitch in their gait or mar on the smooth texture of their glossy coats. "I'll spend some time with you tonight," she promised them in an undertone. She dropped back to bring up the rear, aware always of the quiet solitude of the countryside, only occasionally broken by a house or barn in the distance. "It's gonna be a long trip." Her sigh was deep, her eyes on the man she'd married, who was riding at a brisk trot some hundred feet ahead.

"I'm married, Pa," she whispered. "What would you think if you knew?" Her mouth twisted as she recognized the irony of the query. "Doggoned if I know what to think, and I'm the one who married him," she said beneath her breath. How he'd persuaded her to accept his edict so readily was beyond her comprehension. She just knew she'd rather go with him than watch him ride away again. Her heart thumped as she allowed herself to admit the feelings she harbored for Roan Devereaux.

They stopped to eat when the sun was directly overhead and Katherine had long since quit admiring the warm weather. She was hot. Already, she'd rolled up her sleeves and unbuttoned the top two buttons of her shirt. Not that it helped much, she thought, wiping beads of sweat from her forehead.

"Why don't you take off that hot flannel and put on the shirtwaist I got you," Roan suggested. "It's cotton. Should be a heap cooler."

"It's too nice to wear riding a horse. I'll have it all dusty and sweaty by tonight and then I won't have anything pretty to wear if we stop in a hotel."

His sigh was deep. "Put on the shirtwaist, Katherine. It's gonna get dirty anyway, sometime. You can rinse it out tonight and let it dry on a bush."

"I won't be able to iron it so I can wear it again," she said logically.

"Well, it sure isn't gonna be all smooth and pretty for long, all folded up in your saddlebag. And I'll tell you a secret, Mrs. Devereaux. You aren't likely to come across a flatiron anywhere between here and River Bend, unless we luck out another night and stay in somebody's barn."

"Turn around and I'll change," she told him, bending to search for the white garment he'd chosen in Orv Tucker's store.

He eyed her trim bottom regretfully and turned his back. "We're married, Katherine," he reminded her, rocking back on his heels and considering the clouds that hung low in the west.

Her voice was muffled in the depths of the flannel shirt she was pulling over her head, scorning the undoing of buttons.

"Can't hear you," he said. "Sure you don't need any help?"

She brushed back her hair and slid her arms into the sleeves of the white shirtwaist, rolling them up to the elbow before she buttoned it up the front. "I'm doing just fine. You can turn around now."

He turned slowly, his eyes warm as he saw her for the first time in a truly feminine garment. "You look pretty in that, Mrs. Devereaux."

She flushed at the words, her hands busy as she tucked the shirt beneath the belted waistband of her denim pants. "Pretty's kinda flighty sounding, I've always thought. I guess I've never tried too hard to look thataway."

"Well, that certainly explains the getups you traipse around in," he told her bluntly. "Never saw a woman more determined to look like a shapeless dowdy in my life. I'd say you managed to keep from lookin' flighty, all right."

"What I managed was to keep myself clean and presentable and left alone." The words were sharp in his ears, reflecting the tight-lipped scorn she projected as she faced him. "You didn't marry a woman lookin' for admiration from any man, Roan Devereaux. What you see is what I am. Too plain and too old to be in the market for compliments."

"Well, far be it from me to notice anything about you to admire. Just get your plain old bottom in the saddle so we can get on our way. That rain cloud in the west is movin' fast, and I'd like to be under cover before it hits us full blast."

"Thought we were going to eat," she said, facing him boldly. "I don't know about you, but I'll hold out better if I get something in my stomach. Besides, I need to..." Her voice trailed off as she cast a quick glance around. They'd come to a halt under the shade of a walnut tree, one of a small grove that lined the banks of a rushing stream.

"There's a likely spot for you to wash up a little, back upstream a hundred feet or so," he told her, nodding to a low stand of bushes behind her. He'd simmered down quickly, his irritation forgotten as he recognized her need for privacy. "I'll dig into that sack and find somethin' for us to chew on while we ride."

What he found was dried beef and a soft hunk of yellow cheese. Four biscuits left over from breakfast held all of it nicely. He wrapped two of the makeshift sandwiches in a clean kerchief as she made her way back down the bank of the stream, heading reluctantly away from the cool breeze that flirted beneath the trees.

"This'll have to do," he told her, handing her the small bundle, watching as she knotted the end of the red fabric about her saddle horn. "I'll tighten your cinch," he offered, his voice gruff as he attempted to clear the air between them. They'd come mighty close to having a fuss. Her with her nose in the air, so all fired set on her notion of being too old and not good-looking enough to appeal to a man. Him being so randy and on the edge.

That was probably half his problem, he decided glumly. He had a bride, but what he needed right now was a wife. He'd spent longer than any man should have to without some female companionship, and Katherine sure didn't intend to help matters any, far as he could make out.

"I'll take care of my cinch. I loosened it and I can tighten it," she said evenly, the movements of her capable hands suiting her words.

I pull my own weight, Roan Devereaux, she thought, her shoulders hunched defensively as she checked the stirrup.

"We'll water them at the stream," Roan called back to her, leading the packhorse and the string of yearlings toward the water.

She followed, noting the black filly bringing up the end of the line. She'd been keeping an eye on her since before they left, and the signs were unmistakable. She was in season, no doubt about it. She'd throw a good foal one of these days, Katherine thought, her eyes following the clean lines of the creature she'd bottle-fed. The mare was long-legged, with a delicate conformation, filling in nicely. Katherine admired the horse's rippling hindquarters, the hooves that lifted and fell with dainty precision.

The string of yearlings lined up in the stream, their noses to the water, tossing bright drops that glittered in the reflected light as they shook their heads, enjoying the cool shade beneath the leafy branches.

His packhorse was stoic, already up the bank, waiting for the signal to proceed, and Katherine thought of the stallion they'd left behind. It was a good thing. He'd have scented the filly right off, and they'd have been fighting him every step of the way. It'd been hard enough to keep him separated from the rest back at the farm. There wouldn't have been a chance on the trail.

The clouds in the west were moving fast, Roan noted, chewing on the biscuits, wishing he had a cool drink to wash them down with. The water in the canteen hanging from his saddle would have to do, and he unfastened it, opening and tilting it to his mouth in an automatic motion. No milk for Katherine this noon. The thought came from nowhere, and he wondered at it. He'd lived with her for over a month, picking up on her small habits and likes—not to mention the dislikes, he thought dourly.

Like the thunder they would likely be hearing soon, if the lightning in the distance was any indication. She'd been quiet those few afternoons when a storm blew up quickly, staying away from the door and windows as the thunder boomed and the lightning flashed and glowed about the small house. Charlie'd put lightning rods on the barn, demonstrating his concern for the animals it held. The small house had no such protection, and he'd noticed Katherine's eyes widen as the storms swept past, her reluctance to be caught in the open when it rained.

He added the knowledge to his list. Mice and thunderstorms. He'd have her figured out yet, he thought with a dry chuckle. She wasn't nearly so starchy as she let on, just fearful of...what? Somewhere, somehow, she'd been taught to hide behind the sharp-tongued, drab picture of womanhood she presented to the world. She'd managed to keep the available men at arm's length. All but Evan Gardner... that pitiful excuse for a suitor, who'd probably limp for the rest of his life for his efforts.

At that thought, Roan pressed his heels into the sides of the horse he rode, coaxing her from the trot she'd maintained throughout the morning. Those long legs could cover ground, he thought admiringly. Now was the time to prove it, what with the storm moving in and him with a string of horses and a pouting woman out in the open.

He cast about for a shelter and settled on a cluster of buildings to the south, perhaps a decent sized farm. He altered his direction just a bit to head that way. "Gonna rain," he called over his shoulder. "We need to find shelter."

Katherine's mare edged next to him, her tail flying as she tossed her head and sidled nervously. Damn horse didn't like the approaching weather any better than the woman who rode her, Roan observed with a grin.

"What's so funny?" Katherine asked, an anxious edge making her voice sharp. "I'm not real fond of being out in a storm, Roan."

"Well, I'm not real interested in gettin' wet this afternoon, either. It'll take too long to get things dried out if we travel in the rain. I'm headin' for that farm," he said, pointing into the distance and prodding his horse into a lope that would bring them to shelter in short order.

The farmer was reluctant to offer his barn until he saw the color of Roan's money. The coins he held would buy more than a few hours beneath the barn roof, Roan knew, acknowledging the farmer's wariness.

"Can't be too careful these days," the robust man declared, leading the way to a large box stall, watching as Roan turned the yearlings in together. The dark filly was tied in an open-ended stall, Katherine's mare in the one next to it, and Sugarfoot in a third. Roan's horse was the last one in the barn and he unsaddled her in the wide aisle, rubbing her down as he watched Katherine move from one to another of her animals. She'd deposited her own saddle on a rack, upended against the wall, tended to her horse quickly, then turned to the black filly that stood just a few feet away, twitching her ears and rubbing against the wooden wall of her stall. Her arm about the animal's neck, Katherine ignored the tossing head, speaking soothingly to the dark beauty as she calmed her with the sound of her voice.

"She's caught the scent of the stud outside," Roan told her quietly, standing behind the twitching tail.

Katherine looked over her shoulder at him, her hair disheveled, her face smudged. "I know," she said, intent on pacifying the filly. With a final stroke of her palm against the dark neck, she backed from the stall, reluctant to leave the animal.

"Are the yearlings settled down?" she asked Roan. At his grunt of affirmation she turned toward the outside, peering past him to where dust devils blew in the barnyard. Through the wide, open doors of the barn, the storm threatened to break momentarily, the thunder a dull rumble overhead, the air heavy with the scent of rain.

"They're fine, Katherine. They watered at the stream and I gave them a handful of oats this morning. After bein' hauled thirty miles since sunup, I'll warrant they're happy to be loose of that lead rope for a while." His eyes were intent on her, catching the wariness in her, noting the fidgety way she moved, her hands rubbing against the rough denim of her pants.

"Wanta go up to the house?" he asked her. "Mr. Thomas said we could join his family inside if we liked." Obviously deciding his visitors were just what they appeared to be, the farmer had issued the invitation before he left them alone in the barn.

With another veiled look at the gathering darkness, Katherine shook her head. "I think I'd rather stay here, keep an eye on the animals."

Roan walked to the doorway, his gaze pulled upward by the lowering clouds, scudding across the sky like a flotilla of dark-sailed ships. Shifting and changing in the wind, they gathered the rain, glowing from within when the lightning flashed above them.

A large drop scattered the dust near his boot, and he stepped back into the shelter of the barn. Then, as though a purse string had been cut, the sky opened, the bounty pouring forth, the clouds loosing their burden. Slanting across the barnyard in great sheets of water, the rain poured down, drenching the thirsty ground and running off into the low areas around the buildings.

"Man, that's some storm," Roan said admiringly, having grudgingly given up his post at the door. Rain splattered in, dampening the floor. He reluctantly slid the wide door closed, keeping the weather where it belonged.

With that, the barn was plunged into darkness and he backtracked, opening it a crack, till he could locate a lantern to hold back the shadows. Encroaching from the corners to where Katherine stood in the center of the wide aisle, the dimness surrounded her. She was small and still, only the pale oval of her face and the white shirtwaist she wore making her visible to him.

"I'll get some light in here," he told her. "Soon as I find that lantern I saw when we came in."

"It's up on the wall, just to your right," she said, watching as he turned his head at her direction. Framed in the narrow opening of the barn door, he was a shelter she'd give a bundle to settle into right now, she thought yearningly.

Storms were another matter in her own home place. She could sit in her chair and cover herself with the shawl she kept folded there. The small house was sturdy and the roof tight against the elements. Here, in this great barn, with the rustlings and shadows alive with movement, she felt stranded and vulnerable.

The light blinded her for a moment—the quick flare of Roan's match and the brilliant glow from the lantern as he caught the wick afire. A sigh of relief escaped her lips and she opened her hands, which had tightened into fists in an automatic gesture.

In the corner, from behind a barrel of feed, a pretty calico cat peered at her, and Katherine crouched where she stood, her hand outstretched, her whisper soft as she coaxed the half-wild creature with twitching fingers and high-pitched sounds. "Come, kitty," she called in a singsong welcome. The cat edged closer, its back curved, its tail stiff, eyeing the temptress who beckoned.

"You've got babies, haven't you?" Katherine wiggled her fingers enticingly. "Have we got any more of that beef, Roan?" she asked in the same lilting, coaxing whisper, as if loath to break the spell she was weaving about the shy creature.

"If you think I'm gonna give that barn cat my dinner, you've got another think coming," he told her from where he'd planted himself on a stool near the door. *She's never used that tone of voice with me,* he thought, narrowing his eyes against the glare of the lantern. *All I get is the sharp side of her tongue, till she wants the rest of my dinner. For a cat,* he added silently.

Katherine looked up at him reproachfully. "She's got a litter somewhere, Roan. Just look at her."

"I am lookin'." His eyes took note of the underside of the cat's belly, where she showed signs of having recently nursed her young ones. "She's got her pick of varmints in this barn,

Katherine. She can catch some nice, fresh meat for her dinner."

A shiver passed over her shoulders and ran its fingers down her back as Katherine considered that idea. Her eyes glared with disgust as she turned her head fully in his direction. "Well, give her my share of the beef. I'll just have a piece of cheese and another biscuit."

"Not likely," he told her. "We ate all the biscuits at noon."

The cat had come within inches of Katherine's fingers. Curling her tail about her, she sat, eyes intent on the woman who crouched just out of reach. A rusty sound escaped her mouth, an inquiring purr that brought a grin to Katherine's lips.

"Hear that?" she asked Roan. "She's talking to me."

"Likely tryin' to coax you out of that beef you keep tellin' her about." He reached down for the saddlebag he'd stashed against the wall, his fingers agile as he tore off a piece of the meat. "Here, catch."

She snatched it in midair and flashed a look of triumph in his direction. "I knew you couldn't resist her," she said, shredding the dark beef and holding out a morsel at arm's length.

It wasn't the cat he couldn't resist, he thought dourly. It was the long-haired urchin with the smudged cheek and shining eyes. Crouched on the dusty floor, her bottom cupped in the denim pants he'd bought for her, she was an inviting sight. The material stretched tight across her thighs and calves, outlining the slender, womanly length she'd hidden so well for so long. His eyes feasted on her, the dark tendrils of hair falling against her cheek, the flush of triumph she wore as the cat rose, stretched and yawned, then approached on dainty paws.

"Nice kitty," Katherine whispered, holding out her hand for the cat's approval. The rough tongue touched her fingertip, and the small teeth closed with precision about the treat she offered. She was still wary, chewing the beef, eyes moving to where Roan sat. Then, abandoning the pretense of aloofness, she purred and bent her head to rub it against the extended hand.

Katherine smiled her delight and offered another morsel of meat. The cat, accepting it as her due, settled down next to her benefactress, not moving away even when Katherine lowered her bottom to the floor and crossed her legs.

Outside, the lightning flashed, calling forth the booming thunder, and Roan leaned over to close the door tightly. He watched the woman before him, fascinated by the gentle movements of her hands as she drew the brightly colored cat closer. In moments, Katherine was holding the cat in her lap, tearing the rest of the chunk of meat apart and offering it in minuscule bits.

"You ever had a cat?" he asked quietly.

She shook her head. "Pa always said the mice had a right to be in the barn. I think he just didn't want to be tied down with having small animals about. Made it hard to leave when the time came."

"You still should have had a dog," he told her.

"They're not easy to come by sometimes. A good farm dog is worth something."

"I had three huntin' dogs when I was a boy. Then when my father sicced 'em on a runaway, I decided I never wanted to hunt with 'em again."

"He ran down a slave?"

"Yeah, the dogs were good at followin' a scent. We'd never had a field hand run off before, and my father didn't want to wait for the bloodhounds to be brought out from town. He just rode behind my dogs till they treed that man. Then he brought him back on the end of a rope." Roan's eyes were bleak as he remembered the day that signified the end of his youth.

"What did you do?" she asked quietly.

"Left." He stood suddenly, and the cat dug in her claws as she made her escape, spooked by the sudden movement.

"Ouch!" Katherine winced at the three separate stings the unsheathed claws made in the flesh of her calf. She scrambled to her feet, unwilling to let Roan retreat into silence. "Roan?"

He shook his head at her. "Didn't mean to get you stabbed like that." A grim smile curved his mouth.

"Roan!" She repeated his name, her tone a bit demanding.

"You'd better find a spot to settle down for a couple of hours, Katherine," he said harshly. "This rain isn't about to let up for a while."

"All right," she agreed reluctantly, looking about for a more welcoming place than the hard floor. A pile of woolen blankets in the corner drew her attention, and she stacked them neatly, settling down with her back to the wall, silent beneath his glowering look.

He turned from her and opened the door once more, looking upward to where the rain fell unabated. The door slid shut beneath his hand. He stalked back to the stool, stretching his legs before him as he sat.

"Might's well take a nap if you can," he told her gruffly. And so saying, he tipped his hat forward and closed his eyes.

From behind the feed barrel, the cat ventured forth once more, approaching Katherine's side with dainty steps. Her tail twitched once as she halted, then her legs folded with limber ease, lowering her into a purring bundle of fur, pressed tightly against the warmth of the woman.

The lightning was hidden by sturdy barn walls, the thunder muted by the hayloft above, and Katherine touched the folded ears and rubbed the outstretched head of the cat, who offered her silent comfort.

Chapter Eight

"I don't like the idea of that stallion in the barn." Katherine had taken a stand. From the look on her face, Roan could foresee a battle royal.

"I mean it, Roan Devereaux. I've got a mare ripe for breeding, and you expect me to rest easy with that enormous stud having hissy fits just fifty feet away?" She glared at him, hands on hips, shoulders squared for battle and all flags flying.

What she didn't know about male animals could get her in trouble, he decided, his gaze taking in the flaring color riding her cheeks. The stance she had taken, not to mention the great gasps of breath it was requiring to support her angry accusations, only served to emphasize the womanly charms she scorned. And he was enjoying every bit of it.

"What are you looking at now?" she blurted, moving a step backward, as if to distance herself from his scrutiny.

"Just wondering if your filly is as set against that big old stallion as you are." He spoke with dry humor, his eyes continuing their journey over her trim body. Trim, all but that lush, rounding bosom that was straining at the buttons of her white shirtwaist.

"She's mine," Katherine told him angrily. "She doesn't have to think. I'm making the decision for her. And I say she's not ready to be bred. Besides, he's too big. She could throw a foal that would kill her to deliver.'' Her eyes slid to the back of the barn, where the stallion paced the limits of the box stall where he'd been confined.

As though he responded to her words, the stallion snorted, banging his head against the door of his stall, testing the limits of his freedom. His head came up with a flourish of black mane flying, nostrils flaring, lips drawn back as if to announce his intentions.

"That filly is built like a ... well, she can take him, if it comes to that,'' Roan told her in a low tone, rightly deciding the air was already rife with emotion. Wasn't a bit of sense in him adding to the uproar.

"You're missing the whole point! I don't want her to be bred yet,'' Katherine said firmly. "If there were any way we could saddle up and leave here tonight, I'd do it.''

Roan cocked his head and nodded at the low ceiling overhead. "Hear that rain, Katherine? There's no way on God's green earth you could talk me into headin' out with a storm like this one clobberin' us. And you can't blame old Jed for puttin' his stud inside. He left him out as long as he could in that corral. There just isn't any shelter with the wind blowin' a mile a minute out there.''

He watched her pace to the door and back, the dark swath of braided hair hanging down her back, shimmering in the light of the kerosene lantern. He'd hung the lantern high above the wide aisle, pulling it up on the rope provided, allowing it to illuminate the entire area.

The better to watch you, he thought, his eyes narrowed as he imagined the sight of that marvelous skein of hair undone and flowing against her flesh. Already he'd cursed himself for obeying her order earlier when she'd changed into the shirtwaist. Stood there like a dummy while she stripped down. Probably missed the prettiest sight of the day.

Katherine kicked a block of wood as she passed the stall holding her yearlings, and it hit the wall with a bang, star-

tling the feisty animals into motion. They'd pretty well settled down for the night, and Roan grinned at Katherine's
small fit of temper.

"They'll never get any rest if you keep on rilin' 'em up,
Katherine," he drawled, leaning back against the wall, legs
outstretched into the aisle. He'd perched on a stool, hands
busy with their tack, going over each piece carefully to check
for weak spots or points of strain. "Why don't you simmer
down. Come on over here and quit that marchin' around.
You're gettin' all in an uproar for nothing."

She looked at him over her shoulder, aware suddenly of
the slumberous quality of his gaze, his half smile curling his
mouth beneath the lush mustache. Her gaze fastened on
him, caught by the sudden stillness of lean hands that had
been plying the leather with supple grace.

Laying aside the bridle he held, he leaned forward, fingers splayed against the muscled length of his thighs. His
eyes were dark, deep-set and heavy-lidded. He was quiet
now, as though he waited for her compliance, as if he willed
her to his side.

The filly nickered softly, only feet from where she stood,
and Katherine's attention swerved to the pretty, sleek creature. Before she could step in her direction, an answering
call from the stallion split the air. The floor of his stall
echoed with the stomping of his feet as he tossed his head,
the barn echoing with his shrill challenge.

"Stay out of her stall, Katherine," Roan warned her
tightly. "She's all jittery tonight. You don't wanta take a
chance on her shovin' you against the wall."

"I raised her!" she said sharply. "She wouldn't hurt me."

He shook his head. "Don't chance it. You oughta know
enough about horses to know you can't depend on them
when they're ready to mate."

"Well, what am I supposed to do? Just go up in that
hayloft and close my eyes and pretend..."

He nodded his head slowly. "That's about the best idea you've had all evening, Mrs. Devereaux." He rose slowly, stretching with enthusiasm. The leather he'd been working with lay about his feet, and he bent to set it to order, hanging the bridles on nails, the pack saddle open over the stool he'd been occupying. He nodded at the ladder leading to the hayloft.

"Let's have at it, Katherine. You aren't gonna do any good down here. They'll all settle down once I turn out the lantern."

She cast a last look at the far stall, then again to the filly, who rubbed against the wall, lifting her hind feet in a slow rhythm. Katherine's shoulders slumped, and the gesture twisted something deep inside him as he watched.

She thought she was so blamed invincible, this woman of his. It hurt to see her plumb up against a conundrum she couldn't solve. Yet he rejoiced at the small sign of defeat. It left her vulnerable, her eyes questioning as they turned in his direction once more.

"You sure?" she asked. "I thought maybe..."

"Katherine, you're gonna get yourself up that ladder right now." He stepped to the wall, loosening the rope and lowering the lantern. It hung between them and he nodded at it. "Lower the wick."

She tightened her lips in a show of defiance, her chin lifting in a gesture that pleased him, even though it told him her vulnerability was a moot point. Twisting the key, she lowered the wick, the flame dying gradually as he lifted the lantern a few feet to keep it from being knocked about. In the dark, he felt for the hook provided and wound the rope about it securely.

Her feet rustled in the scattering of hay as she made her way to the ladder. He followed the sound, his body close as she reached to pull herself up the first rung. He lifted her, hands on her waist, and rejoiced as she allowed the small intimacy.

Her feet were sure against the wooden slats, and she pulled herself up to the loft floor in seconds. A window at the near end, fitted with precious glass, revealed the slashing lightning and she flinched, clenching her fingers into fists against her sides.

"It's not letting up any, is it?" she asked needlessly, sensing his presence behind her as he reached the top of the ladder.

"Nope, can't say that it is," Roan replied, heaving himself to his feet. He made his way to where he'd tossed their bedding earlier, atop a mound of hay.

"Come on, Katherine. Take off your boots and britches and slide into your blankets."

"Yes, all right," she answered, her eyes still focused on the window. Another lightning bolt lit the loft for a moment and she got her bearings.

He gripped her shoulder and pressed her down to the floor, where he'd spread out her belongings. "Boots off first," he said, following his own advice and sinking into the hay to work at the tall boots he wore. With a grunt, he levered the first one off, then tackled the other. She followed suit, sinking down till she toppled backward, losing her balance.

A chuckle escaped as she sat up, reaching for her feet and fighting a losing battle against gravity.

"What's so funny?" he asked, squinting in the darkness.

"This is like battling a feather tick. I'm having a hard time keeping my balance."

"Give me your foot." As he reached out, his left hand brushed against her boot, his right hand groping in the dark. He backtracked quickly and snagged it, gripping it tightly and tugging it toward him.

"Roan! You're pulling me with it," she cried, sliding across the hay with his efforts.

"Let me get a better grip." He was grinning, beginning to enjoy this game. Scooting her to his side, he lifted her legs across his lap, holding them there with the weight of his upper body as he bent to his task. One hand on her heel, the other holding her calf, he levered the boot off, repeating the maneuver on the other leg.

She pulled her legs back reflexively. "Let me loose," she said quickly, rolling to escape his hands. They were warm against her, fingers squeezing gently, palms spread on the fullness just beneath the backs of her knees. It felt indecent, she decided abruptly, his handling of her limbs in such a fashion.

"Thank you," she mumbled, kneeling beside him, wishing against her better judgment for another flash of lightning to reveal the whereabouts of her blankets.

As though nature answered her dilemma, the clouds were lit from within, shimmering outside the window for long seconds, illuminating the loft. Her movements were quick as she slid beneath the blanket, tugging it over her and settling down, cushioned by the hay.

Roan watched her scamper about, his eyes becoming accustomed to the dark, able to make out her form, if not the details of what she did.

"Did you take off those britches like I told you?" he asked, intent on removing his own.

"No." She settled lower in the blankets, her voice muffled.

"You'll be sorry tomorrow. You'll be fightin' those tight pants all night."

"They're not tight," she answered defiantly.

"You haven't been lookin' at 'em like I have, sugar."

She was silent, digesting the remark. Her small huff of disagreement was audible. "Well, you picked them out."

He smiled in the darkness, head cradled on the saddlebag, arms folded over his broad chest. "Yeah, I did," he allowed, his eyes slanting to where she lay, close at hand.

"How about my kiss, Katherine?" he said moments later, when she'd all but decided to ignore him and the flaring sky, closing her eyes tightly.

"Is this going to be a nightly event?" she asked primly.

"Yeah, I reckon it's all I get. Unless you're ready to share these blankets with me." His voice held an undertone of sultry heat that reminded her of the rolling thunder overhead.

She was quiet, her breath tightly held as she waited. It was less than a threat, his casual invitation, given so easily. Her mouth opened and she blew out the air she'd held within, aware he'd not moved in her direction. It was still her choice, and she made it with a degree of speed that tickled his funny bone.

Rolling to her side, she lifted one hand to seek his face, meeting the blade of his nose and feeling her way to his mouth. Rising, she placed her lips firmly against his, allowing them to move just a little, as if she felt her way in the darkness. With an audible sound, she released the slight suction she'd brought about and lowered her hand to press against his chest. Then, using him as a lever, she scooted back to her hollowed-out place in the hay and settled down.

She heard him, heard the rustling of his movements, and her eyes widened in the dark, aware of the closeness he'd created between them. Another flash of lightning above the clouds lit the loft, and she stifled a gasp as he rose over her on one elbow, his mouth just inches from her own.

"That was a pretty poor kiss, if you ask me, Mrs. Devereaux. You'll have to do better."

She shook her head. "I don't know how to kiss any differently than that. It's how I used to kiss my father."

His snort was expressive. "Well, I don't plan on treatin' you like my little girl. I'll just have to repeat the last lesson we had on this subject."

He's an arrogant . . . The words were still forming in her mind when he captured her mouth. *Surely this isn't proper,* she thought as his tongue once more explored the seam of her lips, nudging and coaxing his way within. His hand was tugging her closer, fingers spread behind her shoulder, moving up to her neck, where he got a grip and held her in place. She felt the brand of his fingers, cupping the base of her skull, moving through her braid as he loosened the heavy plait.

She drew in air through her nose, her lips so enclosed by his mouth she could only have taken in the breath he released to her. It was not enough. Even the shuddering of her chest agreed with her verdict, and she twisted to escape his hold. His mouth released hers and she gasped, eyes wide, shivers traveling from the nape of her neck down the length of her spine.

"I can't breathe!" she exclaimed against his cheek, turning away from the damp kisses he pressed against her.

"Yeah, you take my breath away, too, Katherine," he whispered with a trace of good humor.

She inhaled sharply, filling her nostrils with his scent, aware of the fresh hay around them and beneath them. It mixed with the soap he'd washed with and the smell of leather that seemed a part of him. Above her, he sighed, the small chuckle that accompanied it telling her the lesson was over for tonight.

And about time, she thought with relief. She was becoming used to his hands on her. The firm pressure of his mouth against hers was almost pleasant, she decided. But there was no point in encouraging him, she thought. If she should decide to go back to Illinois...

Now where had that idea come from? she wondered. She'd about decided she couldn't handle the farm alone anyway. Why would she want to go back? Even if Roan tired of the novelty of marriage and wearied of being denied his rights, she could always manage on the trail alone. She'd ridden a lot of miles with Charlie and Lawson over the years. She could do it again if she had to, and put down roots in a town somewhere. Maybe get a job in a store or livery stable, she thought darkly.

As if the man she'd married would let her. Even now, he was dragging her against him, tucking her beneath his arm and surrounding her with his embrace.

"What if you get tired of being married to me?" she asked suddenly.

"Now what in tarnation brought that on? Do I act like I'm fed up with you already?"

She considered the question. "I feel like you're laughing at me a lot. Maybe I just amuse you, with my old maid ideas."

"Well, I'd say I'm a far cry from bein' amused tonight, honey," he said against the soft skin at her temple.

Wisely, she decided to refrain from answering, unsure of his meaning, unwilling to question him lest he tell her. Folding her arms across her chest and drawing up her knees a bit, she fit herself against his side, unaware of the smile of satisfaction that twisted his mouth as he brushed it against her forehead.

Her head was burrowed against him, the blanket pulled high over her exposed ear, and she missed the first crash of hooves against the stall door. Seconds later, the stud kicked again, and the sound brought Katherine bolt upright.

"What was that?" she whispered, lifting her chin to listen intently.

"Damn horse is bound and determined to get to your filly, Katherine," Roan answered with a touch of aggravation. He pushed at the blanket covering him and reached for his pants, muttering beneath his breath all the while.

"What are you going to do?" she asked, aware suddenly that the rain had stopped and the moon shone through the window above them. It outlined him nicely as he struggled into the legs of his pants, hopping on one foot as he shoved the other in place.

"I'm probably gonna get my brains knocked out," he grumbled, aware of the sound of wood splintering as the huge stallion plowed his way through the stall door. "If I can get to the lantern before he gets in the aisle, I'll be all right," he said, almost as if he were trying to persuade himself of the truth of his statement.

"Be careful," she whispered, already crawling to the hole in the floor, leaning over to peer below.

It was pitch-dark down there, and she sighed.

"I don't think you ought to do this," she told him, squinting through the hole. "You can't see a blessed thing."

Reaching into his pocket, Roan came up with a box of matches. "I'll light one of these when I get to the bottom of the ladder," he told her, holding it before her face. He clamped the metal box between his teeth and backed to the ladder, making his way down the first steps as the barn door rolled open. Revealed in the opening was the figure of their host, clad in a nightshirt, boots pulled on with haste, hair standing out from his head.

"You folks all right up there?" he asked in a rusty cackle, sleep coating his voice.

Roan halted where he was, halfway down the ladder. "I'm headin' down to light the lantern," he said quietly. "Where's the stallion?"

In answer, the horse sounded a shrill challenge, jumping the shattered stall door easily and skidding on the floor as he headed for the stall housing the dark filly.

"Damn, too late," the farmer said, disgust evident in his tone.

"What do you mean, too late?" Katherine's voice came in a loud whisper from the loft above. "He's going after my filly!"

Roan lifted himself back up to sit on the edge of the opening. "Nothing to be done, Katherine. It'd be worth your life to get between those two horses now."

She lay on her stomach and peered below, watching as the big stud approached, hooves clattering against the floor, tossing his head, his mane flying as he followed the scent that drew him. His approach was clarion in sound, his snorting and pawing echoing throughout the barn. He trumpeted again, nosing his way into the stall where the black object of his affections shivered, waiting. He nudged at her left hindquarter, his teeth exposed as he allowed her to feel the edges.

She neighed sharply and shifted, shivering, hampered by the rope that tied her in place. Her scent was strong and the stud's response was automatic. Rearing, he covered her with his considerable bulk, his body plunging as he sought the mating his instincts demanded.

The mare screamed in the darkness, and beside him, Roan heard the sound of despair Katherine could not withhold. He reached for her, his arm unerring as he held her against him, rolling from the opening and holding her tightly to his chest.

She buried her head, lifting her hands to cover her ears. But there was no more to hear. The filly was quiet, the stallion sliding from her with an awkward motion, shaking his head and snorting once more, the sound barely carrying to where Katherine sheltered.

Below them, the farmer spoke in coaxing tones to his horse, catching him by the halter and leading him out the wide doors.

"I'll put him in the corral. You folks can rest easy," he called back over his shoulder.

"Should I go down to her?" Katherine's voice was muffled against Roan's shirt, her eyes squeezed shut as she pictured the scene that had just taken place. So quickly had it happened, she was only now becoming truly aware of what she had seen.

The rearing horse, his movements violent in the dim light from the barn door, the sound of his triumphant squeal as he ... She groaned. Deep within she cringed, holding the memory. She'd seen horses breeding before. Not often, true, but she'd brought her father's stallion to her mare only a few months ago.

He'd been anxious but mature, a mild-mannered stud, if such a thing were to be believed. She almost smiled as she recalled the animal. He'd been uncut, true, but not difficult to handle, even allowing Katherine on his back. And he'd covered her mare with finesse. Eager, biting at her flank, nudging her in place.

Katherine recalled the event, and her face flushed as she moved to free herself from Roan's grasp. She'd experienced feelings on that day in early spring that were still unexplainable. Deep-seated longings had assailed her, emotions she denied as she led the stallion to his stall. She'd returned to release her mare from the ropes with which she'd tied her in place for the breeding, breathless with the needs that simmered within her body.

She blinked, remembering, and shivered. "I'll go down to her," she said hoarsely, pushing against Roan.

"No." His voice was rasping, his grip on her almost painful. "No, you're not going anywhere, Kate. She's all right. You can tend her in the morning." He pushed back from the opening in the floor, taking her with him, his hands hard against her flesh through the fabric of her cotton shirtwaist.

Without a word, he struggled to his feet, hauling her with him, lifting her and carrying her the few steps to where their blankets lay in disarray. Bathed in the moonlight, he was a silhouette, dark shadows forming a man, his face barely discernible. He bent low, dropping to his knees, still clutching her against his chest, his mouth pressed to her forehead. Then, lowering her to the blankets, he followed her down, his weight heavy against her slender form.

Katherine caught her breath, frowning as she struggled to move beneath him. "Roan! What—" His lips swallowed the words she would have spoken. She wiggled silently, her fists pushing against the weight of his chest, her mouth invaded by the sweep of his tongue.

He lifted his head for a moment, his breathing labored and rasping; she flattened her hands, shoving desperately against his shoulders.

"Roan, stop it!" she hissed angrily, her eyes wide in the dim light. The grim set of his jaw as he bent to her once more set off a small spark of fright and she renewed her struggle. *He's too strong,* she thought, aware that her hands were plastered indecently to his chest, her fingers helpless against rock-hard muscle.

His eyes closed and his mouth touched hers again. Stilling beneath him, she was breathless, conscious only of the hot kisses raining against her face, of his murmured words falling softly against her skin.

"Let me love you, Katherine. Kiss me, honey," he whispered, his mouth damp, his voice husky with entreaty.

Deep within her, a restless urgency coiled, releasing a warmth that washed over her like a spring shower. She gasped, shuddering at the sensation, her heart beating audibly in her ears. Her lips firmed beneath his, returning the kiss he offered. And at the silent urging of his tongue, she allowed him entrance, shivering as he searched out the secrets of her mouth. With a murmur of surrender she lifted her arms and twined them about him, clinging to his shoulders. It was a possession she'd never dreamed of, this urgent taking of her mouth, encompassing her with himself, covering her with the heat of his body, his hands swift, moving her beneath him.

With agile haste, he worked at undoing the buttons of her shirt, impatient against the inches of tender flesh he exposed to his sight. She closed her eyes, aware of the gaze he bent upon her, flushing with apprehension as she listened to his wordless murmurs.

It was too much, the knowledge that she was bared to his eyes, that her breasts were almost naked to his view. *He only wants what Evan wanted,* she thought with desperation. *He's going to squeeze me and hurt me.*

Drawing in a breath, sobbing in her throat, she twisted to escape his grasp. Her hands pushed against him, one at his shoulder, the other between their bodies, in a vain attempt to halt his moving fingers before he could bare her entirely.

"Stop it, Roan," she said, the words a harsh whisper. "Don't look at me like that!"

He sucked in a breath and lifted himself from her, gathering his scattered senses, attempting to harness the desires he'd been battling for days. His gaze moved over the vision beneath him, tender as he sensed her wariness, possessive as he allowed his eyes to rest on her mouth, damp from his kisses.

He flexed his fingers, where his hand had buried itself in the fabric of her shirtwaist, exposing the plump flesh of her breasts.

"You're my wife, Katherine," he growled, shifting his big body, groaning as he eased his hunger against the supple strength of her thigh. She gasped again and her breast pressed against the back of his hand, drawing his gaze like a magnet. In the moonlight, the pale flesh he'd brought to view rose and fell with her breathing, and his hand loosened from the shirt.

"Let me touch you," he whispered, his voice guttural with the restraint he imposed. His skin drew tautly across the harsh lines of his cheekbones, his jaw clamped, and his eyes narrowed as he watched her, as if awaiting her words of permission.

Drawing a shuddering breath, she met his look, searching for a sign of the tenderness he'd brought to her with his touch... and finding only the harshness of a warrior in the depths of his dark gaze.

She'd not denied him, Roan thought, not turned him away. She was silent, true, quiet beneath him, but acquiescent, and a surge of joy sped through his veins as he bent to claim the flesh she'd relinquished to his touch. Brushing aside the edges of her garment, he flexed his fingers, carefully fitting them over her ribs, his thumbs almost meeting beneath her breasts. He cupped his hands, moving them upward, then together, until he allowed them to possess the tender underside of her breasts. She was full, firm, and his eyes closed for a moment as he savored the pure pleasure gripping him. He lifted one hand to her face, his fingers brushing back strands of dark hair, smoothing it from her forehead.

"You said..." She bit at her lip, unsure of her ground, her mind focused on his big hand, touching her, possessing a forbidden part of her body. What had he said? That he wouldn't...what? Wouldn't touch her? Another breath shuddered between them as he inhaled again, matching her own trembling gasp.

With eyes widening uncertainly, she watched him bend once more to brush against her mouth. Small kisses showered across her lips, his tension leashed as he tenderly bent her to his wooing. He gentled her as he would a fretting filly, soothing her with his hands, speaking soft words of praise.

Her heart pounding unevenly, her breath catching in her throat, she responded, leaning into his body. Her mouth opened, seeking his, as he sucked gently at the flesh of her lips. The palm that seared her breast moved, carefully kneading, cherishing the plumpness with his big hand. Caressing his prize with callused fingers, he circled the sensitive flesh, cupping her, weighing the fullness within his grasp. Moving slowly, aching to possess the delicate treasure, he held his breath, finally daring to touch the swollen crest with one rough fingertip, brushing against the burgeoning flesh.

Now he'll hurt me, she thought in panic, aware only of the tiny scrap of sensitive flesh. Her gasp was loud, her breath a shuddering movement beneath his hand. "No..." she whispered, trembling, jerking away from him.

His hand tightened, his rough skin scraping across her delicate, budding flesh, and he winced, sensing her panic.

"I won't hurt you, honey," he whispered, attempting to reassure her, even as he recognized it was to no avail.

"No!" She shouted the single word, drawing up her knees, her hands clawing at his, then spreading her fingers widely to cover herself from his view. She turned from his embrace, her shoulders hunching as he released her.

"Katherine..." He lifted himself away from her reluctantly, his voice a whisper.

"Roan, I'm..." She shook her head, her eyes squeezing shut as she pressed her lips together.

Without a word, he rolled away, staggering to his feet. Bending almost double to press shaking hands to his rigid thighs, he closed his eyes, his breath rasping in the silence of the loft.

"I won't hurt you, Katherine," he growled. "You're all right." Turning his back, he walked to the wall, leaning against the rough wood, harnessing the driving need that gripped him. Aware he'd frightened the woman who huddled silently against the blankets.

In a moment, he straightened, making his way back to where she watched him, shirtwaist pulled together with trembling fingers, hair tangling about her face, pale in the moonlight.

"I had no right to jump on you that way," he told her stiffly. "I don't know what got into me."

Katherine nodded. "It's all right," she whispered, and watched him turn away, regret alive within her. "I'm sorry, Roan."

Her eyes closed. *I was almost his wife for real. Almost...if I hadn't...* She silently cursed her own fears, cursed the memory of Evan Gardner, revulsion rising within her as she thought of his hated hands on her flesh.

But Roan is my husband. He has the right. Her eyes opened, seeking his face, as if she could will away the grim expression he wore, visible in the faint light from the window. A small sound from her lips alerted him and he turned.

"Katherine." He spoke her name once and came to where she lay, squatting next to her, reaching to straighten her clothing, smoothing back her hair as he tended her.

She watched him, felt his hands on her flesh and breathed deeply of a new scent that clung to him—musky and enticing, surrounding her.

His hands were gentle, lifting her until he could lie beside her once more. She was unyielding for a moment, unable to bend to his persuasion, her memory fresh and painful as she recalled his rough need of her.

He wanted her, she thought. The way a man wants a woman. But he stopped; he didn't hurt her, not really. Her eyes closed and she allowed her body to unfurl, turning to face him.

Now he embraced her gently, holding himself at a careful distance, giving her the gift of his tenderness. His hands soothed her, and she softened against him, oblivious to the tears dampening her cheeks—aware only of the words of comfort he spent in her ear as he rocked her in the darkness.

Chapter Nine

"That dratted farmer didn't even care. He acted like I should be grateful to be getting his great galoot of a stallion's services." Not satisfied to ride fifty feet behind him, where she must shout to be heard, Katherine gave up, fuming in silence, and rode side by side with Roan.

"I don't want to hear it, Katherine. I've just spent two hours mending a stall door." It was a statement guaranteed to rile her, he knew. He turned in the saddle to glare his frustration, feeling he had a perfect right, seeing as how she was smack-dab at the bottom of his problem. "I can see his point," he said with exaggerated politeness. "He more than likely gets a fancy price for that animal's talents."

"Huh!" The sound was derisive, as was the scalding look she merited for his explanation. "I can't see much talent in what he did. He scuffed up my filly's right flank and probably got her in foal. And her with no choice in the matter."

"Most mares don't get asked for their permission before they're bred," he answered, turning his head to hide the grin that would not be denied. Katherine's logic totally escaped him this morning. For the first time in their acquaintance, she was acting exactly like a woman, spouting off and carrying on as if she'd been sinned against in a mighty way.

"Well, I don't expect she was real pleased, anyway," Katherine said with elaborate patience. She pursed her mouth as she pursued that thought, recalling the shrill scream of her filly. "It still should have been my choice to decide when she was ready to..." She drew in a deep breath and turned away. "Just forget it!"

"If she were out in the wild, runnin' with a pack of horses, she'd already have dropped one foal at least, you know," he said. "She's plenty old enough, and besides, you got yourself a fine stud for her. Old Jed told me he paid a bundle for him. I'll guarantee his bloodlines would match up pretty close to anything my father has in his barns."

She considered a moment, recalling the stud, the pride and joy of their reluctant host of the night before. The stallion was enormous, heavy in the chest, with a thick neck and muscular hindquarters, taller even than her father's stallion. If that horse was a man, he'd probably have every woman in the county after him, admiring his lines.

"Come on, Katherine," Roan said finally, rightly deciding she'd stewed long enough. "You can't do a blamed thing about it. Might as well wait and see what comes of it before you spend any more time havin' fits."

She wheeled away, waiting momentarily until the string of yearlings had passed her by, then pulled her mare into line behind the strangely docile filly.

"If we're close to Cooneyville, why couldn't we stay at a hotel tonight?" Katherine was sitting cross-legged near the fire, intent on the piece of rabbit she held, picking at the meat with two fingers.

"Will you quit your playin' with that," he growled. "Never saw a woman so fussy about her food."

"It's full of buckshot," she sniped, dropping another bit of metal to the ground.

"Well, next time I'll use a rifle."

"Next time, I'll clean the rabbit before it's cooked," she told him, stripping the last of the meat from the bone she held. She eyed him measuringly. "You didn't answer me, you know."

He leaned back against the rock behind him, his feet stretched toward the fire. "We're still a ways from town, Kate. We'll stay right here till morning."

He was not to be moved, she decided, and somehow it wasn't worth the fuss. Tossing the bone into the fire, she stretched toward the spit, tearing another piece of meat from the small carcass hanging there. They'd pulled it from the fire to cool while the can of beans cooked over the flames, and Katherine had snatched the first morsels while Roan readied the coffeepot for brewing.

"Save me some," he told her, watching as she relished the tender meat.

She slanted a long look in his direction. "You ate most of the food at noon."

His shrug was accompanied by a superior look, one eyebrow quirked mockingly. "You turned it down, ma'am. Said you weren't particularly fond of possum sausage."

She swallowed the bite of rabbit she'd been chewing. "I still think you could have found something else for us to eat. Are you sure that's all old Jed's wife offered?"

"You ate most of your biscuits. Still wish you hadn't thrown that good sausage away, though." He sighed as he reached for the rabbit carcass. "Beggars can't be choosers," he quoted solemnly, tearing off a long strip of meat.

"Phooey on that nonsense. We're a long way from being beggars. You paid him for the food and the night's accommodations, such as they were."

"Don't forget, he threw in the stud fee," Roan reminded her blandly, spitting a piece of buckshot to one side.

Her glare encompassed him, taking in the long, lean length stretching toward the fire, the dark silhouette of his head and shoulders against the twilight gloom. She refused to take the bait, and instead gritted her teeth against the words that begged to be spoken.

She'd have willingly paid a bundle to have somebody keep that stallion away from her mare and not have her bred, she thought sadly. Her eyes strayed once more to where Roan sat, engrossed in the can of beans he was eating.

"Want some?" he asked, holding the can in her direction.

She scooted closer and took the can from him, careful to touch only the cloth he'd wrapped it in. "I just knew you were going to eat them all," she said, poking the spoon into the can and peering at the scattering of beans he'd left for her. Glaring at him, she lifted the spoonful to her mouth.

She ate steadily, snatching at a last piece of the rabbit as he slid the bony remnants from the spit. "How will we cross the river?" she asked, wiping her mouth on the towel.

"Flatboat," he told her, rising to dispose of the remains of their meal. The bones went in the fire. The can he buried several yards from where they sat.

"Will it be large enough for all of us?" she asked, waving at the string of horses grazing beneath the trees.

"Some of those rafts are a pretty good size. But we'll more'n likely have to go in two trips." Tossing his blanket to the ground, he bent to straighten it. "Bring your blankets over here," he told her, engrossed in his chore.

She considered his words, her eyes scanning the area they had chosen for a campsite. The trees behind them ran to the edge of the water, a swiftly flowing current determined to dump itself into the big river only a few miles away. It had gradually widened throughout the day, deepening into a small river stream as they followed near its banks. Beneath the trees it was dark, night having crept upon them while they ate, and she felt exposed suddenly, there beside the fire.

He glanced up at her, sensing her disquiet and electing to ignore it. "Let's have that blanket over here, Katherine," he told her bluntly. "You're sleepin' right next to me, just like always." This might prove to be just a little bit sticky, he decided, recognizing the look on her face.

He stood and faced her across the glowing coals. "Look, honey. I'm not gonna jump on you or give you a bad time of it."

She felt the flush creeping up from the open neckline of her shirt. Her cheeks tingled with the blood that pumped its way from her heart, the sound roaring in her ears as she dared a glance at him once more.

"Katherine, the worst that could have happened last night..." He paused and rubbed his fingers across the dark mustache riding above his upper lip, his eyes shadowed and dark. "Well, it didn't happen, anyway," he said finally. "And it won't, not for a while yet. Not till you're ready for it." It was as close to a promise as he could get, he decided, hating the fact he'd felt obliged to make it. Damn, but she made it hard on him. His mouth twisted into a smile at the errant thought. "And that's a fact," he murmured beneath his breath.

"All right," she conceded, rolling to her feet and heading for her saddle and the blankets tied on behind it.

"You need to go out in the bushes any more tonight?" he asked her bluntly, catching the blankets she tossed in his direction and spreading them next to his own.

She blushed again. *I'll never get used to his plain speaking,* she thought, nodding and turning from the fire to make her way through the trees.

"Don't be long, Katherine, or I'll come and find you." The words stepped up her pace, and she hurried to find a likely spot.

His arm was heavy about her waist, and she felt every inch of it as it curled over her, his big hand nestling at her ribs. It was warm, like the rest of him, radiating the same pulsing heat as did his long body, wrapped about her back and touching her from head to toe. His breath blew in her ear as he muttered in an undertone, settling himself, his head resting on his saddlebag again.

"You might be more comfortable with me somewhere else," she said as he shifted once more, lifting her, moving her to rest with his arm beneath her head.

"Damn right!" he muttered, already conscious of the pressure of her bottom against his private parts.

"I can scoot over," she offered, wiggling herself from his grip as she sought to prove the sincerity of her offer.

"Lie still," he growled, scooping her closer and stilling her protest.

She was silent, aware that his taciturn behavior had to do with the proximity of their bodies. In fact, unless she missed her guess, it was about the same problem he'd had last night. Roan Devereaux was needing a woman.

"Will you stop your damn wigglin' around," he grumbled against her ear, his hand easing its way up her rib cage so that the pressure of his wrist was a deliberate wedge beneath her breast.

"Roan?" Her whisper wavered in the stillness.

"I'm not givin' you a bad time of it, Katherine," he told her wearily. "Just tryin' to find a little comfort for myself."

She subsided, only too aware of the pressure he exerted, plumping her breast upward with a gentle urging. *Maybe he doesn't realize what he's doing,* she thought distractedly. And then his hand turned, slowly and with purpose as he cupped his palm, allowing the weight of her breast to fill it.

His grunt of satisfaction banished her hopeful thought and she stiffened within his embrace.

"Don't wiggle," he reminded her again. "I'm almost asleep here and you're disturbin' me."

She had a choice, she decided. She could make a fuss or close her eyes.

She closed her eyes.

Chapter Ten

"So help me, Katherine, if I hear one more word about payin' your own way—" Roan's mouth snapped shut as he cut the flow of words he'd been spewing in her direction.

She gritted her teeth and her chin jutted forward with the movement. Pulling up short on the reins she held in her right hand, she wheeled her mare around and waited for the string of horses to pass her by before pulling in behind the gelding, bringing up the rear once more.

"They're my horses, Roan Devereaux," she muttered, nudging her mare into a quick trot to keep pace.

"You heard what I said, Katherine," he called back gruffly. "Danged if you don't always have to have the last word."

She was quiet for a moment, biting back the words that begged to be spoken—and then gave up her silence as a lost cause. "I know you married me to look after me, Roan," she began stiffly. "But when all's said and done, I'm used to doing for myself, and I'd feel better about things if I wasn't beholden to you."

His sigh was deep. "We already talked about this. To start with, I couldn't leave you back there alone. Things were kinda touchy, and I couldn't face Charlie if I didn't look after you for him." He caught a quick glimpse of her ex-

pression and closed his eyes. Damn, now she was feeling like
a burden he was toting for her daddy.

"Look, honey. It started out that way, but truth to tell,
it's about time I found a wife and settled down anyway. Just
think how pleased my folks are gonna be when I show up all
married and respectable." Never mind the fact he was half
out of his mind with wanting to make a real wife out of the
bride riding next to him.

"I'm sure they're going to be really pleased when they
find out you married a Yankee," she said scathingly. "That
ought to tie a knot in somebody's tail."

His grin was spontaneous. "Yeah, you're right there," he
said, envisioning the look on LeRoy Devereaux's face when
Katherine spoke her howdys in that Illinois twang of hers.

"You didn't mention you were ready to settle down,
Roan. In fact, I had the idea this whole thing, the getting
married part anyway, was kind of a convenience, so I
wouldn't be getting the cold shoulder, traveling around with
a man and not married to him."

"There's several things we've kinda left hangin'. The idea
of maybe stayin' on at River Bend has entered my mind a
time or two," he told her casually. "You might really catch
on to livin' on a big spread like that. Hell, I'll bet you'd even
spruce up the place, once I get you into some decent out-
fits."

"Well, isn't that kind of you," she snapped. "Who said
I was interested in new clothes anyway? I brought along a
dress. I'll have something to wear when we get there."

He looked appalled. "One of those brown things you
were draggin' around in back home?"

"It's black. And quite suitable for church, so I imagine
I'll look decent enough in it to meet your folks."

"Katherine, Katherine." His voice dwelled on her name
lovingly, rolling each syllable with great care. "You're just
bound and determined to fuss at me today, aren't you?" He
shook his head mournfully. "Here I'm tryin' to be good

company and make the ride easy for you, and you just snip and snap at me over the least little thing.''

She frowned, examining the words they'd exchanged, wondering if he was pulling the wool over her eyes or if she'd maybe misjudged his intentions. Probably both.

"I believe you could talk your way around a hanging judge," she said finally, with a scathing glance at his pious expression. "You don't fool me for a minute, Devereaux."

They camped beside the river, beneath a grove of walnut trees. Katherine dropped a line in the water, into a deep spot just off the high bank, and within minutes caught a good-sized fish. "This is the plumb ugliest thing I've ever seen," she told Roan as she carried it to the campsite.

"River cat. Might be ugly, but it sure is good eatin'." He wiped the horses down with handfuls of long grass, finally stringing them out between the trees while he watched her. No other woman he'd met could so efficiently deal with killing and gutting a fish, he decided, watching as she prepared their supper.

The scent of frying fish rose into the evening, accompanied by the rich smell of boiling coffee, and Roan settled back against his saddle, feet stretched toward the fire. "I believe I'll take you on as a cook, Mrs. Devereaux," he told her with lazy approval, watching her deft movements as she worked.

She tossed him a look, her eyes narrowing as she considered him. "If you're planning on eating any of my fish, I'd advise you to pitch in, Mr. Devereaux," she told him. "We could use the rest of those biscuits I cooked this morning. They're in your saddlebag."

He reached behind him for the leather pouches he'd stashed behind his saddle. "Yes, ma'am," he said meekly, undoing the fastenings and retrieving the wrapped biscuits. "Whatever you say, ma'am." Locating the tin plates and cups, he arranged them on a towel next to him, allotting two biscuits to each plate.

Katherine lifted the frying pan, its handle wrapped in a dish towel, and brought it, sizzling and steaming, to where he sat. She took up the fish with her fork, dividing it between their plates, and carried the hot pan away, leaving it to cool in the grass. The coffeepot was dealt with quickly, set aside to allow the grounds to settle, and then she joined him.

"I believe I could be a contented man with you waitin' on me for the next few years," he told her, biting gingerly into a crisp chunk of fish. "You've got a real talent for cookin', Katherine."

"I cut my teeth on campfire cooking," she told him crisply. "My pa wasn't much for doing women's work, and Lawson...well..." She took a bite of fish and chewed carefully, pulling a bone from between her lips.

"Did you get along with your brother?" he asked with casual interest, his eyes carefully intent on her.

She shrugged and picked up a biscuit. "He looked after me when I was little. Used to boss me around a lot. But I didn't mind. Once..." She paused and her look was bleak.

"He...what? What did he do, Katherine?"

She sat up straight, wiping at her mouth with the back of her hand. "Let's just say I found out the hard way not to be too friendly."

"With men?"

"I was just a girl, Roan. Too young to know what men wanted from women and too independent to listen to Charlie when he told me to stay close."

"Where were you then? On the trail?"

She shook her head. "No, we'd been living at a farm in Kentucky for a couple of months. Charlie was training horses, just like always, and I kept house in a one-room cabin, washing and cooking for him and Lawson. I used to watch Charlie work the horses every day, and one of the cowhands was nice to me." She looked at Roan and shrugged her shoulders in a telling gesture.

"He expected you to..."

"He caught me away from the cabin one night and started mauling me, pushed me down on the ground and told me he knew I'd been wanting some loving. He said he was just the man to make me happy." A thin shiver of revulsion slid up her spine and she swallowed the bite of biscuit she'd been chewing.

"Did you get away?" he asked, forcing himself to remain still, forcing his anger under control as he watched her pick up her coffee and sip at the hot brew. His muscles tensed with the effort, and he opened his clenched fist to reach for his own cup, eyeing her over the rim as he drank.

"I couldn't get him off me, and he had one dirty hand over my mouth so I couldn't yell," she told him bluntly. Her lips quivered as she drew in a deep breath and her gaze rose to meet his. "Lawson pulled him off and told me to get. He must have pounded him pretty bad, 'cause the next day the owner came out to talk with Pa, and we had to move on. He said I'd been enticing his men."

"You didn't believe him, did you, Katherine?"

"Well, I made sure no one else ever made the same mistake," she said firmly. "I figured if I quit wearing pants and covered up my female parts, nobody'd ever accuse me of enticing their men again. After that, Lawson stayed pretty close when he wasn't working the horses with my pa."

"Where'd you go from there?" Roan asked quietly, his mind filled with the thought of the girl she'd been, of the life she'd lived.

She shook her head. "To another farm, another town. Pa had a hard time settling down anywhere. We stayed one place in Kentucky for almost two years, though. He trained horses and even had a lady friend, the cook for the family in the big house. I guess she was good reason to stick around," Katherine said with a small smile. "She was nice to me."

The setting sun cast its glow in a final glorious display across the horizon and Roan got up from his position before the dying fire. "I'll scout up some wood to keep the fire going. You better do your washin' up before it gets full dark. I don't want you out in the brush after that."

She looked about their campsite, aware of his care in choosing it. They were beneath the trees, the open, grassy fields spreading before them, the river at their backs for protection. As far as she could see, only waving grasses and shadowed areas of brush met her eye.

"I'll wash here," she told him. "Bring me up some water from the river when you come back. I'll heat it up a little in the coffeepot . . . take the chill off."

His nod was answer enough, and she headed for a nearby cluster of bushes to tend to her needs before nightfall endowed her shelter with dark shadows. Talking about Ned Hastings had renewed old memories she'd buried long ago. Funny she should even remember his name, she thought with a shake of her head. She ought to be thankful, she supposed, for the lesson he'd taught her. The lesson Evan Gardner had reinforced only a week or so ago.

Men were hard and needy creatures, most of them bigger and heavier than she was. Most of them wanting just one thing from a woman . . . the part of her she was least likely wanting to give. She hurried to the spot she'd chosen, silently cursing the frustration of dealing with being a woman while wearing boy's clothing.

It was past midnight when the silence was shattered by a raucous shout, and Katherine felt Roan's big hand press her against the ground as he reached for his gun.

"I wouldn't touch that piece if I was you, mister," a voice called out from the darkness. "I got aim right at your woman's head, and I want you to know I'm a crack shot.

Been practicin' on watermelons. They blow up just about as pretty as a skull full of brains and bone.''

Roan cursed beneath his breath, aware of his negligence. He'd slept soundly, wrapped about Katherine's warm body, sure they were secure in this place. Too late, he'd heard the arrival of the men surrounding them.

His hand rose into the air, empty. ''Leave her be,'' he said quietly. ''We don't have anything worth shootin' us for. Just a string of horses, 'bout as common as they come. Take 'em if you've a mind to.''

Next to him, Katherine inhaled sharply and he nudged her with his knee, pressing against her thigh firmly.

''Well, I reckon you've got more than horses. Let's take a look at those saddlebags of yours,'' one of the men said, stepping closer. He was a dark shadow on the other side of the fire and Roan sat up warily, his eyes on the gun aimed in his direction.

He stood and bent to pick up his saddlebags, tossing them across the fire to where their assailant stood. And then Katherine struggled to her feet.

''Get down,'' he told her roughly, pushing at her shoulder to force her to the ground.

But it was too late; Katherine's face was illuminated by the firelight.

''Will you look at that!'' another voice called from the darkness. ''I'll take the woman. Ya'll can have the horses and whatever else you find.''

A taller, shadowed figure moved into view. Hat pulled low, a full beard revealing only dark, piercing eyes over a flattened nose, he rose menacingly from the night astride a huge horse that blended into the darkness.

''The woman's mine,'' he said in a cold voice, devoid of inflection. ''Tie them both up, and let's get on out of here. If he gives you a hard time of it, shoot them both.''

Chapter Eleven

"Put me down, you ugly bastard!"

Katherine's cry was shrill, carrying to where Roan sat. He lifted his head from his chest. His eyes narrowed against the piercing pain in his head, where a gun butt had guaranteed his cooperation during the early hours of the morning. He'd wakened several times throughout the day, only to see the sleeping figures of several men scattered about a primitive campsite. A lone sentinel stood guard, rifle in hand, but try as he might to catch sight of her, there was no sign of Katherine.

Until now. The sun had blazed its way across the sky throughout the long day. Now, against the brilliant sunset, he made out Katherine's struggles, futile as they were. The man who'd claimed her last night appeared to have her well in hand, lifting her over his shoulder, ignoring the bound fists pummeling his back.

Well, she sure as hell was alive and it didn't sound like she'd been leaned on too heavy, Roan thought. Relief fueled the sigh that emptied his lungs, just as another shriek of promised vengeance split the air. She didn't seem to be roughed up any, just wrinkled and dusty.

"My husband's a Devereaux from Louisiana. When his family finds out you've—" Her words were cut off abruptly as the man who carried her delivered a sharp swat to her fanny, a prime target atop his shoulder.

"I told you to shut up," he growled in the same guttural voice Roan recalled from the dark hours of the night.

"Damn!" It was a hopeless sound, growled between Roan's clenched teeth, followed by a string of fluently uttered curses. The bearded outlaw allowed Roan one long, piercing look from beneath his brows as he heard the low sounds of frustration from his male captive.

Roan watched helplessly as the man carried a subdued Katherine toward a stand of trees. Stretched behind him, his arms were tightly bound, then attached to the tree he leaned against. He'd spent long hours between bouts of unconsciousness attempting to loosen his bonds, to no avail. Still, his fingers twisted and strained as he quietly fought against the rope in a useless battle.

He'd been offered water twice during the day and accepted it thankfully. Aware he was probably living on borrowed time, he'd watched as the camp stirred in the late afternoon, gauging his chances of freeing himself.

Now his teeth ground in futile anger as he saw Katherine's form disappear into the trees, carried like a sack of oats. His senses attuned to her, he heard the words she muttered and he caught a glimpse of the rage blazing from her eyes as her head turned in his direction.

She was furious. Not a glimmer of fear radiated from her flushed face and gleaming eyes. Only the familiar look of Katherine in a snit. And then she lifted her head a bit more and he felt the heat of her gaze sweep over his bound body. Her mouth opened and she drew in a breath, her look one of such caring and concern he could hardly hold still under it. He watched as she attempted to lift herself, pressing her fists into the back of the man carrying her, but Roan shook his head at the movement.

Don't, he ordered her silently. *Don't make a fuss, Katherine.* His eyes begged her, even as they took on a bleak look of fear as he considered her fate. For as sure as the sun would rise in the morning, she was about to become the physical property of the man who carried her.

The bushes closed about them and Roan lost sight of Katherine's head as the two figures disappeared beneath low, leafy branches.

One of the men sauntered close by to grin gleefully at Roan's distress. "Did you see that? I'll just bet Cass is about to have hisself a time with that li'l gal of yours. She sure is a spunky one. Had to gag her to keep her quiet."

Roan closed his eyes, his active imagination already in gear. The thought of Katherine's fine skin and slender form lying bare before another man was almost more than he could abide. He thought of her rich brown hair, the long, shiny length of it wrapped about a filthy hand, and felt the bile rise in his throat.

And then her scream shattered against his eardrums and he dropped his head to his chest, his hands working even more frantically at the rope that bound him.

A lean hand clamped over her mouth and bent her head back against a hard, unyielding body. Katherine's eyes brimmed with tears as helpless rage filled her to overflowing. She drew in a breath through flaring nostrils and choked with the effort.

"If you shut up, I'll take my hand away," said a voice from behind her. It was husky and deep, strangely hushed in the dim light beneath the trees.

She nodded quickly, fearful of gagging on the cough that begged to be released from her lungs. His hand moved cautiously from her lips and she sucked in great gasps of air. She choked again, coughing as she gained her breath, sagging in his grip as he held her with one arm about her waist.

"Don't scream again," he warned her quietly. "That man of yours is already tearing his wrists up tryin' to get loose. You don't want him any more riled than he is."

"I only screeched because you pulled my hair, you big lummox. Why should you care about Roan anyway?" She spit out the words furiously. Her fears for Roan's well-being having been temporarily assuaged, her anger had rebounded in great style.

"Don't say another word," her captor said quietly. "Just turn around and look at me."

Katherine straightened her shoulders and pushed at the arm he'd wrapped around her, turning within his embrace, aware of his hands holding her firmly. Her eyes met the dark cotton of his shirt. Then with an effort, she lifted her chin to gaze fully on his face, the bottom half still covered by a dark growth of beard. Above it, his nose was crooked and flattened. She allowed her gaze to skim the scar slashing whitely across his face, high on his left cheek, and then, with concentrated effort, she stared into his eyes.

They were brilliant blue beneath dark brows, regarding her with sadness, yet filled with a strange warmth. She sensed rather than saw the smile twisting his mouth, noted the reflection of his amusement in the narrowing of his eyes.

"You don't recognize me, do you?" he asked roughly. His fingers squeezed her arms, and he set her away from him. "Take a good look, Katherine," he told her, then stood silently as she raked him with incredulous, unbelieving eyes.

Her fingers lightly touched the growth of beard, brushed against his full lips and then rose to trace the scar marring his flesh. She followed the battered lines of his nose with her index finger and winced as she sensed the pain it had caused him. Finally, she pressed the flat of her palm against his jaw, fingers moving beneath the growth of hair to find the shape of his face.

"Lawson?" The single word was whispered between quivering lips. They pressed together firmly as if she feared to utter it again, lest she be wrong. A single tear slipped from each eye and left a damp path down her flushed cheeks.

His nod was almost imperceptible and he pursed his own lips, as though he fought a surge of emotion. "Yeah, it's me, Katherine. Nasty way to meet up after all this time, ain't it?"

She allowed the tears to flow, closing her eyes and leaning forward to rest her head against the broad wall of his chest. A single sob escaped and she lifted one hand to press her fist against her mouth.

"Lawson, I thought...you were..." She couldn't complete the words, couldn't admit the fear she'd lived with for so long. Forbidden to speak his name, which was tainted with the bitter news of his cowardice during the war, she'd all but given up hope of ever seeing him again.

His arms came around her and he held her tightly, rocking her to and fro for comfort as his shirt absorbed her tears. "Almost was killed a time or two," he said gruffly. "For a while, I wouldn't have cared, except for never seein' you and Pa again. Then, later on, I knew it was too late...and y'all were better off without me."

"Why did you...how come you're..." She couldn't form coherent thoughts, her mind spinning as she tried to comprehend the events of the day. Then her head snapped back abruptly, and she peered at him with concern. "How'd you get your nose plastered all over your face like that?" She smoothed the ruin of his once perfect profile with one finger. And frowned as she remembered something else that had played havoc with her temper all the livelong day.

"Was it necessary to stick that filthy rag in my mouth, Lawson? And just look at the marks on my wrists," she told him, holding out her hands for inspection.

"I had them tie you up and gag you, for fear you'd recognize me today, honey. When I realized you hadn't seen past this beard, I figured it'd be safe to stake my claim and carry you off into the trees for the night. And I did tell them to leave the gag off the last time they fed you."

Katherine shuddered. "I won't even ask you what was in that mess I ate. I only got it down because I didn't know when the next time was I'd be offered anything."

He set her away from him and led her to a dead pine tree, a relic of a long-forgotten bolt of lightning. "Sit down, Katherine," he said. "We need to talk."

She sank limply to the fallen tree and looked at the ground, aware of him beside her, silent and watching. "What will happen to us?" she asked finally.

"Who's the man? Is he really your husband? What did you call him? A Devereaux from Louisiana?"

She looked up at him warily. "What does it matter? For that matter, why did you capture us in the first place? What kind of trouble have you gotten yourself into, Lawson?"

"Didn't have to work too hard to find trouble, Katherine. It came lookin' for me."

She gave him an exasperated glare, her frustration from the long day returning full force. "Are you a wanted man?" she asked bluntly. "What kind of hooligans are you running around with?"

"They're way beyond hooligans, honey," he said quietly. "They're a bunch known as Cass's Raiders. Just leftovers from the war, you could say, makin' their way as best they can."

"Kidnapping and robbing?" She glared at him with exasperation. "Mama would turn in her grave if she knew."

"Yeah, well she doesn't, so don't fret about it. And Pa ain't about to find out, either. Not that he'd care, anyway. After I refused to go fight in the war, he…well, I don't think he considers me his kin anymore, anyway. But I still don't want you tellin' him, hear me?"

She shook her head. "Not much chance of that. Pa died early on in the year, Lawson. He's buried on the farm."

His eyes closed for a moment, and she peered at him in the gathering darkness beneath the tall trees. "Just as well.

I'd shamed him enough already. He couldn't forgive me for runnin', could he?''

She shrugged and reached to lay her hand on his, her fingers squeezing as she offered silent comfort. ''Pa didn't understand, Lawson. He was good at facing up to everything that didn't require him to hang around for long. Going to war was a big adventure to him. Just like packing up and setting off down the road used to be when we were kids growing up. He always told me he went to enlist to save the family from the shame you brought down on us, but I think he was just tired of running the farm and his itchy foot was carrying him right out the door.''

''You hated it, the traveling all over the place, didn't you, Katherine? Nah, don't even answer. I know you did,'' he said bitterly. ''And I hated what it did to you, draggin' from one farm to another. From one town to the next, never a home of our own.''

''Pa bought the farm,'' she said, defending the man who'd fathered them both.

''Yeah...when it was too late for you to have a decent life of it. When you were already marked from hearin' and seein' things you shouldn't have.''

''It wasn't so bad,'' she said stoutly. ''You looked after me.''

He lifted her hand and kissed the back of it tenderly. ''That was my one redeemin' grace, Katherine. I did my best to look after you. There were too many eyes followin' you in those last few years before we settled down in Illinois. Too many men wantin' to try you on, scarin' you and makin' you all grim and tucked away inside yourself.''

She leaned against him, her head resting on his shoulder. ''I'm fine, Lawson. I'm getting untucked, little by little.''

''Devereaux?'' he asked and waited for her nod of admission. ''Where'd he come from?''

''Pa knew him in the war. He dragged Charlie off the field and saved his life. Then they played turnabout and Pa carted

Roan all the way to Philadelphia to get his leg put back together when the war was about over.''

''He come to the farm?''

She nodded. ''Showed up there better than a month ago. I tried to chase him off with that old shotgun of Pa's, but he wouldn't budge.'' Her words were low, her smile laced with the memory of Roan's stubborn refusal to leave.

''How'd you come to marry him? It's not like you to be so headlong about things.''

She grinned at him, barely able to make out his features in the dark. ''He wouldn't leave without me. And he wouldn't take me along unless I was his wife.''

''Is he treatin' you right?'' The question was stiff with promise.

She nodded against his arm. ''He's a good man. He agreed to take care of me and my horses and bring me back to Illinois if I want him to.''

''You're goin' clear the length of the country and back?'' His tone was incredulous.

She shrugged again. ''Maybe...maybe not.''

''Of all the harebrained ideas. Must be you've got him right around your little finger, Katherine, for him to take on such a mess of trouble.''

She stiffened. ''He doesn't seem to mind.''

His eyes touched tenderly on their intertwined fingers, resting against his thigh. ''We got some tall talkin' to do, Katherine. Then I want you to curl up and take a snooze for a while. I've got to figure out what we're gonna do in the morning.''

''Don't let them kill Roan,'' she said carefully, her fingers tight against his as she gripped him with her considerable strength.

''I'll do my best, honey. But I'm not makin' any promises.''

"Lawson..." She pulled him back down beside her as he would have risen from the log. "First, tell me about your nose...."

It was the middle of the night before the camp settled down, the men wide-awake after their daylong slumber. They'd sat about the fire, swapping tall tales, lowering their voices occasionally as they ventured glances toward the stand of trees where the woman had been carried.

"Don't hear nothin' from 'em. Bet Cass settled her hash in a hurry," a lanky, younger man said with a leer.

Roan watched from the shadows beneath the tree. He'd been fed a meal of sorts and given water to drink again. Apparently they weren't planning to starve him to death. It'd more than likely be a shot in the head, he thought with a sense of doom.

If only he knew what was going on with Katherine. There hadn't been a sound from her since the one shrill scream. Either he'd knocked her out or gagged her again, Roan thought. He hoped she didn't know what happened when he... The thought of her defilement was almost more than he could bear, and he dropped his chin to rest on his chest once more. Fighting the rope was a losing battle, he'd decided. He'd do better to save his strength in case this gang decided to move on and take him along. Then there might be a chance to break free and do some damage.

The men had rolled up in their blankets around the low-burning fire, leaving one of the group to stand guard. Leaning against a rock at the far side of the clearing, the guard had tilted his hat forward and appeared to be dozing as Roan looked about. Roan had roused minutes earlier, shifting against the hard ground, wiggling his fingers to circulate the blood within them.

"Don't move and don't make a sound." It was a whisper, a soft voice from behind him.

Roan froze in place, recognizing the husky tones of the leader, who'd not reappeared all night. He turned his head a scant few inches, slowly, his narrowed eyes searching the darkness over his shoulder. The rope binding him to the tree released and he fought to stay upright, his arms numb from confinement.

"Don't move, damn you," the voice ordered again, the husky whisper barely carrying to Roan's ear.

Roan felt the touch of a hand against his, recognized the vibration of a knife sawing at his bonds and in moments realized his hands were free. He sat immobile as other hands massaged his, other fingers squeezed life back into his wrists and arms, scraping against the raw places he'd formed with his silent struggle.

"Monk looks like he's sleepin' over there," the voice said after a few minutes. "I'm gonna give you the knife and I want you to lean over and cut the ropes around your feet. Then sit back up and don't let on you're free. Hear me?"

Roan nodded and received the knife with relief, shifting it in his hand until it fit his palm. Leaning forward slowly, he slipped his hand down the length of his thigh, then sawed quickly at the rope between his ankles, thankful for the leather of his boots as the blade slipped. He completed the task and leaned back, his hands still prickly from the restored blood flow, reluctantly returning the knife to the man behind him.

"Who the hell are you?" Roan rasped in a rough whisper.

"I'll introduce myself in the morning, if we live through this," Lawson said with dark amusement.

"If you've hurt my wife, you won't live past morning." Roan gritted the words between his teeth.

"You talk pretty brave for a man without a gun."

"Where's Katherine?" The words were harsh but quiet, only carrying the few inches to where his rescuer crouched in the darkness.

"Listen to me. I'm only gonna say this once," Lawson said quietly. "I'm givin' you your gun. It's right behind you on the ground. When I give the signal, get behind this tree and look out for yourself. I'll be ridin' past with your wife, leadin' your horse. It's up to you to get into the saddle on your own. If we can make it out of here without any shootin', that'll be fine. If not...hell, who knows what'll happen. It's about the only chance you've got, Devereaux."

"I'll take it. With thanks," Roan answered, his fingers feeling for the promised revolver. It fit neatly into his right hand, and he swallowed against the relief threatening to overwhelm him. Whoever "Cass" was didn't matter. Whatever he'd done to be called leader of this gang of outlaws was of no account to Roan. For some reason, he'd relented and agreed to help them escape. And he'd bet his last dollar that Katherine was at the bottom of it.

The man was slick, he'd give him that, Roan thought with rueful admiration. One by one, three horses disappeared from the tethered mounts strung out beneath the trees. Like a shadow in the darkness, Cass singled out his choices, leading them into the depths of the dense growth of trees. Silently, he lifted the saddles from the ground and carried them from sight, only to return moments later. This time, he snaked a rifle from beneath a tree and slid noiselessly behind the trunk, unnoticed by the sleeping men about the fire.

Roan let his breath out on a sigh of relief, still pondering the situation. It wasn't his place to ask questions at this point, but he was sure storing up a passel of them for Katherine to answer, once he got her shed of this mess.

A muffled sound to his left caught his ear and he tilted his head to look past his shoulder. Three horses, led by the bearded gunman, stood at the edge of the trees, one of them carrying Katherine, who clutched a rifle across the pommel of her saddle.

Roan slowly turned his head back to the fire and muffled a curse. The man on watch, stretching and yawning widely, had risen from his post to relieve himself. Busily undoing the front of his pants, he turned from the fire to walk several yards away, and Roan smiled at the turn of events.

The cooing of a quail, soft and sweet in the early morning air, sounded from behind him. He rose, coming to his feet as the horses made their way to where he waited.

Katherine was an accomplished lady, and obviously birdcalls were only one of her many talents. Her grin told him she'd sent the signal, and he met her eyes with a hooded glare. *Damn woman's all full of piss and vinegar, while I've been sitting here worrying about her all night.* He strode silently past the tree, gun in hand, and caught up the reins of his horse.

But Cass was looking beyond him. "Ah, sh—" he growled. "Watch your head, Devereaux." The warning came almost too late as a shot was fired from one of the gang.

"Damn, they got the boss!" Monk shouted from the far side of the clearing.

The men rolled from their blankets, guns ready to fire, taking aim as they crouched in the dim light. But the rising sun shining through the treetops with glittering shards of brilliance forced them to squint against its rays.

"Get out, Katherine!" Roan said tightly, unwilling to take flight with long guns and revolvers aiming at their backs.

"Not on your life," she muttered, raising her rifle to her shoulder and taking aim. The bullet was true and one of the men rolled about, clutching at his shoulder, even as she took aim once more.

Roan's own gun was empty in no time, each shot reaching its mark. Beside him, Cass fired twice, then slumped to the ground. Roan scooped up Cass's gun and opened fire again. Three members of the gang lay inert on the ground and another ran for his horse. Two more had emptied their guns and dropped to their bellies, snatching up the weapons of their fallen companions.

Katherine's rifle sounded again. One of the gang dropped in his tracks, a hole in the center of his forehead. Even as the report faded, Roan heard her whisper of despair.

"Oh God," she moaned beneath her breath, the words a whispered prayer as the man fell on his face. "I killed him, Roan!"

Roan glanced back at her, caught by her cry of anguish, heedless of the final gunman facing them across the campfire.

"Look out!" The muttered words were a warning from the fallen man beside him. Roan ducked reflexively, evading the bullet meant for him. Beyond him, it skimmed the side of Katherine's head, flying past to bury itself in a tree. Her weapon slid from her hands to hit the ground and Roan spun around, a roar of outrage bursting from his throat. It filled the air, blending with the sound of gunfire from his weapon. The last of the outlaws sprawled on the ground, blood gushing from the wound in his neck.

Catching the reins of Katherine's mare, lest she bolt and run, Roan soothed her with his hands, speaking in a rough growl as he settled her down. She calmed readily, her wild eyes closing, only the flaring nostrils and tossing head offering protest as she responded to his touch.

Katherine! His gaze shifted quickly to where she slumped over the saddle horn, the reins pulling tight beneath her body. Roan lifted her inert form with his right arm. Then, easing the leather from her fingers, he looped the reins over a tree branch.

Katherine clutched his hand, lifting her head, a groan welling within her. Her legs gave way as she slid from the saddle, and only Roan's arm supporting her kept her on her feet.

"Katherine..." It was a muffled groan from the man sprawled nearby, and Katherine pushed away from Roan's support, looking about with a sharp cry of distress.

"Lawson," she whispered, staggering, then scrambling awkwardly across the ground to where he sprawled. "Lawson!" she repeated, her hands reaching for him. She knelt next to his head and bent to lift it to rest against her thigh, holding him in place with one hand, attempting to shift his deadweight.

Her eyes lifted beseechingly to Roan, dark and huge against her pale flesh. "Please..." she cried. "Help me, Roan!" Blood ran down her temple and she brushed at it distractedly, smearing it into her hair.

Roan's gaze wavered as he scanned her wan face, settling on the blood flowing from her scalp. His lips tightened, but he turned to the fallen man, turning him over a bit, careful to support his neck as Katherine slid her legs to one side, providing a place for him to rest. She cradled the dark head tenderly, leaning to brush the dirt from his face.

"He's my brother, Roan," she sobbed, the tears rolling down her cheeks as she blurted out the words, paying no attention to the muffled curse greeting her announcement.

"Katherine," the wounded man whispered again. His eyes fluttered open and he focused on the face above him.

"Pa forgave me, didn't he?" he asked piteously. The words were uttered on a gasping breath and the dying man groped blindly for his sister's hand. He coughed abruptly, and blood flowed from the corner of his mouth. His forehead wrinkling with the effort of his attempt to breathe past the gushing flow, he raised frantic eyes to her face.

"Roan, help him!" she cried, her own vision blurring as her tears flowed unhindered.

"I can't, Katherine," he told her quietly. "He took a bullet in the chest. You need to tell him goodbye, honey."

"Noooo..." The wail came from deep within, a piercing cry of despair.

"Sorry... Take care of..." Lawson's words were indistinct, but Roan read their meaning and leaned closer, intent on offering a last word of comfort.

"I'll take care of your sister, Cassidy." His big hand squeezed the bloody fingers, lifting their lifeless weight from Katherine's palm.

"Oh, God! He's dying," she sobbed, bending down to brush frantic kisses across the lined forehead. "He can't die...he can't," she whispered, her mouth warm against the flesh cooling beneath her lips, her heart squeezing in pain within her chest.

"He's gone, Kate," Roan said quietly.

"There's so much blood." She looked up at him, tears rolling down her cheeks.

"He's dead," Roan repeated. "You have to let him go, Kate." He clenched his hands at the sight before him, helpless to bring her comfort.

"Please, Roan. Put something under his head. I don't want him to lie in the dirt," she said stubbornly, holding him against her legs.

"All right," he agreed readily, taking off his shirt, ripping it in his haste. He folded it over twice, providing a thin pad for the dark head to rest on. Katherine gave way, allowing him to shift Lawson's weight from her.

The sun rose in unerring splendor, casting its brilliance across the bloody scene. The fire burned, the horses bent to search out blades of grass. A mockingbird flew overhead, offering a serenade to the new day.

And Katherine looked about her, only now fully aware of the throbbing pain in her head. Her vision touched upon the bloodless lips of her brother, his eyes closed in the finality of death. A sob vibrated within her as she raised her eyes. "It's not fair," she whispered plaintively.

"Come on, Kate, let me look at your wound." Deliberately, Roan lifted her in his arms, easing her head against his shoulder, uncaring of the blood staining his body. Seeping from her head, it oozed over her forehead and neck to soak into the collar of her shirt. He lowered her to the ground, kneeling beside her. His fingers separated the dark strands of her hair, seeking the source of the flow, and his lips compressed as he watched blood welling from the shallow crease against her skull.

"You're all right, Katherine," he told her gruffly, untying the kerchief hanging around his neck as he spoke. "It's just a scratch, but you're still bleedin'." With awkward movements, he folded the red bandanna, wrapping it tightly about her head, frowning as it refused to stay in place. He looked down at her, wincing at the sight of her bloodless lips and ashen countenance.

But his voice was strong and commanding as he grasped her hand in his and placed it at the site of her wound. "Here, Katherine, hold this for me," he ordered, and her eyes opened. Her fingers spread to hold firm the makeshift bandage. Roan opened her shirt, reaching to rip at the white chemise she wore beneath it. It tore, the fabric giving way to his strong fingers with ease.

"What . . . ?" The word was mumbled as she responded to his touch, her eyes straining to focus on his face.

"I gotta have something to pad your head, honey," he told her, still tearing the front of her chemise until it bared her breasts, leaving only shredded material to cover her ribs. She looked down at her naked flesh and groaned.

"Cover me," she whispered, one hand tugging at her shirt.

"In just a minute, honey," he told her, intent on folding the material he'd scavenged from her underclothing. It would have to do, he decided, until he could get her to a better place and clean the shallow groove.

With careful touches, he moved her fingers from their position and snatched the bandanna from its place. The blood welled more slowly now, having soaked into his kerchief. He pressed the pad firmly against the wound and tied the kerchief in place.

"I think that'll hold for now." His fingers were gentle, touching her carefully, his eyes dark as he scanned her pale features. His gaze fell to the swelling rise of her breasts, where she held one hand protectively, her forearm effectively covering her from his view. From beneath lowered lids, tears flowed, and she lifted her other hand to wipe them.

He reached for her fingers, clasping her hand in his, their flesh sharing the blood of her brother. The stains vivid against the skin of their hands, he rubbed her cold fingers. "Katherine, listen to me. It's over. We're safe. That's what he wanted, you know. He was tryin' to keep you alive."

Her eyes were awash with the tears that streamed unceasingly. "I just found him, Roan. And now he's gone."

"He saved your life, honey. Don't deny him that."

"You're hard, Roan Devereaux," she sobbed. The fine bones of her face stood out beneath the pale flesh, molding a tragic mask of sorrow before his eyes. She struggled to sit upright, snatching her hand from his grip, her trembling fingers working to force buttons into buttonholes. Wisely, he sat back on his heels and watched, until her gaze met his, eyes widening in surprise. Then, lashes lowering, she shuddered, swallowing against the bile rising in her throat. She inhaled deeply through her mouth, sobbing beneath her breath as a line of sweat beaded across her forehead and upper lip. "I don't... " She blinked again and shuddered.

"Don't go faintin' on me, damn it," Roan growled, lifting her from where she sat, rising and looking about, seeking a resting place for her out of the sun.

She was limp against him, her breathing shallow, her head falling back against his arm. And he cursed again as he held her protectively against himself.

Chapter Twelve

His scent was strong in her nostrils, and she rubbed her face against the coarse material brushing her cheek, rousing from the lethargy of her slumber. Her eyes fluttered open, then squeezed shut rapidly against the glare of the sun.

"Katherine?" His voice rumbled in her ear. "Come on honey. I'm gonna stop here. Let me see your eyes."

He bent over her, his hat brim shading her vision from the sunlight. She peered at him, vainly attempting to reconcile the weary-eyed, grimy face above her with the voice of Roan Devereaux.

"Roan?" She struggled against his grip, abruptly aware of her precarious position. Across his lap, riding double on the bay mare, she felt vulnerable, out of control. She was at the mercy of his strength, his arms like iron bands around her, holding her firmly as he gentled the horse beneath him. Unused to the double weight, the mare pranced sideways, tossing her head skittishly as Katherine rousted about.

"Damn! Just lay quiet, honey," Roan told her forcefully, his right hand controlling the reins, his left tucked about her hips.

"Where..." Her whisper was muffled against his shirt, but her movements stilled as she gripped him tightly, her fingers twisting in the fabric.

He bent to drop a quick kiss against her forehead, lifting her against his chest. "I have to get you down, Katherine. I'm gonna pick you up over my left leg and let you slide to the ground. Think you can stand up all right?"

Nodding, she tucked her feet beneath her, helping as best she could to accomplish his goal. Her head throbbed as though a thousand hammers had all aimed for the same place, and she grimaced at the thought. Standing, finally, beside the horse, she took a deep breath and locked her knees to steady herself, valiantly holding back the urge to slide to the ground. Roan had asked her to stand here, and stand here she would, she vowed beneath her breath, her mind cloudy, her thoughts barely coherent.

Beside her, he slid from the saddle and looked over his shoulder, his mind intent on the string of animals following him. One of them bore an ominous burden; his jaw tightened as he considered the next task at hand.

"Katherine, I'm gonna get you under that tree over there, and I want you to rest easy for a bit. All right?"

"Yes," she hissed, more conscious than ever of the pain radiating from a spot just inches from her right temple. "My head hurts pretty bad, Roan. I don't mean to complain, but I must have banged it on something."

"You were shot, Katherine," he said bluntly, lowering her to the ground, where she slumped against the rough bark of a tree.

"Shot?" Her eyes widened, then blinked as she forced them to focus on him. "I was shot." Her whisper was unbelieving. And then she shivered as the harsh memories flooded her mind. "I was shot...I killed a man. I thought he was going to shoot you, and I aimed right for his head."

His smile was grim. "Your pa taught you well, honey. You hit what you were aimin' at. Saved my skin in the process," he drawled. "I'm not sure if it was a good trade, but I'm more than grateful for the favor."

She lifted her chin, stung by his words, drawn from her lethargy as her memory sharpened. "A good trade? I'd do it again, Roan. You're my husband. You know I'll protect you if I have to."

"I think that's supposed to be the other way around, honey," he told her with a gentle chuckle. "I'll have to work at it, won't I?" For a moment, he recalled the terrible anguish of knowing she was exposed to grave danger, and his jaw tightened with resolution. "I was careless, Katherine. It won't happen again."

She looked at him sadly, her thoughts falling into place. "The men who were shot . . . are they all dead?"

His nod was answer enough, and she sighed.

"Lawson?" Her voice wavered on the name.

"We'll bury him here," Roan answered. "I brought him along. Couldn't abide stayin' there any longer than we had to, just long enough to gather up your yearlings. Thought it might be wise to make tracks before we set up camp."

"I'll help you bury him," Katherine said stoutly, scrambling up. "I dug the hole for my pa, you know."

"Well, you're not diggin' this one. Stay right here." He pushed her gently back to the ground and blanched at the thought of this slender woman digging a grave for her father.

She gave in without a murmur, her eyes closing in weary agreement.

He roused her an hour later, his ear attuned to her even breathing, and lifted her against him. "Open your eyes, Katherine. I want to know if you can see me all right."

"My head aches," she told him wearily.

"Don't doubt it, honey." Satisfied she was aware of him, her blue eyes focusing on his face, he relaxed. Gently, his hands clasped her shoulders as he persuaded her to lie back once more against the blanket he'd spread on the ground.

She was acquiescent beneath his touch, her eyelids drooping as she sighed deeply. "I'm still sleepy."

"I know," he told her, his hand smoothing her hair back as she slumbered once more.

It was late afternoon before he roused her for the fourth time. She sat up readily, holding her head at a cautious angle as she looked up at him.

"I'm ready to put your brother in the ground, honey," he said quietly. "Come on, I'll help you up."

His arm supporting her, she walked with him to where the hole yawned, Lawson's body wrapped in a blanket next to it. Roan lowered her to the ground, and she sat watching as he eased the inert form into the shallow grave, then straightened to face her once more.

"You want to say some words, Katherine?"

She attempted a smile. "I'll try."

It was simple. Katherine repeated one of the psalms she'd learned by heart from her mother's Bible, then spoke a short prayer as she delivered her brother into the hands of Providence.

Dry-eyed, she watched as Roan filled the grave, using a flat stone to scrape the dirt back into place. He mounded the top with an assortment of rocks he'd gathered.

Holding her close to his side, he walked with her to where he'd set up their camp. "Just sit easy by the fire while I fix us something to eat," he said. "Then I'm gonna take another look at your head before it gets full dark."

She nodded and he chanced a grin. "You're one agreeable woman today, honey. Must be that bullet knocked all the starch out of you."

"I can get mulish in a hurry if you like," she told him, her glance darting in his direction. The pain had subsided, her vision cleared, and she flexed her shoulders as she hugged her knees, leaning forward to relish the fire's heat.

Roan stirred the contents of the pot he'd hung over the glowing wood. "To tell the truth, I missed you yammerin' at me all day. If you're up to it, I want to hear why you had to tend to your pa's buryin' all by yourself."

She shrugged, leaning her chin to rest on her knees. "It wasn't on purpose. I got Charlie to the house and laid him on the floor. I knew I'd have to bury him by nightfall, so I went up on the rise and dug the hole. Then I rode to town for the preacher."

His keen eyes rested on her. "Didn't anybody else come back with you?"

She nodded. "Oh, yes. Several of the men and Mrs. Tucker, the storekeeper's wife, came out to the place. She helped me, dressing Pa and everything." Her voice faltered and she straightened, looking deep into the glowing fire. "That's about it. The men had to make the grave bigger to allow for the coffin they put together, out in the barn. They were going to send for more folks from town for the funeral, but I just wanted it to be over with. So the preacher gave a good prayer and read from his Bible, and the men carried Charlie up the hill to where I'd dug the hole."

"Did Orv Tucker's wife stay with you?"

She shook her head. "No, no one stayed."

"They left you out there alone?" His voice was harsh in the stillness, which was broken only by the horse's soft sounds as they grazed nearby.

"I was all right. Wasn't any point in anyone staying on. I'd have to be alone sometime."

The silence gathered around them, the fire glowing with flickering flames as he made his way to where she sat, squatting next to her on the blanket.

"Well, you're not alone now," he told her gruffly.

"No, I'm not," she agreed. "I appreciate you taking hold today, Roan. It was good of you."

"Food's about ready," he said. Deftly, he filled their plates, placing hers on the blanket next to her and lifting his own fork to eat.

The darkness settled around them and the night breeze blew sparks from the fire as she looked down at the tin plate he'd given her. Her stomach growled and she realized she needed to eat. The food was warm, and for that she was thankful, chewing and swallowing it in an automatic fashion, uncaring of its taste. She placed the empty plate on the ground and curled up on the blanket, turning her back on the darkness to stare into the fire.

He's dead. My brother's dead. The words were a dull litany in her mind as she absorbed their meaning, her breath shuddering on an indrawn sigh. But her eyes were dry, her tears forbidden to flow as she tucked away the remnants of her sorrow into the dark shadows of her heart.

The night was cool, a welcome change after the heat of the afternoon sun, Roan decided. Indian summer, she'd called it. Whatever name you put on it, it was too blamed hot. October in Louisiana had always been a good time of year, he reflected. Harvest over, time to spend hunting.

The mounded grave beneath the walnut tree caught his eye, a flat slab of rock marking it. Katherine had scratched on it with the sharp point of a small stone. L.C. Two letters to mark the grave of her beloved brother.

Now she lay curled beneath Roan's remaining blanket near the fire, and he watched her, sensing her remoteness, wondering at the visions she saw within the glowing flames. He'd wanted to offer comfort, give her his shoulder to lean against, but she'd shaken her head at his offer, only accepting the blanket he'd covered her with.

"I'm fine," she'd said, pulling the rough covering over her.

He rose and found his pack, pulling out a heavy shirt and donning it. His fingers worked at the buttons and she looked up, her attention focusing on him.

"You'll need your blanket." She lifted herself up on her elbow, ready to unroll from the blankets. "I'll use the one under me to wrap up in."

He shook his head. "I'm all right. Rest easy."

Her frown furrowed the smooth expanse of her forehead as she looked at him, her voice insistent. "You'll need a blanket under you when you sleep."

Katherine at her best, he thought wryly, telling him what to do. His grin denied her offer. "We're gonna share, like always, Katherine. I'll lay down right behind you, honey. Soon's you go to sleep, I'll just snuggle up to your backside, slick as a whistle."

She debated arguing the issue, then thought better of it, aware of the unyielding force of his will apparent beneath the words he spoke. And suddenly the comfort of Roan's warm body held a welcome appeal. She would be foolish to deny herself.

"I'm too tired to argue," she told him, yawning and settling her head in the crook of her arm as she curled once more beneath the coarse blanket.

"Your head hurtin'?" he asked, his eyes narrowing as he noted the care she took.

Her nod was brief. "A little."

"Maybe I'd better take another look at it." He'd already sacrificed one of his shirts, tearing it in strips and folding several sections into thick pads. It had been a chore he would not want to repeat, cleaning the wound where the bullet had sliced its way, leaving a three-inch crease.

She'd chewed on her lip to a fare-thee-well, squeezing her fists and eyes closed as he worked. Only the tears that had escaped those tightly shut eyes had given testimony to her pain. And those she'd have denied if she could have.

"You can holler if you want to, Katherine," he'd told her grimly. "Just don't wiggle around. I'm tryin' not to get this thing bleedin' again."

"Just get it over with and quit talking about it," she'd rasped between her teeth.

Now, he touched the warm flesh of her forehead, sliding his hand to her cheek and then to the back of her neck. "I don't think you've got any fever. But I think we better see f we can get you into a town tomorrow. Maybe let a doctor ook at this.''

"If I get feverish, I've got a drawing salve in my saddle-bag," she told him. "Maybe you better smear some on the bandage.''

"It'll get all over your hair." His fingers tightened at the nape of her neck and he bent to brush his lips against her temple. "I'll wait till morning and see how it looks.''

"Roan?''

"Yeah?'' His hand fit neatly about her head as he slid his fingers into the silky strands of her hair.

"You don't need to wait till I go to sleep, Roan. I don't mind if you keep my back warm.''

He spread the blanket toward him and lowered his long body to curl about her, tugging his saddlebag once more beneath his head as a pillow. His touch was gentle as he lifted her to lie on his shoulder, his callused fingers snagging in her hair as he brushed it away from her face.

"Your pa would have been proud of him, you know," he said quietly, his breath warm against her ear.

She nodded, a tiny movement. "I know. Lawson made up for a lot of things this morning, didn't he?''

"Yeah, I think so. Matter of fact, I'd be willing to bet Charlie knows. Wherever he's at, I'll bet he knows Lawson came through when things got tight.''

She snuggled back against him and turned her head carefully to glimpse his face. "Kiss me good-night. Please.''

His grin was tender, his mouth gentle as he captured her lips. "Go to sleep, Kate." He brushed a second caress against the softness he cherished. "Go to sleep.''

Twice during the night, Roan roused as Katherine shifted in her sleep. He whispered soft assurances in her ear and snuggled her into his embrace. He curved around her back, her woman's scent teasing him with its elusive lure, and his body reacted with a familiar surge of desire. Easing away from her, fearful of wakening her, he scooted back, aware she needed to rest without distraction. But she followed the heat of his body, wiggling to cuddle close to him, and he tightened his jaw, frustrated by her unconscious allure.

It was a long night. Watching the sky turn pink, Roan waited for the rising of the sun, getting up from his place beside her as it hovered at the horizon. She rolled over, her forehead wrinkling as the bandage on her head came in contact with the ground beneath the blanket. Her eyes fluttered open, mere slits against the pale glow of dawn, then opening wide as she focused on him.

He stood a few feet away, tucking his shirt into his pants, his gaze on her, his eyes openly admiring the early morning dishevelment of her. Her braid had come undone during the night hours, and her hair tangled about her face, spreading beneath her head like a dark stain against the blanket.

"Time to get up already?" she asked, her fingers furrowing through the length of her hair as she sat up, loosening and removing the cloth he'd wound about her head. She winced as she pulled the pad from its place, then frowned as she examined the cloth closely.

"Any pus on that bandage?" he asked.

She shook her head. "It looks pretty clean, just a little fresh blood."

"Let me take a look at it." Kneeling behind her, he probed gently at the shallow wound. "We'll find a place to stay and get you a real bath," he told her. "But for now, how about if I just pull your hair back to keep it out of the way? I'll braid it up for you, all right?" His hands busied themselves as he spoke, smoothing their way through the long strands and dividing the thick length into three sections. His fingers worked slowly as he concentrated on forming it loosely into a braid.

"Does anyone need to know what happened?" she asked, her head lowered as he completed his task.

"I kinda doubt anyone is gonna miss that bunch," he said dryly. "We probably don't need to spread the word we killed half a dozen men."

She blanched. "Six? We killed six men?"

"One got away. Guess it was only five." He frowned at her. "Your brother and I did the most of the shootin', Katherine. But your shot there at the end probably saved my life. That doesn't count as a killin' in my book."

She pulled a piece of twine from her shirt pocket and offered it to him. "Tie my braid with this," she said, considering his theory. Somehow it eased the guilt she'd been carrying. Taking a man's life was no small thing. Maybe if she looked at it from Roan's point of view, she could live with it.

His fingers were awkward as he handled the twine, looping it about and tying a knot. "Guess I'd better learn how to do this, hadn't I?"

"I'll be fine in a day or so," she told him. "I need to tend to myself."

"Well, for now, tend to yourself out in those bushes," he told her bluntly, "while I get something cookin' for us to eat."

They rode out less than an hour later, Roan keeping Katherine close by his side as they traveled. By noon, the sun was hot and his gaze was searching as he surveyed the hollows beneath her eyes. He was all for stopping and making camp for a couple of days, but Katherine gritted her teeth.

Within a few hours, though, she gave in gracefully when he suggested an early day, breathing a sigh of relief as she slid from the back of her mare. He eased one arm around her middle and led her to a grassy spot near the river.

"I'm sorry we didn't get closer to a town, honey," he told her as she sank to the ground with a sigh. "You'd feel better with a good soak in a hot tub."

"I'll settle for a pan of warm water," she told him wearily. "And a clean shirt would be nice. But I think I'm out of clothes."

"We've been pushin' pretty hard. How about if we stay here for a couple of days, and I'll wash up our things and let 'em dry on the bushes tomorrow. I think you could use a day to rest."

"I don't want to hold you up," she said staunchly. "I'll be fine."

He was silent, assessing the dark shadows beneath her eyes, the lack of color in her cheeks. "Those horses of yours could use a different pace for a day or so, anyway," he said finally. "Maybe I'll try my hand at workin' with them tomorrow, while you take it easy."

She looked up at him questioningly. "You're going to wash my clothes and tend to my horses?" The thought of Roan Devereaux doing her laundry was a picture her mind found hard to accept, and her mouth curled as she contemplated the idea.

"I've washed out my shirts in a river a time or two already. Yours are put together the same way. Shouldn't be any problem to scrub 'em out when I do mine."

"And I'm going to rest under a tree while you take care of things?" she asked politely.

"Sound's like a good plan to me," he told her.

"You wanta talk about it, Katherine?"

"Am I keeping you awake?"

He thought of the shifting and squirming she'd been doing. His smile was secret, hidden against her hair. "More than you know," he said with amusement.

She stilled, stiffening in his embrace. Curled around her beneath the blanket, he was warm at her back, his arm heavy across her waist, his hand tucked discreetly at her side.

"You dwell too much on things you can't do a dad-burned thing about, honey." His voice was low, carrying to her ear in a hushed reprimand.

She twisted beneath the burden of his arm, and he lifted it to allow her the space she sought. Turning to her back, she searched the heavens as if she might find the answer to her questions there.

"See the Big Dipper up there?" he asked her.

She nodded, her hair brushing his cheek, and his hand lifted to smooth it against her head.

"That was the first thing my mammy taught me about the sky at night. She said that dipper was chuck-full of beautiful dreams, and if I were to close my eyes and think about all the nice things in the world, why, that big old dipper would tip out just the right dream for a little boy like me." His chuckle was tender with remembering, and Katherine found her mouth curving in a smile as she considered the thought of Roan Devereaux as a child.

"Did it work?" she asked after a moment.

"Oh, yeah," he told her cheerfully. "I had the best dreams any little fella could hope for. Of course, the bedtime stories she told me probably helped a little, now that I think about it."

Katherine picked up his hand from where it rested against her waist. Her fingers intertwined with his and she rubbed her thumb against his wrist, idly, without purpose. "I never heard a bedtime story," she confided softly. "But I used to have dreams." She slanted a glance at his profile, there where he'd managed to get just inches from her face. "I always hated to wake up from them," she continued with a sigh. "I'd open my eyes in the morning sometimes and then squeeze them shut quickly and pray I could go back to the dream."

"Did it work?" His fingers twisted against hers and he carried her hand to his mouth, his lips brushing against the cup of her palm.

She shook her head. "No...sometimes I couldn't even hold on to them long enough to remember them through the day."

"What did you dream about, Katherine?" His mustache was brushing softly across her fingers now, his lips warm and damp beneath it.

"Oh, lots of times about having a place to call my own. With a dog, or maybe a cat with kittens, and flowers and a big kitchen garden. I always wanted lilac bushes." Her voice trailed off, and her breasts rose as she filled her lungs with an unsteady breath.

"Did you live alone in your dreams?" He'd somehow gotten her index finger against his mouth and she felt his hot breath on it as he spoke. His tongue moistened the tip of that suddenly sensitive finger, and his lips coaxed it to rest just inside his mouth.

"Sometimes," she whispered, aware of a confusing tingle radiating throughout her body, her whole concentration focusing on the liberties his tongue was taking.

He released her finger reluctantly, kissing the length of it and curling it into the fist she'd made of the other three. Now he concentrated on the vulnerable flesh of her wrist, his mustache brushing back and forth against the fine network of veins that pulsed with her heartbeat.

"Roan...what are you doing?" she asked, her eyes closing as she relished the sensation of his mouth against her skin.

"Just lettin' you know my touch," he said quietly, releasing her hand to lie against his chest, while he turned himself toward her. "Tell me what's goin' through your head, Katherine. Don't lay there broodin' about things. Trouble's lighter if you share it, you know."

She cast him a look of amused scorn. "Did your mammy tell you that, too?"

He shook his head. "Figured it out all by myself. I'm real good at listenin', honey."

She shivered against him, and he tugged her closer. His mouth resting against her temple, he kissed the finely pored skin, careful to leave the wound untouched. They'd decided to leave it uncovered, Katherine vowing the air would heal it better without a bandage.

"Does your head hurt?" he asked.

"No, only if I forget and touch it. It's really only a scratch, Roan. A cut on the head always bleeds like a mortal wound. I remember when Lawson..."

"What do you remember?" he prodded.

Her words were slow as she forced them from her memory, reluctantly visualizing the young boy he'd been. "Lawson was hit by a rock once, when we were coming from school. The bigger boys used to chase us home and tease us because we were new and Lawson didn't want to fight them. Anyway, when one of them threw a rock, it hit him on the back of his head and he bled something fierce. I made him sit on the ground so I could look at it, and I tore a piece of my petticoat to make a bandage."

"Did the boys leave him alone then?" he asked.

"They were pretty impressed that he didn't make a fuss over it. And there was an awful lot of blood. I think it scared them. They thought they'd really hurt him bad."

"What happened then?"

She shrugged. "Nothing. I just thought of it, that's all. Pa told Lawson we all had to take our knocks in life."

"The boys didn't chase you, did they?" he asked quietly.

She laughed with derision. "No, I was too little and scrawny for them to notice. I got my share of attention later on in life. Sometimes I used to wish I wasn't a girl."

He hugged her close. "I'm awfully glad you're a girl, Katherine."

"Don't know how you can tell, with the boy's pants and shirts I'm wearing these days," she scoffed.

He rose above her, supporting himself on his forearms as he allowed his chest to rest gently against her. "Oh, I can tell all right. Every time you twitch that little tail of yours, every time you clamp those long legs around the sides of that mare, I notice how nicely you're put together, Mrs. Devereaux.''

She held her breath, taken aback by his nearness, the sudden proximity of his mouth, as he whispered the outrageous compliments. *He's going to kiss me,* she realized. *Like he did in the hayloft.*

And then her thoughts burst into a thousand small fragments, glittering behind her closed eyelids like sparks from a newly lit pine log, as his mouth enveloped her own and claimed it with tender care.

Chapter Thirteen

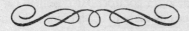

The moon was a slender curve in the sky, just over Roan's left shoulder. Then he shifted, leaning up on his elbow, and the moon vanished, replaced by the shaggy silhouette of his head, hair long over his collar. Katherine watched in silent anticipation as he scanned her pale countenance.

"The moon and stars take all the color out of you. Leaves you lookin' pale and dark-eyed. Makes me feel sorta like I'm takin' advantage of you, Katherine," he told her, his voice holding a tremor she wondered at. Roan with uncertainties was beyond her imagining. Always so sure of himself, so ready to take charge. And now he was hesitant, wondering at her well-being, holding himself back for fear of hurting her.

She smiled at the thought. With all she'd been through during the past few days, she'd learned one thing. Roan Devereaux would never knowingly cause her pain or sorrow. She considered the idea, looking at the man above her with new vision, seeing him with the eyes of her heart. Twice, she'd known him as a warrior, his eyes narrowed and hard, his hands meting out swift judgment, harsh and fearsome in his fury. Then, too, she'd watched him in quiet times, gentling a fretful filly, using those same hands to mend or repair or build anew. She'd listened to him confiding his memories. Good and bad, she'd heard his secrets, some of them at least.

She'd touched him, her fingers sensing the strength of his muscles and the awesome power of his body. She'd known the passion of his caresses, the hard, driving need of his openmouthed kisses against her tender flesh. His hands had held her in kindness and caring, with desire sometimes, and in the simple need for comfort. He'd gentled her as easily as he'd coaxed the bay mare to accept him as her master.

And now he was watching her with a hesitancy she groped to understand. As though he waited for a sign, a signal of sorts. As if he would not encroach on her further without the certain knowledge of welcome on her part.

A rush of emotion filled her, swelling within her breast and causing her throat to ache with longing as she sought to pierce the darkness, see deeply within the eyes of the man whose every breath matched her own. His broad chest touched her tender breasts, only the fabric of their clothing separating the warmth of their flesh. She felt the heat of his body penetrating her skin, soaking into her being like the warmth of the summer sun at noonday. Her heart beat more quickly, her mouth opening as she caught her breath, her mind swirling with the knowledge of her love for this man.

I love him. She heard the words as if they had been spoken aloud, and she blinked, lest her treacherous mouth let them slip from between dry lips. *I love him.* She tried it out again, bravely considering the words as she uttered them in her mind. *I love him.* With firm resolve, her lips silently formed the syllables, and she accepted the truth she spoke within her heart.

He had given her so much already, so freely, with such generosity of spirit. Could she deny him the one thing he needed from her...the giving of her body? Could she expose herself, flesh and spirit, to his scrutiny and allow him the rights he had waited to claim till she should be ready?

"Katherine?" Low and filled with musing wonder, his voice spoke her name. "Kate, what is it?" His breath blending with her own, he bent low to brush a tender kiss across her mouth.

She shook her head, not ready to reveal her new knowledge, unwilling to allow him entrance to her cache of wondering bemusement. She was filled with it, this sensation of yearning, needing to belong to him in the most primitive of ways.

"Open your mouth for me, honey," he told her gently. "Put your arms around me and rub them over my back like you did before. I need you to warm me tonight, sweet Kate."

She did as he bid, her fingers tracing the broad muscles of his shoulders and gripping tightly as his head lowered, his mouth claiming hers with a possession that rendered her utterly breathless.

He sought out the dark secrets of her mouth, his tongue meeting and matching her's, rubbing gently first, then coaxing her to return the favor, as he groaned his pleasure.

He slid his lips from hers, reluctantly, but with firm purpose, breathing hot words of pleasure into her ear as he caught the fleshy lobe between his teeth.

"You smell so good . . . like warm sunshine and cool water. Like sweet woman . . . right here under your ear," he whispered, his mouth claiming the spot as he spoke the words. His hand was at the buttons of her shirt, holding himself up on one elbow, his fingers sliding the buttons from place with ease. Then his mouth followed the path his fingers made, his lips open against her warmth. She wore no undergarment; his searching mouth found no impediment, and he inhaled deeply of the female scent of her breast as his lips captured the jutting peak with a careful, tender possession.

"Roan!" The sharp cry was one of wonder, her hands clutching at his back, sliding quickly up to press against the dark cap of hair, holding him in place. "Roan," she said once more, this time in a whispering plea, her fingers clenching his head as she squirmed beneath his weight.

Her response was more than he'd expected, more than he'd longed for. He chuckled within himself, blessing the honesty of this woman he'd married. She had no false pretenses, no coyness about her, only the generous soul of a woman who could tell no lies, hide behind no subterfuge, who could only give herself with all the courage she possessed.

He raised his head from her, heard the shuddering breath she drew, and paused to drop countless kisses across the expanse of her forehead. His hands were firm in their purpose, stripping her from the shirt he'd opened to the waist. His fingers worked at his own clothing, shedding his shirt, loosening his pants, stripping the belt from its place and tossing it aside.

She lay beneath him, her breasts round and full, the hard, nubbed peaks dark against her flesh. Her hands pushed back his hair, and then, as his bare skin was exposed to her vision, she brushed inquiring fingers over the small dark circles on his chest, seeking them out from the hair surrounding them. Her fingers teased him, her mouth firming as she explored the evidence of his arousal. He watched her from hooded eyes, his nostrils flaring, his mouth dry with anticipation.

"Undo your pants, Katherine," he said finally, when it seemed his urgent need would no longer be stilled.

She slid her hands between their bodies, feeling the brush of hair against her skin, until her fingers completed the task he'd bidden her accomplish.

"Slide them down your legs," he told her, his voice harsh with the desire he held in check.

She hesitated only a moment, then, lifting herself against him, she wiggled her way from the constriction of the denim pants, finally kicking them off her stockinged feet before she lay beneath him in submission.

He'd managed to insinuate himself there, cradled against her belly, her legs drawn up to hold him, and she felt a moment of fear, helplessness inherent in the position she'd assumed. His eyes were narrowed, slits of darkness peering at her. His face was harsh with an emotion she could not name, his flesh drawn tautly over the bones of his cheeks. His mouth was a straight line, firm and ungiving, with no softening to assure her of his concern for her. And yet she sensed it...the tenderness holding him back, the gentleness harnessing his desire.

Unlike the stallion covering the mare with wild abandon, he held his passion in check, struggling with the urgency of his need, but willing to woo her to his bidding. And the knowledge of his patience and understanding brought a smile of sweet surrender to her lips.

Rising up against him, she murmured soft encouragement, her arms pulling him into her embrace, her face burying itself in his shoulder, lips feverish in their pursuit of his flesh.

"Roan..." It was a plea, spoken over and over again as she offered herself to him, rubbing her breasts against the hard width of his chest, reveling in the sensation of need as she lifted her hips to his fullness.

He slid lower, his mouth once more against her breast, urgently seeking the source of pleasure he'd only begun to explore. Her breath caught in her throat as he suckled her with desperate need, first one side, then the other, his big hands cradling and squeezing as he held her to his mouth.

Then he raised his hips and spoke against her flesh, the words guttural and harsh. "Push my pants down, Katherine. Use your hands or your legs, whatever it takes. Just get them off me."

She obeyed, filled with a heated yearning that was sweeping its way through her body with each touch of his fingers and mouth against her flesh. His hands slid behind her, lifting her to meet the warm skin she exposed as she pushed his pants from his body. His arousal was there, pressing between them, demanding and urgent against her belly. She shivered, for a moment fearful as she felt the length and breadth of the insistent proof of his desire.

And then his fingers found her, working gently as he sought her softness, readying her for his taking. Her teeth closed tightly, gritting against the cry of pleasure he drew from her so easily. She rose to meet him, willing him to do as he would, urging him to claim her body as he had her heart.

If he had thought himself a man of experience, if he'd considered himself knowledgeable beforehand, Roan lost those illusions in moments. Nothing in his memory could compare with the female creature he held, nothing he'd felt came close to the anticipation that swelled him almost to bursting as he laid claim to the woman he'd married.

He held her within his embrace, the night air cool against his back, her body beneath him warm and yielding, and closed his eyes as he pierced the evidence of her innocence.

The gasp of surprise escaping her lips brought him a pang of regret—tempered with pride—but it lingered only a moment before it was overtaken by the sheer joy of possession. He rocked against her, clasping her to him, unwilling to complete this act of intimacy, yearning to hold this moment within his breast as a shield against the world about him.

If she could only love him, he thought, holding himself in check, his muscles rigid with the effort. He'd needed to know the love of another human being for so long, yearned to savor this closeness with a woman who'd care about him, whose arms would hold him, lips whisper his name.

"Roan...Roan," she pleaded with soft entreaty, moving beneath him as she grasped for the elusive pleasure his possession promised. If she had expected pain, she'd have been disappointed, for his taking of her body had brought only a moment of discomfort and then a surge of great joy, filling her with such marvel and wonder she could scarce contain it.

With patient urging he led her, coaxing her with words and phrases of endearment. Finding new depths of endurance with each breath he took, he brought her to the final knowledge of passion, hearing with satisfaction the small, eager cries she spent against his flesh. And then he sought his own pleasure, only to find it increased by the evidence of her need as she clung to him, rising to his urging, lifting to his words of praise, riding the storm of his desire until it was satisfied within her warm depths.

She clung to him, unwilling to release him from her embrace, aware of his whispered words of comfort as he rocked her in his arms. And then she felt the damp evidence of her tears, sensing his dismay as he urged her to speak to him, his voice comforting against her ear.

"I'm sorry, Katherine. I wouldn't have hurt you for the world." His hands brushed at her face, wiping the evidence of her weeping, and his eyes sought hers in the darkness. "It'll be better next time, honey. I promise."

She caught her breath in a sob so filled with an almost overwhelming rush of emotion she could scarcely speak. "I'm all right," she assured him breathlessly. Her fingers sought his, capturing them as they dried her tears, squeezing them in a grasp made strong by the sheer joy that filled her being.

"I know damn well I hurt you," he said regretfully. "I'm sorry, honey."

She shook her head vehemently. "No! No, you didn't, Roan." Her laughter was exultant as she lifted his fingers to her lips, kissing them one by one, her mouth holding them prisoner as she caught them between her lips.

He was relieved by her declaration, bemused by her actions, and he sought her gaze, content to remain nestled against her warmth, enjoying the sleek length of her legs as she held him a willing captive. Her eyes still dewy with the tears she'd shed, she smiled in a beguiling manner, her mouth soft and shiny, a bit swollen. His fingers, damp from her kisses, cooled as a vagrant breeze swept through the camp, and his back rippled with the chill.

"We need to get under cover, honey," he whispered, his fingers warming themselves beneath the fall of hair he'd managed to loosen. It lay in glossy, silken strands about her head, only the evidence of her wound marring its simple beauty. And that narrow, dark slash through her tender flesh caught his eye. It was only a crease, scabbed over and healing, but the thought of what it might have been, of what might have happened, stiffened his resolve.

"I think we'd better try to get on a paddleboat and get off the trail," he told her. "We can stop in the next river town and check on southbound steamers."

"Tired of the honeymoon already, Mr. Devereaux?"

The teasing tone, the saucy glance from beneath lowered lids, so unlike the Katherine he knew, unsettled Roan and he lifted himself to lean over her on outstretched arms. He pursed his lips and allowed his eyes to feast on the pale flesh she made no attempt to conceal.

Another surprise. He'd have imagined Katherine wrapping her arms across her breasts or perhaps whispering soft words of protest at his deliberate baring of her body to his sight. But she lay on the rough blanket beneath him, meeting his gaze with all the aplomb of a woman of vast experience, a title she stood no chance of claiming. His mouth twisted in a grin of appreciation as he watched her and saw to his delight an answering grin turn up the corners of her mouth, her teeth gleaming in the faint light of the moon.

"Kinda sassy for a blushing bride, aren't you, Mrs. Devereaux?"

His soft question countered her own, and she lowered her lashes, an unknowing coquetry on her part, as she whispered her answer. "I'm not sure how brides are supposed to act. I can only be myself, blushes and all, Roan Devereaux.''

"Well, to answer your question, I'm not the least bit tired of the honeymoon, Katherine. Matter of fact, I'd like to hole up with you somewhere and spend the next few days just—"

His pause was deliberate, his eyes taking liberties as he rolled to one side, taking her with him, his hand holding her in place. He levered himself up on his elbow and leaned to taste the swollen flesh of her mouth, his kiss tender, gentle against the evidence of his passion.

"I thought we were going to stay here for another day," she said, her mouth answering his summons, her lips returning the pressure of his caress.

"Um...till I get the wash done up anyway," he murmured, distracted by the direction her fingers were taking, following the line of curls trailing down his midsection. "Sweet Kate, if you don't stop that messin' around with my belly button, you're gonna be in a heap of trouble in just a minute or two."

"Trouble?" She squirmed a bit, edging her hip against him, and his attention was caught up by the movement. "I'm just doing a little investigating, Roan."

He reached back to pull the blanket over them, shielding her from the night air, leaving only their heads exposed. "Tell you what I'm gonna do," he said firmly.

Her hands stilled their exploring as she watched him warily. "You don't like this?" she asked with barely concealed reserve.

"More than I should. But I'm afraid I'll do more harm than good if I don't let you alone. At least till morning," he amended quickly. "You were a virgin, honey."

"I know that! I never said I knew a whole lot about this part of things, but I certainly was aware of being—" She turned her head away from the glow of the campfire, her profile an ivory silhouette against the tumbled hair he'd raked about her head.

"Aw...don't get shy on me, Kate. I just don't want to hurt you." He nuzzled her cheek, inhaling the sweet scent of her, the woman smell that surrounded her. "Tell you what, I'll show you something else."

Her head turned just the slightest bit, her eyes meeting his warily. "What?"

He winced at the forlorn look of her. Here he'd spent the past hour or so trying to chase the demons of sorrow from her eyes, and in one fell swoop he'd managed to put them right back in place.

"I'll bet you'll like this, Katherine," he promised seductively. "Just turn back over here and let me show you."

She allowed him to nudge her into place beneath him, her gaze intent on his face, her mouth drawn down in a somber moue. "I feel guilty, Roan," she told him quietly. "Here my brother is, dead only two days, and I'm cavorting around, stark naked under a blanket, forgetting everything that happened."

"You haven't forgotten, honey. You're just doing what comes natural. When folks stare at death the way we did, life gets a whole lot sweeter by comparison. And makin' love is about the sweetest thing we can do. Kinda makes us thankful for bein' alive."

"I still feel like I should have mourned my brother a little longer before I..." She bit her lip and closed her lashes against the limpid beauty of his dark eyes.

"I think you'd already done your mournin' where your brother was concerned, Kate. You gave him up for dead a long time ago, when you heard he'd deserted his company in the war."

Her eyes flew open, surprise evident in her wide gaze. "You knew about that from Charlie, didn't you?"

He nodded. "Yeah. I think that's why Charlie went to war. Like he thought he could make up for Lawson runnin' off the way he did."

"I thought that, too," she told him, relief alive within her. "He was too old to go, almost fifty. I didn't know he'd told you why he felt he had to fight, but—"

"He didn't say so, right out, but we talked a lot, your pa and me," he said simply. "I heard all about you, you know. Charlie said you were his little Sparrowhawk. Matter of fact, we used that for our password. I think it made Charlie proud, kinda. He said it made him think about you every time he was on patrol, guarding the camp, and someone would answer his challenge with the name he gave you."

"He used to tease me." Her smile wobbled just a bit. "I never could see the resemblance, but he called me that for years."

Roan's brow lifted and his grin was mocking. "Oh, I didn't have any trouble a'tall figurin' out where he got the name once I saw you on that porch, pointin' your shotgun at me. You were about as feisty as any little hawk I ever laid eyes on."

"I don't think I'd have shot you," she confided, brushing at a stray tendril of hair on his cheek.

"Well, I wasn't about to take any chances. My leg had about all the damage it could stand and I wasn't gonna give you the chance to make it any worse."

"Has it been bothering you? What with riding so much and everything?" she asked, her brow furrowed with concern.

He shook his head. "Not bad. Just catches me once in a while when I ride hard. What we been doin' is small stuff."

"I don't want to ride a riverboat. I'd rather just do what we've been doing. Unless you think we might get bushwhacked again?"

He shrugged and his mouth was a narrowed line, stern and harsh. "I don't want to take any more chances with you, Katherine. We're gonna run into more folks as we go along and some of them might not be as friendly as we'd like. We'll see how it goes after we leave here.'' He glanced around at the encroaching darkness. ''I feel pretty safe here, the river at our back. But then, I felt like we were safe the other night, too. And look what happened.''

''Maybe we could stay with folks at night. You know, like we did at first.'' She offered it quietly and watched as he considered the idea.

His sudden grin surprised her. ''Maybe we'll stop at a hotel, like you wanted to before. Get you a real bath and wash your hair good.''

Her yawn came from nowhere, and she blinked as she covered her mouth with one hand. ''Oh, my... I didn't know I was that tired,'' she whispered, taking a deep breath and brushing once more at his dark hair. It fell forward as he bent over her, and she laced her fingers through the strands, pursing her mouth as she concentrated on him.

''Maybe I'll wash yours tomorrow, too. Might as well heat enough water for both of us.''

''Thought I'd just dunk you in the shallows and have at it,'' he said bluntly. ''Water's still pretty warm this time of year.''

She shivered and drew back. ''Not if you know what's good for you, you won't. I wash in warm water when it's serious washing. You can just figure out some way of getting enough hot water to do it right.''

His grin teased her, his fingers found her soft flesh beneath the blanket and he slid to lie beside her, curling her against him. ''We'll see about that,'' he said, his voice muffled against her brow, his hands skimming over her warmth.

''Roan? What were you going to show me? A while ago you said—''

"You sure do have a knack of rememberin' things, woman. Thought you'd let that slide by the wayside for sure."

Her sigh was loud in the silence. "I just wondered what you were going to show me," she said in a small voice.

His hand slid up from her waist and cupped the firm weight of her breast, his fingers feathering against the tender flesh. His breath was warm against her ear as he lifted himself to hover over her. His mustache brushed softly against the tender skin of her throat, and he bent lower to tease the plump handful with the same tantalizing touch.

She wiggled, shifting her hip to rub across his belly.

"Mmm..." Her throaty murmur was a dead giveaway, he decided. *She's pretty brave in the dark,* he thought, *rubbing against me right where it'll do the most good.* His grin hidden against her softness, he touched her with his tongue, tasting the sweetness of her, his teeth gentle as he nibbled at the puckered nub of flesh.

She stilled beneath him, gasping at the thrill of his bold caress, tense as she concentrated on the new source of pleasure he afforded.

His mouth left her with reluctance and he heard her gasp of protest, his lips curving in satisfaction.

"Give me your hand, honey," he told her. Clasping her fingers in his, he lowered them to where his aroused flesh pressed to her side in silent entreaty.

Timidly, her fingers explored, and he bent once more to lave wet caresses on her breasts. Caught up readily in the tugging tension his mouth had resumed, she smoothed caresses across his thigh as she followed his lead with eager enthusiasm. He covered her hand with his own, and she obeyed—her fingers curling as he directed her, her curiosity appeased as she measured the length and breadth of his desire. Sliding cautious fingertips over him, she explored the firmness she'd accepted within her body, marveling at the remembrance.

"Are we going to—" She couldn't form the words. Brave as she was, her hands full of his manhood and all, she still found her tongue unable to speak the words aloud.

"Mmm..." he breathed, his eyes closed, his palm flat against her belly, fingers flexing as he edged them closer to the tender flesh he'd vowed to leave be, for a few hours at least. "Maybe we'll..." His groan was one of pleasure as her fingers tightened around him. "I think you're gonna be a fast learner, honey."

And then he gave in to the lure of her woman's flesh, his long fingers tempting, teasing and testing her. His whispers told her of her power over him, his mouth pressing hot, damp kisses in a random pattern as he praised her in silence, and then with growling phrases of delight.

"Roan!" Her cry was wondering, then beseeching as she called his name again. She rose to his touch, her breathing harsh against his chest, and he bent to capture the sounds with his lips. "Ah, Roan," she whimpered, her slender body shivering with delight, tempting him.

He held her closely, her trembling frame secure within the shelter of his embrace. A sob shook her and he felt the damp warmth of her tears against his chest once more.

"You all right, Kate?" he asked warily. "I didn't hurt you again, did I?"

She shook her head. "I just feel so good, so full—" Her laugh was shaky, and she rubbed at her eyes and nose with trembling fingers. "I didn't know it would be like this," she confided quietly. "The loving part. I was afraid of it, before."

He closed his eyes, rocking her within his arms, warming her against the chill of the night air. "I knew that, honey. I just couldn't wait much longer for you to come to me. I need you, Katherine."

His admission was balm to her guarded heart, seeping into the secret place where her grief was tucked, drenching it with the healing comfort of his words. She nodded, her mouth forming the vow she could not speak aloud, not yet willing to surrender this part of herself into his keeping.

I love you. Once more, the phrase curled about her tongue, unfamiliar, forming itself, whispering in silence upon her lips. *I love you.* Her mouth brushed the message against his chest, and she smiled. It came easier now, she decided, forming the words again and again, breathing them in a quiet lullaby as her eyes closed and sleep stilled the message of her heart.

Chapter Fourteen

Five shirts lifted from the bushes in a silent dance, the prevailing breeze from the west catching them in its embrace. It fluttered their sleeves, teased at their hemmed bottoms, billowing them as they dried. Stockings draped over a low-hanging branch and denim pants hanging neatly from a sturdy limb were out of the sun's rays but drying nevertheless, moving in time with the shifting wind.

Katherine tended the fire, adding short lengths of deadwood, coaxing it to bloom anew. Breakfast was a memory, but supplies were short and she hesitated, viewing the small pile of foodstuffs before her.

"It'll have to be fresh meat," she whispered to herself, scanning the bits of flour and cornmeal, the bag of withered vegetables gleaned from her garden. They'd tolerated the journey as well as she could have expected, but the tote sack was near empty now, only a few carrots and a potato left to keep company with several onions.

"What are you muttering about now?" His voice came from directly behind her, and Katherine looked over her shoulder at the man who'd spread their clothing to dry over the landscape.

"All done with the wash?" she asked, ignoring his query.

"Yes, ma'am. Everything's hung to dry. Thought I'd spend some time with those yearlings of yours. They're gettin' pretty frisky, bein' tied so much."

He'd been more than attentive this morning, she thought, what with fixing breakfast, then heating water in a tedious process over the fire in order to do the wash. She'd watched from her vantage point, snuggled beneath the blankets as the sun turned the eastern sky to a dazzling display of color. The clouds had caught the brilliance within themselves, spreading across the horizon, providing them with a pink-and-cerise palette of beauty.

He'd crouched beside her while the coffee boiled and the last of the oatmeal cooked over the fire. His hands had been warm against her shoulders, drawing her into his embrace, lifting her to kneel in the nest of blankets, flushed and nearly naked before him.

She smiled to herself as she recalled his look of satisfaction. He'd brushed his palms over her skin, tenderness in each caress, cradling her, weighing her flesh, his fingers gentle yet insistent. And she'd shivered beneath his touch, her eyes closing as waves of heated pleasure flooded the very essence of her being.

His kiss had been more than welcome, his mouth causing hers to flower and soften into a receptacle for his gentle passion. And then, gathering her closely against him, he'd whispered words of endearment against her rosy cheeks. The phrases had caught at her hearing.... "Sweetheart ... soft and warm..." What had he said? Something about her had struck him as being soft. She smiled wistfully. No one had ever considered Katherine Cassidy to be soft in any way, shape or form. That Roan Devereaux had sunk to the level of wooing her with such words of praise was almost unbelievable.

"Katherine? You're daydreamin' there when you told me you'd find somethin' to put together for our dinner." His voice pulled her from the memories she gathered about her, the moments of pleasure she'd garnered at sunrise.

"Don't get all in an uproar," she told him, turning to face his tall figure, bold and arrogant beneath the noonday sun.

He looked her over with an uncanny eye for detail, his expression softening as he noted the faint shadows beneath her eyes, the still-pallid complexion with a scant feathering of freckles across her nose and cheeks. Swaying on her feet and still ready for battle. His brow furrowed, and he thrust his jaw into a belligerent pose.

"Maybe I'd better tend to the cookin' and you can cozy up under the trees on your blanket for a while," he told her bluntly. "You're lookin' sorta rocky, Kate."

"Well, thanks a whole lot. That's just what every woman likes to hear, I'm sure."

"You look like the near side of a freshly whitewashed shed, honey," he said with flat emphasis. "You're pale as a winter sky right before a big snow." She rolled her eyes and rose to her feet, hands clenched into loose fists at each side.

"I'm sure you're trying to make me feel better with all your compliments, Mr. Devereaux, but I don't need to hear any more about how good I look today. I'm very aware of my lack of beauty without you making an issue of it."

He slammed his fisted hands deep into the pockets of his pants and glared at her hostile expression. "Aw, hell, Katherine! You make everything I say come out the wrong way. I only meant you should take it easy for a while. You got shot in the head, woman! You need to plant your twitchy little butt on the ground somewhere and rest. You are the damnedest confounded female I've ever met!"

She met his glare with equal measure, and her reply sputtered from between clenched teeth. "I'm regretting every nice thought I had about you this morning, Mr. Devereaux. You're about the bossiest man I've ever had the honor of..." Eyes wide and flashing, she ran out of steam, her mouth clamping shut, her nostrils flaring, swaying on her feet as she faced him.

His hands were on her waist even as she blinked her surprise at his rapid movements. He scooped her up before him, holding her at eye level, his gaze piercing as he took her measure. She'd lost the pallor, her cheeks now rosy with the fire of frustration, her eyes sparkling and alive with the spirit he'd admired in her from the first moments of their meeting.

It was more than he could turn down, this vision of female pique and womanly enticement. He bent to her lips, swallowing the words of protest she uttered, claiming the mouth she'd used to scold him with, turning it into a willing vessel for his filling.

With barely a murmur, she shed the indignation cloaking her, curling her arms around his neck and clutching tightly the hard, tensed muscles of his back with spread fingers. His hands against her waist held her with bruising strength, and she lifted herself, wrapping her legs around his hips, holding him with the sleek embrace of her thighs. She rubbed against him, fired by the vivid memories of his loving through the night, and he groaned beneath her onslaught.

"Damn, Katherine, you'll be spread out on that blanket before you know it," he warned her, catching his breath, their lips brushing as he spoke.

She blinked at him, caught up in the desire he'd set afire within her. Then her cheeks flamed anew, her eyes closed before his scrutiny, and, relaxing her legs, she slid down his body, her face pressing against his chest.

"Hey, don't hide like that," he scolded her gently. "I'm not the least bit against lovemakin' in broad daylight, honey. I just wanted you to know where we were headin' before we got there."

She drew in a deep breath and pushed away from his grasp, smoothing her hands over her shirt, tucking it in neatly, repairing the damage she'd done with her twisting and turning in his embrace.

"I've got cooking to do," she said shortly, turning from him to drop to her knees near the fire, where the small store of supplies lay scattered.

Roan's grin was wide as he surveyed her stiff posture. Smothering the chuckle he knew would embarrass her, he walked to where the horses grazed. Even as he selected one of the yearlings to work with, loosing it from the rope he'd stretched between trees, his lips twitched in amusement.

Once more she'd surprised not only him but herself. The fiery woman in his arms was a far cry from the Katherine Cassidy he'd met weeks ago. She'd hidden her passion well, guarding her womanhood beneath layers of drab attire. That he should have been the man chosen to discover the female creature dwelling in such a disguise was more good fortune than he'd ever anticipated. His heart swelling with emotions he was unwilling to name, he led the young horse from the campsite.

Roan's mind focused on the chestnut beauty before him as he attached the lead to the horse's halter. That the words of praise he heaped on the yearling were more generous than usual did not occur to him. His smile was brilliant as the animal responded to his bidding, reflecting the deep pleasure he'd found in Katherine this morning. Somehow she was a part of this and so his hands were gentle, his voice soothing as he handled her young filly. With practiced ease, he worked through the session of training and discipline he'd instigated with the yearling.

Caught up in the chore, he failed to notice as Katherine's slender figure slipped from the camp, long gun in hand.

The shot echoing from the west spun him about as he led the horse back to her siblings. His grip on the halter tightened automatically and his eyes narrowed, sweeping the horizon, piercing the small glades of woodland as he sought its source. A second report focused his gaze on a figure rising from the ground, weapon held at the ready, several hundred yards away.

"Katherine!" The word was thunderous, reverberating in the still air. "Damn woman," he growled. "Leave her sittin' under a tree and she goes huntin'." His eyes were dark with concern, his momentary dread banished by an influx of frustrated anger.

He tied the horse in place and stalked with measured paces to where she stood, hands on hips, frowning at his approach.

"What the hell do you think you're doin', shootin' that thing behind my back? You're lucky I didn't draw on you, woman!"

"You're not wearing your gun," she pointed out succinctly.

His frown deepened. Closing the gap between them, he faced her, the memories of their interlude earlier banished from his mind, his attention riveted on the weapon she held.

"I left you fixin' dinner," he said.

She tilted her head back to look at him through her lashes, squinting against the sun. "So you did. And I decided we didn't have enough to put together for one hungry woman, let alone a big galoot like you. So I went out hunting for something to hang over the fire. Now if you don't mind, I'll go pick up my rabbit and get it skinned and gutted."

Her stance belligerent, her jaw jutting in defiance, she faced him. He gritted his teeth, holding back the words that filled his mind. His eyes feasted upon her . . . independent creature that she was, a small, stiff-necked female armed for battle, facing him unafraid. He felt a wash of unwanted admiration for this woman cleanse his mind of the anger gripping him. The tension eased, and the muscles of his throat relaxed as he allowed his irritation to seep from him. His concern, after all, had been for her well-being, and his relief at discovering the innocence of her gunshots banished the quarrel he'd sought to set into motion.

"I've been killing my own meat for years," she continued, unaware of the softening in his stance.

"Is that so?" he asked, teasing her from her indignant pose.

She tilted her head, eyeing him askance, wary of this new mood. Her nod was quick. "Yes, that's so. And selling off the surplus in town when I needed money for supplies."

"You've made a habit of your independence, haven't you, Katherine?" he asked softly.

She lifted her chin once more. "I've taken care of myself for a long time," she reminded him quietly. And then she handed him the gun, placing it into his hands even as he automatically reached for it, sensing her movement.

Her pace was casual as she walked away from him. He watched, gun in hand, transfixed by the womanly sway of her softly rounded hips. Watched as she pulled the knife from a sheath on her belt and knelt in the grass to tend the carcass of her quarry. In a few swift strokes of the knife, she'd cleaned the large rabbit. Gripping the furry creature by the hind legs, she approached him once more.

"I'm going to the river to wash and skin him out. It'll be a while before I get things together for dinner. You'll have time to finish with the yearlings, if you want to work them."

His hand rose to his temple in a mocking salute. "Yes, ma'am," he intoned solemnly, then watched as a flush rose to paint her cheeks with color.

Her lips narrowed and her gaze searched his. "Don't mock me, Devereaux."

"That's the last thing I'd do, ma'am. I'm not about to bite the hand that's doin' the cookin', so to speak."

She swallowed a reluctant laugh. "You have a unique way of putting things," she said finally, pacing at his side as they returned to the campsite. Bending, she wiped her knife blade against the grass to clean it, then slid it within its sheath. Her eyes scanned him as he strode from her, his only reply a grunt of acknowledgment.

By the time she'd dressed the rabbit and spitted it for the fire, she was reeling. A fine sheen of perspiration covered her beneath the concealing fabric of her shirt, and her fingers trembled as she rubbed them against her thighs to dry the water from them. Then, with an audible sigh, she sank to the ground. Her head resting against her bent knees, she drew a deep breath, and the ensuing shudder caught the eye of the man who approached.

"Kinda shaky?" he asked, unwilling to scold her again.

She lifted her face from its resting place and met his gaze. "A little," she admitted.

His smile was tender. For the first time, she'd allowed him to sense her vulnerability without hesitation. "It's gonna take you a while to get over that crease in your skull. Better let me take a look at it."

She bent her head again, quietly submissive to his suggestion. He knelt beside her, his fingers gentle as he parted the hair to search out the wound.

"It's clean, Kate," he announced quietly, brushing the long strands back to cover the scabbed area. "Want me to braid your hair up for you?" His hands untangled its length, lifting it from her back, allowing it to slide like shimmering silk between his fingers.

She turned her face to slant a questioning glance at him. "You trying to make up to me, Devereaux?" she wanted to know, her tone suspicious.

"Do I need to?" he asked with a cocky grin. "I worked your horses and washed your clothes, honey. I thought that was about all the makin' up I needed to do today."

She shrugged her shoulders in a negligent gesture. "Just so you know, Roan. I pay my own way. I do my share of the chores and—"

His hand, rising to touch her lips with warm fingers, silenced her, closing off the list she enumerated. "This isn't about sharing chores, Katherine. This is about a man takin' care of his woman, lookin' after her.''

''I can look after myself,'' she whispered against the warmth of his flesh, her lips brushing the callused surface of his fingers.

He nodded. ''I know you can. But you don't have to. Not anymore. You're my wife.''

She heard the implied message his final words delivered, and her eyes widened. Twisting her head to rid herself of his restraining fingers, she narrowed her eyes, scanning his face. It was somber, his gaze dark with the message she'd rightly interpreted.

''And you're my husband. That means I look out for you, too.''

He shook his head. ''You can tend to my needs and keep me fed and dressed, and even stand behind me for a backup if need be, but for once in your life, you're about to find yourself on the other end of the stick, Kate.'' He sat beside her on the ground and his hand found hers, his fingers lacing with her narrower ones, forming a grip she would have found difficult to escape.

She frowned at him. ''What's that supposed to mean?''

''I mean you're going to play the part of a wife.'' He looked at her with fleeting amusement. ''Who knows? You might even begin to enjoy lettin' someone else take you on. It means I'm plannin' on lookin' after you. Doesn't mean we aren't partners, Kate. I just want you to know, you don't have to always rely on yourself. From now on, I'll be here for you to depend on.''

''That sounds a little like you're planning a lot of years with me. I thought we'd agreed this was sort of a temporary situation, this being married.''

''Did you?'' His look was piercing as he viewed her from stormy eyes. His hand lifting hers between them, he flexed his fingers, tightening their grasp against hers. ''We're married, Katherine. See our hands? We're joined just as tight as these fingers of ours. If it wasn't a fact before, last night made it so. You're stuck with me."

"Still poutin'?" he asked from the darkness. She huddled before the fire, wrapped in a blanket against the night air, aware of his presence behind her before his voice broke the silence.

It remained unbroken, only her look of scorn acknowledging his query.

Sinking to the ground next to her, he stretched his long legs toward the fire. "Everything looks quiet. I scouted around, but it's pretty much like I thought. I didn't see any new tracks."

He'd been gone since supper, saddling his mare and leaving her alone, only a short few words to let her know he'd be riding out for a while.

Trying unsuccessfully to ignore his return, she'd listened to the sound of his voice as he checked out the string of horses, her ears attuned to the approaching whisper of near silent footsteps.

Now she deigned to answer his challenge.

"I don't pout," she said firmly. "I may keep my thoughts to myself sometimes, but I don't pout. I'm not a child." His gaze raked her slim form.

"Well, I'll have to agree with you there." She cast him a speaking look, unwilling to respond to the suggestive phrasing.

"Gonna be mad all night?" he wondered aloud, his eyes hooded and barely visible to her in the glow of the fire.

"I'm not mad."

"Are we havin' a fight?"

"I'm trying to keep from it," she said after a moment.

"You don't wanna be dependent on a man, do you, Kate? Is it so hard for you to lean on me, just a little?"

"What if you change your mind?" she asked quietly. "I've been thinking. Maybe your folks won't want you married to a Yankee. What then? What if you decide to send me back to Illinois? A lot of things could happen, Roan. You might very well get tired of my ways after a while. I'm not always easy to get on with. And I know I'm not the best-looking woman you've ever laid eyes on.'' She took a deep breath and chanced a look at his profile. "I'm what they call 'long in the tooth' at the livery stable," she said defiantly, as if she dared him to protest the claim. And then in a low whisper she admitted her final fault, the most damaging she could think of. "I haven't got the sort of upbringing your folks will be looking for in your wife."

His disdain was obvious, his scornful look daring her to continue. "My folks can go to the devil, for all I care, Mrs. Devereaux. I married you in Illinois, and I'm plannin' on stayin' married to you in Louisiana. I don't go back on my word. You might just as well set your mind to the fact. I told you this afternoon that you're stuck with me and that still holds true."

She bit at her lip, shaken by his vehement response, for the first time sensing the finality of his commitment to her. The almost overwhelming tide of emotion his lovemaking had released within her surged once more to the surface. That she was willing to give her love into his keeping was a fact she was beginning to accept as truth. But though he would be loyal, that he could ever respond in kind was doubtful.

He'd be true to her. Roan didn't have it in him to be faithless. He'd take care of her. He was a gentleman beneath the facade of hard-bitten warrior, much as he tried to disguise the fact. His fidelity was unquestionable. But faithfulness was a far cry from the love her lonely heart yearned for. Whether he was capable of returning the emotion she felt was a moot question, one she was unwilling to consider yet.

She drew a deep breath, cautious lest she display her vulnerability. "We're married and that's a fact," she told him staunchly. "That makes you my husband, and according to the law, you pretty much get to run things your own way. But I'm used to being on my own. I don't know if I can take being beholden to a man." Her pursed lips and the promise of her stubborn chin warned him of the stand she'd taken. He responded without hesitation.

His hand released hers. Then, slipping his arm about her waist, he gathered her closely to him. Deftly, his other arm slipped beneath her knees, and lifting her to sit on his lap, he arranged her to his liking. One large palm, fingers spread wide against her hair, pressed her head against his shoulder.

His voice was a rumble against her ear and she caught her breath as he spoke once more. "I'll be sure to think of something you can do to keep me happy. Sorta even out the debt, so to speak," he drawled, his arms cradling her against his big body.

She huddled within the blanket, its warmth intensified by the heat of him beneath her, and allowed her body to relax against him. Her mouth curled in a smile as she recognized the implication of the words he had spoken. She twisted against him, ridding herself of the constricting covering.

The fabric of his shirt was rough against her cheek and she eased away a bit, her fingers moving up bravely to release the buttons she'd rested against. His chest lifted in quick reaction, his breathing rough and rasping as her probing touch found the curls beneath the blue fabric. Pushing it aside, she pursed her lips, blowing softly against his flesh, her smile triumphant as she felt the tremor of his response.

With a cry of delight, she nuzzled him, her breath warm, teasing him with the touch of her mouth, her lips open, seeking, savoring the musky flavor of his skin.

"Do you know what you're gettin' into?" he asked roughly.

"Mmm... I think so..." Her hands grasped the material of his shirt, easing it from his shoulders and down his arms.

He was acquiescent beneath her touch, his eyes dark and penetrating, watching the pale, graceful dance of her fingers moving to an unheard melody. Slender and strong, they speared through the curly thatch, seeking what lay beneath, kneading and testing as they went.

She brushed over the small, round nubs, moving her fingers in a slow circle, fascinated by the shivering of his flesh, the sharply indrawn breath he made no attempt to conceal.

"Are you tryin' to make me cry uncle?" he asked, his words like sandpaper, escaping through tightly clenched teeth.

"No..." she whispered, her own eyes closing, savoring the contrasting textures of his body.

He gripped her with steely strength and she gasped, her widespread fingers curling into fists. "Turnabout's fair play," she was warned in a rasping growl. Shifting, surrounding her suddenly with his arms, he turned to lower her to the ground. He hovered over her, capturing her legs between his own, the blanket providing an unwanted barrier between them.

And then her fingers uncurled, flattening, pressing against his chest, captured by his weight. They wiggled their protest and her words begged him, enforcing the message.

"Please... let me touch you." Whispered on an indrawn breath, they offered a challenge, one his aching body yearned to refuse. More than food or drink, he craved the quick, hot pleasure he knew she could provide to his needy manhood. Rigidly, it pressed against her thigh, its throbbing length an urgent message she could not help but comprehend. And yet he hesitated.

"Roan?" Her fingers stilled their tiny movements, her slender frame quivering beneath him, his weight pressing her against the hard ground. She needed his reassurance... awaited his answer.

"You've been touchin' me," he said harshly. "Fact is, I don't know how much more of your teasin' I can take, honey."

A thin shiver of triumph touched the nape of her neck. "Try," she answered with a low, seductive laugh, her eyes opening to seek his gaze.

He groaned his surrender, rolling from her, resting his head on clasped fingers to cradle it from the hard earth. Then waited, aware, attuned to her movements, her scent teasing his nostrils with an elusive sweetness. His eyes closed as her hair touched his forehead, its tendrils brushing their way across his cheeks and down the length of his nose. His lips felt the caress, then his chin and throat as the dark, unbound tresses swept over his flesh.

He sensed her movement, felt the press of her knees against his waist, recognized the soft weight of her breasts snuggling his ribs as she bent low to taste once more the flavor of his flesh. Then she lifted herself from him, her hands on his body, spreading wide from throat to waist, measuring the length of his breastbone, the softer flesh of his abdomen.

And he responded, tensing beneath her fingers. She was gratified by his automatic reflex to her stroking caress, and her chuckle was rich with satisfaction.

"You laughin' at me, Kate?" His nostrils flaring, he fought the terrible urge to conquer, his fingers clenching the back of his head. She'd asked... and he'd determined to allow her the liberties she was taking at his expense.

"Mmm..." It was less than an admission of guilt, more than a denial of the same. Her throaty purr tugged at him, forcing him to tighten the leash he'd put in place as she unwittingly threatened her own precarious position.

She was blissfully unaware of the danger, her fingers busy now at the fastening of his pants, working the buttons from

place, slipping to spread with cool curiosity against the
heated flesh of his belly.

"Kate..." It was a growled warning, and he twitched, his
hips lifting to the beckoning of her fingertips. So close, so
near the throbbing, aching heart of his manhood...yet so
reluctant to bridge the small distance. Her hand hesitated,
fingers brushing in a distracted movement, one slipping into
the small scarred hollow in the center of his belly.

He groaned in frustration and his lips forced themselves
into a pained grimace. Against the denim of his pants, his
hard flesh yearned upward and he urged it on, nudging her
with the evidence of his desire.

"Damn it, Kate! Touch me!" Spewing from him in harsh
syllables, it was a command, a plea, a tortured whisper, demanding her compliance...

And she obeyed.

Chapter Fifteen

The rising sun shed no warmth. It hovered on the eastern horizon in rosy display, promising a splendid day, but for now the air was chill and crisp with a threat of the frosty mornings to come.

Katherine huddled under the blanket, wishing for another to add to its warmth, her back pressed tightly to the hard length of man she'd become familiar with in such a short span of time. She moved her hips against him, lifting her shoulders and stretching the length of her spine.

"What I wouldn't give for just one night in my own bed," she grumbled, squinting into the brilliance of the morning sunrise.

"Are you always so crabby in the morning?" Rough and rasping, the words were muttered against her nape, Roan squirming his way beneath the blanket to find the tender skin he sought. His mouth pressed against the warmth of her neck, biting gently, leaving audible kisses in its path as he levered himself up onto his elbow to search out the hollow beneath her ear. His nose nuzzled there and he growled a wordless message. With a rasping chuckle, he pressed his hand flat against her belly, pulling her tightly against him.

"Roan?" She stilled beneath his touch, eyes wide and startled. "What are you doing?"

"Just rememberin', honey," he drawled, nudging her head up a bit, his mouth pressing damp kisses the length of her throat.

Remembering... Her cheeks grew rosy, her breathing quickened and her eyes closed tightly. *How could I have been so bold, so brazen?* She bit at her lip, recalling the long hours of darkness. He'd responded to her challenge, yielding himself to her as if he were the sacrifice on an ancient altar and she the priestess who would claim the offering as her own.

And she had done just that—had claimed him as if the claiming were her due. Touching, exploring his big body with tentative movements, his murmurs of pleasure assuring her of her competence in this new venture.

Katherine felt the hot blush sweep over her beneath the dual covering of blanket and warm, hard flesh of her husband's body. She turned, then, ducking her head against his firm chest, she breathed deeply of his musky scent... and was thoroughly annoyed by the chuckle that vibrated against her ear.

"Are you laughing at me?" Her tone was aggrieved as she stiffened in his embrace.

"Not on your life, sweetheart!" He rolled with her clutched tightly against him till she could no longer hide her flushed countenance, having been elevated above him, and now finding herself in grave danger of being totally uncovered.

"Roan!" Reaching behind her, she grabbed for the errant blanket, tugging it over the bare flesh he'd exposed so neatly.

"There's not a soul in sight, Mrs. Devereaux," he announced cheerfully, his hands filled with the curves of her bottom as he wedged her between his muscled thighs.

His grin was touchingly youthful, she decided, capitulating with reluctant grace to the position he'd assigned her. Her breasts flattened against his broad chest, her legs held prisoner between his, she cradled his face with the palms of her hands. Strands of dark hair blurred her vision and she blew ineffectively at them as she tossed her head in a vain effort to shake her disordered hair into place.

"I declare, I've never seen you so thoroughly mussed up, Katherine." The drawl he allowed to creep into his words was saucy, designed to tease, and it served its purpose well.

Her eyes lit with challenge. "Probably comes from getting the best of my big, strong husband." She pouted prettily at him and was rewarded with an appreciative grin.

"Never knew you to be so flirty, woman."

Her brow lifted as she considered the thought. "Guess I never had much reason to flirt before," she whispered, bending her head to kiss him with a satisfying smack. Her hair fell in a veil about their faces, the straight, dark length of it freed from its confines throughout the night. He grinned up at her, his pleasure in her apparent, and she delivered another kiss to his waiting lips.

The kiss lingered a bit longer as she bit enticingly at the fullness of his mouth, warmed by his regard and the touch of his big hands as they traveled the length of her spine.

"Am I a wanton woman?" Whispered against his mouth, the words were both a teasing query and a plea for assurance, and he responded with gratifying promptness.

"Don't you know, Katherine, every man wants his wife to be a wanton woman when she's with him." His words were accompanied by a squeeze of both arms as he wrapped them around her middle. "You let me know I wasn't the only one doin' the wantin'. And that's a comfort to a man's soul, you know."

She eased herself up from him and he let her go, releasing his hold. Her gaze swept his face, hesitating on the whiskers he'd sprouted during the past hours, moving on to the narrowed look he offered her, then coming to rest on the tousled darkness of his hair. She smiled, a cunning, feline expression, lifting her hands to spear her fingers through his disheveled locks.

"You look about as mussed up as I've ever seen a man," she declared, repeating his own observation.

"Yeah, well, you oughta be ready to take the blame, ma'am. I don't believe I've ever had a woman who's been so—" He halted the words that had almost escaped his lips, frowning as he considered the damning evidence of his own past.

Katherine rolled from him, taking the blanket with her. She sat beside him, tugging the wool covering around her shoulders, and pulled her knees up to take advantage of its warmth.

"Ah, Kate. Don't look all primed to blow, honey." Naked as the day he was born, Roan went to crouch beside her, his hands clasped between his knees.

"Get your clothes on," she told him quietly. She looked around the campsite, where the evidence of their hurried coupling lay. She allowed one glance at the shirt she'd tugged from his body, another at the pants he'd shed with almost indecent haste, and then spied her own clothing. It too was half inside out, cast aside by the passionate woman she'd become only hours ago.

"Katherine." He called her name in a voice that reminded her of thick molasses drizzling from the jar, warm as a July midday sun, redolent with the Southern drawl that tickled her ear.

She looked up and saw compassion reflected in his dark eyes. Saw the beginning of a sad smile curling his lips and sensed the regret he felt within himself.

"I can't change the number of women in my past, sweetheart. But you'd better know, they don't amount to a hill of beans when I compare them to you. Not one of them is worth your little finger, honey. At least, not the memory of them I've toted around in my mind over the years. Hell, I can't even remember their names, 'cept for a couple. And they weren't important. None of them hold a candle to Katherine Devereaux, and you'd better believe that, sweetheart, 'cause it's the truth, so help me God!''

She melted. There was no other word for it. Deep within, she felt the icy wrappings covering her heart give way, felt the lonely, empty spaces fill with love for the man who faced her. Faced her with regret and understanding painting his dark features. One hand rose from within the confines of her blanket to touch his cheek. Her fingertips smoothed the bristled jaw and traced the furls of his ear as she looked into his eyes. Then his face blurred before her as the melting within became a watershed of tears that coursed down her cheeks.

"Aw, sweetheart, don't cry," he whispered, turning his head to kiss the palm of her hand. He clasped it between his own rough fingers and bent to kiss once more the smaller hand he held.

"I love you, Roan Devereaux." It was a soft whisper, reaching his ear like a welcome spring breeze, and he felt the warmth of it touch his heart.

Reaching for her with both arms, he found himself atop her, their bodies falling to the ground, the blanket between them. Katherine struggled to free her arms, needing the freedom to touch him, her heart crying out for his response.

"Oh Lordy, Lordy, Kate. There never was a woman in the world like you, you know that?" He buried his nose in her throat, nudging the blanket from his path and finding his way to the softer flesh beneath it. His mouth opened to taste the gentle rise of her breast, and his words were a muffled litany of praise to the woman he held.

"Don't for the life of me know how a woman like you could take me on the way you have," he said finally, lifting his head to peer into her teary eyes. "I've wandered around the country for longer than I want to tell you and never found anyone who cared about me. I left a family back home that was only interested in havin' fancy things around them, and gettin' more things gathered up as fast as they could. My mother and my pa...well, they just didn't see eye to eye with me on much of anything. I already told you that."

"I thought you were the one who took me on," Katherine reminded him. "You married me and dragged my horses along. You even got into a gunfight because of me."

His brow puckered into a frown. "Now how the hell do you figure that?"

She shrugged beneath him.

"Don't you know, Katherine? Don't you know I wouldn't have married you if I hadn't wanted to? Have you any idea how hard it was for me to...do you know how much I wanted to—" He sighed, unable to speak the words. But his eyes gave her the message. His body moving against hers through the blanket told her in no uncertain terms what he was unwilling to voice aloud.

Her smile was suddenly winsome, her eyes sultry as she peered over his shoulder to look around the surrounding area. "Are you sure we're all alone here, Devereaux?"

"Yeah, I'm sure." His movements became more focused, his body settling against hers with a compelling motion.

Her lips sought his ear, and her whisper was welcome as she issued the invitation. "Why don't you join me under the blanket for a while? Maybe we could talk about things."

"Things?" It was a rasping croak delivered from a throat that was suddenly dry with the remembrance of what she had offered so sweetly throughout the night hours.

Her hands framed his face once more, and the kiss she delivered to his eager mouth spoke volumes as she repeated the word against the dampness of his lips.

"Things."

* * *

All things considered, Katherine decided they'd done well to be on the trail by noon. What with folding all the laundry and packing the saddlebags, she'd taken longer than she'd expected. Roan had worked the yearlings for an hour while she sorted out the campsite and made a meal of sorts. Then they'd lingered over the coffee and biscuits and decided on a plan of action. Rather, Roan had decided and Katherine had agreed somewhat grudgingly to settle for a boat trip.

Now they were strung out along the trail, Katherine in the lead, Roan riding beside her for a while, then dropping back to keep a close eye on the string of horses behind them. It was late in the day when she spied the outline of a town against the horizon, and her heart lifted with the thought of the pleasures to be found in a hot bath and a soft bed.

"What town is that?" She pointed to the scattering of buildings ahead of them.

"Should be St. Maria, I think." His horse nudged hers as he fell into place beside her.

"Sounds like a priest founded the town."

Roan laughed, a short, disdainful sound. "If one did, he must've left before he had much influence on things, honey. It's just a river town, 'bout like the rest of them. Couple of saloons and a general store. Maybe a church if the right folks settled there."

"There'll be a hotel, won't there?" Katherine leaned over the pommel and lifted her hand to her brow, peering at the fast-approaching settlement. Scenting the livery stable, the horses had stepped up their pace without urging. Even as she spoke, they rode past several houses surrounded by picket fences and spaced along the trail, which was fast becoming a dusty road. A small child raised a hand in welcome from where he sat on the front steps of a whitewashed house.

Katherine's own hand lifted in response and her smile was brilliant. "A real town," she breathed, as if such a thing were a wonder to behold.

Roan glanced at her and chuckled. "Sure doesn't take much to tickle your fancy, does it?"

She jutted out her chin and granted him a look of scorn. "Probably not, since you've managed to tickle it once or twice." Then she blushed at the implication of her words.

His shout of laughter only served to bring a darker rosy hue to her cheeks, and she dug her heels into the sides of her mare, riding on ahead.

There was indeed a hotel, one sporting a satisfactory bathtub. Filled with hot water and contented woman, it presented a pretty picture to the man entering his assigned room, bundle in hand.

"You're supposed to bathe behind the screen, Kate. Anybody in the hall could look in here and see you."

Katherine opened her eyes just a bit, jarred from her state of languid pleasure, sitting erect as she stirred from the sloped back of the tub. Her hair, secured firmly only minutes ago to the top of her head, had begun to fall around her ears in dark strands. She blew one stray lock from in front of her eyes and glared accusingly at the man who'd interrupted her leisurely bathing.

"Seeing as how you and I are the only ones having keys to that door, I don't see how anybody else could peek in here." She lifted her washcloth and rubbed the bar of soap against it. Satisfied with the suds she produced, Katherine sniffed at the cloth and smiled.

"Smells like lilacs in the spring." She ran the soapy cloth the length of one arm and across her breasts, then upward to her throat, her eyes closing as she reveled in the tactile pleasure. "What's in the package?" she asked idly.

Roan's footsteps were silent against the rug. He knelt beside the tub and leaned over the rim, his lips puckering as he blew a warm breath on the soap bubbles covering her breasts. "A new dress for my wife." Spoken in a husky whisper, the words brought a smile of delight to her mouth.

He blew once more, watching the shimmering soap bubbles break, revealing her pale flesh.

She shivered. Her eyes opened and her mouth puckered. The temptation was too much for him to resist. He bent farther, capturing the words she would have spoken, his mouth settling on her lips with unerring accuracy. Without opening his eyes, he grasped the cloth she held and took up the route she'd chosen in her bathing. He swept across her shoulders, then made a detour to the arm she'd not washed. Obligingly, she lifted it from the water, holding it aloft for his ministrations.

Mouth moving beneath his kiss, she whispered, "You didn't wash between my fingers."

His chuckle was spontaneous, and he leaned back to grin at her. "You sure know how to mess up a mood, sweetheart."

She shrugged, lowering her arms into the warm water, hiding the smile she wore. "If you're going to do a job, you'd best do it right the first time."

Roan stood and glared at her with feigned annoyance, tossing the washcloth into the water with enough force to splash her face. Elaborately, she wiped the water from her left eye and lifted the brow just a bit, scanning his towering frame.

"I always figured you'd be prickly about taking criticism," Katherine said with an air of disdain. Casually, she searched for the washcloth beneath the surface of the water and once more brought up a lather with her bar of soap. Lifting one leg, she washed its length, bending her knee to better reach her toes. Then in turn she lifted the other limb, pointedly ignoring him as she washed every inch of calf and foot.

"Would you believe me if I told you you'd missed a spot?"

Katherine glanced up and smiled sweetly. "Nope."

He leaned over and pressed a long forefinger to the flesh just inches above her knee. "Right here."

Her leg slid with haste into the water and she sniffed, spurning his advice.

"Just tryin' to be helpful," he said with a sigh.

"You bought me a dress?" She slanted a look from beneath lowered lids.

"Yup. I told you I would."

"How do you know it's going to fit?" She lifted one eyebrow as she dribbled a stream of water from the washcloth over her shoulder.

His eyes lit with amusement. "You forget I'm pretty familiar with the way you're built, ma'am."

She sniffed and looked away. "Go away, Devereaux." It was a casual dismissal, accompanied by the lackadaisical wave of one hand. That her mouth was curved in a satisfied smile did not fail to escape his notice, and he stuffed his hands into the back pockets of his pants, rocking back on his heels as he surveyed her slender form.

She was really coming out of her shell. Like the hermit crab he'd watched as a child on a trip to the shore in New Orleans, she was wary of exposing herself. She'd pulled back from him, shielding herself from the start, unwilling to let him too close. Until the past few days, when he'd broken down the barriers of her innocence and brought to life the passion she'd guarded so carefully.

"Think you can get out of that tub in time for supper? I'd be more than happy to help you dry off and put on your new dress."

"If you get yourself out of here, I'll be ready for supper in fifteen minutes. I can probably manage to dry off all by myself," she told him firmly. "Been doing it for more years than I can count."

"Make that an hour," he said, turning away. "I'm goin' to the barber across the way to get my hair trimmed and a decent shave. Maybe I'll get a bath over there while I'm at it." He scooped up a clean shirt and a dark pair of socks from the clothing she'd piled on the bed and headed for the door.

"Don't forget to lock it behind you," she called out. "We wouldn't want anybody paying me a visit."

His mouth tightened at her words, and when he left the room, he checked the doorknob twice before he was satisfied. The man he'd spotted on the dock had looked familiar. With just a glance, he couldn't be certain, but that fleeting look had sure as hell rung a warning bell. It had been the slouch, the leather vest and the furtive gestures that had caught his attention. Too late, the man had turned away, but Roan had long since learned to trust his intuition. His frown deepened as he trotted across the dusty road to the small barber shop.

"Any strangers in town?" It was a polite opening query and the barber accepted it as such.

"Besides yourself?" He shook out the striped cloth and draped it around Roan's neck, stepping back to consider the shaggy length of dark hair.

Roan chuckled obligingly. "Thought I saw a fella I used to know, down by the dock earlier. He didn't come from hereabouts. Thought maybe he was passin' through."

The barber slashed the air with his scissors. "Coulda been. We always got folks comin' and goin', what with the riverboats dockin' here every couple of days."

Roan nodded. It was just about the answer he'd expected. He'd have to do some looking around on his own. It wasn't likely that the lone gang member to escape would show up here, but it wouldn't do to rest too easy, he decided. He closed his eyes as the first snip of hair fell to the floor.

It had been a simple matter to purchase tickets for the trip. The horses would be accommodated in the stern of the boat. He and Katherine would have a small stateroom on the second deck. Satisfied with his arrangements, Roan turned his steps toward the hotel, aware he'd lingered longer than he'd expected.

His bath had been lukewarm and he'd hurried through it, scrubbing and singing in time with the movement of his hands over his body. He'd rinsed with clean water, standing in the tub, shivering as the cool stream floated the suds from him. He grinned, remembering the pleasure Katherine had taken in her leisurely bathing. Sure didn't take much to make her happy. Give her a tub of hot water and bar of soap and she was in hog heaven.

The hotel lobby was crowded, and Roan stood for a moment, taken aback by the suppertime crowd, most of them travelers planning on boarding the riverboat in the morning. Then, as if she drew his gaze with conscious intimacy, he became aware of Katherine. Halfway down the curving staircase she'd paused, her eyes meeting his across the fifty feet or so separating them. Her hair was braided and coiled around the crown of her head, a severe arrangement, only serving to better display the finely drawn lines of her forehead and cheek. Her beauty stunned him with its simple form.

His indrawn breath was audible to his own ears, and he blinked quickly as though he must regain control of his emotions. She was exquisite, this woman of his—this lady of grace and dignity. His lady—his woman. The blue dress he'd chosen for her was simple, its lines classic, clinging to her lush breasts and fitting to her waistline. From there it cascaded to the floor, its yards of fabric swirling about her feet as she descended the stairway.

She walked across the lobby to join him, her eyes never leaving his, her mouth curved into a half smile, as if she delighted in the stunned expression he wore.

"Katherine." He could speak only her name. He wanted to tell her how lovely she looked, but the words would not form on his tongue. Only the name that rolled from his mouth like a liquid melody and pleasured his very being as he gave it voice.

"Katherine," he said once more, and she took his hand and allowed her gaze to sweep over his damp hair and cleanly shaven jaw.

"You're looking mighty fine, Mr. Devereaux." Her voice was husky, her look flirtatious, as if she tested her new power over him.

"I see the dress fits." It wasn't what he wanted to tell her. He wanted her to know how lovely she looked, how proud he was of her. *Later,* he thought. *I'll tell her after a while, when I help her take the dress off.* Taking her hand, he placed it on his arm and led her to the wide archway and through it into the hotel dining room.

A girl in a white apron stood there, ready to usher them to a table in the already crowded room. Katherine followed her and Roan brought up the rear, his gaze intent on his wife. Her hair was dark, with mahogany highlights gleaming from the lamps overhead. The nape of her neck looked fragile and vulnerable beneath the heavy, coiling braids. Her back was slender, narrowing to a slim waist he knew would fit his hands with unerring precision. Then his eyes caught the gentle sway of her skirts as she moved between the tables, and he envisioned the sleek length of her legs and the lavish curves of her hips.

By the time he'd seated her and slid into his own chair, he was halfway to a state of arousal that was well on its way to being embarrassingly obvious. Blessedly, the approach of the waitress, menus in hand, took his attention and he concentrated on ordering their evening meal.

They ate with extravagant appetite. Katherine wrinkled her nose at the rare steak Roan ordered, but fell to with enthusiasm when her own roast beef was served. After the scant rations they'd been reduced to over the last two days, they'd ordered a veritable feast. Katherine's index finger traced the edge of the china plate she ate from, her gaze admiring the floral design. She lifted the heavy silverware with a careful touch, her fingertips intrigued by the splendor of the carved pattern.

Roan watched her, his eyes narrowed as he noted the movement of her hands. That she was unfamiliar with fine linen tablecloths and silver tableware was not a surprise to him. Her easy acceptance of their surroundings was, and yet he would have expected no less of her. Though raised in the rough-and-tumble world of horses and men, she'd somehow retained a feminine grace that served her well tonight.

He'd admired her skills for weeks—her abilities with the horses she loved, her adaptability to the life on the trail they'd traveled. Now he caught another glimpse of the woman she'd been concealing beneath her frumpy clothing and bristling demeanor.

His Katherine was a lady. There was no doubt about it. Did it come from the mother she scarcely remembered, or had Charlie held the seeds of gentility somewhere in his rough makeup? Perhaps it was her own determination, her own stalwart sense of self that allowed her to put on the gentle airs of a lady as easily as she had donned the dress he'd provided for her to wear.

No matter, she fit as well into this room of genteel men and women as if she'd been raised in the finest drawing rooms of the East. That her fingernails were short, her hands bore calluses and her feet were more accustomed to boots than the shoes she wore was of little matter. What counted was the grace and dignity she displayed, even as she ate with delicate enthusiasm. He found his mouth curling in a smile, observing her as she chewed and swallowed, watching the movements of her hands and the delight she displayed in her surroundings.

It was almost a letdown when the meal was over, when they'd replaced their napkins on the snowy tablecloth and had, by mutual, unspoken consent, deigned to leave the table.

Once more, Roan followed her as she made her way through the maze of tables. He watched her with vigilant eyes, his stern countenance a warning to the admiring men who dared to cast their gaze in her direction. And then, he moved behind her, up the staircase, down the narrow hallway, past the flickering lamps that lit their way to the door of their room.

And within that room, he fulfilled his fantasy, removing her dress, undoing the ties of her petticoat and sliding the leather shoes from her feet. In silence, he came to her, his hands as gentle as his eagerness would allow. With hushed murmurs, she accepted his attentions, bending and swaying to his every urging. And with a tenderness of touch he fought to maintain, he wooed her. Stifling the eagerness that cried to be spent upon her slender form, he worshiped her with careful caresses and passionate words.

She blossomed beneath his attentions, her flesh responding to the care he lavished upon every inch. From the top of her head to the soles of her feet, he imprinted his touch, the warmth of his desire, the heat of his harnessed needs. He pleasured her, courting her with all of the skill within him ... until she writhed in his arms, her whispered words a pleading for his possession.

And with a gentleness that knew no limits, he took her, only in the final moments of their loving allowing himself the luxury of unbounded passion.

Chapter Sixteen

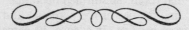

"Sure as hell got all fancied up since the last time I saw her." Abel Sloan slouched in the shadows, his gaze fastened on the woman at the rail of the boat just a few yards distant. Just moments ago, he'd watched as Devereaux loaded the string of horses on board, eyeing with greed the sight of beautiful horseflesh just out of reach.

"I coulda had one of them mares," he muttered beneath his breath. "Hell, I coulda had all of 'em, given half a chance." Magnifying it in his mind, he recalled the gunplay around the campfire. "All that damn smoke got in my eyes. Couldn't get a clear shot."

Now he shifted, easing his way beneath the eaves of the warehouse, careful to shade his features with the wide brim of his hat. The blue-clad female had turned her back, making her way down the lower deck to pause near the stern of the paddle wheeler. Sloan glanced at her briefly, certain she'd paid him no attention. His steps became less furtive, his manner more aggressive as he neared the gangplank and made his way aboard, offering his ticket to the man waiting there.

"Goin' down to Memphis, are you?" Giving him a casual glance, the boatman waved him on board, obviously unimpressed by the sorry condition of the new passenger.

Sloan hurried toward the bow of the boat, unwilling to expose himself to the scrutiny of the woman he watched. She was still watching as her man fussed with his horses back at the stern. They'd probably be heading for their dinner as soon as the boat left the landing, he figured. Seeing to those horses would sure be his concern if they wore his brand. His mouth almost watered as he remembered the sleek lines of the mares.

A man could set himself up right well with a bunch like that in his corral. They'd bring a pretty penny if I was to sell 'em outright. His eyes lit with a speculative gleam as he considered the future he planned for himself.

Not only did the man called Devereaux owe him plenty for shooting up the gang he'd been part of for over a year, he'd also made away with all of the booty the bunch had managed to snag from the pair's saddlebags—and then some.

"Damn lucky I was to even find my boots," Sloan grumbled aloud, remembering the roundabout return he'd taken to the campfire. Barefoot and without a mount, he'd surveyed the ruin of a year's work, at the same time developing a healthy portion of hatred for the man called Devereaux and his woman. He'd managed to run down a horse and equip himself from the motley assortment of belongings lying about the campfire, before setting out for the river.

"Sure never thought I'd lay eyes on 'em again," he said beneath his breath. Slouching on a wooden bench, his hands hanging between his thighs, he scanned the other passengers with furtive interest. Now he just had to stay out of Devereaux's way till he made his move.

"I hear tell the food's real good." Roan, stripped to the waist, peered at himself in the small mirror, his hands busy at the chore of removing his whiskers.

Katherine sat on the bunk behind him, swinging a foot impatiently as she watched his endeavors. "It'll all be gone before we get there," she said pointedly.

His eyes crinkled at the edges as he fought back a grin. Wouldn't do to get too cheerful while he was working on his throat, he decided. He leaned forward after a moment, splashing his face in the basin and wiping it on the small towel provided.

"I'll make sure you get enough to eat, Katherine." His gaze found her over the edge of the cloth he used. She'd changed into the other dress he'd bought her, a deep shade of maroon with white touches at the collar. It fit her well, hugging her narrow waist, and he complimented himself on the choice.

"What's the matter? Do I have dirt on my face or something?"

"Nope. I was just admirin' your getup. You look good in that color. I noticed it fits you pretty snug around the middle. And above—there where—"

Her head dropped forward and she frowned, her eyes wary as she examined the bodice of the dress. "I didn't think it was too tight," she exclaimed indignantly. Her fingers tugged at the fabric outlining her bosom, vainly attempting to loosen it.

Roan reached her in one easy step. His hands covered hers and stilled their movement even as his head ducked to allow his mouth access to her face. She looked up at him, still perturbed by his comment, and he dropped a quick kiss on the end of her nose. She wrinkled it and shook her head, as if she would brush aside his caress.

"Roan?" It was a demand for confirmation. "It's not really too tight, is it?"

He shook his head. "Naw. It just fits nice and snug, the way I wanted it to. Now the only problem will be to keep every other man on board from lookin' at what belongs to me."

Her blush was expected and he relished it with good humor, even as she denied his worry.

"There's not a man on this boat who'll be taking a second look at me. Not when they get a good look at the women I saw when I came on board." She pursed her mouth as she recalled three young females, all gussied up with fancy dresses and ribbons tied in their hair.

"They're performers, honey. They give shows at night and keep the passengers entertained." He brushed at a speck of dust on her shoulder and allowed his hand to rest at the nape of her neck as he spoke. "Not one of 'em holds a candle to you, sweetheart. You're a lady from stem to stern, and when all's said and done, that's what a man's lookin' for."

Her glance was skeptical, delivered with a lifted eyebrow as she murmured a delicately derisive snort. "Don't tell me you've never given one of those performers a second look, Devereaux."

He shrugged, dropping his hand, tucking his shirt into place and fastening his pants once more. "Not today. Not the way you mean, anyway," he told her bluntly. "You're enough woman for me, Kate. I don't need to look any farther if I want to see a good-lookin' female."

Her glance was measuring as she stepped closer, her fingers reaching to busy themselves with the top buttons of his shirt. In the confines of the room, they were bound to stumble over each other during the next days, she'd already decided. Might as well take advantage of the close quarters and let him know in no uncertain terms how much she appreciated his words of flattery. Her hands spread against his broad chest as he fit his fingers around her waist. And then he waited, as if he knew what was to come.

She rose up on her toes to reach his face, her mouth seeking the warmth of his, parting in anticipation of the meeting of their lips. Roan let her have her way, holding back the need to crush her against his body. It was the first time she'd taken the lead since the night on the trail when she'd dropped the barriers of her inhibitions and claimed him as her own. His hands firm against her, he absorbed the slender length of her as she leaned into his strength. He breathed deeply of the sweet scent rising from her body, allowing her the liberties she sought, his lips softening as she brushed them with slow movements, her mouth damp and plush.

It was almost too much, Roan decided. Katherine could turn him on faster than any woman he'd ever taken a fancy to and that was for sure. His hands tightened around her waist and he grunted a soft command against her lips.

"You better stop now or forget about dinner."

She settled back down on her heels and shielded her eyes with dark lashes. "You really do like me, don't you, Roan Devereaux?"

His chuckle was more than humorous. Dark and filled with sensual promise, it pleased her, and she smiled in return. He bent low to whisper in her ear, and the words earned him a look of disbelief.

"I don't believe you ought to make promises you can't possibly keep," she said with primly enunciated words, careful to move back from his embrace. She turned to the door, her hand on the brass handle.

"That's one promise I'll personally guarantee, Mrs. Devereaux." She hesitated for only a moment before she opened the door to escape the confines of the stateroom, smiling as she contemplated his words.

The evening sun cast a golden glow on the muddy water of the Mississippi. "Sure is pretty for a dirty brown river," Roan observed. "Leastways at sunset."

Katherine peered beyond him. "A river's a river, far as I can tell. I'd just as soon be on a horse, riding along that trail over there." Her eyes turned longingly to the tree-lined bank. "How long are we going to be on this boat anyway, Roan?"

"Don't fret, Katherine. Three, maybe four days should get us to Vicksburg."

"That soon?" Katherine's voice rose in surprise. "I'll venture to say we'd have been on the trail another week or so at least. Three or four days I can probably handle."

"We're makin' good speed, even with this river meanderin' back and forth the way it does. Probably coverin' seven or eight miles an hour." He cast a sidelong look at her from his vantage point at the rail. One foot propped on a small crate, he leaned nonchalantly against the wooden railing while Katherine stood in the shade of the deck overhang.

She peered past him at the white water splashing from the paddle wheel, where it mixed and blended with the glittering golden reflection of the setting sun. Her swallow of determination was almost audible. "When will we dock somewhere?"

"You feelin' puny, Kate?" His brow furrowed as he considered the stiffness of her posture, her hesitation to approach the rail.

She shook her head quickly. "No, not really. I just appreciate the river more from a different angle. Preferably from the bank. I've never been real thrilled about getting into water over my head, Devereaux."

"You can swim, can't you?"

She nodded. "Lawson made sure of that when I was about five or six. Threw me in a pond and laughed when I swallowed half the water in it before I managed to get to the shallow part." Her smile was tremulous, and she blinked at a suspicion of moisture behind her eyelids. "He said I'd thank him one day—but I never did."

"Well, he's got my thanks," Roan declared. "I'd sure as hell hate to be stuck with givin' you swimmin' lessons at this late date. That's somethin' better learned when you're still a tadpole."

His eyes were keen on her face, sweeping her features with an all-encompassing look. His final teasing remark had served to banish the mood of melancholy at least. Now she wore an indignant frown, her glare turned in his direction.

"I'd be willing to match my skills with yours whenever you say, Mr. Devereaux. I'll beat you at shooting and riding and maybe even swimming any day of the week. You won't be needing to give me lessons anytime soon."

His voice was smooth as butter from the churn as he acknowledged her claim, establishing one of his own at the same time. "Maybe so, Mrs. Devereaux. But I think I've managed to teach you a thing or two lately." His eyes lit with triumph as he heard the small gasp of air she inhaled.

"Speechless, ma'am?" He slid his foot from the crate and sauntered to where she stood, stopping just inches from her side. One long finger slipped beneath her chin, and he turned her face to meet his gaze. His voice sank to a whisper, audible only to her, and he leaned just a bit closer as he spoke.

"You're givin' me dirty eyes, sweetheart, and takin' deep breaths till I can't hardly keep my hands to myself, what with watchin' your bosom and admirin' the blue sparks flyin' in my direction."

"Try your very best, Devereaux. We've got us an audience, and I'm not much for putting on a display in public." She turned from his touch and sauntered down the deck toward the stairway leading to the cabin area.

His look was guarded as he glanced toward the stern, where several roughly dressed men sat on bales and crates. They averted their eyes at his look of warning, and one turned his back to lean negligently against the wall of the lower deck. Roan's gaze narrowed, focusing on the slump-shouldered man. But the sound of Katherine's voice from the top of the stairs broke into his thoughts.

"Are you coming? Or shall I go on without you?" Behind her the lights of the cabin where the evening's entertainment was about to begin had been lit. She stood in the waning light, the finely sculptured lines of her face enhanced by the gleam of the lanterns. His heart quickened as he gazed his fill.

"Roan?" She was sultry, a new quality she'd acquired in the past few days. She'd been appealing before, but the addition of dresses, petticoats and finely textured undergarments had revealed a new facet of this woman to him. As though the feminine clothing had performed some sort of metamorphosis, she had emerged from the flannel shirts and denim pants with all flags flying. No doubt she could as easily become the campsite companion he'd set out with, take away the dresses and doodads. But for now, he delighted in the rarity of Katherine as a lady.

A lady who was waiting for him with toes tapping impatiently.

He grinned and took the stairs two at a time, arriving at her side in seconds. "Hear that fiddle, Kate? That's a call to action if I ever heard one. I'll bet the cabin's all set for the show."

Her eyes lit with anticipation and her voice became a murmur, filled with repressed excitement. "I've never seen a riverboat show, Roan."

"Well, this isn't really what you're thinkin', honey. Not a full-fledged entertainment. Just a couple of girls, all dressed up and kickin' their heels a little. They have to keep it nice and clean for the ladies on board."

She shook her head impatiently. "It might not be much to you, but I've never seen real performers before. The only women I've heard sing were in saloons and they probably were more talented doing other things."

He chuckled and gripped her elbow, ushering her into the main cabin, where tables had been cleared since suppertime and now awaited the arrival of the upper-deck passengers for the evening's entertainment. "These ladies might earn a little money on the side, too, sweetheart." He bent lower to whisper against her ear. "Besides, what do you know about the other things those saloon ladies did for a living?"

She cast him a glance from beneath lowered lids. "I've been finding out lately, haven't I?" Lowering herself into a wooden chair, she watched as Roan settled back next to her, his feet crossed at the ankles, hat tipped back and grin well in place.

Her face sobered. "Roan...how can they do that? I mean, with one man after another?" Engraved on her memory was the pure intimacy of the acts of marriage she had explored with this man. That another man should touch her or look at her as he had was beyond her comprehension. She shivered and her eyes were vulnerable as she lifted her gaze to meet his.

The smile curving his lips grew tender and he reached to clasp her fingers within his wide palm. "Kate, there's no way to compare what you've been doin' with me to what you're talkin' about. There's women who find themselves with nowhere to go and nobody to look after them. Some of 'em end up with a handful of nothin', instead of bein' dealt four aces. I reckon they just do the best they can."

Her eyes grew dark, and she squeezed his hand. "I couldn't."

"No, I don't believe you could, Katherine. You'd scrounge and scrape and make do somehow, if you had to eat dirt. You've got gumption, and that's the truth." He scooted his chair closer to her and draped one long arm around her. "You belong to me, Kate. You got any idea how proud that makes me feel?"

Her eyes widened at his words. "Why I declare, Mr. Devereaux. You are becoming more of a Southern gentleman with every mile this boat travels." she teased. "I don't mind belonging to a gentleman tonight, I suppose."

"I used to be a Southern gentleman," he told her. "Suppose you can settle for a gamblin' cowhand for tonight?"

She frowned her brow. "The cowhand I can figure. Where'd the gambler come from?"

"After the show, I'm goin' to escort you to the cabin and spend an hour or so dealin' a hand of cards."

She sat up straight in the chair. "I can't watch? You're going to tuck me in bed and sit around and play cards?"

"Don't get all huffy, Katherine," he said quietly. "It's not called playin' cards when there's money involved. Then it gets to be serious gamblin', and I don't need you lookin' over my shoulder. Matter of fact, I'd feel better if I knew you were locked up in our cabin, safe and sound."

Only a burst of music from the two men on the stage stopped her from the quick words she yearned to speak, and she swallowed them as music filled the cabin. The fiddle twanged in time with the piano, and the agile fingers of the pair began to play a tune in fine style. Katherine glared at Roan's smiling face, his attention caught by the music and the three garishly dressed women who had appeared on the raised stage at the end of the cabin.

Their gowns were scarlet and royal blue, with sequins and ruffles in abundance, and their hair was piled in curling profusion, falling in ringlets down their backs. They posed and pirouetted in time to the rollicking tune, finally breaking into song. The lyrics were simple, repeated often and sung with vigor, and soon the entire crowd of gathering passengers joined in.

Without a moment's pause, the music swung into another song, and the women onstage went through a series of dance steps, lifting their skirts to expose trim ankles and rounded calves as they circled the small area. The audience clapped with enthusiasm at the final flourish of skirts, then listened with rapt attention as the three took turns singing ballads to their eager public.

For an hour they performed—singing, dancing, telling small singsong jokes that set their audience to laughing with a delight Katherine did not share.

"They're just on the edge of being—" She was lost for a word to describe the nature of the humor she was being exposed to.

"Naughty?" Roan supplied.

She shrugged. "It just isn't as shiny as I thought it would be," she admitted in an undertone. "They look sort of...used up, don't they?"

Roan smiled at her. "You're growin' up, Kate. All the women in the world aren't at one end of the scale or the other. There're those in the middle. Not upstairs doxies, but certainly not ladies like yourself. Just a few steps up or down, whatever the case may be, makin' do with what talent they got."

"It's full dark," Katherine said suddenly, looking through the doorway to where the night sky was barely visible over the upper railing of the boat. The floor beneath her feet vibrated with the muffled engine's rhythm. She sensed a moment's sadness as she thought of the daily routine of the women who had performed, and the innocent joy she'd felt disappeared. "I think I'm ready to go to bed."

"Let's go." Roan rose without hesitation and grasped her arm, leading her to the nearest doorway and out onto the narrow deck. "It's about time for the serious gamblin' to start anyway. Let's get you safe and sound for the night."

"You're determined to do this, aren't you?"

He nodded. "I've spent a lot of hours on riverboats, Kate. Most of them makin' money."

Her mouth opened and she halted abruptly. "You're a gambler?"

He moved her ahead, nudging her with his arm around her waist, catching her as she stumbled. "Only when I know there's money to be made."

"Well, I never—" She walked across the threshold of the cabin and waited while he lit the lamp on the wall. Her skirt billowing around her, she flounced onto the edge of the bunk and watched him.

"We're gonna run low on funds, Kate, and I don't want to hear about your money," he told her, stanching the words she was about to spout in his direction. "Now just behave yourself for a while and wait in here for me."

"What if you don't win?" Her eyes snapped her indignation as she taunted him.

His smile was quick and laden with promise as he tipped his hat and backed out the door. "Don't worry, sweetheart. I never lose."

Chapter Seventeen

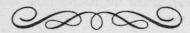

"Can't tell if that's your heart thumpin' or the paddle wheel hittin' the water." His muffled words buried against her breast, Roan voiced his thoughts. Shifting his head just a bit to the left, he grunted contentedly, his mouth opening, allowing his lips to close over a particularly succulent piece of flesh.

"I don't think I'm even speaking to you, Devereaux."

"Hmm... hush, Kate. I'm tryin' to figure this out."

"I know exactly what you're trying to do and you might as well know right now—" Her squeal of surprise and his chuckle of amusement were simultaneous. Sliding up her body to claim her mouth for his own, Roan halted her scolding midway. His arms tucked her snugly against him, and his hands roamed at will down the length of her slender back, settling on the curve of her backside.

"This isn't going to get you anywhere, you know," she grumbled against his mouth.

"Already got me right where I wanted to be." His announcement was smug, his words teasing as he nibbled at her lower lip.

"I have an aversion to gambling."

He sat up, his hair tousled, his brow drawn into a frown of disbelief. "Well, I'll be double damned! Is that what this's all about? You're mad because I won a few hands of poker last night?" Rising from the bunk, he stalked to the small square window on the outer wall of the stateroom. Magnificently naked, his body rippled with the play of muscles, his back sloping from the solid width of his shoulders to the narrow measure of his hips. The length of his thighs, tightly drawn and thick with the strength of a horseman, drew her eyes, and she focused on the scarred expanse above his right knee.

"I've never seen your wound before," she whispered. A tenderness she could not conceal washed the words with a warmth that cleansed his anger.

He turned quickly, attempting to hide the evidence of his injuries and surgery from her sight, and she cried out her objection as he gathered up his pants from the floor.

"No! Don't hide from me, Roan." She moved quickly, crossing the narrow space between them, her arms reaching to hold him. Then he was in her grasp, and her shuddering breath was hot against his chest. She slid like a slender wraith the length of him, her arms and hands swift against his flesh, until she knelt before him, bending to press her mouth against the purpled scars wreathing his thigh. The flesh was mended now, but the pain of the mending was apparent to her and she groaned within herself at the suffering he had experienced.

His hands tugged at her, gripping her shoulders as he murmured her name. "Kate, come on, honey. It's all right. Only gives me a little trouble now and then. Kate!"

But she would not be soothed. Her mouth opened as she touched the most severe scarring with the tip of her tongue. Then, tracing the line of knotted scar tissue where stitches had pulled flesh to cover the gaping wounds, she delivered damp kisses and tender touches of hands and fingers to his leg. Bending almost double before him, she bowed as a supplicant, unaware of the clenched jaw and glittering eyes of the man she had married.

"You've seen it before, Katherine," he said gruffly.

She shook her head, her hair brushing against his knee. "No... only in the moonlight and from a distance. I didn't know—" She clasped his knee between her palms and rubbed the flesh with gentle movements, shaking her head, ignoring the tears that flowed without ceasing. Then with a final brush of her lips, she leaned back, her legs folded beneath her, and looked up to meet his gaze.

"You were hurt dreadfully, weren't you?"

He grasped her hands and lifted her to stand before him, molding her hips beneath his palms, only the fragile fabric of her gown between them. A mocking smile curled his lips as he drew her closer. "I reckon the surgeons did as much damage as the shot they dug out of me. 'Course, by the time they got to me, it was pretty loaded with pus and dead flesh. Your pa did his best, but there's just so much a man can do with no doctorin' skills and nothin' to do it with."

She wiped her eyes with quick swipes of her fingers and cleared her throat, sniffing the tears out of existence. "I'm glad he did what he could for you. He said he owed you for dragging him from the battlefield in Virginia. He told me you saved his life."

"I guess we were even then, Kate. Didn't matter who did what anyhow. We all just did the best we could. By that time we'd begun to wonder what the fightin' was all about anyway." His voice held a tinge of bitterness and she hugged him tightly, as if she would gather to herself the harshness of his memories.

"Did you ever wonder how things happen to be, Roan?" Her voice was muffled against him, and he bent to bury his face in her hair, inhaling the sweet, early morning scent of it.

"Yeah. I've often wondered if Charlie knows. You know, he told me to look him up after the war. Told me he'd have a horse for me. Said he'd train one special."

She laughed, a silent movement of her shoulders and a quiver of her breasts against his stomach. "And you got the special one I'd worked with instead."

"You were pretty mad at me, weren't you, Kate?"

"I guess so. You took her away from me. With a few little whispers and some tugging on the reins, you had her going in circles for you. When you got on her, I almost hoped she'd dump you in the dirt."

He laughed, a sound of muted triumph. "Nah... by the time I got on that sweet little filly's back, she knew we were goin' to be just right together. I just had to sweet-talk her a little and coax her into likin' me."

She lifted her head and eyed him with new knowledge. "Is that what you did with me, Devereaux? Sweet talk and coaxing and whispering promises in my ear?"

He shrugged indifferently, trying without much success to hide the grin fighting to curl his lips. "I'll have to admit, you're one fine filly, Kate. But the sweet talk and the coaxin' weren't just to nudge you into my blankets."

"No?" She waited, willing to be persuaded, hoping for the reassurance of his words of...what? Love, perhaps? No, not Roan Devereaux. He wanted. He might even need. But the words of deeper emotions would not come easily to that wide, mobile mouth. He would give her assurances, tell her how much he was drawn to her curving female flesh. He could make her think she was almost beautiful, in the depths of the night, when his hands made magic against her skin and his mouth gave her pleasure beyond her wildest imaginings.

"No. You're my wife, Katherine. I needed you like a man needs his woman. You drew me like a bee to a honey tree right from the first, and you knew it. You saw me cuttin' my eyes at you every chance I got. I knew I was bound to lay claim to you one way or another if I stuck around."

"Is that why you left?"

He nodded. "I was wantin' you more than was good for either one of us, Kate. But then I couldn't do it. You know damn well I didn't get very far before I turned around and came back."

"A good thing you did, too. Did I ever thank you?"

He shook his head. "Nope, never did. I figured gettin' you to marry me was thanks enough. And look what it got me."

He held her away from him and his gaze traveled down the length of her, from the shadowed tips of her lush breasts to the pink toes curling against the wide planks of the cabin floor. Beneath the gown, she felt a flush paint her flesh. She lifted her hands to push against him and felt the curling brush of hair enfold her fingers as they pressed against his broad chest.

Against the soft flesh of her belly, his arousal made itself known, and she caught a breath at the evidence of his need for her. For her. Not for just anyone, but for Katherine Cassidy. No, Katherine Devereaux . . . his wife. She leaned against him, her thoughts of turning away set aside. Later, she could dress and prepare for the day. Later, she could find her way to the cabin where breakfast would be served. Later, she could think about seeing to her mares. For now, there was a man who deserved the assurance of her love. For if he could never tell her the words, it would matter little to her. She would lavish upon him all of the love her heart held, until some of it would surely overflow and take seed within his own being and there be nourished until it bore fruit.

Her hands framed his face and her mouth formed the sounds of love he'd learned to listen for. He bent to meet her lips. For now, he could forget the suspicions festering in his fertile mind. He could ignore the faint pangs of hunger nudging at his stomach. He could even put from his mind the string of horses he must tend to within the hour. Katherine was here, waiting, willing and warm against his hard, rigid frame; and there was nothing in the world more important.

The string of mares and yearlings trailed behind Roan. He looked over his shoulder as he kept his mount to a trot, grinning while he watched the animals tugging and pulling at the restraint of their lead ropes. The side-wheeler had drawn tightly to a bank and dropped the wooden plank from deck to ground. They would only be there for a couple of hours, he'd been warned by the captain, and with those words still ringing in his ears, he'd headed for the edge of the small town where they'd moored.

A grove of trees beckoned from a half mile or so ahead. He quickened the pace of the mare beneath him, anxious to allow the horses an hour of exercise before they were once more tied in place in the stern of the boat. The yearlings were feisty this morning, he thought with a satisfied grin, and he kept check on their frollicking behind him. The packhorse had been left behind, content to stand on three legs and rest in the humid morning air.

Katherine had argued a bit, wanting to come along, but his time was limited, he'd told her, and she'd have to change clothes and saddle up. Besides, she'd been wanting a bath, and the captain had assured him that a tub was available, with two strong deckhands to deliver it to their cabin forthwith. His smile widened as he thought of her pleasure in the warm water and leisurely splashing she was so fond of.

So intent on the yearlings with their scampering about at the end of their lead ropes, he missed the stealthy figure of a man who had been watching him for just such an opportunity for two days. Even now, Abel Sloan slouched on the seat of a wagon he'd rented at the livery stable, clutching the reins and ambling along on his trail as if he were heading for his own spread of land. Only the intent stare from beneath lowered brows gave away the malice he held like a finely honed weapon against the man exercising the small herd of horses beneath the grove of oak trees.

Somehow the bath wasn't nearly as enjoyable as she'd expected. The water was nicely heated, the soap was fragrant, and the cabin was warmed by the morning sun streaming through the small windows on the outside wall. Katherine had peered out anxiously before she climbed into the metal tub, estimating the eye level, should anyone on the riverbank be looking toward the windows. Finally satisfied, assured of privacy, she'd shed her gown and climbed into the warm water, relishing the scent of lilacs as she plied the soapy cloth over her body.

It was quiet. Only the far-off cries of children and the thump-thump of the engine at rest stirred the air. An occasional call from another passenger broke the silence. But the voice Katherine's ear was attuned to was absent, and she moved restlessly within the close quarters of the tub.

"I should have gone with him," she murmured, squeezing the water from the cloth and hanging it over the rolled edge of metal. Her fingers searched out the bar of soap and clutched it firmly, leaning over the side to locate the wrapping paper. She knelt in the water, folding the precious fragrance in the flowered covering that had contained it since the bath in the hotel in St. Maria.

Katherine smiled, remembering the diffident expression on Roan's face as he'd presented her with the soap and the new towel. She rose, rubbing her hair with the thick, soft fabric, her memories filled with the pleasure of his thoughtfulness.

"Decided you could use somethin' a mite softer than that old feed bag you were usin'," he'd said gruffly.

Her smile widened and she shook her head vigorously, the long strands of dark hair flying about her. Her brush was already laid out and she reached for it, bending from the waist to scoop her hair into one hand. With brisk strokes, she eliminated the snarls, then her fingers snaked through the strands, braiding quickly.

Naked, she surveyed the cabin. Roan's neatness had extended to her belongings; her pants and shirts were piled in a tidy stack on a chair, fresh from the hotel laundry in St. Maria. She snatched the topmost pants and reached into her saddlebag for fresh undergarments. Not the fragile beauties Roan had bought to go with her dresses, but the practical cotton drawers she'd made. A camisole top came to hand and she pulled it on, buttoning it quickly, tucking it into the elastic-banded underwear she'd donned. Her slim boy's pants were next and then the flannel shirt.

The mirror across the cabin reflected her slender figure and she blinked as she recognized herself in the almost unfamiliar getup. "Three days dressed like a lady and I'm forgetting what I really look like," she grumbled, tugging her boots in place.

The long braid fell down her back, making a damp line down her spine. She grabbed the hat she'd stashed in her saddlebag and punched it into shape before placing it squarely atop her head. A quick look around assured her of her readiness, and she unlocked the cabin door, pulling it closed behind her. The key turned in the lock and then dropped into the pocket of her pants, her index finger stuffing it all the way to the bottom, lest it work its way out and be lost.

A deckhand approached and nodded, looking her over with unveiled curiosity. "Ma'am? Are you going ashore now? Cap'n says we only got a little better than an hour till we push off." His eyes roamed the length of her, pausing on the slim-fitting boy's clothing she wore, coasting over the fullness of her bottom and down the slender legs.

Katherine tilted her chin and viewed him with narrowed eyes, defying his assessment with one of her own. "Mr. Devereaux has taken my mares out for exercise, and I intend to join him. Can you direct me?"

The deckhand swallowed and bobbed his head. "Yes, ma'am. He headed south of town. Shouldn't have gone too far, I don't reckon. Cap'n told him to watch the time."

"Thank you." Offering him a cool smile and the back of her head in quick succession, Katherine strolled from the boat. Crossing the patch of water on the plank without looking down at the muddy flow that rocked the boat with a gentle motion, she made the bank and headed at a quick trot for the road running through the small town.

A livery stable stood next to the general store and she peered into the dim interior, squinting to locate a human presence. The scent and sound of horses met her, and she inhaled, pleased with the familiar surroundings.

"Help you, ma'am?" From the shadows a young boy ambled toward her.

"I need a riding horse for about an hour." Her fingers slipped into her front pocket in search of coins and she grimaced as they came up empty. "I haven't any money with me," she apologized. "But the gentleman who just rode out of town with a string of horses is with me and he'll pay you when I bring the horse back."

The boy scratched his head and eyed her skeptically. "I dunno, ma'am. We don't generally do business thataway."

"I'll pay a quarter when I come back," she offered.

He looked at her, taking in the slender form encased in boy's clothing, the damp braid and rumpled hat. His smile broke through the doubting frown and he nodded. "Leave me your boots and I'll let you take the horse."

Katherine bent to tug at her leather boots without hesitation. It wouldn't be the first time she'd ridden barefoot. Probably not the last, either, she thought with a grin.

"I don't need a saddle. Just stick a bit in his mouth and I'll ride anything you've got back there," she told him.

The boy led an undistinguished mare from the rear of the stable, bridle and bit in place, and offered Katherine the reins. He scooped up the boots and placed them on an overturned bucket inside the door.

"Don't fergit ya owe me a quarter when ya come back," he reminded her quickly as she hoisted herself to the broad back of the aging mare.

Her feet wrapped around the mare's ribs and she nudged the animal with her heels. "I won't forget. I'll be back in less than an hour." Urged into a trot, the mare made her way down the road, past a small white church, past a scattering of homes and toward the open country beyond.

Katherine's hand shaded her eyes as she peered into the distance. He couldn't have gone far, not in the half hour or so head start he'd had. The sun was bright and glittered on the harness of a lone horse, probably half a mile down the road. Hitched to a wagon, it stood beneath a small stand of trees.

Katherine's brow furrowed. Roan would have no use of a wagon, surely. Perhaps he'd gone in a different direction. She looked around, squinting against the sunshine, but to no avail. Nowhere did she see a tall man astride a bay mare, nor, for that matter, was there any trace of three yearlings and a pair of mares on a lead rope.

It seemed the grove of trees was the only spot he could have headed for, and she turned the mare she rode in that direction. The animal broke into a slow lope with Katherine's urging, and her scent rose, pungent and ripe.

"That bath was a waste of time," she said aloud. "I'm gonna smell like horse and dust, and Roan spent a quarter on warm water for nothing."

She slowed as she neared the trees, catching sight of a slumped figure on the wagon seat. He'd cast a look in her direction and then back at whatever he watched through the trees, and she narrowed her eyes to make out the face that turned once more in her direction.

With furtive movements, he picked up the reins and slapped them against the back of the horse. The animal lurched in movement and the wagon pulled from beneath a shady tree to wend its way south.

"What's going on?" She whispered beneath her breath, then dug her heels once more into the sides of the mare she rode. Obligingly, the animal broke into a gallop, heading for the shady grove before her. Katherine's heart thumped in an unsteady rhythm as she approached the section of wooded area.

"Roan?" she called out. "Are you there? Roan?"

From within the trees came a whinny, then another, and the horse she rode answered with a call of her own.

"Roan?" Katherine nudged the animal forward, ducking her head as she passed under an overhanging branch. Here, past where the wagon had been sitting only moments ago, she could catch sight of her yearlings, each on a lead, Roan holding the ropes and allowing the gamboling youngsters to circle him. He was in a patch of sunlight in a clearing within the clustered trees. His shirt was off, lying on the ground to one side. His big body was gleaming with sweat, the muscles of his arms flexing as he controlled the playful yearlings with the tremendous strength of his shoulders.

Katherine watched, her mouth dry as she inhaled deep breaths of morning air, her heart still hammering with a combination of apprehension and sudden awareness of the man she'd married. She glanced over her shoulder quickly, hoping to catch sight once more of the wagon, but it was too far away now, rolling into the distance, turning off the road even as she watched.

"Roan?" Her voice was quiet, but his ear was ever attuned to her and he wheeled quickly, holding the ropes over his head as he turned to face her. The yearlings continued their romping, bucking at the end of the lead ropes, shying at the breeze that brought fluttering dust devils to life about their feet. But the man facing her was intent on the woman who rode bareback atop a livery stable mare.

"What are you doing here, Kate? I thought I left you in a bathtub."

"You did. I got out of it." She smiled at him with tremulous lips. That he could affect her so was more than she could fathom. The sight of Roan Devereaux, shirtless, sweaty and, unless she was mistaken, about to take her head off, was about the best thing her eyes had lit on in at least an hour or so. Since the last time she saw him, anyway, she decided.

"I wasted two bits on hot water for you," he told her, frowning in her direction. "Now I'll warrant you smell like a horse that hasn't seen a curry comb in a month of Sundays."

She shrugged. "Probably." Sliding from the mare's back, she approached him, her eyes intent on the frollicking yearlings.

"Stay back." His words were brusque, his hands busy as he gathered up the lead ropes he held, pulling the young horses closer with each twist about his arm. They came reluctantly, slowing their pace, tossing their heads, until they were caught in a circle around him. He led them to a rope he'd strung between two trees and clipped their leads in place, several yards apart.

Then he turned to the woman who watched his every move. His hands tucked into the front pockets of his pants, he approached her. "Couldn't stay away from me?" His brow was still furrowed, his chest was a bed of curling dark hair, and his pants rode low on his hips, leaving him exposed to below his belly button.

It was there her eyes focused. A drop of sweat perched on the edge of that small indentation, and, defying the force of gravity, it hung, swaying as he walked. She felt her tongue thicken in her mouth and her eyes grow heavy-lidded, as if they were too weary to open fully. But there was no need. He stood before her, within reach, and she lifted a trembling finger to trace the line of sweat that flowed from his throat to the middle of his chest, where it was lost in the dark curls. From there it once more slid in small, round drops to pool in the sensitive spot she'd come to appreciate with intimate knowledge.

Her voice was thick with an emotion he tried to recognize. She was enthralled with his belly for some reason, but there was something else about her, some sense of apprehension perhaps, that coated her throat and made her words slow and her tones deepen.

"Kate? What is it? What's got you upset?" His hands reached for her, cupping her shoulders, drawing her against him, his head dipping to nuzzle the lilac scent of her damp hair. He looked over her head, eyes seeking movement behind her, aware of the tensed muscles beneath his fingers.

"What happened? Did you get scared? Was somebody after you?" His questions shot at her rapidly as he held her closer, and he felt the quick shake of her head against his flesh.

"No...nothing, Roan. I just needed to come find you. I don't know why. I was sitting there in that tub, enjoying the warm water, and I decided I should have gone with you." She lifted her head to look into his eyes and the sense of apprehension eased at the tenderness of his gaze. Shaking her head again, she attempted a grin.

"Maybe you're right. I just couldn't stay away from you."

"Somethin' scared you, Kate. You were almost quiverin' under my hands for a minute there."

"There was a man in a wagon watching you," she said unsteadily. "He left when he saw me riding from town, pulled off the road up ahead."

"Where?" Roan set her aside and stalked through the stand of trees to look into the distance. She followed quickly, trotting at his side.

"I don't see him now. Oh—" She pointed at the scattered buildings of the town to the north. "Maybe that's him, there near the livery stable. I can't make out from here if it's the same horse or not."

Roan shrugged. "Don't matter much now, anyway. He's too far away to tell. Probably just caught sight of the horses and stopped to watch." His mouth was tight, his eyes dark as he turned abruptly from her and strode back to where the string of horses cropped grass, tails swishing and ears twitching.

"Damn," he muttered beneath his breath.

She hurried to join him. "Roan? What do you think? Why would somebody sit the other side of those trees and watch you? Maybe it isn't the same man," she said soothingly. She waved her hand in the distance. "He's probably long gone, on his way home."

"Yeah." He unsnapped the lead for the black filly and led her into the clearing, loosening the rope from his hand as he turned, allowing the animal to trot and then lope in a circle around him. The mare shivered in the sunlight, the ripples in her gleaming coat catching his eye. He smiled in pleasure at the grace of her posturing as she lifted her head and nickered softly.

"You don't name your horses, do you, Kate?"

She looked at him in surprise. "No, I don't suppose I do. Not the ones I know I can't keep forever."

"You're gonna keep this one, honey. You'd better come up with a name for her." His hands were deft on the lead rope, wrapping it around his palm and turning with the horse in a slow circle as she slowed her pace and approached him warily, tossing her head as he tugged gently on the rope.

"I'll keep her if I can afford to," Katherine said quietly. "I may have to sell her one of these days, if my money doesn't hold out." She watched as he stroked the mare's gleaming coat, his hands firm but gentle against the slope of her head.

"You'll never have to sell her, Katherine. I'll see to that," he told her gruffly, leading the horse to the line and clipping her lead once more in place. The animal lifted her head and snorted once, tossing her mane, testing the rope that held her. "She's a beauty, all right," he said softly, watching as the mare ducked her nose into the verdant grasses beneath her feet.

"Do we need to get back to the boat?"

"Soon as I let Mama here kick her heels a bit," he said over his shoulder, leading the chestnut mare into the clearing. Once more he went through the same routine, giving the mare her head, turning in a slow circle while she set her own pace. Stretching her long legs into a trot, then a lope, she tucked her head down as her muscles bunched with the quicker gait.

Katherine's lips curved. "Mama." Her eyes were misty as she considered the man who exercised her mare with gentle care. His voice lifted and fell as he spoke to the chestnut mare, nonsense words, cajoling her, urging her.

"All right, that's enough for now, girl," he said finally, pulling her gradually to his side, walking with her, one hand under her jaw as he spoke his praise. Gathering up the long line, he untied it from the trees and led the string of horses to where Katherine waited.

"Here you go, Mrs. Devereaux. Time to get back to the boat before the captain decides to leave without us." Katherine reached for the line and held it, the horses herding together in front of her, her eyes filled with the gleaming beauty of her babies.

"I don' t want to ever sell any of them, Roan," she said softly, aware he could not hear her halfway across the clearing, intent on fetching his own mare.

"Let me take them, Kate." Reaching down from his seat, Roan eased the rope from her fingers and nudged his mare into a trot. The yearlings and mares strung out behind him, and he watched with careful eyes as Katherine once more hoisted herself atop her own mount. She bent forward and scooped up the reins, and the mare plodded into motion, bringing up the rear of the train of horses.

"I owe the boy at the livery stable a quarter," she called out as Roan left the trees and turned toward the small settlement.

"What'd he do? Keep your boots as ransom?" His eyes flicked to her bare feet, hanging down the round sides of the nondescript mare she rode.

"Yes! Matter of fact, he did." Her grin was wide, the sight of Roan with her babies in tow bringing a quick sense of contentment to her troubled mind. His answering smile reassured her.

"I'll settle your debt, Kate. Never fear." But the wary look in his eyes belied the teasing note in his voice, and his gaze was vigilant as they approached the town.

"Slide down off that horse," he told her, halting in front of the livery stable. The young boy came into the sunlight, blinking as his eyes adjusted to the brightness of the noonday sun.

"Brought him back, did you?" he asked with a shy grin, once more taken with the slender woman who rode with a skill he couldn't help but admire.

Katherine nodded. "Where'd you put my boots?"

His hand waved at the doorway. "Right inside. I'll get them for you, ma'am."

Roan flipped a quarter at the youth. "Here's for the use of the mare." The lad caught it midair and nodded his head, then turned to deliver Katherine's boots to her. His appreciative look at her posture as she slid her feet into them did not go unnoticed, and Roan's voice was gruff as he called her name.

"Katherine. Give me your hand." Reaching to her, he lifted her easily to sit across his lap, and his heels pressed against his mare as they headed for the boat.

"Did you see anyone?" Her words were quiet, her eyes scanning the area they passed.

"No." One word, spoken abruptly. But his tension was apparent as his arm tightened around her.

"You're squeezing me." She wiggled beneath his touch.

"Hold still, Mrs. Devereaux. I've got the right to hang on to you. I've got a notion we came up lucky this morning. I won't be so careless next time. You can mark my words."

"You really think—"

He shook his head, and she felt the movement above her own. "I don't know. Just a feeling, I guess. At any rate, I'll keep a sharp eye out."

The water was cool, and a faint scum rode the surface, but Roan stepped into the tub with a sigh of contentment. "Get me a bucket of hot water sent up, will you, Kate?" he asked, closing his eyes and leaning his head back against the curved edge of the tub.

She eyed him doubtfully. His knees were drawn up and his greater size had raised the water level past his waist. "I don't know if you have room in there for a bucketful, but I'll see what I can do."

There was plenty of room, she found out as she poured the hot water down at the foot end of the short tub a few minutes later. Returning the bucket to the deckhand waiting outside the cabin, she smiled her thanks and closed the door. Roan groaned his pleasure as the water rose to cover most of his chest, bending to allow his arms and hands to loll in the depths.

"I'll wash my feet in there when you get finished." Katherine watched from the edge of the bunk, then with a quick movement snatched up the cloth she'd used and approached with soap in hand. "I'll scrub your back for you," she offered, kneeling by the tub and sudsing the cloth.

"You'll make me smell like a damn flower garden." He grumbled the words in a token act of resistance, but his head bent and his shoulders hunched as she scrubbed at the long line of his spine. "I'll give you about fifteen minutes to quit that," he muttered darkly, enjoying the rough cloth and the strong strokes she employed as she rubbed at his muscled back.

"Sit up and I'll do your front, too." Her voice was coaxing and he glanced at her.

"If you think for one minute I'm gonna turn down that offer, you've sure got another think comin'," he told her bluntly. Straightening his spine, he shifted in the short tub, leaning back once more to rest his head on the edge, his chest half-exposed, the rest of him hidden in the clouded water.

"Have at it, lady." It was a growling invitation and she dropped a quick kiss on his parted lips as her hands dipped into the water and began their chore.

"It's almost time for dinner, you know," she teased, her fingers pressing his flesh through the cloth.

"Yeah? Well, they'll save us some. You've got fifteen minutes to get me clean, sweetheart. Think you can manage?"

Her cheeks were rosy as she bent to her task. "I'm new at this." Her tongue was tucked to one side, just the tip showing between her lips as she concentrated on the territory her hands explored.

His sigh was pure contentment as he tilted his head back farther and his eyes closed, concentrating on the pleasure of her touch. "Ah, but you're a fast learner, Katie girl. I've got faith in you, sweetheart."

Chapter Eighteen

Katherine's blue dress gleamed like a jewel amid the dark animals. She was quiet, her murmurs barely audible to the man who watched. As she moved slowly from one to another, her hands and voice paid homage to the mares and yearlings at the stern of the paddle wheeler. The tall black mare drew her attention finally, and she nuzzled her face against the long jaw of the animal.

"You're probably going to drop a foal next year, baby," she whispered. Her hands were firm against the dark coat of the mare, fingers pressing, scratching a bit, delivering their message of affection. Ears twitching almost in time with Katherine's soft crooning, the horse pressed against the woman as if she sought the connection, and relished it.

"Roan's right, you know. You're plenty old enough to be bred. You've got lots of space to carry a foal. And that big old stud was a dandy, you'll have to admit." Katherine chuckled to herself, remembering the virile beauty of the stallion. "Sort of overwhelmed you, didn't he?"

"Nice bunch of horses you got, Mrs. Devereaux."

From behind her, the voice was low and rusty, its owner a lengthening shadow against the straw that littered the deck where she stood. Katherine's breath caught in her throat as a chill made its way down her spine. Her eyes widening, she watched as the sunlight turned to shade at her feet and the shadow crept closer.

She turned, her hand still curved under the jaw of the horse, intent on facing the intruder. He was close, a couple of yards away, near enough for her to smell the unwashed garments he wore, close enough for her to see the grizzly whiskers covering his dark skin.

"What do you want?" She held her ground, unwilling to give way to the sudden shaft of fear piercing her chest. Where was Roan? He'd stopped to talk to the captain after breakfast. Surely he'd be along any minute.

"Just takin' a look at those horses of yours, ma'am." His words were slow, exaggerated, almost as if he would pacify her, calm her apprehension.

It didn't work. "I don't want anyone near my animals. Kindly get out of my way." Katherine was proud of the firm, unwavering tone she'd managed. Chin jutting forward, she waved her hand imperiously, as if she would usher the intruder from her presence.

"My, ain't you the fancy piece in your new getup." With a sneer, he stepped a bit closer. "You didn't look near so ladylike first time I saw you, ma'am. Layin' there with that man of yours all tucked around you. Still don't think it was fair that the rest of us didn't get some of that cuddlin' you looked to be so good at."

"Who are you?" Katherine's words were a frozen whisper as she peered with narrowed eyes at the dirty-faced intruder.

"You owe me, lady," he snarled. "Reckon I'll get the pleasure of your company long enough to get me a taste of your—"

"You filthy scum!" Katherine's mouth curled in disgust and her fingers drew into fists.

"Shut up! Yer too mouthy by a long shot." He stepped closer, and his big fist moved swiftly to fasten in the front of her dress, causing the seams to give way with the force of his grip.

"Roan!"

"Won't do no good to holler for yer man, honey. He's up top, talkin' to the captain. Can't hear you over the engines no way." His free hand settled with force over her mouth, and he dug his fingers into her cheek.

Katherine's stomach churned at the smell of his unwashed flesh beneath her nose, and she shuddered as she recognized the press of his knuckles against her breast. *Where are you, Roan?*

They're puttin' that gangplank down any minute now, lady. And then you and me are takin' this string of horses to shore, and we're gonna ride off." He shook her, his fingers tearing the fine material of her dress. "Got that?"

She shook her head, no easy task with his hand gripping her so tightly, twisting her face with his grimy fingers.

"If he comes a-lookin' for you, I'll put a bullet in him."

The words were enough to still her struggle. Roan wouldn't be expecting an ambush. Her mind searched frantically. Had he worn his gun this morning? She couldn't remember...she couldn't remember! Inhaling through flared nostrils, she swallowed hard against the sour bile roiling up from her stomach.

"That's better, lady." His fingers relaxed against her breast, and he shoved her backward till she thumped against the far wall of the stall. He slipped his hand to his side, and a gun gleamed dully in his fist. "Put a bridle on this horse."

It was an order. She recognized the futility of arguing and reached for the leather straps and bit she'd only recently begun to use with the black mare. Unused to a rider, barely acquainted with a saddle, the horse would never accept his weight—and Katherine knew it. Her hands shook as she lowered the bridle over the gleaming head, the horse shifting nervously as she scented the unease of her owner.

"It's all right, girl." Her whisper was meant to reassure, and it did the job. The black mare nickered softly and swished her tail, stretching her neck as she felt the bit against her mouth.

The man nudged Katherine with the barrel of his gun. "Get over there." He pointed to the next mare, Katherine's own chestnut beauty. "Bridle that one, too." His words were harsh, his eyes furtive as he scanned the area.

Yesterday, there had been several passengers around every time Katherine or Roan had come down to check on the animals. This morning, the stern was deserted. Probably everyone was getting ready to go ashore. It would be only a short stay, not long enough to take the animals off the boat to exercise them, Roan had said at breakfast.

Katherine's hands moved slowly, fitting the bridle over her mare's ears, snapping it into place with as little speed as she could manage. From the corner of her eye, she caught sight of the revolver once more, its barrel pointed in her direction. At all costs, she must keep it from aiming at Roan. To that end, she'd cooperate with this outlaw for now.

"Now what?" she asked quietly, holding the reins in one hand, turning back to face the stranger.

"I've been followin' you, Mrs. Devereaux. Picked up your trail just before you got to St. Maria. Been watchin' you and yer man."

His whining words of accomplishment rang a bell in her memory. Katherine shook her head, angry at her own blindness. "You were on the wagon yesterday. You're the one who got away."

His grin was evil, his teeth discolored and crooked. "Old Cass turned traitor 'cause of you, lady. Don't know how you managed it, but you sure got him wrapped around your finger in a hurry, didn't you." His mouth drew back in a feral grin. "Too bad I don't have time to sample some of what you handed out to him. Musta been good to set him against the gang fer you."

"He was my brother." She whispered the words. Her face pale in the dim light, she gritted her teeth against the pain of her loss. "He was my brother." Quick tears washed her eyes. Unwanted, they blurred her vision, and she shook her head to dispel the effect.

"He was a fool." Ignoring her distress, Sloan grabbed her wrist and, dragging her behind him, moved to where the string of yearlings were gathered against the far side of the boat.

His voice was guttural, rasping against her ear. "Untie these horses and hitch that other mare on with 'em."

Katherine stepped back, frantic to put space between them. His hand released her, and he snarled an oath at her reluctance. "Do as you're told, lady, or I'll shove you overboard and save myself the trouble of totin' you along."

Her eyes widened. A shudder swept through her slender frame and his grin was triumphant. "Thought that'd get you movin'. Can't imagine you'd want to drown in that muddy water, would you now?"

Katherine refused the gibe, her hands working at the ropes holding her yearlings. "They're tied," she whispered.

"Now, get those reins in your hand and lead those two mares outa here." The gun was unwavering as it pointed in her direction. "I'll be right behind you, lady. If you holler fer that man of yers, I'll put a bullet in him and shove you over the side."

And he would. Deep in her heart of hearts, Katherine believed every threat he'd leveled in her direction. Grasping the reins of the black and her own chestnut mare, she walked slowly from the livestock area in the stern of the boat, heading with even steps toward the gangplank.

Wide enough to hold two horses, the gangplank stretched from the lower deck to the bank. She shuddered, swallowing hard as she considered the water flowing beneath her feet.

"Katherine. Where the hell you goin' with those mares?" From the deck above, Roan's shout was pure irritation, his voice harsh.

Her eyes sought him, blinking against the brilliant sunshine, and her mouth opened with words of warning to spew in his direction. From behind her came a snarl of impatience and the hard pressure of a gun against her spine.

"Shut yer mouth." It was a warning growl and her lips pressed together obediently.

"Damn!" Roan's single curse blistered the air and she closed her eyes at the anguish visible on his face. "Take the horses and get. Leave the woman." His snarling words reached her ears with the force of a tempest.

Behind her, Sloan laughed, a triumphant sound, accompanied by the nudging of his gun as he urged her forward. "Too late, Devereaux," he taunted. "You shoulda been payin' attention to yer woman instead of jawin' with the captain. Now you get to watch us ride off together."

"Not likely," Roan retorted. Frozen in place, he'd already decided using his own weapon was not an option. Katherine was too close to her captor. And then it became a moot point as Sloan shouted out an order.

"Throw yer gun down here, Devereaux." His eyes gleamed with vicious intent as he watched the tall man on the deck above. "Either that or I shoot yer woman. What'll it be?"

Slowly, Roan slid his revolver from the holster and dropped it to the deck below. His hands gripped the rail once more and he watched through narrowed eyes as Sloan nudged Katherine onto the gangplank.

"Get on that horse." Sloan's head nodded to Katherine as he pushed her toward her mare. With no saddle and with skirts hampering her agility, she floundered for a moment, one hand grasping the mane of the chestnut. "Damn, I'll shove you overboard in a minute. Let that man of yours go after you."

"No!" Katherine's denial was frantic. The thought of being swallowed up by the murky water sent a chill of despair through her body.

"Can't swim? Ain't that a pity!" His mockery brought her around, and a glare of anger flashed from the depths of her eyes as she faced him.

"I need to cross the gangplank and get on with the help of a bale or crate or something. If you push me over the side to drown, you'll have Roan Devereaux on your neck so fast you'll never know what hit you."

His eyes squinted at her knowingly. "You may be right, lady. Get movin' then." Walking between the mares, they crossed the wooden bridge, the four horses strung out behind them. Above, Roan watched, his gaze unwavering as he clenched his teeth, waiting his chance. The gun was firm against Katherine's back and he couldn't risk any movement that might spur the outlaw into action.

Passengers had halted all around him. Several men on the dock were enthralled by the drama they'd stumbled upon, none of them eager to interfere. It didn't pay to stick your nose in another man's business along the waterfront.

The yearlings milled about, excited by the commotion, unused to the scent of the stranger in their midst. Roan's gaze focused on the blue dress and the woman within its folds. Surrounded by horses—she looked small, fragile almost—and his heart thumped against his chest as he considered the odds of her situation. His hands tightened on the rail, his body tensing as he gauged the distance to the deck below.

Sloan grabbed at the reins in Katherine's hand. "I reckon you'll be more good to me in the river than on that horse, now that I think about it," he growled against her ear. His fingers were tight about her arm as he twisted it with cruel strength, shoving her to the edge of the bank.

Roan moved with instinctive grace. He cleared the rail, landing on the balls of his feet on the lower deck, one hand reaching for the knife inside his boot. As Katherine hit the water, the knife left his hand.

Sloan felt the blade pierce his back. Clutching at her mane, he dragged himself atop the black mare. She danced sideways, snorting and rearing at the unexpected weight. Sprawled across her back, Sloan struggled against the pain, wheezing to catch a breath, frantic to seat himself upright. The mare's shrill whinny was loud in the morning air. Her neck arched and she bucked once, scattering the yearlings. Without a sound, Sloan slid from her back to sprawl on the grassy bank, blood flowing from his mouth.

Roan's feet hit the gangplank, his eyes searching the water. From several yards downstream, Katherine's head broke the surface. She sputtered and shook her head, her arms and hands moving to hold herself afloat.

"You okay, honey?" Roan's long steps carried him to the bank where several men had been spurred into action by the sight of Katherine's struggle. One tossed a rope to her, and it floated just beyond her grasp. She reached out, her fingers snagging it with ease.

Her eyes sought Roan, and she shoved long strands of wet hair from her face. Wrapping the rope around her wrist, she pulled herself closer to the men who leaned to help. Eager hands grasped her, lifting her from the water.

Katherine plucked at the wet dress, pulling it from her legs. Her teeth chattering, her legs trembling, she shivered in the sunlight. "Am I all right? No, I'm not all right!"

"Get that mare!" Roan's shout brought Katherine's head erect, and she abandoned her efforts to put herself in order. The black mare was trotting down the riverbank, shivering and tossing her head. His hands full calming the string of horses and holding firmly to Katherine's chestnut mare, Roan watched as two men approached the black horse. Her reins dragging in the dust, she was an easy target, and within seconds, she was captured.

Katherine drew a deep breath, but it wasn't enough. Her vision blurred and she faltered, aware only of blinding sunlight and the voices around her. As her legs trembled beneath her, she felt a firm hand grip her waist. With ease, she was lifted and carried, her slender body held tightly.

"Roan?" It was a trembling whisper.

"Yeah, I've got you, Kate. You're all right."

"I'm telling you, I did not faint." Steam rising around her, Katherine scrunched down into the bathtub Roan had helped drag into their stateroom.

His eyes lit with amusement. If Katherine could argue, she was well on her way to recovery. "Well, honey, if I'd a known that, I wouldn't have gotten all wet, luggin' you in here."

She sniffed and rubbed at her nose with the back of her hand. "I could have walked. I just got a little dizzy for a minute." She bent her head, scooping the trailing length of her hair into one hand and swishing it through the hot water. "Hand me that soap, would you, please?"

Stripped to the waist, Roan knelt by the tub. "I'll do better than that. I'll wash it for you."

Her eyes closed and she sighed with anticipation. "Reckon I could handle that. Besides, you owe me, Devereaux."

His brow rose as he bent to the task he'd assumed, his big hands making suds in her dark hair. "How do you figure that?" Gentle against her scalp, he rubbed the residue of the river from the long strands.

She hid her smile, burying her face against her knees. "I could have drowned, and all you cared about was the horses. You left it to strangers to pull me out of the water."

He tangled his fingers in her hair and pulled her head up, leaning to breathe his words against her mouth. "If I'd let anything happen to those babies of yours, I'd never have heard the end of it, lady. Anyway, I asked you if you were okay.''

She blinked at him, her eyes tearing from the soap.

He shook his head in disbelief. ''Don't you dare cry, Katherine, you hear me?''

''I'm not! You've got soap in my eyes.''

He frowned at her, one hand lifting the cloth to splash clear water across her forehead. ''Mad at me, Kate?''

She took the cloth from him and squeezed it out, washing her face quickly, then holding the cloth to her burning eyes. His hands turned gentle as he rubbed her hair, waiting for her to speak.

''Duck your head, so I can rinse the soap out,'' he told her after a few moments. She complied, lowering herself to swish her hair in the water. ''You all clean yet?'' He scanned the long locks with a critical eye.

She nodded, her flesh warming nicely from the hot water.

''Then raise up here, and I'll rinse your hair with this bucket.'' He grasped her elbow and lifted her. She knelt obligingly and he poured the warm stream through her hair. Her fingers working the soap from the long strands, she sighed her pleasure, relishing the slow drizzle of warm water over her head and shoulders.

He leaned close, and his warm breath brought chills to her skin as he repeated his question. ''You mad at me, Kate?'' It was a silky whisper, meant to entice.

Her head turned, and her look was pained, as though she hurt for him. ''You killed him, didn't you?''

''Yeah, I did.'' His mouth tightened and his eyes were dark and hooded. ''It wasn't the horses, Kate. We coulda lived without them. But I don't want to ever be as scared as I was when I saw that gun in your back. He could have killed you, honey. And I don't want to even think about life without you.''

Her arms rose to encircle his neck and she drew him closer, her mouth seeking his. "I was never mad, Roan. I knew you wouldn't let me drown. Now, if you'd let anything happen to my horses, I'd have been after your hide." The words were whispered against his lips, and she laughed as he grunted his disbelief.

His hands grasped her waist, and he lifted her to her feet and over the side of the tub to stand before him. Still kneeling, he wrapped her in the towel and dried her with long, steady strokes. His hands were tender, gentle against her skin, his eyes feasting on the feminine flesh he cared for with a lavish touch. He patted carefully at her breasts, his eyes narrowing on the reddened area that had known the touch of Sloan's hand.

His voice was guttural, anger roughening the words he spoke. "I could kill him again for hurting you. I'm sorry, Katherine. I didn't look out for you the way I should've."

Her smile was warm, teasing and welcome to his anguished gaze. "I like having you on your knees, Devereaux," she told him, her whisper husky and inviting. Her hands slid from his shoulders to his back and she clasped him to her, bending to press her cheek against the top of his head. "I'm chilled again. Do you think you could get me warm?"

It was an invitation he would have been a fool to resist. And no one had ever called Roan Devereaux a fool.

Chapter Nineteen

Riding astride in a dress was not her first choice, but Katherine was determined not to meet her husband's family clothed in a pair of britches and a boy's flannel shirt. She fretted, tugging the fabric down until only her ankles showed, thankful for the fullness of the skirt. Lifting her right hand, she patted her hair once more, tucking a stray strand behind her ear.

"You look fine." From beside her, Roan's reassuring words were small comfort.

"I'd feel better if we'd gotten here after dark. Getting off this horse is going to expose a whole lot of me," she grumbled.

"Ridin' up to a dark house isn't too healthy, honey. You don't want a shotgun pointin' our way, do you?"

She slanted a look in his direction. "You'd know all about that, wouldn't you?"

He refused to swallow the bait, and his shrug was genial. "Just up ahead, around that bend in the road, we should be able to see the house."

Katherine stood in her stirrups and leaned forward. Her eyes glistened a bit as she considered what this confrontation would mean to the man she'd married. Pray God they would welcome him with open arms. Her head bowed for a second as the petition wended its way through her mind.

A dog barked directly ahead, and from farther away, another joined it. Katherine's heart beat faster as they rounded the bend in the narrow road. Before her was a plantation house, in need of repair, but still standing and showing no outward sign of damage. The front door opened and a man stepped out onto the long porch, hesitating as he spotted the approaching riders. Then, one hand lifted to shade his eyes, he moved closer to the steps.

His piercing gaze rested on Roan, and as if he considered the tall, silent man to be of little consequence, he looked at the woman beside him. Dark beneath bushy eyebrows, his eyes took Katherine's measure, and his head nodded in an almost imperceptible movement. Looking beyond her, he assessed the string of horses in her wake. Dismissing the packhorse with a derisive glance, he took stock of the yearlings, his eyes narrowing as he caught sight of the black mare bringing up the end of the string.

Roan was immobile in his saddle, back straight, reins held in an easy grip. A sardonic smile twisted his mouth as he noted the older man's inability to hide his interest in Katherine's horses. LeRoy Devereaux had never been able to resist a beautiful filly.

"If you're interested in sellin' those animals, I just might be interested in the black filly." Drawled in the fashion of a Louisiana plantation owner, the words were directed at Roan. LeRoy Devereaux had just extended a truce of sorts.

Roan shook his head. "Sorry about that. The horses aren't mine to sell. They belong to my wife."

The dark eyes narrowed and rested once more on Katherine. "You married to him?"

She glanced at Roan, rigid and ungiving as he waited beside her. Her gaze returned once more to the man facing her. "My name is Katherine Devereaux. The horses are mine. But they're not for sale."

LeRoy's shoulders lifted in an expressive movement. "We'll see. Maybe I can change your mind."

"Maybe you're in for a surprise," Roan offered. "Kate's not one to give up what belongs to her. Hell, she wouldn't let 'em out of her sight all the way from Illinois."

"You've had a long ride. Were you planning on coming in?"

"Yeah, I reckon we could do that," Roan allowed. Dismounting with an ease Katherine envied, he untied the lead rope from his saddle horn and faced his father once more. "You got any hands livin' here?"

"Yep. In fact, Jethro is headin' this way right now. Maybe you'd let him take those horses and put them up."

Roan's eyes warmed as he watched the husky, dark-skinned man approaching from the barn. Snatching his shapeless hat from his head, he headed directly for the tall visitor.

"I knew that was you, Mr. Roan. When I saw you a'sittin' on that horse, I knew." His grin was wide, and his hand was extended.

Roan accepted it with pleasure. "I didn't expect to see you here. Thought you'd have headed out, after the war and all."

Jethro cast a quick look at the man on the porch. "Yore pa and me come to an agreement," he said in a low, rumbling tone.

"Can you put those horses up in the stable, Jethro?" LeRoy's voice boomed the query.

"Yassah, I sure can." Jethro nodded his head quickly and took the lead rope from Roan. "Want your mares taken care of, too?" His words were directed at Roan, but his eyes were on the chestnut animal Katherine rode. "Sure is a pretty lady," he said respectfully.

"The mare or my wife?" Roan's voice was amused.

Jethro looked at him askance. "I wouldn't mean no disrespect to your woman, Mr. Roan. You know better'n that." His grin reappeared quickly, and his voice lowered. "They's both mighty good-lookin', though."

Roan stepped to Katherine's side, and his hands lifted her from the saddle, tight about her waist as he swept her from the horse. Holding her before him, he clasped her firmly, sensing the weariness she was trying to hide.

"You all right, Kate?" She was wrinkled a bit around the edges, but she stood erect now, and unless he missed his guess, she was good for whatever came next.

Katherine's hands brushed at her skirts and she nodded at Roan. "I'm fine. I could do with a drink of water, though."

LeRoy watched from the veranda, and his eyes were piercing in their scrutiny. "I could offer you some tea, ma'am."

Katherine inclined her head in a graceful gesture, almost that of a queen accepting her just due. "That would be fine." Now where the hell had she learned that sort of thing? Roan wondered, watching with barely concealed amazement as his wife approached the wide step leading to the verandah. His father met her there and extended a hand. That Katherine's own fingers were callused, her flesh tanned to a golden brown and her hair beginning to escape its confinement appeared to matter not at all to the old man.

He led her onto the porch and toward the door, Roan following. Behind him Roan heard Jethro's low chuckle and cast him a look of inquiry.

"Sure am glad you're home, Mr. Roan," the dark man said, his grin wide as he led the horses away.

Roan stepped onto the wide boards of the covered veranda and shook his head. Kate seemed to be in control here, and he'd be damned if he was going to break up her party. Cool as a cucumber she was, nodding and smiling at his father like she owned the place.

"You comin', Roan?" LeRoy held the screened door open for Katherine and looked back at his son.

From within the house a woman's voice called out. Then the slender form of his mother filled the doorway, and she spoke again. "Well, well! Valderone! I declare, I thought I heard your daddy sayin' your name."

Roan took several quick steps and held out his hands. His mother hesitated only a moment, then reached out and clasped his fingers, her pale skin a contrast to his tanned flesh.

"We'd about given up hearin' from you again," she said. Her eyes swept his tall form, hesitating for a moment on his leg before they rose once more to meet his gaze.

"I wasn't sure I'd be welcome." It was a blunt statement.

Her shoulders lifted in a delicate shrug. "You're heir to River Bend, Valderone. You've made some poor choices, to my way of thinkin', but that won't keep you from bein' your father's son. This is your home."

Roan's eyes darkened. "I didn't get the feelin' you were gonna welcome me with open arms, Mama. My last letter from you wasn't too lovin'. Seemed like a good idea to make myself scarce around here."

Her shrug was deliberate. "Well, you're here now. Might as well come on in and we'll—"

"Mama, I've brought my wife to meet you."

Letitia Devereaux's gaze moved to where Katherine stood, then her eyes sought those of her son once more. "You're married?"

"This is my wife, Katherine." He stepped back to her side, his arm sliding behind her, his palm warm against her back, and Katherine was suddenly grateful for the unspoken message it implied.

She smiled and inclined her head. "Mrs. Devereaux. I'm pleased to make your acquaintance."

Letitia's brow furrowed. "You're from up north?"

"She's a Yankee, Mama." It was plain and simple. If they couldn't accept Kate right off the bat, he'd head out before they stepped foot inside the house.

Letitia's smile was strained, but she buoyed it with a restrained wave of welcome, leading the way through the doorway into the room beyond. "Y'all come on in now. I'll get Susanna to bring some tea."

"A Yankee bride, eh?" LeRoy shook his head. "Guess you can't help what you are. Come along, Miss Katherine. Tell me how you met my son."

"She threatened me with a shotgun," Roan said bluntly.

Katherine had the grace to blush at his words. It was hard enough playing the part of a lady without Roan making things difficult. "I didn't know who he was. He rode onto my place and I—"

"She threatened to shoot me." Roan's accusation was mildly spoken as he lowered himself to sit on a chair before a wide fireplace.

LeRoy waved a hand at him in dismissal. "Let her tell it. Why don't you go on out and help your mama find some refreshments for your wife."

Letitia came through the doorway. "Susanna's comin' directly. Sit still." She took her place in a matching chair and folded her hands in her lap.

"Katherine was just tellin' me how she met Roan, Mother." LeRoy ushered Katherine to a long sofa and urged her to sit down.

"Roan knew my father during the war. In fact, he saved my father's life," Katherine said. "Later on, when Roan was wounded, my father took him to a hospital in Philadelphia. They lost track of each other after that. A couple of months ago, Roan decided to look Charlie up, and found me instead. I was alone. Seemed like a good idea to go to the door with my shotgun."

"Is your father well?" Letitia asked politely.

"He died early this year," Roan put in quickly. "Kate's been on her own a good while."

"Well, she's got you now," LeRoy said, his white hair glistening in the sunlight that entered the windows.

Kate sent a grateful look in his direction, meeting his dark gaze and scanning the stern features. "He favors you, Mr. Devereaux. He has your nose and eyes. You wear the same look."

"Managed to get my temper, too," LeRoy said gruffly. "Always goin' off half-cocked and makin' rash decisions."

Katherine smiled at the pronouncement. "Maybe he's grown up a little in the past few years then. I haven't seen much trace of bad temper, anyway."

"He couldn't have considered too long and hard about marryin' you, Miss Katherine," the older man said.

Roan nodded agreeably. "Probably the smartest move I ever made, to tell the truth."

Katherine blushed and concentrated on the floor, certain that all eyes in the room were focused on her. "He liked my horses."

"So did Evan Gardner, but you didn't marry him," Roan offered. "Not that I'm complainin', mind you."

"Well, you're welcome here," LeRoy said from his end of the sofa, his eyes taking on a glow of welcome as he watched Katherine. He leaned closer and spoke in an undertone. "Who's this Gardner fella?"

Katherine cast Roan a look that should have quelled his mischief. "Just a man from the town near my farm."

"Kate decided she didn't like him near as well as she did me," Roan said mildly. "And I figured she'd be welcome at River Bend as soon as you caught a glimpse of her string of yearlings."

LeRoy glared at his son. "I do admire a nice-lookin' filly, and I don't mind sayin' so. But Miss Katherine's got a welcome of her own here. Isn't that right, Mother?"

Letitia's smile was delicate, her eyes cool as she surveyed her son's wife. Then her gaze went toward the wide archway and she welcomed the dark-skinned woman who carried a tray into their midst.

"Bring it here, Susanna. We'll let Katherine pour the tea." Her slender hand waved at the table sitting before the long sofa.

"Sure hope you got somethin' stronger than hot tea for Roan and me," LeRoy said abruptly.

Susanna nodded quickly. "Brought you in a tall glass of buttermilk."

His sigh was deep and his head shook sadly as LeRoy looked at his son. "Not much to offer. Not like the old days, is it?"

Roan shrugged. "I've got nothing against buttermilk, Pa." Rising, he walked to where Katherine sat and took the seat next to her. "I'll give you a hand with this, Kate." He lifted the napkin covering a plate and sighed deeply. "Looks like Susanna still bakes good bread, Mama. And there's jam tarts, too. I expect we'll manage to tide over till dinnertime."

The bedroom door had barely closed behind them. Katherine giggled, smothering her laughter with her hand, and sat on the edge of the bed. The feather tick gave way beneath her weight and she closed her eyes in pure enjoyment, flopping back to lose herself in the cushioning expanse. Another giggle escaped her and she gazed at Roan, her eyes crinkling with laughter.

"What's so blamed funny?" Busily stripping off the dusty shirt he wore, he paused to glare in her direction.

"Valderone? Valderone?" She giggled again, raising her hands to capture the sound of laughter.

His grin was sheepish. "My mama was fond of French names when we were born. My brother's named Gaeton and my sister is Yvonne. Guess she thought my daddy's ancestors needed to be remembered some way or another."

"Where are they? Your brother and sister?" Katherine's face was suddenly sober. Sitting up, she rose from the bed and presented her back to Roan. His fingers moved to the buttons holding her dress closed and undid them quickly.

"Jethro told me Yvonne left here with a Yankee colonel. He'd made this his headquarters and took a shine to her. Guess that's why it's still in good shape. Jethro said most of the other places between here and the river are pretty bad off."

"She married a Yankee?" Katherine's tone was unbelieving. "No wonder your mother wasn't too happy about me. She's already got one Northerner in the family."

Roan turned Katherine to face him and his hands slid down her back, warm through the layers of fabric she wore. "Mama's gonna have to get used to the idea, I reckon. I'm assumin' Yvonne married the colonel. Jethro didn't say."

"What about your brother?" Katherine slid the unbuttoned dress down the length of her body and leaned against Roan's solid form. Her head turned to rest against his shoulder and she closed her eyes, suddenly weary.

"He left. Got on his horse and rode west, from what Jethro said." Roan's hands swept the length of Katherine's back and pressed her close. His head bent and he nuzzled his nose against her hair. "He was in a Yankee prison, Kate. I guess when he came home, he just couldn't face all the ruin hereabouts. Maybe he thought River Bend could make it without him. I don't know—"

Katherine leaned back and looked at Roan, her eyes wide. "He just abandoned your mother and father. Just walked way?"

Roan's expression was grim. "Appears so."

"Are we staying?" Katherine stepped from the folds of her dress and bent to pick it up. Watching Roan, she approached the washstand and picked up the pitcher to pour water in the flowered bowl.

"Don't know, Kate. Maybe for a while, till spring anyway. I told you I'd take you back to the farm."

She dampened the cloth and rubbed soap over it. Lifting the warmth to her face, she washed, relishing the clean scent and the luxury of warm water. "Think I could have a real bath before we go to bed?" she asked, lashes drooping as she drew the cloth over her throat and around the back of her neck.

"Reckon you could." He watched her with hungry eyes. "You sure make a production out of gettin' clean, lady."

Katherine slanted a look in his direction. "Warm water is a luxury, Roan. I appreciate it. I'd just appreciate it more if I could climb in a whole tub full of it."

"If you let me help, I'll scout up a tub after dinner and see what I can do about hot water."

Her eyes widened at his words. "Dinner! What on earth will I wear to dinner? I just took off my only decent dress."

Roan measured her with narrowed eyes. "Think you might be close to Yvonne's size. Maybe she left something you could wear. I'll find out, soon as I get washed up."

"I could wear my pants," Katherine offered sweetly.

He shook his head. "I'm not sure River Bend is ready for my wife in a pair of britches just yet. You've got them thinkin' you're a lady, Kate. Let's not burst the bubble, yet."

A somber Letitia provided a dress of her own. Garbed in a summery print that almost fit, once the hem had been taken up with wide stitches, Katherine found her way to the dining room. The meal was scant, with only a stewed chicken and more vegetables than meat to offer, but she paid little attention. Watching Roan act the gentleman took her mind from the scarcity of food. Fresh bread and churned butter filled the gap, and she relished the treat, after days of stale biscuits eaten from a saddlebag.

"More stew, Katherine?" Letitia asked.

She shook her head quickly. "No, thank you. It was wonderful."

Susanna stood in the doorway. "We got sweet potato pie, missus."

Letitia nodded. "That will be fine. I believe we're finished now, Susanna."

"Yes, ma'am." Nodding agreeably, she came to the table and began clearing the dinner plates.

Letitia stood and went to the sideboard, removing smaller plates and bringing them to the long table. Returning to the burnished mahogany buffet, she opened a drawer and found forks. "We find ourselves short of help these days," she said to Katherine. "Most of the people from the house left us after the war."

"I'm not used to being waited on," Katherine told her quickly. "I can help out if you'll let me."

"Kate's a good cook, Mama. She bakes pret' near as good as Susanna."

Letitia's head swung from one to the other. "No...no, I couldn't let you do that, Katherine. You're a guest here."

"If we're staying awhile, we'll both pitch in, Mama." Roan's voice was firm and he looked to Katherine for agreement.

"I want to do what I can to help," she echoed. "I'm used to—"

"What Kate means is she's used to runnin' the whole show. From trainin' horses to raisin' the food, she's about as capable as any woman you'd ever want to meet up with."

LeRoy Devereaux lifted his eyebrows in surprise. "You train horses, ma'am?"

A blush suffused her cheeks and Katherine nodded.

"Those are really your animals? I thought Roan was funnin' me, tellin' me they belonged to you."

"They're mine, all right. I raised them and I've been training them. After my pa died, I was all there was."

"Maybe you'd like to go out to the stable after dinner and take a look at my animals," LeRoy said, his eyes alight with interest.

''Watch your back, Kate. He'll have you talked out of that black mare before you know it,'' Roan warned her quickly.

She shook her head. ''I doubt it. I'll be needing to get on her back before long. If we do any hard riding, I won't want to be riding my mare much longer.''

LeRoy looked puzzled. ''That chestnut got a problem?'' Katherine shook her head quickly. ''No, not really. She's due to drop a foal early in the spring.''

''You got a mare breeding?'' LeRoy leaned forward over the table. ''Where's the stud?''

''You won't believe this story,'' Roan put in.

''Well, eat your pie before you start talkin' horse talk,'' Letitia said politely. ''I declare, this is not fit conversation for the dinner table, LeRoy.''

''Eat up, Katherine.'' The older man nodded at the pie being served and picked up his own fork. ''We'll go to the stable as soon as dinner's over.''

''You didn't get to show off your horses, Kate. Are you mad at me?'' Roan stretched out on the bed, arms behind his head, sheet pulled haphazardly to cover his long body. He watched, his eyes half-hidden beneath hooded lids, as Katherine languished in the tub of water he'd provided for her.

She looked at him over her shoulder and pursed her lips. ''You left me with your mother.''

His grin struggled to be apologetic. ''Pa wanted to talk, Kate. To tell the truth, he didn't know which he wanted more—to take you out to the barn, or spend some time hashin' over some bad memories with me.''

Katherine nodded, reaching for a towel from the chair nearby. ''He said he'd rather look my yearlings over in the daylight.'' She stood and stepped from the cooling water, wrapping the length of towel around her. Her hair was slipping from the pins she'd used to anchor it with and she lifted both hands to twist it atop her head. "Your mother holds grudges, doesn't she?"

He nodded, his eyes intent on the towel that clung precariously to her breasts, its length barely covering the tops of her thighs. "Mama always was one to nurse a sore spot. I knew she wouldn't be gettin' out the fatted calf for me, Kate."

She glanced at him. "Do you suppose there is such a thing around here? I have a notion that meat on the hoof is pretty scarce these days."

"Pa said they've got a good sow left and she produced a big litter this year. There's pork salted away from fall butchering and the smokehouse is in pretty good shape. They had three good-sized pigs that they kept. The rest they traded off for supplies in town." He sat up in bed and shoved his pillows against the tall headboard, scooting up to lean against them.

"I heard chickens after supper. I think Susanna was out feeding them," Katherine said, leaning to dry her legs with a second towel. The hair she'd piled and pinned with haste fell forward, unable to resist the power of gravity as she bent to pat her feet. "Drat... I swear I'll cut it off one of these days," she mumbled, her forearm rising to brush it from her face.

"Not on your life," came the lazy reply from the man who watched. "I like your hair."

She muttered a hasty word beneath her breath, then turned to glare in his direction, the dark strands falling over her shoulders in tangled disarray. "You aren't the one who has to keep it brushed and combed and out of the way."

He grinned and waved invitingly. "Come on over here and I'll brush it all you like."

She shook her head. "I want to hear what your father had to say. If I climb up on that bed, you'll—"

"I'll tell you while I do your hair," he coaxed. He watched as she pulled her long nightgown from a drawer, his frown deepening as she lifted it over her head and allowed it to fall in place down the length of her body. She stepped aside and picked up the towel she'd disposed of in the doing, then placed it to dry over the wooden rack behind the washstand.

"You gonna wear that thing?" His tone was aggrieved.

She cast him a scornful glance. "I'm in your mother's house," she said.

His eyes were genuinely puzzled. "What does that matter?"

"It matters." Picking her way across the floor, stepping over his boots and pants with exaggerated precision, she paused to snatch her brush from the dresser. "I'm not picking up your things, Devereaux," she warned him.

"Hell, if you take that damn tent off, I'll do the wash, honey. Yours and mine both," he offered.

She stood before him, brush in hand, smelling of soap and warm woman, and his breath caught as he inhaled the scent of her.

Her eyes narrowed, her gaze directed to the flush rimming his cheekbones, rising to the gleam of desire lighting his eyes. Then in a languid survey that seemed to penetrate the covering sheet, she focused on the masculine arousal he made no attempt to hide. Her smile was faint, curling the corners of her mouth. "Got a problem, mister?"

One hand snaked from where it had rested against his thigh, snatching her wrist in its grasp before she could step back. Her gasp was pleasing to Roan's ear. "You shouldn't tease a sleeping giant, ma'am," he told her, his voice deepened by the desire he'd been harboring for the past half hour. Watching Katherine bathe was becoming one of life's greatest pleasures, he'd decided.

Her frown was a facade, her struggle to rid herself of his grip halfhearted. The warmth of his fingers was a prison she felt no need to escape, and she gave in without a whimper. One knee lifted to the edge of the bed and he tugged her the rest of the way. Brush in hand, she fell across his chest and he narrowly escaped being smacked by the wooden handle as it flew from her fingers.

"Wanna talk now or later?" It was an offer he felt duty-bound to make, having promised to answer her questions. His hope was that she would take the latter option. Hell, they had all night to talk, he figured. Right now, his arms were full of curves and hollows he yearned to explore.

She peered at him, her hair tangled and half hiding her eyes from his view. "Brush my hair first?"

"Take off that nightgown?" His grin was eloquent, his hands already tugging it up her legs.

She sighed and tried unsuccessfully to present a somber demeanor. "You drive a hard bargain, Devereaux."

His fingers smoothed over her hips, taking the gown with them, lifting it higher, his palms cupping the firmness of her breasts as he slid them beneath the cotton fabric. "It's almost off, Kate." He squeezed with delicate pressure and her indrawn breath told him what he wanted to know.

"I want the sheet over me," she said from beneath the enveloping folds.

He pulled it over her head and tossed it to the foot of the bed. Reaching down, he tugged at the sheet and held it high, allowing it to fall over her as he held her against his chest. "Happy now?"

She sighed, stretching a bit, shaking her head to toss the hair from before her eyes. "After you brush my hair I will be."

He turned her, spreading his legs to settle her between them, her back to him. Then, picking up the brush, he set to work, his strokes long and slow, his fingers untangling as he went, intent on smoothing the strands, deft and gentle against her skin.

Her pleasure was audible and he grinned as she tipped her head back, allowing him access. "You could do this all night," she said, her words a slurring sound.

"Five minutes, Kate." Bending forward, he kissed her nape. "I've got other plans for the rest of the night."

Chapter Twenty

The kitchen garden was a plot of overgrown weeds with only a few cabbages and turnips left to harvest. The tomato plants were tangled and dry, the squash and cucumber vines trampled into the dirt. Chickens poked beneath the brown leaves that remained, seeking a morsel, cocking their heads to watch for any stray movement. Roan leaned one shoulder against the springhouse, his expression grim as he contemplated the remains of his mother's prized garden. "I don't know how my folks have made it by themselves, with only Susanna in the house and a handful of help in the fields."

"A summer garden always looks pretty worn out by this time of year, Roan," Katherine told him. "Susanna's put up a good lot of vegetables. Your mama just wasn't much of a help to her in the kitchen." Or anywhere else, she thought privately.

He shook his head. "This..." His waving hand encompassed the bedraggled area. "It should have been cleaned up. When I was a child, Mother would have one of the hands pull the vines and rake up the plot. Only there isn't anyone to do it now."

"I'm here." Katherine hugged herself, a chill gripping her as the wind swept between the outbuildings, promising a drop in the temperature. "I'd like to work the garden, Roan. It needs to be made ready for spring and I can do it."

"You can't do everything, Kate. You're flyin' around from one place to another already. I've been watchin' you scrubbin' the stairs and washin' windows to a fare-thee-well. Today you've been up to your neck with cleaning the parlor since right after breakfast. I told you, there's no point in tryin' to make away with years of dust in one fell swoop." His frown deepened. "You'll be fightin' a losin' battle anyway. This place is too big for one woman to keep up."

She gave him an exasperated look. "Your mother just needs a hand. I don't think she ever learned how to do much cleaning, and Susanna is busy with meals and doing the wash."

He reached to pull her next to him, his arm curving around her waist and fitting her neatly against his side.

"You can't even find time to spend with your horses, Kate. My father's been tryin' for three weeks to get you on that black mare and you always have some excuse or another."

She grinned at him and shook her head. "He's having a good time working with her. He's been throwing a sack of feed over the saddle and I even caught him draped over it himself, getting her used to the weight."

Roan looked down at her, this woman who had become almost indispensable to his parents' household in such a short time. She had blossomed here, between sorting through musty linens and hanging fresh curtains in the bedrooms and helping Susanna get ready for the cold weather. The chickens had been culled, the young roosters put in a separate pen to fatten for the dinner table. The garden had been neglected, but then his mother had always said there wasn't much sadder a sight than a dried-up pile of watermelon vines. And Letitia Devereaux had finally begun to perk up a little, to his way of thinking.

Kate was the reason. As sure as the sun would set in the west, his wife was determined to set this place to rights. Letitia had balked at first, insisting Katherine was a guest. But she'd had that notion banished in a hurry.

"I'm a member of the family now," Katherine had told her firmly. "If I'm living here, I'll pull my own weight. Besides, it looks to me like you need a hand with things."

And she'd given it. Not only a hand, but the whole of her energetic body. As if she had stored up an abundance of energy during the trek southward, she burst into activity, leaving a stunned Letitia to follow her about the house. Until, finally, they had begun to work together in a way that had put a smile on the face of LeRoy Devereaux and a song about the golden stairs and heavenly gates upon the lips of Susanna.

"He'll have that mare stolen away from you if you're not careful," Roan warned her as they watched the sun set with a brilliant flourish of color against the twilight sky.

"He's having a good time." Katherine's shrug was eloquent. Some days she was astonished at what little time she spent even thinking about her string of horses. That they had been moved from the forefront of her thoughts to second or third place was a conundrum she had not ventured to solve. Family was what counted right now. What did it matter who trained the mare to carry a rider? Somehow, during the past days, the importance of the sleek animal had become overshadowed by the magnitude of work to be done at River Bend. The mare could wait. Katherine had decided she wasn't going anywhere for a few months, anyway.

One session with LeRoy in the barn had convinced her of his ability to manage her horse. His hands, so broad and callused, became things of beauty when they touched the silken mane and the velvet nose of the black mare. He'd begun calling her pet names, gruffly and beneath his breath at first. Then, to Katherine's surprise, he'd asked at the dinner table one evening if she would have any objections to him giving the filly a name.

"Doesn't seem right to be talkin' to a creature every day and not be namin' her, Katherine," he'd said abruptly. "Always made it a practice to put me a wooden sign on every stall. I wrote the letters and Jethro burned them on with a hot poker. Don't suppose you'd cotton to me callin' that black mare by a proper name, would you?"

Katherine had nodded slowly, as if the idea met with reluctant approval. "I suppose it wouldn't hurt," she'd said. "I was thinking a while back, if I were to call her something, it might be Journey."

LeRoy chewed slowly, contemplating his daughter-in-law with a thoughtful frown. "Don't know as how I'd have come up with that particular name. Any special reason?"

Katherine had sent a look at Roan, who had followed the conversation with silent appreciation. "She'll have reason to remember her first long trail ride." Smiling, she'd sipped from her water glass. "It just sounds like a good name to me."

LeRoy had acquiesced. "Journey," he'd muttered, as if he were trying the name on his tongue, and then he repeated it. "Journey. I reckon it'll do, all right."

"I suppose he'll be namin' the rest of your animals, if you don't come up with some suggestions for him," Roan told her now, watching as her smile widened.

"He's having a good time, isn't he?"

"Yeah." He nodded agreement. "It's kinda put a sparkle in his eye, playin' with your babies, Kate. You know, he's not the same man I knew ten years ago. He's changed."

"Maybe you've changed, too." She tipped her head back to meet his gaze and hers was challenging. "You never told me if he whipped the slave that day, Roan. You said he ran him down with your hunting dog. But then what happened?"

"I don't know. We had an argument while Jethro stood there with a rope tied around his neck, followin' along behind my pa on his horse. I was so mad, seein' it . . . like for the first time, I knew I couldn't own another man. Hell, Jethro was my friend growin' up. He taught me how to spit between my front teeth, and how to make a willow whistle and a couple other things I don't think I'm gonna tell you about." His grin was a welcome respite from the grim look he'd worn. His eyes were warm with remembrance and he chuckled. "I used to sneak out after I was supposed to be sleepin' at night and we'd run off and sit together and talk for hours, down by the stream."

"Did your father know?"

Roan shook his head. "I doubt it. I could climb out that window and down the oak tree like greased lightning."

She thought once more of the man tied to a rope and wondered aloud, "You didn't tell me before that it was Jethro." She considered for a moment. "Jethro doesn't seem to hold a grudge." And it was the truth. Between the two men there appeared to be an unspoken agreement, LeRoy Devereaux in charge, but Jethro holding his own as he managed the several field hands who lived in cabins behind the barn.

"Jethro said they have an understanding. I think what it is, Pa understands he couldn't get along without somebody to take charge, and Jethro understands he's got a place for his wife and family to live and food on the table."

Katherine's smile dimmed. "Things are hard, aren't they? The war left some pretty deep scars."

"It'll never be the same, that's for sure," Roan said flatly. "But maybe, one of these days, it'll be better. Pa's hired on six of the men who used to be slaves here, for a place to live and whatever else they need. After the war they left for a while, but when they found out how hard it was to scrabble out a livin', they came back."

"It's not much different for them now than it was then, is it?"

"They're free, whatever that means." His laugh was harsh. "Hell, we're all tied to the land, hereabouts. Most everywhere, I guess. Nobody's really free, what with havin' to sow and reap and hope for good weather so the crop comes in good. The only freedom any of us have is the choice of where we do it. I figure the big difference is that those men don't owe their soul to LeRoy Devereaux anymore."

He laughed suddenly, a rueful sound in the silence of the gathering darkness. "The strange part is, they're workin' harder now than ever before and not gettin' any more out of it. Except they each got their own little piece of land and their cabin to call their own."

"Their spirits are free, Roan."

"How about yours, Kate? Is your spirit feelin' tied down here? Are you countin' the days till we head north in the spring?"

She nestled closer, gathering the warmth he radiated and allowing it to seep into her chilled body. Turning, she leaned against him, her arms lifting to circle his neck. She peered at him, wondering at the turnabout he'd effected with his quiet questions. Like a stone dropped in still water, forming circles in an unending fashion, his query had caught her off guard, shaken her out of her comfortable rut. She'd just begun to settle here, and he'd brought up another change. One she'd planned would come about, but perhaps not so soon. And if she went home, what would happen next? Would he want to stay with her in the rolling farmlands, where his slow, Southern drawl made him a stranger?

"I'm too busy to be counting days, Roan." Her tone was curt as she silenced the nagging doubts that surged within her. Would the ties they'd forged during the long night hours be strong enough to bind them during the years of hard work facing them back at the farm? Would he be satisfied with her life there? She clutched at the strength of his muscular shoulders, her fingers gripping him with a silent plea. *Just love me,* she wanted to tell him. But the words she spoke were all her cowardly heart would allow.

"I told your mama I'd help get all the rugs out on the line tomorrow. She asked Susanna to get one of the men to beat them good for us."

He squeezed her gently, his hands firm against her back, fingers yearning toward the tempting fullness of her hips. His look was approving as he spoke his praise. "You've done more than your share, Kate. You just pitched in and took on the whole house, like it was your calling, didn't you?"

"Your mama needed me," she said, as if that were enough reason to tie her to the fading glory that was River Bend. "Besides, it's fun to live in a house where everybody's got room to put their belongings without tripping over them every time you turn around. Your pa's got books in the library I never thought I'd get a chance to read, Roan. And there's pictures on the wall of your pa's folks, painted and framed just like in the museum."

"You don't mind the hard work?" His fingers obeyed the urging of his fertile mind and curved around the firm flesh of her hips.

She wiggled against him, aware now of the awakening of his body to her nearness, and her lips formed a secret smile she managed to hide against his chest. "No, I don't mind working. I never did. And I don't work any harder here than I did on the farm." She tilted her head to the side and considered his flashing grin, white teeth visible beneath the mustache he had trimmed just this morning. "I probably don't work as hard, some days. Fine things are easier to keep up, somehow. Your family has a houseful of beautiful things."

"Pa said they hid a lot during the war. Jethro buried a heap of stuff in a cache way out in the swamp east of here.

Took the best horses out there and kept them from the armies that went through.''

"Your father owes him, doesn't he? When he could have run off, Jethro acted like he was part of the family."

"Guess he was, really. He'd been here since he was born, and then when Gaeton went off to fight and I was gone, Pa had to depend on him more than ever."

"Your mother told me they've only heard once from your sister. She was settled in New York. I think your mama misses her terribly." Katherine's voice held a sadness Roan recognized. It was the same yearning, wistful sound he'd heard from her after Lawson was killed, the lonely cry of a woman without family.

"She's lucky she's got you then, isn't she?"

His rasping words rumbled against her ear and she lifted her head from its place against his chest. "I'll never be able to take the place of a daughter," she stated unequivocally. "Yvonne is your mother's own blood."

"Yvonne was a spoiled little girl who didn't care enough about her folks to stay here and take care of things." It was a judgment he'd made and carried about silently for weeks.

Katherine lifted her shoulders and sighed. "We're all different, Roan. Don't be judging her. You weren't here to know what happened."

He snorted his disagreement. "Pa told me that the Yankee officer took a shine to Yvonne right off, and the way the war was goin', it made sense for her to head out with him when he left. Hell, Pa doesn't even know if he married her."

"Surely..." Her voice trailed off pensively as Katherine considered the alternative. All men weren't cut from Devereaux cloth, and Roan Devereaux himself was a rarity among men, she admitted with a thankful heart. He'd married Katherine Cassidy without a second thought, knowing he couldn't cart her away from her home without protecting her with his name.

"We need to be gettin' inside, honey," he told her with a final squeeze of his arms before he set her apart from him. "The dew's fallin' and the night air is beyond chilly. You're gettin' cold."

"Yes." Her agreement was automatic as she felt the warmth she'd relied upon taken from her. How cold her world would be without the arms of Roan Devereaux to hold her fast, how dreary would be the nights, how lonely the days. The thought brought a shiver of dismay that sent her seeking his touch. Her hand reached to clasp his and he shot a look of surprise in her direction, then tightening his grip, he held her closely to his side as they made their way to the kitchen door.

"We've always celebrated Christmas," Letitia said brightly. Breakfast was over, the table cleared, and Katherine was dusting her way around the molding that rose high over her head. A long pole with a cloth draped over its end made the journey from one corner to another, and her mouth was pursed in concentration as she worked.

"Christmas?" As though she had just, for the very first time, heard the word, she turned a startled glance at her mother-in-law.

"Don't you observe Christmas?" Letitia's query was hesitant, as though she might tread on sensitive toes.

Katherine nodded. "Of course. It's just that I'd forgotten it was so near." She lowered the pole, which was causing the muscles of her shoulders to cramp with its weight. "I used to go into town on Christmas Eve for services. It was always beautiful, riding home alone in the night, thinking about the shepherds and how they must have felt." She grinned suddenly and her eyes flashed with mischief. "I always wanted to hear the angels sing. I thought they must be much more talented than Mrs. Wellman. She had the loudest voice in the church choir and I used to wonder if she'd be allowed in the angel choir in heaven. My pa said that death makes all of us perfect, so we'll be fit for the pearly gates.''

Letitia's eyes moved slowly over the young woman who stood before the window, gazing pensively into the yard beyond. ''You have no family, have you, Katherine?''

Katherine's head shook slowly. ''No. Lawson was the last. Now there's just me left.''

''You have Roan.''

Katherine turned to face the older woman. ''Yes, I have Roan.'' Her smile was like a ray of sunshine on a dreary day. ''I thought more than once that maybe he was an angel God had sent to me when I needed—well, when I was alone.'' She shook off the mantle of sadness that threatened to cover her, remembering instead Roan's laughter, his constancy, his early morning cheerfulness on the trail. Her eyes crinkled as she considered the thought. ''He can't sing, you know. He'll never make the choir in the church back home.''

Letitia's brows rose in silent inquiry.

Katherine laughed aloud. ''Have you ever heard him sing? He'd put a bullfrog to shame, I swear.''

Letitia shook her head. ''Do you think he'll go to church with you...back home?'' Her voice rose with a delicate emphasis on the last words.

''I don't know.'' Katherine shrugged. ''The matter didn't come up.''

''He wasn't much for church-goin' as a boy,'' his mother confided quietly. ''He was sort of...rebellious, once he got his growth and started feelin' his manhood comin' on.''

Katherine's mouth firmed. ''He hated what happened to Jethro. And then I think he felt guilty because he left before finding out what his pa was going to do about the running away business.''

Letitia shivered. ''I declare, I hate to think about that day. LeRoy was so angry. Probably angrier at himself than Jethro or Roan, come to think of it. He'd never done that before…used a dog to track down a slave, then led him back with a rope around his neck."

"Jethro was Roan's friend." And that made the difference? For a moment, Katherine considered the thought. If it was wrong for Jethro to be treated so, then it was wrong for any man to be shamed that way. It wasn't so much owning a man that was hurtful, though that was sin enough, it was the shame of the treatment that man received from his fellow man.

"He let Jethro go when Roan rode out of here," Letitia said quickly, as if she must still Katherine's solemn pondering. Her eyes were anxious on the younger woman's face. "He didn't whip his people, you know. LeRoy wouldn't do that."

"I'll tell Roan. I think he's wondered if his pa hadn't taken it out on Jethro when his son left in such a temper."

"And he won't ask for himself."

Katherine shook her head. "No, he's not been able to yet. I think men tend to go roundabout, rather than facing head-on sometimes. I remember when Pa and Lawson would—"

Letitia's eyes were moist with tears at the grief inherent in Katherine's voice as she spoke the names of the men in her past. Her hands stilled on the silver she'd been cleaning. "I'd like to think we could be your family now, Katherine." Her head ducked a bit as she rubbed her cloth against the carved pattern of the knife handle she held.

Katherine looked startled, her glance settling on the older woman. "You've treated me well, ma'am. Better than I expected, coming out of the blue the way we did. Roan should have warned you he was bringing home a Yankee."

"That used to be almost a profanity here," Letitia said sadly. "The country hereabouts was almost devastated, you know. It's hard to be forgiving, like the Bible says we must. And then to think of my son in that terrible prison in Elmira. He was almost a broken man when he returned home."

"Roan doesn't understand how he could leave you and his father," Katherine ventured quietly.

"Roan wouldn't have done it," his mother said. "He left thinking that Gaeton would always be here, as the oldest son. He thought Gaeton would inherit someday. Now we don't even know for sure where he is."

Katherine put the pole down on the floor, careful to gather the dusty cloth into a ball to hold the accumulated soil within. She stepped around the table where they'd eaten their morning meal and stood beside the woman who'd made the hesitant offer, as if she'd expected it to be refused.

"I'd like to claim you as my kin, now that I'm a Devereaux in fact." Her knees bent in a gesture of submission to the older woman, and Katherine knelt beside her chair. She looked sad, Katherine thought, lonely perhaps, her eyes damp with unshed tears, her mouth quivering.

Letitia's hands left the silver she'd been tending and settled on either side of Katherine's face, her fingers caressing as she moved them across the fine cheekbones. "I desperately need a daughter these days. Roan coming home answered a prayer I've spoken every night for years. I'm so pleased that he brought you to me, Katherine. I only hate that you'll be gone in the spring."

"My home's in Illinois, back at the farm. My father bought it for me, for a home place. He knew I needed a settled spot to be my own, where I could count on seeing the same walls every morning when I woke up. Where I could look out and see the sun set every evening and know that the land around me was—" She smiled, a blush moving up to cover her cheeks. "I'm sorry. I didn't mean to go on so about the farm. It's just that . . . it's my home."

Letitia nodded knowingly. "We all need a home place, Katherine. Especially a woman. Where she can make her nest and settle in and feel comfortable."

Katherine felt relief sweep over her. For the first time in her life, another woman shared her thoughts, understood her feelings. Her hands rose to cover the slender fingers of Roan's mother, and she held closely to the cool flesh. "Thank you for understanding, for knowing how I feel."

Letitia nodded. "I know how you feel, but knowin' won't make it any easier to see you leave, come spring."

Chapter Twenty-One

"I've never spent a lovelier Christmas, Roan." Spoken on a sigh, it was a pronouncement that pleased Roan Devereaux beyond imagining.

Katherine turned to face him and caught sight of the smile he wore. "Does that surprise you? That I've never enjoyed Christmas more than I did today?"

"It pleases me, I reckon. To think that one of your finest memories will always include me."

She inhaled deeply, his aroma as always a part of the attraction that drew her to this man. The fresh outdoor scent he carried with him, on his clothing and in his hair. The faint, musky perfume of his flesh, which fired her imagination with memories of their loving. Even the aroma of his father's slender cigars, clinging to him when he left the dinner table, having taken up the sharing of LeRoy's evening smoking ritual.

"Most of my best memories include you," she told him quietly. "I love you, you know."

She hadn't said it lately. He'd begun to wonder why, and the words spoken now made him realize how much he'd missed the soft declaration from her lips. She'd said it first in the heat of their loving, almost reluctantly, their coming together all but forcing it from her, as if she could not contain the emotion welling up within. But never in daylight, or while the candlelight shone on her face.

He'd tried. He'd formed the words with his lips, whispered them silently against the silken strands of her hair, his face buried against her dark tresses. Now she faced him in the flickering candlelight of their bedroom and whispered them once more. And he felt the sting of unfamiliar tears beneath his heavy-lidded eyes. Thankful for the dim light, he nodded, accepting her love, and bent his head to cover her mouth with his own.

"Kate...you're the best thing that ever happened to me." Each syllable brushed against her lips, his voice harsh as he tempered it into a whisper. His mustache was soft, moving the caress to her cheek and then to her temple as he left a line of kisses across her face. The words had never come easy to him. He remembered his mother asking for them in a small game they'd played at bedtime.

"Do you love your mother, Valderone?"

And he'd nodded his dark head solemnly. "Yes, Mama."

"Do you love me, Roan?" As if she echoed that long past question, Katherine repeated the query, her voice trembling. His proud, strong woman was asking for his love—or at least the declaration of it—and he was shamed by the thought. She deserved better than Roan Devereaux, gunman, sometimes gambler and wanderer. All the qualities she'd scorned in her menfolk, she'd managed to find in a husband. And now she'd been forced to ask assurance of his caring.

"You know I do, Kate," he said finally, gruffly and against the cushion of her hair.

Her sigh was a release of the pent-up breath she'd held in abeyance as she waited his reply. She leaned against him fully, knowing he would accept her weight, confident in his strength, aware of his tender concern for her. But did all that add up to love? He'd acknowledged her plea, he'd couched his answer in words of agreement, and with that she would be satisfied. It might be all she'd ever get from Roan Devereaux and it was certainly more than she'd ever wanted from any other man. Her voice was cheerful, determinedly so.

"Your mama had a good time, didn't she? Singing all the old songs and serving up the spiced tea. She said she hadn't used the old trimmings around the house in years. I thought Jethro would have a fit when she made him climb a tree to get down a ball of mistletoe for her."

Her fingers had been busy with the buttons of his shirt as she spoke, her voice amused, the fondness for Letitia Devereaux apparent in her words. Now she spread wide the sides of his garment and placed her hands flat on the triangle of curls that covered his chest. She dipped her fingers beneath the dark hair and tangled them there, tugging to get his attention.

She needn't have gone to such pains. His whole being was focused on the woman before him. From the first words she'd spoken when they entered the room until now, he'd not taken his attention from her. She'd sashayed before him, the new dress Letitia'd made her for Christmas swirling about her ankles as she walked. Slipping the soft shoes from her feet just inside the door, she'd traveled on stocking-clad feet to where he stood, chattering all the time, her words barely making an impression.

Until she'd spoken the declaration of love. Those words had penetrated his mind, traveled throughout his body and lodged firmly in the place where his heart pounded in a solid, steady beat. Hell, if he couldn't tell her what she wanted to hear, he'd just have to show her. Let his body speak for him.

He turned her around with easy pressure on her shoulders until her back was to him, her head bent as she waited for his fingers to work the buttonholes, which were still stiff from Letitia's fine stitches. His hands were clumsy and he silently cursed their tremors. Like a callow youth, he trembled in anticipation, knowing what he would find beneath the fabric. The finely pored flesh he would uncover, the narrow span of her shoulders, the slim waist and flaring hips that held him in thrall. She lured him with her presence. Unknowingly she brought him to the edge of his endurance, his manhood rising as he touched only the clothing she wore.

Kate...the very word caught at his heartstrings. He smiled as he considered his musing thoughts. She had him making poetry these days. Heartstrings...a fancy word for a part of his being he'd never known existed until now.

His hands smoothed the dress over her hips, and he watched as it drifted to the floor about her feet. Carefully, he turned her within the circle of fabric, his fingers gentle against her bare shoulders. "Help me, Kate. I think I'm probably gonna tear something if you don't give me a hand here." His gaze was dark and piercing as it traveled the length of her body, pausing for long moments as he watched the telltale changes his scrutiny brought about.

Her hands rose to cover her breasts and she flushed, the pink color rising from the rounding of her bosom to settle against her cheeks.

"Don't." His fingers gripped her, lifting her hands to his mouth, turning them until he was able to cover her palms with soft, damp kisses. "Don't hide from me, Kate. You've no reason to cover yourself. I know what my lookin' at you does to them. Don't you know it makes me proud to see it?"

She shook her head and breathed her reply. "No...I just know it happens when you look at me like that." Her chin lifted in a gesture that pleased him and she took her hands from his and set them to work with the ties and hooks that held her underclothing in place. "I'm glad I please you, Roan." The petticoat fell to the floor and she lifted the chemise over her head. White underpants were next, a small encumbrance as her hands disposed of them quickly. Her slender legs were covered with white stockings, held above the knees with narrow garters, and she bent to roll them down over her calves.

His hands stopped her and he brought her erect once more. "Let me do that." It was an order, roughly given, harshly spoken from a mouth that barely moved with the words that passed through it.

Her eyes widened at the tone and she smiled, a siren's acknowledgment of her effect on the man she lured so easily. He knelt at her feet and his fingers were gentle, careful lest he snag the precious stockings, rolling them till they lay about her ankles. Then he picked up her feet, one after the other, while she held his shoulder to brace herself. The white stockings lay in small circles on the rug, and he picked them up with one long index finger, lifting them to her waiting hand.

"Thank you." Her voice was amused and he shot her a glance of narrowed appraisal. She'd disposed of the stockings on a nearby chair and raised her hands to her hair, unpinning it from the top of her head, where braids had been arranged in a complex design. The heavy plaits fell over her shoulders and her fingers busied themselves with the untwining of them while she watched the man who knelt at her feet. Proud and unfettered, her breasts rose with each breath she took. Trim and sleek, her body gleamed in the candle glow, her legs rounded and slender, her hips filling his palms as he fit his hands against her flesh.

Her indrawn breath told him she was not immune to his touch. Her involuntary shiver brought a smile to his lips. But it was the soft speaking of his name that brought him to his feet.

"Roan." More than a whispered entreaty, it was an invitation, spoken in a tone he'd become familiar with. "Roan." *Love me,* it said. *Hold me close, touch me, make me tremble, pleasure me . . . give me your body and take mine in return.* "Roan." She spoke it once more, in a yearning, coaxing appeal he had no inclination to refuse.

"Let's celebrate Christmas, Kate," he said with a smile that spoke the words he could not utter. His clothing came off with haste, even as his eyes held her gaze. Only when he bent to remove his boots did he break the look he'd held her with, and that only for the moments it took to free himself from their leather hold.

Lifting her in his arms, he carried her to bed, lowering her to the sheets, and then followed her down into the feather mattress. "Happy Christmas, sweetheart," he whispered, his hands sliding through the crinkled length of her hair. His mouth pressed against hers, his lips damp and seeking, and then he groaned as her tongue made the first advance.

"Kate..." It was a sound of pure pleasure, the calling of her name, as his hands found the fullness of her breasts, his mouth opening to receive the abundance of her kiss and his body settling itself next to her. His firm muscles cushioned by the softness of her woman's flesh, his long legs given space between hers, he lifted himself to where he yearned to be. His heart beating and pulsing, the blood flowing at a quickening pace throughout his big body, he sensed his readiness for this act of loving. And yet he waited, wooing her with his mouth, his loving phrases, his hands and the movement of his body against hers. Until she told him she was ready for his possession. With softly uttered words, with smothered gasps and the moans she could not contain, she brought a smile of satisfaction to his tightly drawn lips.

And then with careful, gentle touches, with hands that moved her to his pleasure, he gave her the gift of himself and received the warmth of her love.

"Did my boy buy those britches for you?" LeRoy Devereaux's brows were lowered over his dark eyes as Kate entered the barn. The shirt Roan had purchased those long months ago in Illinois had shrunk somewhat. It no longer tucked down over her fanny beneath the boy's pants she wore, and the front of it was filled nicely with her bosom.

She'd taken a second look in the mirror before she left the bedroom and had eyed her own burgeoning figure with doubt. But there was nothing to be done. If she wanted to ride the black mare, she needed to wear her pants. The clothing intended for a young boy had fit her during those weeks on the trail. Somehow her rounded figure, combined with multiple washings of the cotton fabrics, now produced a snug fit.

"Yes, your son bought me these clothes. And yes, I know they're a little bit—" She looked down at herself and bit her lip.

The eyes that reminded her of Roan every time she looked into their depths sparkled now as LeRoy grinned at his son's wife. "I didn't say I didn't like the outfit, girl. I just wondered how Roan had the nerve to turn you loose in it."

A deep chuckle from the far stall announced the presence of a third party. "She won't be goin' anywhere but right here. And I reckon I'd better invest six bits in a pair of bigger britches for her next time I go to town." His eyes reflecting the residue of passion from their early morning loving, Roan approached his wife.

"You ready to finally climb on that animal of yours? After my pa's gotten her all nice and gentle for you, it shouldn't be much of a challenge, I reckon."

Katherine ignored both men, her cheeks wearing pink flags, her mouth pursed as she took the reins of the mare she'd named Journey. She moved to stand in front of the dark head, her hands rubbing the long nose, tugging at the black forelock, and her voice speaking nonsense to the animal in a low, tender tone. Journey tossed her head and a low whinny rumbled from her throat. Katherine laughed and wrapped her arm beneath the neck of the animal, her face rubbing against the silky mane.

"You gonna stand there all day?" Roan's big hand grasped the bridle just beneath its bit and he wrapped his arm around Katherine's waist. He felt the telltale thumping of her heart against his arm and his look softened. "You're not worried, are you, honey?"

She shook her head. "No, of course not. I'm just . . . I've waited a long time to ride her, Roan. She's been my baby since she was born and now she's all grown-up and she's going to be a mother."

He bent to drop a kiss of reassurance on her temple. "Come on, sweet, she's waiting for you. Climb on and I'll take you out into the yard with her."

Katherine nodded and eased herself smoothly into the saddle, making her weight as evenly distributed as she could. Journey shifted once uneasily beneath her and then lifted her chin, as if she would free herself from Roan's restrictive grasp under her bit.

"All set?" With one look at his wife, he led the horse into the sunlight, where several men stood watching.

"Jethro, aren't you supposed to have these people working somewhere?" LeRoy's stern tones were attention-getters and the men looked at him quickly, their expressions uneasy. But Jethro was not so easily affected.

"We didn't want to miss Miss Katherine's first ride on her mare." Delivered with a smile, his message was clear. Not for anything would these men choose to work elsewhere when the horse that LeRoy Devereaux had spent so many hours with was about to be taken for her first ride by the new young missus.

LeRoy grunted a reply and lounged against the outside wall of the barn. Roan watched with guarded interest. Not like the old days, he decided, when his father would have stormed and carried on in grand style if his men weren't nose to the grindstone all day long. Between the owner and his tenants, there had formed a new understanding, and Roan, not for the first time, was watching the results.

Katherine held her reins loosely, control of the horse between her legs more a matter of pressure from her knees than her grip on the leather reins. Journey lifted her feet with dainty steps, not content to stand idle, and Katherine gave her a nudge with her toes. In a dancing trot, the mare went the distance to the far side of the dirt drive, and then, at Katherine's urging, she broke into an easy lope as she headed down the long, tree-lined drive that led away from the plantation house.

Katherine's hair streamed behind her as she rode. The wind was in her eyes, certainly the reason for the tears that fell to her cheeks and dried there. Beneath her, the frisky mare stretched out her long legs and ran, her muscles bunching, her hooves reaching as she felt the relaxed hold upon her bit. Katherine bent low over the dark mane, flinching as the heavy hair brushed her face, yet choosing to ride with her eyes half-closed as she whispered her praise to the animal she'd raised from birth.

Too soon, the plantation house was out of sight and she slowed Journey with a tightening of the reins. Too short a ride, but Roan would be worried if she failed to reappear when he deemed it appropriate. She knew he was concerned, yet the look of pride he'd worn as she left him watching had warmed her heart and assured her of his confidence in her skills.

The ride back was taken at a slower pace, but to the woman who rode with buoyant ease, it seemed to be but seconds until she caught sight of the barn and the men gathered there. She rode into their midst and LeRoy grasped the bridle as she dismounted.

"Isn't she wonderful?" The words were automatic as she stood before Roan. Her cheeks were rosy with triumph, her eyes alight with pure joy.

"Yeah, I'd say she's about the most wonderful thing I've ever set eyes on." But the female creature he bathed with glowing pride was not a black mare but the woman standing before him.

Roan Devereaux was a man in love, his daddy decided. If ever a young man was more enthralled with a woman, he surely hadn't stood where LeRoy could see him. Maybe except for himself and the woman who had been watching from the back door of the plantation kitchen. He tied the reins to a ring on the barn door and brushed at the already gleaming coat of Katherine's mare. There was no doubt in his mind. The only way he'd ever lay claim to this animal was if Katherine made River Bend her home. The mare was hers. No matter that he'd spent days and weeks in nurturing and training the creature, her heart belonged to Roan's wife. And unless he missed his guess, Roan was in about the same state.

A triumphant Katherine graced the dinner table, more suitably garbed, to be sure, but just as jubilant.

"She didn't even flinch, did she?" For the second time, and between bites of food she scarcely tasted, Katherine sang the praises of her mare. Her gaze went to LeRoy, whose own appetite was unfettered. He ate with gusto, his plate piled high with the food Katherine had helped prepare for her celebratory meal.

"You rode her first, didn't you?" she said. It was less than an accusation, more like a fond reproof, and LeRoy took it as such.

"Couldn't have you takin' a tumble, could I?" he asked. "I just took a turn around the corral yesterday, made sure she was nice and gentled."

"Well, with all the time you spent on her, I about expected her to turn cartwheels and stand on her head for Kate." Roan's droll pronouncement brought LeRoy's chewing to a halt.

"I didn't waste one hour on that animal," he blustered. "Just a few minutes here and there. You think she means more to me than any other horse on the place?"

"Yes." Katherine's quiet response brought identical pairs of dark eyes to rest upon her.

''Yes?'' LeRoy made the single syllable a sound of rebuttal.

Katherine took up the challenge. ''I think she means a whole lot to you, sir. I think you're about half in love with my mare and I don't blame you one bit. In fact, I have a proposition to make you. I'm willing to pay you for the work you did with her.''

LeRoy shook his head, a vehement gesture that would have called halt to a lesser woman.

Katherine blithely ignored his frown. ''When Journey gives birth, I want you to have the foal.''

As if he were thunderstruck, LeRoy's mouth fell open and his eyes sparkled with an excitement he made no attempt to hide. ''You'd give me your colt?''

''It might be a filly.'' Katherine picked up her fork and, with a smile of satisfaction well in place, lifted a piece of meat to her lips.

''I don't believe so,'' LeRoy said stoutly. ''She looks to me like she'll—''

''You've just got your heart set on a new stud for the place.'' Roan's quiet observation brought a chuckle from Katherine.

LeRoy's eyes narrowed as he considered the young woman his son had married. ''You gonna bring that foal back down here all the way from Illinois?''

At the reminder, Katherine placed her fork beside her plate and rose from the table. ''Excuse me, please,'' she muttered beneath her breath, almost gaining the doorway before the last syllable was uttered.

''Go after her, Valderone,'' his mother urged.

But Roan had needed no urging. On his feet, napkin slung helter-skelter on the chair, he was fast on Kate's heels.

He followed her at a distance, unwilling that she should send him back, needing to watch over her as she struggled with the words his father had spoken. She walked quickly, past the barn, past the corrals and past the outbuildings.

Her steps took her beyond the cabins and their fenced-in yards and gardens, where dark-skinned children played in the fading light.

Finally she halted, arms wrapped about her, the wind blowing her skirts against her slender form. Before her was the fallow land that waited a spring planting, the sun fast falling to the horizon in the west. The ground had been cleared and plowed last year, a tedious process. Now it awaited the proper time for the seed to be sown, the soil dark and rich, almost seeming eager to put forth a bounty of cotton.

Her skirt a bright flag against the barren field, Katherine faced the future of River Bend, the hope of spring, the land that the Devereaux family had planted for three generations. And behind her was the last of the men who would plant this land.

She had known he would follow, had heard with the ears of her heart his footsteps as he came in her wake. Had known he would not intrude on her thoughts, that his innate respect for her solitude would keep him at a distance.

And suddenly she could not abide the space between them.

"Roan." It was the calling of his name that had signified her need in the past. Now he heard it as a cry for comfort. For a need so great, it was beyond her ability to voice the words that would ask his understanding. And he responded, as she had known he would, as he would always respond, coming to her with long, silent strides through the grass.

His arms slid around her, his hands clasping hers and holding her in the way she knew so well. Her back was warmed by his presence, her whole being supported by his greater strength. And she leaned with wholehearted confidence in the man who held her, allowing him to take the weight of her body against his.

"Kate?" It was a single word, holding a plethora of questions, and she pondered for a moment, weighing the choices she must make. The sun was sinking rapidly now and she watched it. Watched the pink-and-blue rays that rose from the orb, painting the clouds with a vision of beauty that promised fair weather for tomorrow.

"My daddy bought me the farm, Roan." She felt his nod against her head. "He wanted me to have a home. Someplace I could settle in and make things my own. A place where I'd be able to stay for the rest of my life if I wanted to, and nobody could ever take it away from me."

The man behind her was silent. "And then you came along and took me with you. You married me, when you didn't have to—"

His grumbling words halted her. "That's where you're wrong, lady. Marrying you was the one thing I had to do."

She smiled, knowing his meaning, and continued. "Hush now. Let me talk." His deep sigh gave permission.

"Anyway, you brought me here and promised me we'd go back to the farm, come spring."

"I'm not renegin' on that, Kate. I'll take you home, whenever you say."

She nodded impatiently. "I know you would. You're a man of honor, Roan. If I haven't learned anything else about you, I've learned that. You'd leave this place without blinking an eye and trot me right back up the river to Illinois." She breathed deeply as if she must gain strength for the words she prepared to speak.

"I'm not going back. I want to stay here. I want to watch the cotton bloom and I want to help pick it. And I want Journey to have her foal here and watch your daddy's face when it's born."

She turned in his arms and he released his hold so she could press herself against him, her arms unfolding to slip about his shoulders. "I want to stay here, Roan. With you

and your folks and Jethro and Susanna and the rest. I want
you to be my family.''

"What about your home place?" Idly spoken, the words
were far from unimportant. The farm had been her heri-
tage from the father who had managed to give her little else.
It had been the most important thing in the world to her,
aside from the family of horses they'd dragged clear down
the length of the river.

"You're my home place, Roan. Wherever you are, when
I'm with you, I'm home. I found that out today, when I had
to face the thought of leaving here. If going north is what
you want to do, then we'll leave. If staying here is your
choice, then it's mine, too. Your family is mine. I have no
other, but that doesn't make me bereft. While I have you, I
have all I need. I told you I love you. This is what it means
to me. I want to be with you, no matter where that is.''

His heartbeat vibrated against his ribs as Roan heard her
declaration. His throat was strangely filled with a thickness
he could not swallow and his eyes were blurring, casting
Katherine into a gauzy mist. But the words that spilled from
his lips were honest and true and the voice that trembled in
the speaking was deep and vibrant with the emotion he
could not contain.

"I love you, Kate. I love you with all I have to offer. We'll
stay here if you're sure it's what you want. I'm all my folks
have, besides a handful of help and a barnyard of animals.
And the best daughter they could ask for.'' The final words
were spoken slowly, his smile warm as he pronounced his
judgment on the woman he held.

"My mother loves you, you know. And my pa is pleased
as punch to have you for a daughter.''

Her answering smile crinkled the corners of her eyes and
forced the tears that had been hovering to slide down her
cheeks. "Really?" It was a word filled with longing and he
could no longer resist.

His lips touched hers, a kiss of promise, a message of commitment she could not fail to grasp, and she responded with wholehearted joy. Their lips held, meshing in a familiar yet ever new blending that brought pleasure and an unspoken vow of passion to come.

"Sweetheart?" He held her gently, firmly, with arms that promised her his support for all time.

"Hmm?" She basked in the warmth of his embrace and rubbed her face against his cheek.

"When were you gonna tell me?"

She stilled. Her eyes opened and she looked up at him warily. "Tell you what?"

"Did you think I didn't notice you were gettin' a little big for your britches and your shirt was snugger'n a snake's skin in the spring?"

"I wasn't sure myself, Roan. Now you've ruined my surprise."

"It won't be any surprise, sweetheart. Susanna's been singing lullabies in the kitchen for almost two weeks. She does your washin', you know."

Her face flamed and she ducked her head. "When will you ever learn that there are some things a gentleman doesn't mention to a lady?"

"You're my wife, Kate," he said quietly. "Anything that concerns you is my business. Especially when it's my baby we're talkin' about."

Her eyes were hopeful as she met his gaze. "I want you to be happy about it."

His grin was brilliant, his teeth gleaming in the twilight, and his arms were strong as he lifted her to hold her against his chest.

"Roan, I'm too heavy! Put me down!" Her cry was startled, but the arms that slid about his neck held him in an embrace that gave him permission.

"We've got a couple of folks sittin' in there waitin' to hear what's goin' on," he told her, his long strides carrying them both on a return journey to the house. They passed the cabins, the corral and the barn, her face buried against his neck, her words of love whispered against his ear.

And on the back porch stood two people who couldn't wait any longer at the dining table to hear the words that would decide their future. Their faces were wreathed with smiles as the form of their youngest son strode toward them. In his arms was the woman who would form the nucleus of this home in the future years. And within her was the hope for generations to come.

Roan Devereaux had come home.

* * * * *

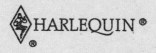

A baby was the last thing they were

EXPECTING!

But after nine months, the idea of fatherhood begins to grow on three would-be bachelors.

Enjoy three complete stories by some of your favorite authors—all in one special collection!

THE STUD by Barbara Delinsky
A QUESTION OF PRIDE by Michelle Reid
A LITTLE MAGIC by Rita Clay Estrada

Available this July wherever books are sold.

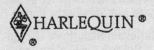

HARLEQUIN ®

BRIDE'S BAY RESORT

UNLOCK THE DOOR TO GREAT ROMANCE AT BRIDE'S BAY RESORT

Join Harlequin's new across-the-lines series, set in an exclusive hotel on an island off the coast of South Carolina.

Seven of your favorite authors will bring you exciting stories about fascinating heroes and heroines discovering love at Bride's Bay Resort.

Look for these fabulous stories coming to a store near you beginning in January 1996.

Harlequin American Romance #613 in January
Matchmaking Baby by Cathy Gillen Thacker

Harlequin Presents #1794 in February
Indiscretions by Robyn Donald

Harlequin Intrigue #362 in March
Love and Lies by Dawn Stewardson

Harlequin Romance #3404 in April
Make Believe Engagement by Day Leclaire

Harlequin Temptation #588 in May
Stranger in the Night by Roseanne Williams

Harlequin Superromance #695 in June
Married to a Stranger by Connie Bennett

Harlequin Historicals #324 in July
Dulcie's Gift by Ruth Langan

Visit Bride's Bay Resort each month wherever Harlequin books are sold.

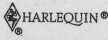

HARLEQUIN ®

BBAYG

Harlequin® Historical

Bestselling author **RUTH LANGAN** brings you nonstop
adventure and romance with her new Western series
from Harlequin Historicals

The Jewels of Texas

DIAMOND	February 1996
PEARL	August 1996
JADE	February 1997
RUBY	June 1997

Don't miss these exciting stories of four sisters as wild
and vibrant as the untamed land they're fighting to protect!

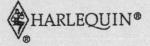

HARLEQUIN®

Coming in August from

Another exciting medieval tale
from award-winning author

Margaret Moore

The next book in her ongoing Warrior Series:

The Baron's Quest

"Ms. Moore is a genius of the genre..."
—*Affaire de Coeur*

"Margaret Moore has a bright future ahead."
—*Romantic Times*

Keep your eye out for THE BARON'S QUEST
wherever Harlequin Historicals are sold!

WARRIOR96

Harlequin® Historical

If you're a serious fan of historical romance,
then you're in luck!

Harlequin Historicals brings you
stories by bestselling authors, rising new stars
and talented first-timers.

Ruth Langan & Theresa Michaels
Mary McBride & Cheryl St. John
Margaret Moore & Merline Lovelace
Julie Tetel & Nina Beaumont
Susan Amarillas & Ana Seymour
Deborah Simmons & Linda Castle
Cassandra Austin & Emily French
Miranda Jarrett & Suzanne Barclay
DeLoras Scott & Laurie Grant...

You'll never run out of favorites.

Harlequin Historicals...they're too good to miss!